Eric **Malpass** was born in Derby in 1910 and worked in a bank after leaving school, but his firm ambition was to become a novelist and he wrote in his spare time for many years. His first book, *Morning's at Seven*, was published to wide acclaim. With an intuitive eye for the quirkiness of family life, his novels are full of wry comments and perceptive observations. This exquisite sense of detail has led to the filming of three of his books. His most engaging character is Gaylord Pentecost – a charming seven-year-old who observes the strange adult world with utter incredulity.

Eric Malpass also wrote biographical novels, carefully researched and highly evocative of the period. Among these is *Of Human Frailty*, the moving story of Thomas Cranmer.

With his amusing and lovingly drawn details of life in rural England, Malpass' books typify a certain whimsical Englishness – a fact which undoubtedly contributes to his popularity in Europe. Married with a family, Eric Malpass lived in Long Eaton, near Nottingham, until his death in 1996.

ERIC MALPASS

BEEFY JONES

HOUSE OF
STRATUS

Copyright © 1957, 2001 The Estate of Eric Malpass

This edition published in 2001 by House of Stratus, an imprint of Stratus Holdings plc, 24c Old Burlington Street, London, W1X 1RL, UK.

www.houseofstratus.com

Typeset, printed and bound by House of Stratus.

A catalogue record for this book is available from the British Library.

ISBN 0-7551-0199-5

To
Muriel Gladys

Bless her heart

CHAPTER 1

For some time a decaying tooth had been trying to get a message through the rock-like structure of Beefy's jaw. At last it succeeded. It reached the brain.

No one could call Beefy's brain a precision instrument. But it knew a pain when it felt one. "Hey, Beefy," it called. "You got face-ache."

But Beefy Jones did not hear. He was sitting in the warm darkness of the Majestic Cinema, wearing, as always, a blue and white striped singlet and blue serge trousers. His thick fingers were spread across his bulging thighs. Mouth open, breathing somewhat heavily, he gazed entranced at the vast screen just above his head, where the Sheriff and his men were recklessly pursuing the villains. The cinema was loud with horses galloping, guns firing, bullets whining. This was the moment Beefy always loved. He gripped his thighs more tightly. He breathed more heavily. One of the bad men had turned in the saddle, and was taking careful aim at the hero. You saw his finger tighten on the trigger –

"Hey, Beefy, you got face-ache," his brain called again, just a trifle irritably this time.

"Take me home," cried the decaying tooth, in a thin, pain-racked voice. "Take me home."

Beefy rubbed his jaw. Nasty, nagging face-ache, just when the hero was facing disaster! He thought longingly of his

1

ERIC MALPASS

bed, that roll of linoleum into which he fitted so snugly, of the old hassock that was his pillow. Sleep, and forgetfulness.

He turned to his neighbour. "Heck," he said. "I got face-ache."

Heck's eyes did not leave the screen. Beefy looked anxiously at his idol's thin features, at the sharp nose, the stylish black side-whiskers, the lank, greasy hair. Perhaps he hadn't heard. "I got face-ache," he repeated plaintively.

Heck continued to watch the screen, but he spoke out of the side of his mouth. "What you expect me to do about it?" he asked.

"Oh, nothing," Beefy hurried to say. "I just thought I'd go home. Get to bed early, see."

"Oh, don't fidget," Heck said irritably. Eyes glued to the screen, he pulled a fresh piece of gum out of his pocket, unwrapped it, put it in his mouth.

"Take me home," moaned the tooth, but Beefy sat, motionless, so as not to disturb his friend, until the film ended.

It was followed by an advertisement that showed a beautiful girl coyly and winsomely offering ice cream to the patrons. Then the lights went up, and there, scowling at the citizens, was Bessie Brown, one eye on her tray of ice cream and the other up the chimney, symbolizing the change from the tinsel world of make-believe to the grim world of reality.

The tooth screamed. "Take me home, take me home, take me home."

Beefy pondered. He'd only seen the programme round once. And if he went home at this early hour he might not be able to get in. And Heck might be annoyed.

Then he thought of his cosy roll of linoleum, with an old stone ginger-pop bottle, full of boiling water, pushed up one end, and himself pushed down the other. The vision was unimaginably attractive. It drew him like a magnet.

2

"You stay and see it round again, Heck," he said. "I think I'll be getting along."

Heck grunted. Beefy looked at him anxiously, hoping that he would give some sign that he was not cross. But Heck seemed already to have forgotten his friend.

Sadly, Beefy came home early. And, by so doing, discovered a plan that threatened to rob himself and several other worthy citizens of their *pied-à-terre*, of their little bit of comfort in a harsh world, of their very home.

There can be few places more unattractive than the Midland town of Danby.

Dirtier places, yes; even, perhaps, uglier places; but for sheer downright mediocrity, Danby is supreme. It is as tasteless as a stale bun; as characterless as a station waiting-room.

In fact, in some ways it is not unlike a station waiting-room. All day, all night, the trains go screaming through, bearing fortunate people to exciting places, to the deer forests of Scotland, to the gold-paved streets of London, along the sunset track to Wales. And the inhabitants, like the porter in the waiting-room, watch the fiery beast drag its chain of cosy, bright parlours into the primeval dark; and they sign, and throw a little more coal on to the fire, and think wistfully, of far places.

Nearly two centuries ago, money was poured out, and men sweated and died to cut canals through the sad Midland plain. Like the railways, these canals converged on Danby. Through the long days of forgotten summers, the slow, patient horses dragged the gipsy-painted coal barges beside quiet meadows; and, in winter, the ice rang and sang to the lash the skates. But now the horses have gone, and the bargees with their golden earrings. The sedge grows beside the canal, the channel is narrow, and all Danby comes out on a Sunday morning in wellingtons and scarves, with a rod and line and a tin of bait, and a sandwich or two, and sits, meditating, beside the still waters.

The great, metalled roads lead out of Danby in all directions. If you take one you come to Leicester; if you take another you come to Coventry; and if you take a third, Heaven help you, you come to Birmingham.

When writing about Danby, it is perhaps natural to begin by discussing the ways of getting out of it. But we are not getting out of it. Resigned, we are staying in the place. We are going to take a look at the Parish of St Jude the Obscure.

There are twenty parishes in Danby; some high, some low and one, St Jude's, betwixt and between.

St Jude's is as unattractive as the rest of the town. It has a population of fifteen thousand. It has two cinemas, the Majestic and the Regal; five fish and chip saloons, frying daily; a fine selection of public houses; and the Kosy Kaff.

It has a dusty park with a wrought-iron, green-painted bandstand, where hot men in thick uniforms play Gems from the Operas on blue-serge-suited summer Sunday evenings.

Everyone does the Pools, and all but a few intellectuals have Television.

Sunday is the day when Dad gets a lie-in and there's a bit of real meat in the newspapers.

Intellectually, the parish ranges from the Reverend John Adams, MA, to old Lizzie Tubb, who assumes that the world is flat and that the stars are a painted backcloth; from little Miss Titterton, who writes such amusing sketches for the Dramatic Society, to old Lord Wapentake, a dim flame if ever there was one; from Heck, who is smarter than a wagon-load of monkeys, to Beefy.

The church itself is a horror of yellow brick. Built in the early nineteen hundreds, it is fussy, fretful, and as over-decorated as a Victorian barmaid. A narrow tower supports a needle-narrow metal spire. The spire supports an ornate and top-heavy weathervane. Fancies and whimsies cover the exterior like sores on an already ugly and foolish face. Even the door of the coal-hole has grotesque wrought-metal hinges.

On the other hand, the interior of the church is gaunt, cold and bare. At evensong, with the lights on, and the candles blowing draughtily on the altar, there are sinister shadows lurking in the high roof. But at early Communion, on a foggy morning, the church is as cheerless as a tomb.

And yet, for fifty years, men have left these doors with a warm feeling in their hearts for their God and for their fellow men. They have seen visions here, and talked with God here, and taken into their mouths the Body and Blood of Christ.

So it is with the Parish of St Jude the Obscure, with the drab, ugly Parish of St Jude. If you want to, you will find beauty; though you will have to search as you search for violets. But beauty is there, sure enough. The warmth of sunlight on old brick; the look on a mother's face as she watches her sleeping child; and sometimes in Heaven they turn the snow on and blot the whole place out for a few merciful days with sparkling, celestial icing sugar. There are no cloud-capped towers, but there are little homes with men returning to them in the evenings. There are no gleaming mountains, piled, like clouds on the horizon; but, sometimes, there are clouds piled like mountains. Lift up your eyes, when you tire of Danby, for even Danby has an English heaven.

But Beefy, coming home through streets lit by an afterglow in which the lamps burnt like stars, Beefy did not lift up his eyes. He walked with them downcast. Heck hadn't liked him coming out and leaving him, Beefy was sure of that. And his face-ache. It was chronic. Like someone trying to prise his gum open with a pickaxe.

Now he had left the main road where, day and night, the great green buses roar. He was in poor back streets, with a few late children playing and the houses rising from the pavements like red brick cliffs. Nearly home now. He came to a dreary crossroads. On one corner was the Lord Nelson, on another a chip shop, on the third a beer-off; and on the fourth, starkly silhouetted in all its hideousness against the clear afterglow, was St Jude's Church Hall.

Beefy went up to the door, pulled out a bunch of skeleton keys, and let himself in.

CHAPTER 2

The Parochial Church Council of St Jude's was in earnest session.

In the chair was the Vicar, the reverend John Adams, MA, a four-square young man in pepper and salt tweed jacket, flannels, and clerical collar; his fair, freckled face wearing its usual expression of benevolent, but slightly baffled, exasperation.

If only, he seemed to be thinking, if only my problems would put on human form and a pair of rugger shorts, then I should know just how to tackle them. Grab 'em resolutely below the knees, bring 'em down, that was the way. But you couldn't grab a debt of £15,000 below the knees. You couldn't get your hands on it at all, somehow. It was like playing rugger against a team of ghosts.

On the Vicar's right was the spare, erect form of Mr Edward Macmillan, people's warden, manager of the Danby Branch of the Northern Counties Bank; a cold man, the Vicar thought; a man who would know you through and through, but who would never let you know him. Next, the quite negligible figure of the vicar's warden, Mr John Smith.

Scribble, scribble, scribble went little Miss Titterton, secretary to the council, on the Vicar's left, like a little mouse, putting it all down, all the wisdom and the nonsense, and the kindliness and the laughter; all to be reduced to a soulless, precise Minute.

Facing the Vicar were the councillors; twelve gentlemen and nine ladies; twenty-one Incalculables who would agree to spend £500 at the drop of a hat, and then argue for half an hour over a bill for half a crown; who regarded the Vicar very much as Parliament regarded King Charles I; and yet who, if trouble threatened, would be behind him to the last man.

Tonight the last two items on the agenda were as follows:

> Confetti at Weddings.
> Erection of New Church Hall.

Of course, the item everyone was really interested in, that would call for long and earnest discussion, that the Vicar was burning to get his teeth into, was the last. But somehow the meeting had got itself bogged down on the penultimate.

There had been a short, friendly, sensible discussion on various ways of fighting the confetti menace at weddings. Several suggestions had been made, including that of having printed notices requesting the congregation not to throw confetti in the churchyard or the church. Everyone agreed this should be done, and then someone said, What colour should the notices be, and the fun started.

Blue, said Miss Fribble, firmly.

We didn't want any damn namby pamby colours, begging the Vicar's pardon, said George Bloodshot. We wanted something that would catch the eye. Red. Couldn't beat red. They'd see it all right if it was in red.

The Vicar was getting restive. "Will someone propose that we have white cards with red printing?" he asked. He looked round hopefully.

But the meeting was uneasy, unwilling to commit itself without further thought and discussion.

"I have a feeling – mark you, it's only a feeling. I may be wrong, but I have a feeling that red might clash with the altar curtains," said Mrs Fosdyke.

Miss Austin thought yellow was such a nice, cheerful colour. Made you think of daffodils and things.

Bert Briggs liked black.

Joe Grayson got a laugh by saying, "We was talking about weddings, Bert, not funerals."

John Adams banged his gavel. "We're wasting time, ladies and gentlemen," he said. "Will someone propose that we have white cards with blue printing?"

"Blue cards with white printing might be rather effective," suggested Cyril Mayflower, an artistic young man whom, secretly, the Vicar thought was a bit cissy.

The debate continued; until George Bloodshot and Bert Briggs, realizing that, if something wasn't done quick, they'd be calling "Time" at the Poet and Peasant before the meeting finished, proposed, and seconded, that a small committee of ladies be appointed to go into the matter and report back to the council.

Those in favour? Carried unanimously.

John Adams glanced at his sturdy wrist watch. "And now," he said solemnly, "we come to the most important item on our agenda for tonight; probably the most important item on this council's agendas for many years. The erection of a new church hall."

This was a matter very close to his heart. The present hall, where they were at this moment, was a shrine of Victorian ugliness and gloom. It was hopelessly inadequate for a live and growing parish. It was dark, cramped, and unutterably depressing. But in the Vicar's mind's eye was another church hall, bearing no resemblance to the present one than the New Jerusalem bears to the Old. It was light, and gay, and roomy, all green and cream, with plenty of cloakroom accommodation, a well-equipped stage, and bright, airy rooms. And in this pleasant place the healthy, well-nourished children of the New Age would look back to the Manger and the Star, and forward to the Brave New World that was theirs for the asking.

But could he get this vision across? Could he fire the council with his own enthusiasm? For without their co-operation he was helpless.

He looked at the council. Yes. He had their attention. Miss Titterton sat, pencil poised. Old Willie Ironmonger noisily shifted his humbug from port to starboard. Twenty-four pairs of eyes gazed expectantly at the Vicar. They were his, he realized exultantly. His to mould and influence into the acceptance of his vision.

He began to speak, confidently, convincingly. Then, to his horror, old Lord Wapentake rose to his feet, looked round to gather attention.

"I wonder," he said, "whether we are right in thinking that red is a startling colour. May it not be used as a danger signal simply because it is the colour of blood?" He put his hands in his pockets, settled himself more comfortably. "I have known colour-blind people who are quite unable to distinguish between dark red and brown," he continued.

John Adams, frustrated in a tense moment, did not quite know whether he wanted to snap or to laugh. He decided he wanted to laugh. "You're on the wrong item, Lord Wapentake," he said. "We're discussing the new church hall now."

"Oh," said Lord Wapentake. He looked round with a "Why wasn't I informed?" sort of expression. He sat down. The Vicar tried again. Lord Wapentake began telling his neighbour about a feller he'd known in Simla who'd been *absolutely* colour-blind. Saw everything grey. "And the joke was," said Lord Wapentake, his voice suddenly bursting forth loud and clear like a wireless set when you turn the volume up, "the joke was, the feller was a colour sergeant." He chortled loudly to himself. "Colour sergeant," he underlined, "and he couldn't tell crimson from flaming yellow."

The old gentleman subsided, mopping his streaming eyes. A little coldly, the Vicar began again.

But he soon warmed to his theme. He told his dreams. He spoke of the inadequacy of the present room. But there was plenty of space near the church to build a new church hall. He spoke of the bright, airy rooms, of the big hall with its stacking chairs, of the numbers of washing basins. His eyes glowed. He was carrying the council with him, he could feel it. It was like running up the field, the ball under your arm, outstripping or outwitting the opposing backs, and seeing the touchline clear before you.

At last he stopped. Mr Macmillan spoke into the silence.

"Can the Vicar give us any idea how much this project is likely to cost?" he asked.

The Vicar set his jaw. "About fifteen thousand pounds," he said firmly.

A gasp of sheer horror went up from the council.

"Will the treasurer tell us how much we have in the bank?" Mr Macmillan asked.

"Nine pounds, three shillings and four pence," said the treasurer.

Joe Grayson was in form tonight. He got another laugh by saying, "Leaves a bit of a balance to find, don't it."

"We shall find it all right," said John Adams.

But to his dismay he saw that the members of the council weren't with him. They wouldn't meet his eye. The whole scheme was too big. They were frightened.

"Let's try to reduce the figure," he pleaded. "I scared you with my fifteen thousand pounds. But we can expect some help from the diocese. And don't forget that we already have this hall that we are in now. I'm quite sure one of the factories round here would be only too pleased to buy it for a store-house."

He paused, and looked at their faces. They were coming round a bit. But they still weren't with him. Oh, why couldn't they see his vision? Why hadn't they got faith? Somehow he'd failed.

But at that moment there was a diversion; a noise outside the door, the unmistakable noise of someone sneezing.

"Excuse me, Vicar," said George Bloodshot. "Those kids again." He hurried to the door, wrenched it open.

The door led on to a short, lofty passage. On one side of this was the door into the kitchen. On the other the outside door. And above, high in the wall, attainable only with a ladder, was a door leading into the loft. George Bloodshot switched on the light. To his surprise, the passage was empty. No kids. He opened the outside door. This led on to an unlit alley that ran between the church hall and a high brick wall. And in the darkness it seemed to George that a thickset man in a striped singlet was just whipping out of the alley into Rockefeller Avenue, the grim back street in which St Jude's church hall was situated.

George didn't give chase. He returned to the meeting. He went in, quietly shutting the door behind him.

"What a nuisance those kids are," said Bert Briggs. "No discipline, nowadays."

"It wasn't kids," said George. "I think it was a man."

Miss Fribble asked nervously. "Do you think someone was listening to us?"

"I hope not," cried the Vicar, suddenly inspired. He banged the table with his fist. He leapt to his feet. "I hope no one was listening to us, being craven when we should be bold, being afraid of a little work, a little giving, when we should be on fire to give this parish the kind of hall it needs; being afraid to give our children, and our children's children, a place of which we could be proud." He sat down, his hands trembling. He stuck his pipe in his mouth, took it out, peered at the tobacco packed into the bowl, put the pipe on the table. Breathing rather quickly, he glared at the council.

Miss Titterton sucked her pencil. Definitely not for the minutes, she decided.

The council looked thoroughly embarrassed. Not quite English, this sort of outburst.

But then they began to wonder. Was this not, perhaps, the way the Church Militant should speak on occasion? They considered.

The Vicar sighed. The moment was passing. But then, to his delight, he saw the firm, solid figure of Alfred Mason stirring. It rose.

Alfred Mason had a strange light in his eyes. "I propose," he said, speaking slowly, "that the Vicar be authorized to instruct the church architect to produce plans for a new church hall adjacent to the church, at an approximate cost of fifteen thousand pounds."

"Will anyone second that motion?" the Vicar asked quietly.

There was a long, thoughtful silence. Everyone was wrestling with his thoughts and his conscience.

George Bloodshot rose. "I second the motion," he said.

The Vicar kept the happiness out of his voice, but it shone in his eyes. "Those in favour?" he asked.

Every right hand sprang up. John Adam's heart rose within him. "Those against?" he asked.

They sat as still as mice. "Carried unanimously," said the Vicar.

The meeting broke up. "Mauve's a pretty colour," said Lord Wapentake as they helped him into his coat.

Chapter 3

Black night now. All things came home. The little furry things flickered into their holes, they curled up in the darkness, almost safe for a few hours. Birds settled down uncomfortably in the hedgerows, while Earth, shuttling like an old goods train along its little branch line in space, lumbered once more through the tunnel. Dogs dozed and twitched by dying fires. Only the cats still stalked, bringing the terror and majesty of the jungle to grubby backyards.

George Bloodshot and Bert Briggs, whistles wetted, came out of the Poet and Peasant and turned homewards. Lord Wapentake, gulping his whisky, told his wife they'd spent the whole damn evening arguing about colour schemes for some new altar curtains. The Reverend John Adams let himself into his great, gaunt vicarage, and was greeted by nothing friendlier than the familiar smells of gas, and damp, and boiled cabbage. He ate some bread and cheese, and drank a cup of cocoa.

And Beefy Jones came back once more to the now deserted church hall and let himself in with his skeleton keys.

He put the kettle on in the kitchen. Then he propped the ladder against the passage wall, climbed up into the loft to get his ginger-pop bottle, and brought it down to fill it.

But he didn't want any supper. It wasn't only his face-ache. He'd had a nasty shock this evening.

14

Usually when he came home the church hall was empty. The Guides, or the Cubs, or the Men's Fellowship had left. One of the disadvantages of making your home in a church hall without the knowledge or consent of the Vicar was that, if you came home early, you found the place still occupied. Beefy, seeing the light under the door of the small room, hearing the murmur of a voice, had not dared to risk putting his ladder into position and going up into the loft.

Instead he went and put his eye to the keyhole. He couldn't see much. There was the parson, on his feet, talking, and sitting on his right a pale, tall man who looked as though he didn't go much on what the parson was saying.

Beefy hadn't gone much on what the parson was saying, either. He didn't quite understand it, of course. In fact, unless things were explained to him very slowly and carefully, he never did. But he understood enough to know that they were going to sell his home to a factory. And then where would he be? Nightwatchmen, police; he foresaw trouble with all kinds of unsympathetic types. Then, before he could hear any more, he'd sneezed, and had to run for it.

Sadly he filled his bottle. He climbed the ladder into the loft, and slid into his roll of linoleum. The hassock was hard to his aching face. Lying there, in mental and physical discomfort, he stared at the naked electric light bulb, and wished the boys would come. The boys were clever. They'd know what to do.

As usual, when he was in trouble, he turned his thoughts to the distant village of Shepherd's Delight. That was where he was going to retire to, one day, when he'd got a bit of money. He'd have a little cottage there, with a garden, and a pig, and a few hens. And on summer evenings he'd lean over the gate of the sty and scratch the old pig's back with a stick until she rolled over with a faraway look in her eyes. Then he'd go inside and get himself a bit of supper and then go up to a little room with a sloping ceiling and sleep in a real bed until the sun came peeping into the room again. No more crime. No more face-ache. And, somehow, he'd have learnt to read by then. He would read Westerns all day long.

Of course, he hadn't been to Shepherd's Delight since he was a boy, since he used to go and see his Auntie Nellie, and play with his little cousin Sally. He liked Sally. She was pretty, and kind, and cheerful. He wondered where she was now. For the first time it occurred to him that she would no longer be a little girl. She'd be – what? Beefy reckoned he must be about thirty. And Sally was five years younger. He counted on his fingers. Goodness, Sally must be a woman of twenty-five. He'd be afraid of her. She'd laugh at him, with his big, red hands and clumsy feet. Perhaps she was married, to a clever, smart man who would turn his nose up at Beefy.

He didn't like his thoughts now. He turned them back to Shepherd's Delight.

By now the village was half-memory, half-fantasy. It was set high, and you came to it by a grassy track that ran beside a wood, and behind it was a mountain, blue, remote, mysterious. Often, in his dreams, Beefy walked along the track, his feet rustling the autumn leaves, and he saw the blue smoke crawling up from the chimneys of Shepherd's Delight; but he never reached the village. Always he awoke too soon, to the grey dawn creeping through the dirty fanlight of the loft, and the snores of the boys.

But here were some of the boys at last. He heard the door downstairs being opened, footsteps on the ladder. The loft door was pushed open. Peg Leg Evans' face appeared on the threshold.

Peg Leg was completely bald. His head looked as though it were carved out of teak, well treated with linseed oil. On each side of the thin-lipped mouth two deep lines had been chiselled from nostril to jaw. The eyes were a hard yellow.

"You're home early, Beefy," he said. "Didn't you see the picture round?"

"Only once," said Beefy. "I got face-ache."

Peg Leg Evans pulled himself into the loft. "Pore old Beefy," he said. "Have you tried rubbing it with brandy?" He pulled out a flask. "Here. Put some of this on."

"Thanks, Peg," said Beefy. Without much hope he rubbed some of the brandy on his gum. It tasted nasty. Beefy's favourite drink was dandelion and burdock.

A little, cheerful face appeared in the doorway. "Hey, Joe," Peg Leg addressed it. "What you do for face-ache in Russia?"

Joe Vodka pulled himself in. "Pliz, what is face-ache?" he asked.

Peg Leg made anguished pantomime. Joe grinned. He understood. He pulled out a flask. "Vodka! Much Vodka," he said, giving the flask to Peg Leg.

Peg Leg passed it to Beefy. "Have a good swig, chum," he said kindly.

Beefy had a good swig. It tasted awful.

Lofty Longbottom and Willie One Eye came in. "What's wrong with Beefy?" they asked.

"I got face-ache," said Beefy. "And I feel sick."

"Can't beat whisky," said Willie One Eye.

"Gin's best," said Lofty.

They produced flasks. Willie pushed a whisky-wet finger into Beefy's mouth and rubbed. Lofty did the same with gin.

"Any better?" they asked.

"A bit," lied Beefy kindly. "I got some bad news," he managed to say at last.

But at that moment Heck arrived. "Just been talking to Ida," he said. "She's called a board meeting for tomorrow morning. Downstairs, here. As soon as the old woman's done cleaning up." He looked at himself in the cracked mirror, lifting his long upper lip like a dog to reveal his unsavoury teeth.

Beefy groaned. He didn't like board meetings. They made him nervous. And he'd got face-ache. He groaned again. "What's wrong with him?" Heck asked.

They told him. He went on studying his teeth. "I know," he said. "He was binding in the pictures."

The men forgot to ask Beefy about his bad news. They began getting ready for bed. Heck took off his corduroy jacket and folded it carefully. Willie One Eye removed his glass eye and put it in an old cup, a proceeding that always fascinated Beefy. Lofty Longbottom stretched his great length out on the floor. "Hope you'll get some sleep, Beefy," he said kindly.

"I got bad news," repeated Beefy. He made a great effort to marshal his words. "They're going to sell this place to a factory."

He was rather pleased with the reaction. No one ever took much notice of Beefy as a rule. But this time they really were interested. Lofty propped himself anxiously on an elbow. Heck stopped smearing margarine on his hair and stared down at Beefy's head protruding sadly from its roll of linoleum. Peg Leg Evans, who had been hanging his trousers carefully over a disused bier, froze into listening silence. Even Joe Vodka caught the prevailing apprehension. "Pliz, what is factory?" he asked.

Heck squatted down beside Beefy. "How do you know?" he asked.

"I heard them talking downstairs," Beefy said. "They're going to build another church hall and sell this one to a factory."

There was a stunned silence. "We've got to stop this," said Peg Leg. "Somehow."

"Not a very nice way of going on," said Lofty Longbottom. "Selling somebody's home to a factory. I thought better of them than that."

"But they don't know it is our home," pointed out Peg Leg, who liked to get things right.

"Well, if they did they wouldn't let us stay here anyway," said Lofty. "So it comes to the same thing."

Beefy tried to work this out, and felt more sick than ever. But the ethics of the case left him cold. All he knew was that someone was threatening the nearest thing to a home that he had known since he left Grandma's cottage and went into the world; and he felt lost, and frightened, and quite helpless.

Heck was still squatting beside Beefy, staring at him with his cold, pale eyes. He said, "You'll have to bring it up at tomorrow's meeting, under 'Any Other Business'. Ida may be able to suggest something."

Beefy looked with horror at his friend. "Me bring it up?" he cried. "But I shouldn't know what to say. I ain't educated, see."

Heck said a rude word, stood up, and went back to the mirror.

"Wouldn't *you* bring it up at the meeting, Heck?" pleaded Beefy. "You'd know what to say, like."

"You make me sick," said Heck, studying his teeth.

Peg Leg Evans, who always slept with a towel wrapped round his head, mumbled, "You ought to do it yourself, Beefy. You know what it's all about, see."

"But I don't," desperately cried Beefy, who had very little idea what anything was about.

"Aw, go to sleep," said Heck. He stretched himself luxuriously on a mossy bank, an old stage prop from St Jude's Dramatic Society's production of *A Midsummer Night's Dream*. "Put the light out, somebody."

No one moved. So Beefy extricated himself from his linoleum, climbed down the ladder into the passage, switched off the light, climbed back into the loft, groped his way back to bed, and wormed himself in. Through the grimy fanlight the stars wheeled, clean, aloof. Beefy watched them. Sleep did not come. His tooth swelled, and jumped, and cried out. But his mental suffering was even greater than his physical. Not only was he faced with homelessness; but in the morning he'd got to say something at the meeting. He'd got to make a speech, answer questions maybe. "Any other business?" Ida would say, and then everyone would look at Beefy and he'd have to stand up and say –. What? He tried to think what he would say. But, to Beefy, words were like minnows in a stream. There they were, still. And you put in your hand to grasp them and suddenly they'd gone, scattered. You never caught one. And even if you did manage to grab some, and put them in a jam jar, by the time you wanted to use them they were floating, silvery, useless corpses, on the surface of the water. He knew that untold agonies awaited him on the morrow. He groaned aloud. "Aw, shut up," murmured Heck in his sleep.

Uncaring for Beefy and his troubles, the morrow's sun rose relentlessly. Down in Rockefeller Avenue old Lizzie Tubb rolled out of bed and pulled a jumble-sale jumper over her underclothes. She climbed into a skirt that Mrs Fosdyke had given her, and slipped on a pair of off-white plimsolls that she had salvaged from heaven knows where. On her head she put the mob cap she had bought herself for her sixtieth birthday, and she clipped her steel-rimmed glasses over her ears. Lastly she put on her apron, a sack stamped with the words "1cwt Finest Bone Meal". She gave Blackie a bone, and shuffled off to the church hall and cleaned up.

When she came away Beefy was watching her from the big fanlight. He did wish he knew what it said on her apron.

Could it be her name? Or her address in case she forgot where she lived? Not for the first time he wondered whether he might ask one of the boys. But he was sensitive about his lack of education, and disliked having attention drawn to it. Anyway, he was too worried to bother much about it this morning. He'd got to make a speech. Life was moving inexorably towards that terrible moment when Ida would ask, "Any other business?"

He came down into the kitchen. There was great activity here. Heck was shaving. Lofty was getting the Mothers' Union cups out for breakfast. Joe Vodka was grilling kippers.

"How's your face-ache, Beefy?" asked Peg Leg Evans. "You don't look very cheerful."

"I got problems," Beefy said miserably. He spoke furtively. "If I was to tell you a speech, Peg, would you write it down? Then I should know what to say."

"But you wouldn't be able to read it if I did, Beefy," Peg Leg explained kindly. "On account of you ain't educated, see."

Not for the first time Beefy wished that, like Peg, he had a clear incisive brain that went straight to the heart of a problem.

"I hadn't thought of that," he muttered. He wandered off into the other room, thinking till it hurt. " 'Any other business?' Ida says, and then I stand up and say, 'Ladies and gentlemen, they're going to sell it to a factory on account of they're going to build another. I'd got face-ache, see, so I came home early, only saw the big picture round once, didn't even find out what it was about quite on account of only seeing it round once. They're going to build another one near the church.' "

That sounded pretty clear, he decided. And it had got to be clear so that they wouldn't all start asking him questions he couldn't answer. But, however clear it was, he knew he'd forget it all before the time came.

The assorted spirits seemed to have done his face-ache good. But he didn't want any breakfast. He was too worried.

Lofty and Willie One Eye began getting the room ready for the meeting. They set chairs round the table. They gathered up old agenda papers left by the church council, and put one before each chair. Heck fussed busily with his minute book.

There was the sound of a skeleton key in the lock. The outside door was flung open. Ida, twice as large as life but not half as natural, stood beaming in the doorway.

CHAPTER 4

Ida's face was brightly painted. Her hair was dyed bright auburn. She bulged all round a black silk dress, her pallid flesh, where visible, hanging in folds. Her fingers were fat and crinkled. Her ankles hung over her high-heeled shoes. She looked as though her idea of heaven would be to sit for ever in front of a large fire, eating peppermint creams washed down with stout, and reading the Sunday newspapers.

Only her eyes gave her away. They were alive, humorous, and, in their way, kind.

For Ida was a woman with a mission, a person of considerable vision and imagination. She was not satisfied with the *status quo*. Like all those born before their time, she wanted to mould things nearer to the heart's desire.

Crime does not pay, but it ought to, she had taken as her thesis. But why didn't crime pay? She had tried to analyse the problem.

Generally speaking, overheads were low, and the Commissioners of Inland Revenue, with unparalleled generosity, made no claims on the profits of the criminal. Also, the malefactor had no social position to keep up, and was not expected to entertain lavishly. And yet, in an England of unparalleled prosperity, there were two classes whose standard of living entirely failed to reflect the economic wealth of the country; the middle, and the criminal, classes.

So far as Ida was concerned, the middle classes could go hang themselves. But she was criminal class through and through. And if, before she died, she could do something to help this depressed minority, then she would go on her way happy.

She had given much thought to the problem. It seemed to her that the criminal was still living too much in the world of the little, free-enterprise, man. Rather like England at the turn of the century. Now Ida was no Socialist. She was not ideologically opposed to free enterprise. She just thought that the day of the little man was passed.

The people in the money nowadays, she realized, were the big, highly organized limited companies. You could struggle along on your own for ever and not get anywhere.

So she formed her own limited company. True, it had no certificate of incorporation, no memorandum or articles. It hadn't even got a name, being known simply as the Company. But it had a board of directors, under the chairmanship of Ida, and its aims were, one, to make money; two, to raise the prestige of the criminal; three, to canalize his efforts.

So far all three aims had failed completely. The Company continued to make enough money to pay modest fees to the directors; but that was all.

Plant and machinery consisted of a battered yellow van, a collection of jemmies and skeleton keys, and a second-hand printing press for producing thousand-pound notes. Since, however, in the post-war years, the mere sight of a thousand-pound note would attract every policeman within a radius of fifty miles, this last item was a wasted asset. Ida would have liked to sell it and buy a fruit machine, but there were no takers. It wasn't the sort of thing you could advertise on a postcard in a newsagent's window, she reflected sadly.

Ida entered the church hall, and took the chair. Her directors filed in and sat down. "Good morning, gentlemen," she said cheerfully.

"Morning, Mr Chairman," they said dutifully. She looked round. Queer bunch, she thought. But what could you expect? She'd found Heck, her secretary, in a pin-table saloon. She'd picked up Peg Leg Evans, masked, just descending by ladder from the bathroom window of a house at two o'clock one morning. She'd never really believed his story that it was to have been an elopement but that the girl had changed her mind.

Willie One Eye, Lofty Longbottom and Joe Vodka, she'd met as they came down the prison steps. And Beefy! She'd never forgotten the look of sheer joy on his face when she'd asked him whether he'd like to be a company director. "Me?" he'd beamed, putting down his barrow of coke and scratching his striped vest, for at that time he earned an honest living running errands for people. "Me? A company director? One of those geezers in silk hats?"

The silk hat would perhaps come later, she had explained. That depended on the prosperity of the company. And the prosperity of the company would depend on – Beefy.

She looked at him now, doodling morosely on the back of a church council agenda paper. Something on his mind, she thought. On his what? she asked herself. She laughed mirthlessly.

"May we have the minutes of the last meeting, please?" she asked.

Heck the Sec. rose. He read the minutes. Reverently he laid the minute book before the chairman.

The chairman looked at her directors. "Am I to sign these as a true and correct record of the goings-on at our last meeting?" she asked.

Four right hands were raised in confirmation. A fifth right hand continued doodling.

"Beefy!" the chairman called reproachfully.

Beefy looked up to find all eyes watching him, and blushed. The very thing he always tried to avoid! Now he'd have to talk in front of everybody.

The chairman still sounded reproving. "Beefy, you don't deserve to have a Sec. what can write." Heck modestly studied his fingernails. "You didn't hear a word of them lovely minutes."

"I was taking notes," stammered Beefy lamely.

"Let me see them."

"Oh, no, Ida." Beefy, dismayed, stared down at his striped vest.

She held out an imperious hand. Beefy, blushing furiously, passed up his paper.

Ida studied it for some time. "You want to see one of them psychiatrists," she said at last. "They can do things for people like you."

"Such as like what?" asked Beefy defensively.

Ida settled her vast bulk back in her chair. "Deep down in your unconscious," she explained kindly, "there's a nasty, festering tooth what's poisoning your whole system. A psychiatrist would pull it out, see."

The thing you noticed about Beefy was his jaw. His cranium, covered with sandy bristles, was small and negligible, like that of some primeval monster; and, if the eyes are windows on to a man's soul, Beefy, you felt, kept the blinds down. But his jaw! It was hard and strong as iron; it was like the prow of a battleship; it was the Rock of Gibraltar.

Now he put up a great fist and rubbed it, producing a sand-papery noise. "It don't ache no more, Ida," he said, puzzled.

The Chairman sighed, and changed the subject. "Matters arising," she said. "Item four in the minutes." She began to read. "The chairman said that crime did not pay, but it ought to. The balance sheet refused to show an increased profit. Members were asked to produce for the next meeting plans for increasing the profit-turnover ratio."

She looked round. Six pairs of eyes steadfastly refused to meet her gaze. "Well," she demanded. "Who's got any ideas?"

Silence.

"You lousy bunch of pinheads," said the chairman. "Hasn't anyone got an idea?"

Silence.

Ida tapped irritably with her pencil. "I suppose no one's noticed that the bankers of this town are having a dinner dance at the Assembly Rooms on the fifteenth of October," she said coldly.

"So what?" asked Peg Leg Evans, voicing the sentiments of all.

Heck the Sec. had been librarian during his last stretch, until the prison authorities, amazed at the sudden popularity of Burton's *Anatomy of Melancholy*, found that he had pasted a copy of *Wakey-Wakey* inside the tome and was lending it out at a couple of fags a go. He liked to air his book knowledge. "I know," he said. " 'On with the dance! let joy be unconfined;' But hark; what's happened? The Company's surrounded the place. It's a hold-up."

"I got it," chimed in Lofty Longbottom, his pale face strained with thought. "We keep 'em covered, and Peg Leg Evans stumps round, holding out his hat, and says, 'Help the lifeboat, ladies. Drop your tararas in the old titfer.' "

Beefy was getting overexcited. His words came tumbling out in his eagerness. "And I follow him round with my sweet persuader and I blows down the muzzle like the cowboys and I say, 'And any lady who don't feel like helping the lifeboat had better think again, unless she wants to see her gentleman friend stretched lifeless at her feet.' "

"Boys, boys," cut in Ida. "You got me wrong. There won't be no tararas at this particular shindig." Beefy's face fell. "These won't be no pearl and diamond toting dames; they'll just be solid middle class."

Beefy still looked blank and disappointed. "What you might call members of the *petite bourgeoisie*," Ida explained.

Beefy brightened immediately. "French dames?" he inquired hopefully.

"No, you fool." The chairman exploded, then straight away regretted it as she saw the hurt on Beefy's rock-hewn face. "Now, listen," she said. "The keys to every bank safe in town will be in the Assembly Rooms that night. All we got to do is collect those keys from the gentlemen, and label them. Then one party will stay behind and keep the gentlemen covered, while other members go round the various banks and empty the cash safes. Then the outdoor members come back to the Assembly Rooms, pick up the inside party, and we're miles away before they've even found that the telephone wires have been cut." She sat forward, elbows on table, and waited for the cheers.

Silence.

"Any questions?" she asked testily.

"Pliz, what is bank?" asked Joe Vodka. "And what is keys? And what is Assemble Rooms?"

"Oh, tell him, somebody," snapped Ida.

They told him.

"There'll be an awful lot of keys," pointed out Lofty Longbottom. "How shall we know which banks they fit?"

Ida produced her trump card. "Heck used to work in a bank," she said, proudly. "He knows all the local personnel."

A gasp went up from the assembled company. Heck, in a bank! They weren't sure they approved. It seemed to give a taint of respectability to their proceedings.

Heck hastened to justify himself. "I was a messenger," he explained. "Got the job on forged testimonials, and only stayed a month. You wouldn't believe how fussy they are in banks. But it was valuable experience."

The board relaxed. Obviously Heck had stooped to the job rather as a great author might stoop to road sweeping; for the sake of his art. But Beefy was staring at his idol, entranced.

"You wore one of them silk hats, Heck?" he asked. The side-whiskers, the pointed shoes, the gold teeth; and now above all, a silk hat. For the hundredth time Beefy thought wistfully how wonderful it must be to be Heck; clever, able not only to read but to write, polished, and now, with the knowledge no one could ever take from him, that he had once worn a silk hat.

The chairman banged the table with the cosh she used as a gavel. "Order," she cried. "Let's get down to details."

She spoke for a long time. The board listened, with strained, if bewildered, attention. "Now," she said at last. "Will someone propose that my suggestions be adopted?"

Peg Leg put up his hand. Lofty seconded. "Those in favour?" asked Ida.

Five hands went up. "Beefy!" called Ida.

Beefy stopped doodling, smiled seraphically. "It's all right this time," he said. "I was drawing Heck in his silk titfer." He put up his hand.

"Carried unanimously," declared the chairman. "Now then. Is there any other business?"

Beefy studied his drawing of Heck. Yes, it was good. He'd show it the boys afterwards. They'd like it. They'd say, "Good ole Beefy."

Then he became aware that someone was kicking him persistently on the ankle. He looked up crossly, and found his fellow directors nodding, winking, or frowning at him. What had he done wrong now, he wondered.

"I don't get it, boys," he began.

Peg Leg Evans put his face next to Beefy's and hissed, "Any other business?"

"Oh!" cried Beefy. "Oh!" He scrambled to his feet and stood there, his mouth opening and closing, like a bewildered codfish. "Any other business?" That was his cue. But his mind was as empty as a weekday church. Swept, garnished. Not a word in sight. His fingers played frantically with his pencil.

"What is it, Beefy?" Ida asked, a trifle irritably. She was feeling a bit low. She'd been going to knock 'em cold with that lovely plan of hers about the bankers' shindig. And what happened? They'd taken it all as a matter of course. No thanks. No appreciation. Disappointment gnawed at her.

Beads of sweat stood out on what there was of Beefy's brow. His great fingers twisted and twisted at the pencil. Ida was getting cross now. This was even worse than he had imagined. Then, like a little cloud floating in a summer sky, a word drifted into the uncharted spaces of his mind. He clutched at it. "Factory," he gasped. "Factory."

"What do you mean, factory?" Ida asked, sighing. She bet a bank chairman didn't have all this frustration when he asked for "any other business".

"They're going to build one," Beefy said hurriedly. "Leastways, not a factory. They're – " Oh, if only all those eyes would stop watching him.

Something snapped. It was the pencil. Beefy looked at it stupidly. He'd been proud of that pencil. A bright, enamelled yellow, and now it was broken. He wondered whether Ida would give him another, or whether she'd be cross.

An irritable, impatient voice cut in. "Beefy's trying to say," Heck explained, "that he heard the parson say they was going to sell this place to a factory and build another hall near the church. And what he wants to know is, where's he going to perishing well sleep if they do."

Beefy gazed at his friend in admiration. The whole thing had been presented, clearly, in a few words. He saw Heck's brain dipping into a great barrel full of words, picking out just the ones he wanted, getting them quickly into the right order, stringing them like beads on a thread. Wonderful gift, that, thought Beefy.

But Ida seemed unimpressed. She was getting tired, and the matter-of-fact reception of her plan still rankled. She sat forward, plump elbows on table, and taking out her mirror and lipstick, repainted the great orange cupid's bow of her lips. She put the things back in her bag. She fixed the now uneasy meeting with a glinting eye. "Listen, boys," she said. "I'm your chairman. I'm your brain. I got you organized and I'll see that you stay that way. But I ain't your nursemaid. I ain't going to feed you or tie your bibs on or tuck you up in bed. And if you get turned out of this place I'm not going to find you alternative accommodation. You can find it yourselves. OK?"

"OK, Ida," they said sheepishly.

"Any other business?" she asked, hands on table, ready to lever herself to her feet.

Beefy rose. "Yes?" snapped Ida.

Beefy looked at his broken pencil. Then he looked at Ida's flashing eyes. He had second thoughts. He sat down.

"It's all right, Ida," he murmured sadly. The meeting was closed.

Ida went back to her hotel. The boys rather sheepishly climbed the ladder. "We got to do something," Beefy kept muttering hopelessly.

"Such as what?" asked Heck nastily.

Beefy looked at him in astonishment. "It's no good asking me," he said. "I ain't clever, see." He cheered up. "You'll know what to do, Heck," he went on. "You got brains."

Heck removed a pin from behind his lapel and picked his teeth. "We could try delaying tactics," he mused.

"What's them?" asked Beefy hopefully. He'd know all along Heck would think of something.

But Heck didn't answer. He threw himself on to his mossy bank, and began to read a ten-cent Western, his shoes pointing heavenwards like two diminutive steeples. Beefy sat cross-legged on the floor, watching Heck, and wondered what delaying tactics were.

His mind wandered. "Heck," he said. "Those silk titfers. Are they heavy?"

"No," Heck replied, not looking up.

Beefy wanted to ask so many things about silk hats. Whether they made you feel different from ordinary people, whether folk treated you differently, whether it mattered if you got them wet. But he was not good at framing questions, so he said, after a time, "They *look* heavy, somehow."

Heck did not reply. There was a long silence.

"Wisht I was educated," said Beefy, staring at his white plimsolls.

Heck sighed, and closed his book on a finger. "You went to school, didn't you?"

"They never learnt me nothing," said Beefy wistfully. "They tried. But after a bit they seemed to get discouraged, like."

Heck went on reading. There was silence, while Beefy tried to frame his next sentence. It was an important one.

"Would *you* learn me to read, Heck?" he asked, gazing shyly and anxiously at his friend.

"No," said Heck.

"That's all right," said Beefy, kindly.

Thoughtfully Willie One Eye scratched his glass eye with a nail file. "After the fifteenth of next month you'll be able to pay someone to read to you, Beefy," he pointed out.

What with one thing and another Beefy had forgotten about the fifteenth. Now he remembered. He was going to be rich! All they had to do was to get hold of a few keys, and help themselves to all the money they needed. Then, Shepherd's Delight, here I come! He would buy his cottage, and his hens and his pig. He would see the sun go down behind the blue mountain.

"Think I shall call my pig Emily," he said, smiling radiantly at Willie One Eye.

CHAPTER 5

October came, bringing clean grey pavements under clean, grey skies, or the serene, majestic days of the summer's old age, or high, windy days that tossed the birds down the sunlit wastes of sky.

In the great vicarage, that had once been noisy with children, proud with butlers, busy with servants; in the great vicarage John Adams washed up his tea things and wondered when he was ever going to get a new housekeeper. He'd been looking after himself for three months now, ever since old Miss Jenkins had had to go and nurse her aged brother. Not having a housekeeper wasn't too difficult in the summer, but it was going to be damned uncomfortable in the winter. If only he could find some good, capable woman to take the job on! Lizzie Tubb came in to do, of course. But, with all respects to Lizzie, she wasn't a great deal of help.

He finished washing up, hung the tea towel on the gas stove lid. He went to his study. Dark already. How the days were drawing in. He switched on the light, and looked happily at the sketch plans on his desk, plans of the new church hall. He hadn't wasted any time, he reflected. Only three weeks since the council meeting when he'd first raised the matter; and already he'd got the architect to produce plans; rough ones, of course, but good enough to present to the parochial church council at the special meeting that he had called for this evening.

For a time he examined them once more, his mind translating them into bricks and mortar, into bright, cheerful rooms, into the recreation room of a happy parish. Then he rolled them up, put them under his arm, and set off for the church hall.

In his eagerness he was early. None of the council had yet arrived. He switched the light on in the small room where the council held its meetings, and put the plans on the table while he took his coat off.

What he wanted now, he decided, was the blackboard, to fasten the plans to. It must be in the big room. He went through. The Guides were there. He had a word with them. Then he lugged the blackboard back into the small room. George Bloodshot and Bert Briggs had arrived.

"Hello, George. Hello, Bert," he said.

"Evening, Vicar."

"Just hold these plans against the blackboard while I stick the drawing pins in, will you," he said. He looked at the empty table. "Where *are* the plans?" he asked.

"What plans, Vicar?"

"The plans for the new church hall. They were on this table. Have you been looking at them?"

"Haven't even seen them," said George Bloodshot.

"Nothing on that table when we came in," said Bert Briggs.

The Vicar looked at them pleadingly. "But you *must* have had them," he said.

Bert and George looked hurt. Did he think they went around pinching plans?

"Are you sure you brought them, Vicar?" asked George. He knew parsons. Absent-minded lot. Old Canon Tumble, the late vicar, was always coming to church on his bicycle and then trudging off home without it.

The Vicar was getting a little testy.

"Of course I brought them," he said.

"Bet you anything you like they're still at the vicarage, sir," said Bert. He, too, knew parsons.

Joe Grayson arrived, and found the Vicar peering under the harmonium.

"Lost something, Vicar?" he asked.

The Vicar straightened up, red in the face. "It's a most extraordinary thing, Joe," he said. "But I put the plans on that table five minutes ago and they've simply disappeared."

Joe knew parsons. "Sure you brought them, Vicar?" he asked, with a scarcely concealed grin.

"Quite certain," the Vicar said shortly.

Mrs Fosdyke arrived. It wouldn't surprise her, she said, if the plans weren't still in the Vicar's study. She'd never forget how old Canon Tumble used to forget things. Not that she was saying anything against Canon Tumble, mind. He'd been a real gentleman, had the Canon.

Miss Titterton arrived and said, well, she was quite sure she'd never had the plans, so she couldn't have lost them. Now the Vicar was quite sure in his own mind, wasn't he, that she'd never had them. She wouldn't like anyone to think –

Lord Wapentake said plans! What plans? You didn't need plans for new altar curtains. Oh, plans for a new church hall. That was different. Yes, some feller had drawn up plans once. When? Oh, long before Old Tumble's time. If he remembered right they were at the bottom of the linen chest on the vicarage landing.

Cyril Mayflower and Willie Ironmonger, coming in late, both had an idea. Perhaps the Vicar had forgotten to bring the plans with him.

Still somewhat red in the face, the Vicar addressed the meeting.

"At seven twenty-five," he said, almost pleadingly, "I came into this room with the plans for a new church hall under my arm. I put them on that table while I went into the next room to fetch the blackboard. When I came back George Bloodshot and Bert Briggs were here, and the plans had completely disappeared. Now can anyone throw any light on this extraordinary business?"

Uncomfortable silence. "Sure you brought them, Vicar?" asked Alfred Mason, who had only just arrived.

The Vicar said yes so coldly that Alfred shut up quick.

"Has anyone looked in the loft?" asked Joe Grayson, hoping for a laugh.

He didn't get one. "No one's been up there for years," snapped the Vicar. "So why should the plans suddenly find their way up there?"

"Now that's a point I've been meaning to bring up for some time," said Mrs Fosdyke. "That loft must be a perfect junk room. I thought that, if the Vicar agreed, we might get the Scouts to clean it out sometime." She laughed gaily. "There's no knowing what we might find," she added.

"*Can* we keep to the matter in hand, Mrs Fosdyke?" pleaded the Vicar.

Uncomfortable silence.

"Ponsonby!" said Lord Wapentake so suddenly that everyone jumped. "Ponsonby! That was the feller!" He seemed to become aware that the meeting was not quite keeping up with him. "Feller who drew up those sketch plans," he explained. Dim-witted crowd, he thought to himself. If you didn't explain everything in words of one syllable they just sat and looked blank.

The Vicar rose. He was very pale. There was an uncontrollable tremor in his voice. He said, loudly, "This meeting is closed," and stalked out of the building.

The next day he visited the architect and, after a somewhat heated interview, secured the promise of a new set of sketch plans. He received them on the thirteenth and called a meeting for the fourteenth, at which he showed them to the council, who quite approved of them. He went home, locked the plans in his desk, and went to bed well pleased with his efforts.

The fifteenth dawned bright and clear. "Yes, we have no bananas, we have no bananas today," sang Beefy as he descended the ladder to breakfast. It was his one song. Grandma had learnt it him, when he was a little boy at Shepherd's Warning.

How happy he was! Today was his last day of poverty. Tomorrow he'd have all the money he wanted. They could sell the church hall as soon as they liked, now. They could even have his roll of linoleum. For the thousandth time he saw himself entering his little cottage at Shepherd's Delight, lighting the lamp, drawing the red curtains, and settling down for half an hour with his Western before going up to bed under the eaves. "But, YES," he carolled, as he stepped on to the floor of the passage. "We have no – " He saw Heck scowling at him, and stopped suddenly. Heck didn't like Beefy to sing. Heck said Beefy was tone-deaf.

"Sorry, Heck," said Beefy humbly.

The fifteenth! Old Lizzie Tubb put on her apron with its adornment of "1 cwt Finest Bone Meal", and set off to do for Mrs Fosdyke. But first she looked anxiously at Blackie, sitting morosely in his box. She saw, with the eye of love, the greying hair round ageing eyes, the listless effort to wag the stump of tail, the stiff plumpness, all the sad look of a dog growing old.

"Shan't be long, Blackie," she mumbled, her voice a caress for the one creature that loved her. "Shan't be long." She shambled off, into the golden day.

The fifteenth! Edward Macmillan telephoned the Vicar. Would it be possible for him to see those plans? He'd like to study them at his leisure. Perhaps effect a few economies. So at six o'clock in the evening the Vicar called at the Northern Counties Bank House and gave the plans to Edward Macmillan. "And for heaven's sake don't lose them," he laughed.

Mr Macmillan did not laugh. He seldom did. "*I* shan't lose them," he said. There were people, the Vicar gathered, who might lose plans. But Edward Macmillan was not one of them.

Rather reluctantly the Vicar handed over the big roll of papers. "We've got this meeting with the Archdeacon and the architect tomorrow morning at eleven," he said. "Will you bring the plans along?"

Mr Macmillan's tight lips flickered in a smile. "I'll bring them," he said. "Don't worry."

The Vicar left. He didn't quite like letting those plans out of his sight, even to anyone as efficient and trustworthy as Macmillan. There'd be a most awful rumpus if this lot disappeared. But how could they, he consoled himself pedalling thoughtfully down the High Street.

The lights were out in the banks. All over the outskirts of the town, in neat little semi-detached houses, in villas with tidy gardens, bank clerks sat and scrubbed in hot baths, while bank clerks' wives dabbed powder on their noses, each wondering whether she would be the only lady in the Assembly Rooms to be wearing last year's frock.

But Mr Macmillan was not one for parties. He wasn't going. He developed a headache, and decided that he'd have a quiet evening in his study with those plans; and, if he wasn't going, neither was Mrs Macmillan. That was that.

In the loft of the church hall Beefy happily cleaned his revolver, and sang, "Yes, we have no bananas", and dreamed of the woodsmoke-sweet village of Shepherd's Delight, where falls not hail, or rain, or any snow, nor ever wind blows loudly.

Everything went like clockwork. At precisely eleven p.m. the gang marched into the bankers' dance, just in the middle of the tea break.

Peg Leg Evans went up to the deserted bandstand and clashed the cymbals. Like the rest, he was wearing a rather dramatic mask.

"I want all the gentlemen to proceed to the cloakroom in an orderly fashion," he bellowed.

He was disappointed. He had expected his dramatic announcement to be greeted with screams from the ladies, cries of rage from the gentlemen. Instead, there was an amused titter. This was something new in cabaret turns. Wasn't he a funny man!

Annoyed, he fired a couple of shots at the chandelier. "Come on, get going," he barked.

This time he got a real laugh.

But gradually the guests began to wonder what was happening. Rough men with nasty-looking guns were herding the gentlemen towards the cloakroom. They went, furious, bewildered, anxiously balancing cups of coffee and plates of meringues.

In the cloakroom Ida was seated at a card-table, a packet of labels in her hand. She had put on evening dress for the occasion, and her hair had turned an even brighter auburn. Behind her, Heck leaned against the wall, nonchalantly waving a revolver.

The first gentleman was marched up to the table.

"May I have your bank keys, please?" Ida sounded firm and business-like.

"My what?" gasped the gentleman.

"Come on. Your bank keys," snapped Ida.

"No, I'm hanged if I do," said the gentleman.

Heck stopped waving his gun. He pointed it at the gentleman's waistcoat. "I'm going to count three," he announced. "One, two – "

"I left them at home," said the gentleman.

"Search him," said Ida.

The gentleman put down his coffee cup, fished in his pocket, and flung a heavy bunch of keys on to the table.

"Which bank?" Ida asked.

Silence.

"Western National," said Heck briefly. "Next gentleman, please."

The business proceeded smoothly. At last Heck called, "Here you are, Beefy. That's all the keys to the Western National. Off you go."

Trembling with excitement, Beefy scooped up the great pile of keys. He ran through the ballroom, where Willie One Eye was keeping the dames covered, out of the entrance, guarded by Joe Vodka, leapt into the Company's van, and drove furiously to the Western National Bank.

He went to the side door, and was relieved to find that it was in a quiet, dark street. It was just as well. He tried key after key. None of them seemed to fit, but in the darkness he found it difficult to make sure that every key had been tried. Baffled and worried, he slipped the borrowed keys into his pocket, and pulled out his own skeletons.

It was easy with those. Within a few minutes he was inside the vast marble halls of the bank.

A faint light filtered in from a street light outside. Beefy looked round, listened to the empty silence. "Wisht I wasn't alone," he muttered. There were strange shapes, sinister shadows all about him. Then, in the dimness, he saw a heavy steel door set flush to the wall. This was it. Behind that door there was undoubtedly enough money to keep Beefy and his friends in luxury for the rest of their days. Carefully he flashed his torch. The door seemed to have three keyholes.

Beefy took out his borrowed keys, and went to work on that door. Half an hour later he stood back, looked at the unmoved square of steel with frustration and loathing, and kicked it. "Take that," he muttered. Not a single key had fitted. All that money, lying there, asking to be took, and this door just stood, refusing to be moved.

Unfortunately, no one had given Beefy any instructions covering such an eventuality, so he just didn't know what to do. He daren't go back empty-handed to the Assembly Rooms. Ida would shout. Tears of rage filled his eyes. He kicked the strong-room door again. Then, nonplussed, he wandered round to the counter, and began flashing his torch into the various drawers. There was so much money in a bank, he thought; they were quite likely to leave a few hundreds lying about.

But they hadn't. All he found was four twopenny stamps, an Egyptian piastre, and a lot of forms.

Forms fascinated Beefy. People of education, he knew, spent many happy hours filling them up; yet to him they were but a symbol of gracious living.

There were green forms and red forms and white forms. I bet that red one's an application for a million pounds, and the green one for under a million, he thought. Dear sir, I wish to apply for two million pounds. Yours sincerely… And then, the flourished signature. But no one would ever give Beefy a million pounds. He couldn't fill the forms in. He sighed.

Disconsolately he wandered to the back of the office. And, suddenly, his heart stopped beating. He couldn't believe his eyes.

His disappointment over the unyielding strong-room was forgotten. So were the empty tills. For there, shining in the faint light, august and serene, was a messenger's silk hat.

Meanwhile, Mr Macmillan had been having a pleasant evening with the sketch plans for the church hall. By midnight he decided that he'd saved the church a thousand pounds. With a sigh of pleasure in work well done he sat back. Now for a quiet ten minutes with the *Financial Times*; and then, bed.

But where was the *Financial Times*? Oh dear, he must have left it in the manager's room in the bank. Wearily he rose, and went to the door. Then he remembered the Vicar's anxiety about those wretched plans. He came back, unlocked his private drawer in the desk, stuffed the plans inside, locked the drawer again, and put the key in his pocket. Then he went down into the bank.

For a long time Beefy stood and gazed at the silk hat. Then, breathless, he picked it up and stroked its sleek surface. Finally, like an heir apparent trying on the crown, he put it on his head.

A light was switched on. "Great Scott!" said an astonished voice. Then: "May I ask what you think you're doing?"

Beefy spun round, whipping out his sweet persuader. "Reach for the sky," he snapped.

The newcomer reached for the sky. "Don't be such a fool," he said testily. "And for heaven's sake take that damn silly hat off."

Beefy was deeply hurt. He was terribly proud of his new hat. He kept it on.

"Who are you?" he asked.

The newcomer was tall, lean, and middle-aged, with a long, strong nose and a high forehead. He remained silent.

Beefy took careful aim with his sweet persuader. "Who are you?" he repeated.

"I live here. I happen to be manager of the bank you are trying to burgle. Or had you just decided to get a hat?"

Beefy thought this over. "You say you're manager here?" he asked.

"I am."

"Then why," asked Beefy accusingly. "Why don't none of your keys fit your perishing safe? And why aren't you at the dance?"

The manager looked at the revolver, "I had a headache, so I stayed at home. I still have a headache," he added wearily. "And holding my hands up in this ridiculously melodramatic position isn't helping it."

Beefy was very sorry about the headache. But he was firm. His mind raced at a most unusual speed. With his left hand he flung the borrowed keys at the manager's feet.

"Open that safe," he ordered. "And no funny business. This gun goes off easy."

The manager stooped and picked up the keys. He examined them.

"You'll never open my safe with this bunch," he said.

Beefy's suspicions were confirmed. Incredible though it seemed, Heck must have made a mistake. Telling him those were the keys to the Western National! Golly, the chairman of the Company wasn't half going to blow her top over this lot.

Then he froze. An awful thought had swum into the turgid waters of his mind. Suppose – suppose it wasn't Heck who'd made the mistake!

"This – this *is* the Western National Bank, isn't it?" he faltered.

"Western National? Great Scott, no! This is the Northern Counties."

Beefy had an awful, sinking feeling in his stomach. He said, miserably: "I was sure it was Western National. But I can't read, see. I couldn't check up. It's on account of I'm not educated." He trailed off. "I bet you can read," he said suddenly.

"I've mastered a few simple words," said the bank manager. "But the question is, what do we do now?"

He looked at the sweet persuader. It was still pointing uncomfortably at his waistcoat.

What indeed? It was bad enough having lost the lolly, and let the boys down. But now Beefy had acquired a bank manager, and he just didn't know what to do with him. If he let him out of his sight for one moment he'd be ringing the police or doing something equally unco-operative. And if he didn't let him out of his sight – well, they'd just stay here chatting till the staff arrived to open up the bank in the morning. And Beefy, even with the sweet persuader, couldn't tackle a whole staff.

Besides, the messenger would want his hat back.

It was then that Beefy had his idea.

It was probably the first idea that Beefy had ever had in his life, and at first he didn't know what to do with it. To begin with, he couldn't quite get hold of it. He put out his hands, and it faded, like flowers grasped in a dream. He took it in his arms, and it wriggled away, supple and slippery as a serpent, into the virgin jungle that constituted so large a part of his mind.

But at last he had it firmly. He knew what he was going to do now. He, Beefy, was going to strike out on his own. He was going to kidnap the bank manager, hold him to ransom, and, while they waited for the ransom to be paid, the bank manager was going to learn Beefy to read!

It was a whale of an idea.

Beefy dug his revolver into the manager's ribs. "There's a van outside," he said. "You'll get into the seat next to the driver. And if you utter one peep you're a dead man."

"Don't you think this nonsense has gone far enough?"

"Go on. Walk."

The manager ground his teeth. "By Jove, you're going to regret this. Can I fetch an overcoat?"

"I'll come with you," said Beefy.

They went into the Bank House. The manager got his coat. In doing so, he managed to knock an umbrella stand over. The noise reverberated through the silent house. Beefy was annoyed. "Now run," he ordered, poking the gun into the gentleman's side.

The street was deserted. Beefy put the bank manager into the van, and hurried round to the driving seat, keeping his victim covered through the windscreen. The door of the Bank House opened. A shaft of yellow light fell across the road. "Edward," called a woman's voice. "Where are you going?"

Beefy started the engine. The woman ran onto the pavement. "Edward," she cried.

Beefy let in the clutch. The woman grabbed at the door handle, missed. They were away, round a corner, tearing across the empty market place, swinging now into a wide road that ran past little shops and dingy pubs, past big villas, past a red rash of outlying houses, into the silent, waiting countryside.

Beefy drove with one hand. With the other he still held the sweet persuader against his passenger's ribs.

The bank manager's voice sounded a little strained. He was remembering all he had read of people being taken for rides, of inconvenient corpses tumbled from cars on lonely roads.

"May one ask where one is being taken?" he asked.

Beefy said happily, "We're going to see my Grandma."

"Angels and ministers of grace defend us," ejaculated the manager.

"What say?"

"Nothing."

Beefy looked suspiciously at his passenger. He hoped he wasn't trying to take the mickey. He didn't like people who took the mickey. It was nicest when everyone was kind, and friendly, and polite. In an effort to promote friendliness he said, "You can call me Beefy."

"Thanks very much."

Somehow the ice remained unbroken. "What's your name?" asked Beefy, still trying.

"Macmillan."

"Hiya, Mac," said Beefy.

Introductions had now been effected, but the passenger still seemed remote and aloof. Actually, he was watching the fuel gauge. Short of an accident, or a puncture, his best hope of escape seemed to be a halt for petrol. But the gauge still showed more than half-full.

"Where does your Grandma live?" he asked.

"She don't live nowhere."

A madman, thought Mr Macmillan wretchedly. A madman with a gun. Oh, heaven help all poor bank managers on a night like this.

Beefy tried to keep the conversation going. "Leastways, she lives in a cottage. But the cottage ain't nowhere."

"It must be somewhere."

"It ain't. It's halfway up a mountain."

Mr Macmillan groaned. "What's the nearest village?"

"There isn't one. Leastways, Shepherd's Warning is five miles away."

"And where is Shepherd's Warning?"

Beefy had never considered this question. Grandma lived near Shepherd's Warning. Shepherd's Warning was near where Grandma lived. And that, felt Beefy, was all ye know and all ye need to know.

But Mr Macmillan obviously wanted to take the thing a stage further. Beefy tried to help. "It's not far from Shepherd's Delight," he said helpfully.

Mr Macmillan gave up, and watched the needle flickering on the halfway mark. Beefy drove on, while the stage-scenery trees swung close and slipped away behind, while the white line and the cats' eyes were sucked endlessly into the mouth of the van.

He began to be aware of a vague disappointment. Finally he tracked it down. Heck the Sec. had been wrong. Silk hats *were* heavy. His was like a massive iron band round his temples, giving him quite a headache.

He daren't use his revolver hand to take it off. He slowed down, let go of the steering wheel for a moment, and lifted his hand to his hat. Quick as a flash Mr Macmillan grabbed the steering wheel, wrenched it to the left, and the van careered off the road. For a few seconds it ran along the grass verge, then its nearside wheels found the ditch. The van hung poised, then it toppled sideways.

Unfortunately for Mr Macmillan the door on his side was jammed under a foot of muddy water. Now he'd not only got Beefy's gun pressing into his ribs; he'd got Beefy as well.

Somehow they disentangled themselves and struggled out of the van and onto the grass verge. They were both panting heavily. Beefy was annoyed. "What did you want to do that for?" he asked. "You've bust the van. Now we've got to walk." He remembered something. Still keeping Mr Macmillan covered, he put his hand into the van and groped around. He pulled out the top hat, felt its smooth shape in the darkness. "Might have damaged that, too," he grumbled. "Silly thing to do. Thought you'd have had more sense."

They began walking, with Beefy firmly grasping his victim's arm. They walked for miles. It was horribly dark, after the bright headlights, but eventually the earth began to take on a certain form. Trees were no longer a darker night; they became things of bark, and bough and leaf. The stars hurried from the sky. Behind the hill a cock crew, and little birds in the hedgerows woke, muttering. And Mr Macmillan, trudging along the hard road, saw, all about him, the black, still-sleeping mountains.

They came at last to a lane that wandered away up the hill. "Shepherd's Warning 1/2 mile," said the battered signpost, in the sad light of dawn. Surely, Mr Macmillan thought, I shall find some means of escape in the village. There must be a policeman; someone is sure to be about.

But there was no help from the grim, sleeping hamlet of Shepherd's Warning. A dog snarled at their ankles. A cat, sitting on a wall, put out vicious claws to scratch Mr Macmillan's face. An evil countenance, framed in yellow lamplight, peered furtively from a lattice. That was all.

"Are there any policemen in Shepherd's Warning?" Mr Macmillan asked casually.

"No. The villages don't hold with them."

Mr Macmillan groaned. They plodded on. The lane dwindled to a track, and set off up the mountain.

The greyness of dawn lightened to the cold greyness of English daylight. Mr Macmillan felt his stubbly chin. Suddenly he was overcome by his preposterous position. This was the hour when he should be in a hot bath, preparing to spend another day looking after the affairs of his customers. Before long the staff would be arriving at the bank, sheep without a shepherd.

And where was the shepherd? Tired, stiff, unshaven; toiling up a blasted mountain with a lunatic in a top hat. He stopped dead.

"Now look here," he said furiously. "I demand to know where we're going, and why."

This was what Beefy had been dreading. He had always known that, if a person of Mr Macmillan's education and strength of character turned awkward, he, Beefy, would be nowhere. Whatever happened, he mustn't get involved in an argument. He took decisive action. He fired at the ground about two inches from Mr Macmillan's left foot. The bullet ricocheted off a rock, and whined away up the hillside.

"Shut up and get going," said Beefy.

The bank manager got going.

The road wound uphill for miles. And at last, in a fold of the mountain, they came to a tiny, tumbledown cottage, and as they looked an old lady in an apron shuffled out and emptied a teapot onto the garden.

She peered at the travellers.

"Why," she cried. "It's Beefy."

"Hello, Grandma." Beefy kissed her. "This is my friend, Mac."

Grandma's wrinkled little face beamed. "Come inside, both of you," she said. "Beefy always used to bring his little friends to see me, didn't you."

They went into the small, dark kitchen. A bright fire in the grate, china dogs, a welter of furniture, geraniums on the windowledge.

"That's a fine hat you've got, Beefy," Grandma said admiringly. "What are you doing, now?"

Beefy smiled happily. "I'm in finance."

"I thought it looked a finance sort of hat. I bet you're doing well."

Mr Macmillan wasn't listening. His mind had turned to food. Surely they'd give him some breakfast. He was just about starving.

"Ask your friend to sit on the sofy, Beefy," she said. "Your little friends always used to sit on the sofy and have a biscuit," she recalled. She went to the sideboard and lifted

BEEFY JONES

out a tin biscuit barrel in the form of a terrestrial globe. Mac and Beefy perched side by side on the sofa. Grandma removed the Arctic Circle, gave the open tin to Beefy.

"Give your friend an alphabet biscuit," she said. "You remember this tin, don't you."

Mr Macmillan sat and munched. Grandma picked up the kettle. "I'm going to make you a nice cup of tea," she said. "You talk to your friend, Beefy, while I go and fill the kettle at the stream." She pottered outside.

Beefy was getting awfully tired of holding his sweet persuader. He wished there were some other way of keeping Mr Macmillan prisoner.

The bank manager was evidently thinking along the same lines. He swallowed the last of the biscuit, and said, "If I gave you my word of honour not to try to escape before lunchtime, would you stop poking that confounded gun in my ribs?"

Beefy thought this over. "No," he said at last. He explained. "You see, Heck's my friend. But if Heck said to me, 'Beefy, I give you my word of honour not to do this,' I should know he was going straight out to do it. Well, you're not my friend, see; not a close friend, anyway, so –" He trailed off.

Of course, he knew what he ought to do. Pinch Mac's trousers. But a natural delicacy prevented him from giving the necessary orders. Besides, Grandma might not like it.

Then he had another idea. "Take your boots off," he commanded.

"No."

The sweet persuader dug viciously into Mr Macmillan's side.

Groaning, he took his boots off.

Beefy threw them on the fire.

Grandma came in with the kettle, and looked at Mr Macmillan's grey socks.

"Has your friend got sore feet?" she asked.

"Yes," said Beefy.

"Perhaps he'd like to sit with his feet in a bowl of water for a bit," suggested Grandma kindly.

"No he wouldn't," said Mr Macmillan.

"Used to do Beefy's dad's bunions a lot of good. He'd sit there for hours."

"I haven't got bunions."

Grandma looked doubtful.

"Can we stay for a few days?" Beefy asked.

"Of course you can, dear. As long as you like. You won't mind sleeping with your friend, will you."

"Oh, this is too much," exploded Mr Macmillan. Boots or no boots, he'd got to get away somehow.

Suddenly, with intense excitement, he noticed something; a shotgun propped in the corner. It was a symbol of hope. If he could once get hold of this, even if he hadn't any cartridges, he could use it as a club. Perhaps things weren't as bad as he'd imagined.

The kettle boiled. Grandma made the tea. She filled three pint mugs, and gave one to Mr Macmillan.

It was a black, hellish brew, but he drank it greedily. Over the rim of his mug he watched Grandma struggling into an ancient coat. She jammed a cherry-laden hat on her head, and picked up her basket.

So Grandma was going out. The bank manager tried not to show his excitement. Soon he would be alone with Beefy who must, in the nature of things, drop his guard sometime. Then, grab the gun and fight level. The sight of the possible weapon, plus the powerful tea, had given Mr Macmillan new heart.

Grandma turned to Beefy. "I'm just slipping down to the village for something for dinner. You'll be all right? Don't let your friend play with fire."

She went to the door. She turned back. Oh, please go, you silly old woman, prayed Mr Macmillan silently.

Grandma put out a hand and picked up the gun.

"Might get a shot at something on the way back," she said. "Ta-ta."

Mr Macmillan's shoulders slumped.

Beefy rose and stretched. "I'm going outside," he said. "Got to think."

He strolled to the door. "I got problems," he said.

"Good," Mr Macmillan said unfeelingly.

Beefy went outside and sat on an upturned bucket. Now that he had time to think he didn't like the look of things at all. Up to now, the failure of his mission to the Western National Bank and the wreck of the van had not worried him too much. Ida would be furious, of course. The boys would be reproachful. Well, he would let them have their say. Then, casually, he would pull £50,000 out of his pockets and say, "By the way, boys, I got this to share up. Ransom money."

"Good ole Beefy," they would say. "Always knew we could rely on Beefy."

But now a problem had arisen that, in the first careless rapture of kidnapping Mr Macmillan, he had not foreseen. How was he to demand a ransom when he couldn't write?

It didn't seem fair to ask Mac to write the letter. Grandma could write, but she might not approve. You never knew with Grandma. She was funny about some things.

Beefy tried to think. He beat his low forehead. But making his brain work was like cranking a car with a flat battery on a frosty morning.

Mr Macmillan, wearing Grandma's bedroom slippers, crept furtively out of the front door. Beefy sent a couple of warning shots across his bows.

Mr Macmillan went inside.

How long, Beefy wondered, would it take Mac to teach him to write. Quite some time, he decided. And he'd have to be able to read, too.

Mr Macmillan must have climbed out of the kitchen window. He was toiling up the mountain behind the cottage.

Absent-mindedly Beefy took a pot shot. There was a savage spatter of earth in front of Mr Macmillan's nose.

Mac turned and shook his fist at Beefy. He went back to the cottage.

Beefy wondered whether there was anyone in Shepherd's Warning who would write the letter for him. But the friends of his youth were scattered; they had settled in far places, Dartmoor, Pentonville, Strangeways. Beefy sighed. There was only one thing for it. He'd have to write that letter himself.

He went back to the cottage. The door was ajar. He pushed it open. A heavy saucepan full of boiling water fell on his head.

It was very fortunate that he was still wearing his top hat. The brim saved his face from the scalding water by acting as a sort of watershed; and the hat took the force of the savage blow that Mr Macmillan aimed at him with a poker.

Beefy's great fist caught the bank manager exactly on the point of the jaw.

When he came round, ten minutes later, Beefy said to him, "Would you like to do something for me, Mac?"

"I'd like to kick you in the teeth, if that's what you mean," Mac said unkindly.

Beefy ignored this lapse of taste, and said: "I thought you might learn me to read and write, Mac."

Mr Macmillan struggled to his feet. Beefy, studying his face anxiously, knew that he would have to find some other way.

Grandma came back, carrying a dead rabbit. "I dare say you boys are getting hungry," she said. "Can your friend skin rabbits, Beefy?"

"No," said Mr Macmillan.

"He'd better peel the potatoes, then. Get the bucket for him."

Together they prepared the meal. Soon Mr Macmillan found the smell of cooking almost unbearable. He had never known hunger like this before. He kept bending over the pot, smelling the sweet savour of it, peering in at the tender, white morsels of rabbit meat. Oh, would the meal never be ready?

The table was laid. And at last, Grandma took three hot plates and went over to the pot, and seized a huge ladle. Mr Macmillan watched her, the saliva running down his stubbled chin. Another minute, another thirty seconds, and he would have some of that rich, steaming food between his teeth.

"Mac don't want no dinner, Grandma," Beefy said.

Mac looked at his captor piteously.

"Of course I do. I'm starving," he said.

Grandma looked at Beefy questioningly.

"He don't want no dinner," Beefy repeated firmly. "His doctor won't let him. 'Might be fatal, eating dinner,' he says. We don't want no sudden deaths, do we, Grandma?"

Grandma filled two plates. Beefy turned to Mac. "You wouldn't think again about learning me to read and write, I suppose?" he whispered.

Mr Macmillan swallowed. "No," he said.

Grandma and Beefy enjoyed their dinner. Beefy finished mopping his plate round with his bread. "Doctor says he don't want no tea, neither," he said. "Nor no supper."

"Be silly to take any risks," agreed Grandma.

CHAPTER 6

In the study of St Jude's Vicarage a clock struck eleven. The architect fiddled with his pencil. The Archdeacon crossed one gaitered leg over another and glanced surreptitiously at his wristwatch. He'd got another meeting before lunchtime.

The Vicar stuffed tobacco into his pipe. "I'm sorry we can't be looking at the plans, sir," he said to the Archdeacon, "but Mr Macmillan's bringing them with him." He struck a match. "He should be here any moment now."

There was thirty seconds' silence. The Vicar puffed. He peered into the bowl of his pipe. He struck another match. "Lovely autumn weather," he said. "I really think it's my favourite time of year."

There was a minute's silence. The Vicar produced unspeakable filth from his pipe with a pipe-cleaner. "Not like Macmillan to be late," he said.

There was silence for five minutes. The Vicar blew down his pipe. It erupted like a volcano. He dusted the burning ash off his trousers on to the carpet and said, "He can't be far away."

When the clock struck quarter past he picked up the telephone and spoke to the Northern Counties Bank. He had quite a long conversation. When he put the receiver down he was rather pale. "I – I can't believe it," he stammered. "There seems to have been some sort of raid on the Bankers' Dance at the Assembly Rooms last night, and Mr Macmillan appears to have been – abducted."

"With my second set of drawings, I suppose," the architect said drily, standing up and reaching for his hat.

"No. No, please, gentlemen." The Vicar waved him back into a chair. "I'll speak to Mrs Macmillan. Perhaps she can throw some light."

But Mrs Macmillan was not prepared to throw light. She made it quite clear that, after the loss of her husband, the loss of the plans seemed to her relatively unimportant. Rather grudgingly she went and looked in his study. No plans. Yes, of course she knew what she was looking for. Yes, there were several locked drawers where the plans might be. No, she certainly hadn't got the keys.

She put down the receiver. The architect picked up his hat. The Archdeacon gave John Adams a rather amused smile. "Sorry, Vicar," he said, "but I shall have to go."

John Adams saw them out. Then he flung himself into his chair and drummed his hands furiously on the arms. He had never felt so frustrated since he broke a collarbone at the height of the Rugby football season.

It was a homely scene in the little kitchen that evening. The fire burned brightly. A quick column of smoke rose from the paraffin lamp. Grandma's knitting needles clicked merrily, and so did her false teeth. Mac and Beefy sat side by side on the sofa once more.

'And what does C-A-T spell?" Mr Macmillan was asking.

"Cat," replied Beefy, promptly. His eyes shone. "I always wanted to be educated," he said proudly. "If I'd of been educated before, I shouldn't of gone to the wrong bank, and you wouldn't of been here now."

Wistfully, Mr Macmillan agreed with him.

But the next morning Beefy was feeling less enthusiastic about his education. He'd had an awful night. The unwonted mental exercise had left his brain too agitated to sleep, and Mr Macmillan was an energetic sleeper, dragging the bedclothes round him, flinging his limbs about, and snoring like a hedgehog. Beefy, after losing the tussle for the bedclothes, had been awake all night, shivering with cold, deafened, kicked, prodded and scratched by the wallowing Mr Macmillan.

He came to a decision. He couldn't face any more nights like that. He'd just have to find someone to write that letter for him.

After breakfast he said, "Just going down to Shepherd's Warning, Grandma. Back for dinner."

"Get me the *Financial Times*", Mr Macmillan called out, almost cheerfully. Now, at last, his chance had come! Once Beefy was out of the way he'd soon deal with this old creature.

He watched Beefy out of sight down the mountain. Then he said to Grandma, "Now, my good woman, I want a pair of your late husband's boots; and quickly, please."

Grandma, who was peeling potatoes, looked far from friendly. "What do you want boots for?" she asked.

"I just thought I'd like a stroll. And my own boots seem to have been mislaid."

Grandma's little apple-cheeked face was definitely hostile now.

"Oh, no you don't. You're staying here."

Mr Macmillan didn't bother to argue. He made for the door that opened on to the stairway. He'd find some boots if he had to turn the house upside down.

A knock came at the door.

"Come in," Grandma called. The door was pushed slowly open.

A large, plump, friendly-looking woman came into the tiny room. "Beefy in?" she asked pleasantly.

"No," said Grandma. "He's down in the village. Funny you didn't meet him. He must of went the other road."

"Mind if we wait?" the visitor lowered herself into a chair. Suddenly she produced a bellow like a sergeant major. "Come in, boys," she yelled.

A dark gentleman with side-whiskers entered, followed by another who appeared to have a wooden leg. The latter put his head out of the door. "Come on, you lot," he said. "We want to give Beefy a nice surprise."

The room was already full, but several more men pushed their way in. "Pliz," one of them was asking anxiously, "What is nize surprize?"

"Are you some more of Beefy's friends?" Grandma asked.

"We certainly are," said the lady.

Grandma went to the sideboard. She got out the biscuit tin.

Poor Mr Macmillan was wedged tightly into the darkest corner of the room. All he could see was the broad back of the gentleman who was leaning against him. He tapped this back. "Excuse me," he said.

Slowly a head came round. A pair of cold eyes looked at him inquiringly.

"Look," said Mr Macmillan, urgently. "You've got to help me get away from here. I'm being kept a prisoner."

The eyes stared at him without emotion. Mr Macmillan prepared to drop his bombshell. "This Beefy that you've all come to see" – he lowered his voice even further – "do you know, he's criminal!"

To Mr Macmillan's horror, the gentleman meditatively scratched his left eyeball with an alphabet biscuit. "Are *you* kidding?" he asked.

Someone had taken a great jar of honey, and had spread it, thick and golden, over the dreaming countryside.

Beefy, the sun warm on his face, his silk hat, which he carried in his hand, shining and glinting as he turned it this way and that, Beefy began to cheer up. He'd always liked the country. It was quiet, and friendly. "Yes, we have no bananas," he began to sing. Despite his slightly rolling gait he went quickly and surely down the hill, and soon came to the noisome village of Shepherd's Warning.

Not much help there. Old Mother Truggitt looked up and scowled at him as she drew a pail of water from the pond. Joe Moggs, throwing open the doors of the Stoat and Weasel to admit a crowd of gin-sodden customers, looked at Beefy and spat. So did the gin-sodden customers.

Beefy felt unhappy. There was no one here whom he could ask to write a letter for him. They were more likely to stone him out of the village.

Next door to the Stoat and Weasel was the village shop. Beefy, remembering Mr Macmillan's *Financial Times*, peered in at the little bow window, at the striped wasps crawling frenetically over the striped humbugs, at the dead flies, wings outstretched, upside down on the currant buns, at the dog-eared horror comics. He went inside. An aged man brushed a cat off the cooked ham, picked up a vast ear-trumpet from a tray of cakes, and said, "What yer want?"

"I want the *Financial Times*," said Beefy.

The old man weighed out a pound of sausages. "Anything else?" he barked.

Beefy began to feel helpless. "The *Financial Times*," he repeated.

"Two bob," barked the ancient.

"No," stammered Beefy. "No." He backed towards the door, slipping a horror comic into his pocket on the way. The

61

old man snatched up a carving knife. "Two bob," he screamed, trying to head Beefy off.

Beefy managed to get outside. "Thief! Robber! Stop thief!" cried the shopkeeper. Several unsympathetic-looking types outside the Stoat and Weasel straightened up, lazily pulling coshes and knives out of their pockets. They began to move, slowly but determinedly.

Beefy ran. The way back to Grandma's was barred. He ran the other way. After half a mile, puffing badly, he slowed down and looked behind. The loungers had gone back to their lounging, he saw with relief. Panting, he sat down on the parapet of a little bridge; there, in front of him, was a little white signpost that said, "Shepherd's Delight, 4 miles", or so Grandma had always told him. And Beefy realized suddenly what it was that he had been wanting to do ever since he came to Grandma's. He wanted to go to the village of his dreams.

And why not? Mr Macmillan would be quite safe without his boots. With a mounting excitement he set off up the hill.

He was taking a road that he had not taken since the world was young. Much of it he thought he had forgotten, but when he saw it again he found it had been there, all the time, in some deep, unvisited cave of his mind. He came to the track beside the wood, and scuffled his boots happily in the crisp leaves. Soon, now, he would see it. You came to a bend, and there was a gap in the trees, with a tree trunk to sit on, and through the gap you could see the village. He wandered on, filled with a strange content. He came to the old tree trunk. He sat down, and gazed.

The village, clustered about its little green, slept in the noonday peace. The remembered woodsmoke stood up straight from the remembered chimneys. On the pond ducks, upended, lifted dignified bottoms to the sky. In the high elms a wood pigeon lazily bubbled his note. A path wandered up the blue mountain, and no one followed it. And there was the smell and the haze and the deep content of autumn over all the land.

"Nice," Beefy whispered softly. "Nice." His imagination began to work. "There, Emily. Good pig," he muttered. He wondered which cottage he would have. Old Mordecai Wainwright's was a nice one, up a little track from the village. Was old Mordecai still alive? Anyway, once Beefy got the ransom money, he could build himself a house if he wanted. No difficulty there. Or Mordecai might have an accident. Not a painful one, of course. Just fatal.

To Beefy's delight, a rabbit popped out of his hole, snuffed the air, lolloped towards Beefy, began hungrily cropping the grass. Beefy uttered a long, tender "Ah!" Animals were nice. They were never snappy, like humans. They never made you feel small because you couldn't read. *They* couldn't read, either.

Beefy was so entranced that he did not hear footsteps approaching on the dry grass. Two hands came round and covered his eyes.

Cops, was his first thought. But policemen's hands were not soft and sweet-smelling as were these hands.

He struggled to his feet, and spun round. The hands fell away from his eyes. "Sally," he cried, beaming all over his face.

"I knew it was you, Beefy," she said. "You haven't changed a bit."

They stood, smiling at each other, her white hands resting lightly in his great, thick fists. He looked at the light shining in her eyes, at the small, white teeth in her laughing mouth. She was alive, she took the sunlight and the breeze, and made them a part of herself.

"Whatever are you doing here, Beefy?" The questions came tumbling out. "Are you coming to see Mother? What are you doing, these days?" She saw the hat, laid carefully on the tree trunk. "Is that yours? Wherever did you get it from?"

"I'm in finance," Beefy said proudly. "That's my finance hat."

She gave a puzzled little frown. "You shouldn't wear it with a striped vest, you know," she said kindly.

Beefy was anxious to learn from anyone as kind as Sally. "Why not?" he asked.

"You need a morning coat with a top hat," she said, wondering whether Beefy had the faintest idea what she was talking about. Deciding that he hadn't, she changed the subject. "Come on," she said. "Let's go and see Mother."

She slipped a cool arm in his. Beefy blushed happily. Picking up his hat, he let her lead him into the village, into a cottage garden ragged with chrysanthemums, into the cool gloom of a stone-flagged cottage.

She danced in ahead of him. "Mother, look who's here," she called.

"Well, if it isn't Beefy!" said Beefy's Auntie Nellie. "I thought you'd have been run over long ago. All them motor cars," she explained, vaguely and mournfully.

"Beefy's in finance," Sally said.

"Then you'd better get Sally a job in finance, too," Auntie Nellie said. "She's had such a good job, housekeeper at the vicarage, but now the old Vicar's gone and died. And they're having a new man with a wife and four daughters. So they don't want Sally no more. Have a drink of camomile."

Beefy wondered whether it was nasty, like brandy and gin.

"No thanks, Auntie," he said politely.

"If your Uncle Bert had drunk more camomile he'd have been alive to this day," Auntie said warningly. She looked at Beefy with foreboding. "You're getting just like him," she said. "Fleshy. Puts a strain on the heart."

"Oh, Beefy's all right, aren't you, Beefy," laughed Sally, putting a cool hand on his.

"Yes," said Beefy with feeling. In this dark, tiny cottage, sitting with people he had known from his youth, he was relaxed, unafraid. He could talk, without the words getting all jumbled up as they came out. He was sorry when Sally got up and went into the kitchen. "Is old Mr Wainwright still alive?" he asked his aunt.

"Be better if he wasn't. They have to do everything for him. *Everything*," Auntie Nellie repeated darkly. And from this, with practised ease, she slipped into a comprehensive survey of the bodily afflictions of the village. Beefy listened politely. The recital went on. But at last there was a pause. Beefy, trying to keep his end up, said, "Last week I got face-ache."

"Joe Grummitt died of face-ache," Auntie said promptly. "It wasn't a tooth at all. It was *something nasty*."

"Mine's better now," Beefy said hopefully.

"So was his, for a time. But it soon came back. Horrible, it was. Funny how often people think they've just got face-ache, or a bit of indigestion, and it turns out *something nasty*."

Beefy began to feel depressed. But then Sally came in, like sunlight, with a large slice of cold rabbit pie, and a crusty loaf, and butter with the dew on it, and a large beaker of milk. She put them on the table. "Here you are, Beefy," she said. "Pull your chair up."

He smiled up at her gratefully. She had put on a little flowered apron, and she looked very feminine, with her chestnut-coloured hair and her brown, serene eyes. Suddenly Beefy had a strange and disturbing vision. He wasn't alone with Emily his pig any longer. Sally was in his cottage, wearing the flowered apron, tripping lightly from kitchen to living-room, curling up at his feet while he read his Western. He felt himself going very red. Suppose Sally knew what he was thinking! She'd never forgive him. Or she'd laugh. Eyes downcast, he sat at table. Sally stood at his side, pouring milk for him, and he smelt the sweet freshness of her. Then she sat down, and, smiling, chatted away to him. Auntie Nellie knitted in the window seat.

Beefy enjoyed the food. He was shy again now, but while he was eating he didn't have to talk. He just nodded with his mouth full. Then, as he finished chewing his last bit of pie, he remembered Mr Macmillan, left alone with Grandma. Conscience told him he ought to be getting back. "I got to be going," he said.

"I'll walk with you as far as the tree trunk," Sally said, and took off her apron.

"Ta-ta, Beefy," said Auntie Nellie, kissing him.

Beefy picked up his hat. They stepped out into the bright warmth of the afternoon sunshine.

They walked in silence. Beefy was too shy to speak first, and Sally seemed lost in her own thoughts. In silence they came to the tree trunk. She held out a hand. She looked at him very hard. There was a sad, yet amused expression on her face. "Goodbye, Beefy," she said. "And I'm glad you've grown up so – nice."

"Me – nice?" gasped Beefy, staring at her in utter astonishment.

"I think you're the gentlest and humblest person I've every met," she said. Putting her hands on his shoulders she touched his cheek lightly with her lips, and then she was gone, swift as a wild thing, in the shimmering afternoon.

It was a long time before Beefy moved from that sacred spot. Someone thought he was nice. Someone had noticed him enough to think that he was gentle. He couldn't quite believe it. People talked to him, of course, and swore at him, and told him to do things; but he could never believe that he was a real person whom people might think nice, or gentle, or humble.

And, of course, the miracle was that the person who had noticed him was Sally; Sally, who had grown up to be more beautiful than he had ever imagined possible; Sally, who was the kindest person he had ever known.

She had long disappeared from sight when at last he moved. And the autumn afternoon had lost a little by her going. A haze had come between sun and earth, and a little chill wind scurried over the grass and tore a few early leaves from the trees. The once-bright paint of the trees and the fields was getting a little shabby, and the gay booths of summer were putting up the shutters for the season.

But to Beefy, at this moment, it was eternal spring. Sally thought he was nice. Heavy though he was, he ran like a young goat upon the mountains. The skeleton leaves of other summers rattled like dry bones at his feet. Down the hill he came, skirted the village of Shepherd's Warning and up the hill to Grandma's. Gaily he pushed open the door. "Couldn't get the *Financial Times*, Mac," he called cheerfully. "So I brought you a horror comic. It was all they'd got." He broke off. "Why, Heck!" he cried. "Ida! What you doing here? How did you know I was here?"

"Oh, I just looked up your file," said Ida, proud of her paper work. "Found you came from Shepherd's Warning. The rest was easy. Especially," she added nastily, "when we saw the Company's van in a ditch a few miles away. *We* had to come by long-distance bus."

She was feeling just the teeniest bit bloody-minded today. The Bankers' Dance venture had failed completely to show a profit. Shortly after Beefy had left to go to the Western National a man had arrived to photograph the bankers.

He had been suspicious of Joe Vodka. And when Joe had threatened him with a gun in the entrance hall his suspicions had been confirmed.

Either through panic or out of sheer malice, he had dropped flashbulbs all over the entrance hall. A retired banker, a veteran of Mafeking, heard the uproar, cried: "The relieving force, by gad!" hooked his walking stick round Ida's neck, and tugged.

Heck shot him in the ankle. But the damage had been done. The bankers, led by the hero of Mafeking, rose to the attack.

A good general knows when to retreat. Ida gave the command. The Company retired in good order, without losses, but also without profits.

Unless, of course, Beefy had saved the day and could be persuaded to co-operate.

"Nice of you to come, Ida," Beefy said, uncomfortably licking his lips. Somehow the visit of his friends did not seem to fill him with unmixed delight.

"Nice of you to have us, Beefy," Ida said. "This here's an extraordinary meeting to investigate what you done with the lolly from the Western National."

"But – but there wasn't any lolly," Beefy was perspiring. "It's on account of I can't read, see. I went to the wrong bank."

"Beefy," said Ida sweetly. "We want that money. We want it bad. We've come a long way to get it, see, and it's not been easy. You know a long bus ride always makes Joe Vodka sick."

"But there ain't no money, Ida. I went to the wrong bank. The keys wouldn't fit."

Heck broke in. "You know, Beefy, we're disappointed in you. We thought you was a friend. A loyal friend," he added in a broken voice.

Beefy's eyes filled with tears. "But I *am* your friend, Heck," he pleaded. He wrung his hands in mental torment. Here he was, actually telling the truth for once, and no one would believe him! It was very hard.

"Is the money in this cottage?" asked Ida. She looked like an adult beginning a long and wearisome game of "hunt the slipper" with a child, except that usually, in such circumstances, the adult is not pointing a dainty little revolver at the playmate's left eye.

"I got an idea," Lofty Longbottom burst out. "Lock Beefy in the bedroom while we search the cottage. Then, if we don't find no lolly, and if, through someone being a bit careless with a cigarette end, the cottage was to get burnt down, well, be a bit hard on Beefy, wouldn't it."

Beefy's nerves were beginning to crack. "I tell you I ain't got no money," he shouted.

Grandma, who had been out to fill the kettle at the stream, came back at this moment. "Beefy," she said reproachfully. "You ain't spent your post office Grandad gave you?"

Mr Macmillan had the instincts of an English gentleman. No matter what the consequences, he could not stand aside and see injustice done. He pushed his way to the front and said, "What Beefy says is perfectly true. He came to the wrong bank."

Ida looked at the unkempt Macmillan with distaste. "Who the devil are you?" she asked.

Mr Macmillan stepped forward. He thrust out his stubbled chin. "I am a bank manager," he began.

Ida gave a great shout of laughter, and slapped her thigh. "So you're a bank manager," she roared. "OK, brother. I'm the Queen of Sheba." She went off into peals of laughter.

The board of directors were beginning to enjoy themselves. Heck the Sec. minced forward. "Ectually," he drawled, "I'm the editor of the *Economist*."

Joe Vodka stroked an imaginary beard. "Me Bulganin," he beamed, joining in the merry fun.

Ida stopped laughing, wiped her eyes, hiccuped, and called the meeting to order. She looked sorrowfully at Beefy. "So you got an accomplice, Beefy. We wasn't good enough for you. You had to get this broken-down social outcast to go in with you." She dropped her voice. "Why wasn't we good enough for you, Beefy?"

Beefy was too overcome to speak. To add to his troubles, Mr Macmillan turned on him.

"For heaven's sake tell them who I am, you great oaf," he shouted.

"We know who you are all right." Heck cut in roughly. "And if Beefy can't remember where he put the Western National money, perhaps we shall be able to persuade you to remember."

"I am a branch manager of the Northern Counties Bank, and I am not intimidated by a bunch of – hoodlums like you," Mr Macmillan said bravely.

The directors looked hurt.

"Listen," cried Beefy. "It's true. That's who he is. I've kidnapped him, and I'm holding him to ransom. Only there don't seem much future in it on account of I ain't wrote to nobody demanding a ransom on account of I ain't educated, see."

Ida worked this out. "Beefy, are you sure there ain't no lolly from the Western National?"

"Sure, Ida."

She looked at him searchingly. "See this wet, see this dry, Beefy?"

He nodded dumbly.

"So you pinched this geezer instead?"

Another nod.

"Beefy," said Ida. "You done well. You showed drive and initiative." She turned to Heck. "Mr Secretary, record in the minutes that Beefy showed drive and initiative. Oh, and write to the head office of the Northern Counties Bank and say we got one of their managers and they can have him back for fifty thousand pounds cash down, the ransom money to be paid over the counter in pound notes to a masked man who will call any day they say. And if they breathe a word to the police or try any funny business we'll blow every one of their branches sky high. Got that?"

"What address shall I give?"

"Tell them to reply through the personal column of *The Times*."

She looked at the proud and smiling Beefy. "Nice work, son," she said.

"Madam, you don't really expect my head office to reply to this outrageous nonsense?" exploded Mr Macmillan.

Ida regarded him coolly. "If we don't hear nothing in a week, we'll maybe send them an ear," she said thoughtfully.

Grandma had always liked Beefy to bring his friends in; but this time she did feel that the cottage was a bit overcrowded. She and Ida slept in one room; Mr Macmillan, Beefy, and the rest of the boys slept in the other.

All the boys complained about Mr Macmillan. They never got one good night's sleep. "Sounds more like a dog worrying a slipper than an honest banker taking his rest," said Heck the Sec. They began to get rings under their eyes. Some were for packing in, but as Ida said, after the bit of unpleasantness at the banker's shindig the other night the police might quite well be asking a lot of tomfool questions, and the present moment was quite a good one for the directors to relax quietly in the country. But they had overlooked the van, lying in its ditch. The police began piecing all sorts of facts together. They made their plans.

They pounced. Fortunately everyone except Beefy, Grandma, and Mr Macmillan was down at the Stoat and Weasel in Shepherd's Warning.

Mr Macmillan, eventually, established his innocence. Grandma flatly refused to be charged with anything. Poor Beefy caught it all.

But he didn't get a long sentence. In the first place, for the life of them, they couldn't decide what it was that he'd been trying to do. And at his trial so many irrelevancies, red herrings, and non sequiturs were tossed to and fro about the court, like tennis balls, that at last, in sheer desperation, they gave Beefy six months, and the judge adjourned the court and went to bed with a couple of aspirins and a sick headache.

At the next meeting of the board, Ida rose solemnly. "Gentlemen," she said. "We have a vacant chair. Let us stand for a few moments in memory of a loyal, but absent, friend."

The board rose. Heck blew his nose. "Poor old Beefy," he said. "Staying at his post, that day; even though we all knew the police were coming."

"But Beefy didn't know," pointed out Peg Leg, who had a logical mind. "*We* all knew. That's why we cleared off to the Stoat and Weasel. But Beefy didn't know. Nobody told him."

"It wouldn't have done for the police not to find anybody," said Lofty. "They wouldn't have been satisfied."

Willie One Eye spoke simply. "He took the rap for all of us," he said quietly. "Good old Beefy."

"Good old Beefy," they echoed. They dried their eyes. They went on to the minutes.

CHAPTER 7

Spring came, a bedraggled lady, to the parish of St Jude the Obscure. A few sooty snowdrops kept their dirty faces averted from public gaze. A few crocuses pushed through, and were promptly torn to pieces by the juvenile delinquents of the sparrow world. Blossoms, like great blobs of blood-soaked cottonwool, appeared on the flowering Japanese trees in suburban gardens, and were immediately swept off by the savage winds of May. Grey clouds scudded over grey roofs, raindrops danced and spat in the gutters, sunlight flashed in the little park and in the hearts of men. A regiment of women, armed with dusters and brooms and paint brushes, driven by some primeval urge, went into spring-cleaning action.

No one had had a very pleasant winter. Lizzie Tubb went about worried and silent, a tense, sick feeling in her stomach, for Blackie was nearing the end. Sometimes, when she returned home, he would rise to greet her and stand on stiff legs, conscientiously wagging his tail. More often he would look up from his basket with despairing eyes, and remain lying there.

Mr Macmillan went back to banking and tried to forget the ignominy to which he had been subjected, rather bluntly refusing to address the Rotary on "The Mind of the Criminal".

Heck and the others were still encamped in the church hall loft. Quite against Ida's principles they had subsisted during the winter on a few small, individual jobs, a burglary or two by Willie One Eye, three confidence tricks by Heck, a little shoplifting by Ida herself. Peg Leg had even got honest work with the government. For Ida, after the Bankers' Dinner job, was like an author who has written an unsuccessful novel and is afraid to start another. She just hadn't any more brilliant ideas, and, even if she had, she would not have dared to put them into execution.

The Reverend John Adams had spent a cheerless winter without a housekeeper, returning from evening meetings to an empty, cold vicarage, coming home from early Communions to prepare his own breakfast. He hadn't had a single game of rugger. He hadn't even seen one, for in Danby no one played anything but a bastard variation called soccer. And his new church hall was still a source of endless anxiety. True, Mr Macmillan had come home from that ridiculous business of letting himself be abducted, and had produced the plans from his desk; which, incidentally, if Mrs Macmillan had shown the slightest gumption or co-operation, she could have forced any time at all. But there had been endless snags. So many different people were involved that at times he thought the thing never could be built. And, apart from that, it seemed almost as though some maleficent influences were at work. Little Miss Titterton, returning one winter's night from a council meeting, was stopped by a dark, tall man who demanded, not her life, her honour or her handbag, but her minute book. The vicarage mail went hopelessly astray. Certificates from the Town and Country Planning Authority, letters from the architect and the archdeacon, all failed to be delivered, so that the Vicar spent half his time dealing with angry, querulous, and downright incomprehensible telephone calls. He began to wonder whether that new postman, the chap with the wooden leg, wasn't thoroughly incompetent.

But one spring morning the same wooden-legged postman brought him a letter that really did cheer him. It was from a Mrs Mary Phillips, who had been housekeeper for thirty years to a lately deceased Rural Dean, and now wished to apply for the post of housekeeper to the Vicar, which she had seen advertised in the *Telegraph*. She enclosed references.

The letter was courteous, friendly, and well written. The references were excellent. Whistling gaily, the Vicar pulled a sheet of writing paper towards him and wrote to Mrs Phillips, asking her to visit him as soon as possible.

And, that same day, Beefy came home. He was disgruntled. The judge had been cross with him when he sent him to prison. Beefy hadn't liked that. And then, when they set him free, they had refused to give him his skeleton keys back. It wasn't right. Heck had always said they had to give you *all* your things back. Otherwise tell the Governor, he said. But Beefy hadn't. Somehow he felt that he wasn't quite the type to tell prison governors things. Heck was, of course. He'd soon make them feel pretty small. But not Beefy. He wasn't clever enough, like.

But he was through with crime. He didn't like it. People got cross with you. He was going straight in future. But first he must see about his lodgings. He had thought about three things in prison: one, Sally, and about how she had said he was nice, and had kissed him; two, that cross judge, and all the nasty things he had said, or at least such of them as Beefy could understand; three, his cosy roll of linoleum.

But by now, of course, the church hall would probably be a factory, and Beefy would be a homeless wanderer.

His heart beat more quickly as he came within view of the hall. It didn't seem to have changed much, anyway. And the front door was open. Stealthily, he went in.

It was already dark inside. Old Lizzie Tubb was cleaning up after the Brownies, preparatory to locking up. She had not bothered to put the light on. And then, to her horror, she saw a squat, powerful-looking man in a singlet coming into the passage. She gave a squawk.

The man looked at her, and advanced towards her.

His first words did not reassure her. "What's that what's wrote on your stummick?" he asked.

She looked at him fearfully, backing away a little.

Beefy followed her. "It says something," he said. "I've always wondered what it said."

She looked at him now. "What yer want?" she asked fiercely.

Beefy recapped. "There's something wrote on your stummick," he explained patiently. "What's it say?"

Lizzie looked down at her apron. She saw the "1 cwt Finest Bone Meal". She understood.

"I – I don't know," she stammered.

"Perhaps you're looking at it upside down," said Beefy helpfully.

Lizzie hung her head. She was cornered.

"I can't read," she admitted, shame hanging upon her like a garment.

But Beefy could have taken her in his arms. "Can't you really?" he asked. "Can't you really read?"

"No," said Lizzie. "I tried to learn, but – " She trailed off.

"You know what?" said Beefy jubilantly, his face alight in the gloom. "You know what? I can't read either!" He stood watching her, waiting for her round, moon-like face to light up too.

It did. "I always thought everybody could read except me," she said with a catch in her voice.

"I always thought everybody could read except *me*," Beefy laughed happily.

"Never knew it *did* say summat on my stummick," said Lizzie. "Wisht I knew what it was."

"We'll ask Heck," Beefy told her proudly. "He'll know. He's educated. He's my friend."

"You like to come and have a cup of tea my place?" asked Lizzie in her flat, grating voice. "I'm just going."

Beefy felt Lizzie's friendship wrapping him tight and warm, rather like his roll of linoleum.

"Yes, if you like," he said, "But don't lock up. I live here, me and the boys."

"Now you're joking," said Lizzie with a sudden cackle.

"No, I ain't. I live here, but I lost my keys. We live up there." He pointed to the loft. "Only don't tell nobody."

"Oh" Lizzie lost interest. "I never clean up there. Don't know what's up there. You know anything about dogs?"

"My Grandma and me had one once. He was called Blackie."

Lizzie looked impressed. "That's funny. Mine's called Blackie, but he's ever so poorly. I got him some medicine, but I can't read whether to give it him or rub it on him."

By now they were in Rockefeller Avenue. Lizzie let Beefy into her dark little house and lit the gas in the kitchen.

"There he is," she said, indicating the limp little body.

Together they looked at Blackie. At last: "I know what's wrong with him," Beefy said sadly. "He's dead."

Lizzie gave a strangled sort of moan. "He was a good old dog," she said.

Beefy hated touching dead things. He was very surprised to hear himself say, "I'll bury him if you like."

To his dismay Lizzie said that would be nice. He went out into the backyard, and dug a hole in the sooty square of earth, and buried Blackie while the thin rain fell. When he came in Lizzie gave him a mug of tea. She swallowed. "He'll be all right, out there," she said.

"Yes," said Beefy. Noisily he drank his tea. "Going out," he said. "Be back in half an hour."

He was back in ten minutes, a large, wriggling, excited puppy dog in his arms.

"Found him on the Leicester Road," Beefy said. "He might of got lost."

The puppy licked his face. Then it licked Lizzie's.

"Ah," cooed Lizzie.

"Ah," cooed Beefy.

"He's nice," said Lizzie. "Not as nice as Blackie, but he's nice."

"There's something wrote on his collar," said Beefy.

"P'raps his address," Lizzie suggested.

"We don't know, do we, on account of we can't read," said Beefy.

"No," said Lizzie.

"Not much good, is it," said Beefy, "if we don't know what it says."

"No," said Lizzie.

"No good keeping it, then," said Beefy, taking the collar off and throwing it on to the fire.

They gave the puppy a saucer of milk and, together, listened to his happy splashings.

"If we could of read what it says on his collar we could of taken him back where he belongs," said Beefy.

"That's right."

"But we couldn't," said Beefy.

"He'd nearly fill Blackie's basket already," said Lizzie.

"Put him in," said Beefy, "and see."

And the little creature, full of milk, sniffed his way round three times in the basket, curled up and went happily to sleep.

Seeing this reminded Beefy of his own bed. He went across to the church hall, climbed the ladder, and to his delight there was his roll of linoleum, just as he had left it. He didn't bother about a hot-water bottle. He just slipped himself inside. Wouldn't the boys be surprised!

"Why," they cried. "It's Beefy," when at last they returned.

"How'd you get on, Beefy?" Peg Leg asked.

"They kept my skeleton keys," said Beefy.

"Didn't you see the Governor about it?" Heck asked sharply, his eyes irritable and angry.

"No," said Beefy. He took a deep breath. He'd got a very important announcement to make. He wished really that he hadn't gone to bed. It was difficult making an important announcement when your head was level with your hearers' feet.

"I ain't going to need skeleton keys no more," Beefy said firmly. "I'm going straight."

"Yeah?" said Heck nastily.

"I don't like crime," Beefy said sulkily. "It – it ain't honest," he explained.

Peg Leg came to the rescue. "OK, Beefy," he said. "So you want to go straight. Well, that's OK, isn't it, boys. Beefy can go straight, but he can still live here, can't he."

Willie One Eye wiped a tear from his glass eye. "We shall be losing a colleague. But we shall not be losing a friend," he announced sententiously.

Beefy sniffed. It was sad, this closing of a chapter in his life, this end of an epoch. But there was still a little worry nagging at him.

"What's Ida going to say?" he asked anxiously.

"Oh, Ida isn't one to come between a man and his ambitions," Peg Leg said reassuringly. "She'd never think of trying to hold back anyone who wanted to get on."

"Don't you think so?" asked Beefy gratefully. So that was all right. He drifted into sleep, his future bright, and happy, and assured.

The next morning he set off for the Labour Exchange. But on the way he just called in at Lizzie Tubb's. The new puppy was cheerfully eating the table leg.

"Nice, isn't he!" Lizzie said, watching the animal with delight and love.

"What you going to call him?" Beefy asked.

"Whitey," said Lizzie.

"That's a nice name," he said. He put two and two together. "On account of he's white, I suppose," he added, impressed by his own acumen.

He was aware that Lizzie was looking at him with an adoring expression. She groped for words of gratitude. "I was sorry about Blackie," she said. "I'd had him a long time. So it was nice having another dog straight off. It – it took me mind off it, like."

Beefy was horribly embarrassed. He stood on one leg. "That's all right," he muttered. "Better be going now." He set off for the Labour Exchange.

But he never got there. For on the way he met a funeral. Sympathetically he eyed the coffin. "Poor departed geezer," he thought. "Poor dead perisher," wondering vaguely what it felt like to be dead. But trying to use his imagination always rather hurt, so he forgot about it. And then, suddenly, he saw something that shook him to the core. The funeral cars had stopped outside St Jude's Church, and a number of men *in silk hats* were getting out of the cars. And not only silk hats. Black frock coat, black gloves. That's what Sally must have meant when she said he didn't ought to wear a silk hat with a striped vest. He had to admit that it did look nicer with one of those long black jackets.

Beefy, breathing heavily, hurried up and watched them closely. They were lifting the dead geezer out now. Didn't look as though you needed much education for that job. And six of them to lift one. Why, Beefy could have managed it on his own.

"Well, it's a very funny thing, Mr Jones," William Smith, undertaker, was saying two hours later. "But we have got a vacancy, as it happens. First we've had since the war. Poor Robinson. They fished him out of the river round about dawn. The job must have preyed on his mind."

Beefy looked around. Over a table lay a frock coat; on the frock coat was a pair of black gloves and a silk hat. It was sad, like, seeing them lying there, knowing poor Robinson would never wear them again.

Very sad. Very sad indeed.

But there was nothing sad about Beefy the first time he rode beside the driver of the last funeral car. Lodged just above his sandy eyebrows was a silk hat. About his thick, compact body was a black frock coat. And the hands lying in his lap had actually been forced into the late Mr Robinson's gloves.

He sat there, happily waggling his thumbs. He'd never seen his hands in gloves before. They looked nice, real gentlemanly. You couldn't tell they were red and horny now he'd got gloves on.

The procession stopped outside St Jude's Church. Beefy, watching the other top-hatted gentlemen carefully, descended. They carried the coffin into church, and then came back and sat in the cars.

There were quite a few people about, and Beefy, his hat on his head, one gloved hand elegantly supporting his chin, knew the proudest moment of his life. All sorts of people were walking about on the pavements, wearing raincoats, and cloth caps, and flannels. And here was he, Beefy, sitting in a Rolls Royce, dressed up to the nines. He coughed genteelly, so that he could lift his gloved hand to his mouth same as like what he had seen Heck do.

And then, with awful suddenness, Fate struck. Beefy, happily watching the common people go about their common tasks, was afflicted with terrible misgiving. For, coming down the road towards him, casually but inexorably, was a gaily chattering group of people. There was a plump, auburn-haired woman; there was a tall man with black side-whiskers, a postman with a wooden leg, a flat-faced Slavonic type, a tall man, and a man, one of whose eyes stared glassily before him.

Beefy should have been glad and proud. But he wasn't. His instinct told him that trouble was on the way. He no longer sat up. He cowered. Hat pulled down over his eyes he crouched so low that the driver of his car looked at him with interest and asked, "What's up, mate?"

"I got a pain," moaned Beefy.

The driver grunted. Beefy, head down, heard the laughing group draw nearer. He could even pick out Ida's rather husky voice now. He shrank down farther.

With the inevitability of Greek tragedy the group moved on. Out of the corner of his eye Beefy saw them drawing level with his car. They reached the bonnet, they were passing the driver's seat now, another second and they would have passed. Beefy held his breath. Could he be going to escape after all? No. "Well, if it isn't old Beefy," cried a loud, uninhibited voice.

Beefy jerked his head down lower.

"Old Beefy, dressed up like a dog's dinner," said another.

"Just off to Ascot, I shouldn't wonder," said a third.

A silence. Then: "Too proud to speak to his old friends now." Ida sounded hurt.

Beefy lifted his head a fraction. "Hush," he pleaded. "We got to be quiet. It's a funeral, see."

"Look at him, gloves and all," cried Peg Leg.

Beefy was almost in tears. "Please go away," he begged. "You'll get me the sack. And it's such a nice job. The nicest job I've ever had."

With delight Joe Vodka recognized the top hat as a symbol used by cartoonists in the *Urals Advertiser*. "Bloddy imperialist capitalist warmonger," he cried merrily.

"Ida. Heck. Please go away, please," besought Beefy.

"Very good, my lord," said Heck, dropping an elaborate curtsey. That amused the boys, and Ida. They didn't half laugh. And at that moment Mr William Smith came out of the church to summon the bearers. He couldn't believe his eyes. He strode forward, pushing his way furiously through the laughing group. "Please," he begged. "Please. Have you *no* sense of decorum?"

Laughing, the boys dispersed. Mr Smith glared at the wretched Beefy. "I'll see you later," he hissed.

And see him he did, scowling at him furiously over his desk. "For fifty years," he said, between clenched teeth, "I, and my father before me, ran this business on the basis of dignity and decorum. Today, thanks to you, we had about as much dignity and decorum as a circus. Take that hat off," he ordered.

"But – " began Beefy.

"Take it off!"

Sadly, Beefy obeyed.

"And that frock coat."

Beefy obeyed.

"And those gloves."

Beefy tried to obey. But his hands were sweating, and anyway he wasn't used to taking gloves off. There was a loud, tearing noise.

"I'm ever so sorry," Beefy said.

"Never mind," Mr Smith said bitterly. "You've ruined my business reputation. You might as well tear my gloves to pieces as well." He paused for breath. "If I thought they could do anything I'd hand you over to the police like a shot."

"I'm ever so sorry."

"Get out," Mr Smith said savagely.

"But – " said Beefy.

"Get out!"

Beefy went to the door. "I'm ever so sorry," he repeated pathetically.

Mr Smith seized a large paperweight, shaped like a coffin. He threw it at Beefy. He missed. Politely Beefy picked it up and put it back on the desk. Then, disconsolately, he turned and walked out of the door, and out of the job that had been his heart's desire.

Somehow, at the moment, he didn't want to see Ida and the boys. It wasn't their fault, of course, that he'd lost his job. They just hadn't realized how dignified one had to be on these occasions. But desire for sympathy led him instinctively to Lizzie Tubb's. He had to tell Lizzie about it. And, in his wounded pride, he wanted to hide in the cramped darkness of her little house.

A flicker of pleasure passed over her plain face when she opened the door to him. "Are you coming in?" she asked. "The teapot's on the hob."

He came in. Whitey flew at him and began to eat his trousers. Lizzie gave him a mug of tea. He drank it slowly. Lizzie set the puppy on her knee and stroked him fondly.

"He's nice," she told Beefy. "He's a nice little dog." She gave him a shy look of gratitude.

"I lost my job," said Beefy. "I reckon you don't know any jobs?"

"Only job I know is Vicar wants a housekeeper," Lizzie said. "But I don't think – "

"My cousin's a vicar's housekeeper, at Shepherd's Delight," Beefy said. "Leastways she ain't no more on account of her vicar died and they set a new man on with four daughters."

"She'd better come and look after our Vicar," said Lizzie.

Beefy was suddenly filled with joy. Sally, living in the same town as himself! Sally, where he could sometimes meet her! It would be wonderful.

"Does he really want someone?" he asked hopefully.

"Want someone? He's desperate. He'll have her, if you can get her to come."

Beefy drew despondent again. "But I can't write to her about it on account of I can't write," he said. "And I can't go and tell her on account of I ain't got no money and it's a long way."

Lizzie rose. Without a word she went to the mantelpiece, and lifted down a vase. She groped inside. She gave Beefy two pound notes.

"Will this help?" she asked.

Beefy shied away. "I couldn't take that," he said.

"You got me a dog, didn't you. When I needed one, bad," she said fiercely. "Well, then. Here, take it." To Beefy's embarrassment she jabbed the notes clumsily and angrily into his pocket. "Now you go and tell that cousin of yours."

"But suppose she comes and then the Vicar don't want her?"

"He'll want her all right. He'd have almost anybody now. Any road, there's plenty more jobs in Danby, even if he didn't want her."

"I don't like taking your money," began Beefy. But he couldn't argue. The events of the morning had left him shaken. He hadn't liked that man being cross. And the thought of going off to the friendly quiet of Shepherd's Delight, and, above all, of seeing Sally again, was too much for him.

"I'm going to live at Shepherd's Delight when I retire," he told Lizzie. "I'm going to have a pig called Emily, and – " He was off. Lizzie listened devotedly. "I hope you get there, Beefy," she said in her cracked, hoarse voice. "It'll be nice. I've always liked the country. Me – I suppose it'll be Rockefeller Avenue all me days. But I'm lucky. I've got me own little house."

Beefy made a sudden decision. "You could come to Shepherd's Delight and keep house for me," he said. "Be nice. I'm going to learn to read before then. I could read you Westerns in the evenings."

A warm glow came into Lizzie's eyes. "Be nice, Beefy," she agreed. "I must think it over." She pulled Whitey's ear. "But somehow I think it will be Rockefeller Avenue for me."

The next day Beefy set off for Shepherd's Delight. He wasn't going to spend more of Lizzie's money than he need, so he hitch-hiked all the way. He did not arrive until the village was wrapped in a blue evening mist, and the cottage windows were yellow squares of soft light.

He went straight to Auntie Nellie's, and knocked.

Sally came, and stood in the open doorway, with the lamplight behind her, and she was so lovely that Beefy found himself completely speechless.

She looked a little anxiously at him, standing there in the dusk. Then she threw the door wide open. "I didn't recognize you," she smiled. "Come in. We've thought such a lot about you."

Beefy stepped into the lamplit parlour, where Auntie Nellie was knitting. He had thought up something funny to say to her. He grinned broadly. "Hello, Auntie," he said. "I ain't died of face-ache yet, see."

Auntie did not seem very amused. "If you've come to stay," she said, "you'll have to sleep on the sofa."

"That's all right," Beefy said. He marshalled his words preparatory to dropping his bombshell. "I know a vicar what wants a housekeeper," he said.

"Beefy! Do you really?" cried Sally. "Mother and I had just been arguing about a job for me. That's why she's a bit bad-tempered."

"She wants to leave me all alone and go and work in the town," Auntie snapped.

"There's nothing for a girl of my age in Shepherd's Delight, is there?" Sally appealed to Beefy. "I've done nothing all winter. Do you really know someone who wants a housekeeper?"

"Yes. He's a vicar. He wants one bad."

"How old is he?" asked Auntie, clicking her needles irritably.

Beefy wasn't prepared for such irrelevancies. "I don't know," he said. "I only seen him once. Through a keyhole."

"Look. I'm coming to see about this," Sally said. "Where does he live?"

"In Danby. Quite near me," Beefy told her.

Auntie Nellie wiped away a tear.

"I dare say I shall be gone when you come back, Sally," she quavered. "I shan't last much longer."

"Oh, nonsense, Mother. You're as strong as a horse."

87

Auntie Nellie shook her head. Sally appeared to waver. "I can't really go and leave Mother, Beefy," she said.

"Just like you to go dashing off on a wild-goose chase like this," said Auntie Nellie.

"It might be more sensible to write and apply for the job," Sally decided.

Beefy was getting impatient with all this arguing. The Vicar wanted a housekeeper. Sally wanted a job as a vicar's housekeeper. Well, then, why the fuss?

"You don't know the first thing about him," pointed out Aunt Nellie.

"He's ever so nice," Beefy said.

Auntie turned on him. "You've only seen him through a keyhole," she snapped.

"Lizzie says he's nice," Beefy said.

"Who's Lizzie?"

"She's got an apron with something wrote on it," he explained.

Auntie groaned. "I'm going to bed," she announced. "Take your boots off before you lie down on the sofa, Beefy."

She went to bed. Sally fetched some sheets and pillows and made a bed up for Beefy. A last log in the fire burned low, flared up, broke and clattered in the grate. Sally lit a candle from the lamp. She smiled at Beefy. "Did you really come all this way just to tell me about a job?" she asked.

Beefy looked down at his boots. "That's all right, Sally," he muttered.

"It was kind of you," she said, quietly. "Sleep well, Beefy."

She went then, tiptoeing up the creaking stairs, closing behind her the little door that opened on to the staircase. But the warmth and the fragrance of her were still in the little room, mingled with the humid smell of the geraniums on the deep window ledge, and the scent of the crumbling pine log on the fire.

Beefy sighed, and took off his boots like Auntie said. He turned out the lamp. Then, in the last dying flickers from the fire, he climbed into bed.

It was even more comfortable than his roll of linoleum. He groaned with sheer pleasure, and stretched himself out, watching the shadows dance jerkily on the pictures of Queen Victoria and Prince Albert, listening to the vague, restful noises of the countryside. It was comfy, here. He did hope Sally would go back to Danby with him. It would be nice, showing his pretty cousin to Lizzie and the boys. They'd like her.

A drowsiness enveloped his mind, as soft and warm as the bed that enveloped his body. He was going up the blue mountain now. He was nearly at the top. He was struggling hard to get there, for at the summit was something wonderful, something he had always wanted, something that was worth endless searching.

Now he was on the last few difficult steps of his pilgrimage. Almost, the summit was within his grasp...

And then someone was shaking him urgently by the shoulder.

He opened his eyes. Sally, in yellow candlelight, her warm body wrapped in a flowered dressing gown, her dark hair a tangled glory about her face and shoulders, her eyes big and dark with anxiety, was bending over him.

"Beefy, it's Mother. She's ill," she was saying.

Beefy struggled into wakefulness. He looked fondly at his lovely cousin. "What time is it?" he asked.

"Oh, never mind the time. Mother's very ill. You must go for the doctor. Do you remember where he lives?"

Beefy's mind began ticking over. If Auntie was ill, Sally wouldn't be able to leave her. Then he'd have to go home alone. But Auntie didn't want Sally to go.

The whole thing stood out a mile. "She done it on purpose," he said sulkily.

"Please hurry," Sally begged. "I'm going to fill her a bottle. Now you're sure you remember where the doctor lives?"

Beefy thrust out his lower lip. "She done it on purpose," he repeated. Then, suddenly, he was aware of the pleading in Sally's face.

"OK, Sally," he said quickly. "I'm going."

"Thanks, Beefy." She hurried into the kitchen. Beefy swung out of bed and put his boots on. He went out, under the burning stars, and fetched the doctor. Later, much later, he sat with Sally drinking a cup of tea, while the grey dawn filtered in through the parlour window, and the ashes lay cold in the grate, and the lamp burned yellow and smoky in the coming clear light.

"I'm afraid I shall have to say goodbye to that job, Beefy," Sally was saying. "The doctor says she's going to need nursing for some time."

Beefy looked at her with compassion. There were delicate blue shadows under her eyes, her face was pale and sad. He wanted to put his arm round her, to say, "I'll see the Vicar doesn't get another housekeeper till you can come," but he thought she might hit him if he touched her.

Noisily he gulped his tea. "Don't worry, Sally," he said comfortingly. "Perhaps your Mother won't last long. Then you can come, after all."

To his dismayed astonishment she began to cry. He felt completely helpless. Fishing in his pocket he produced the rag he used for cleaning the windscreen of the van. Mutely he held it out to his cousin. "Don't cry, Sally," he pleaded.

Eyes bright with tears, she looked at the rag, then at Beefy's horror-stricken face. For a moment she sat, the tears welling in her eyes, her lips parted tragically. Then, slowly, she began to laugh, dabbing away the tears with her own handkerchief. "Oh, Beefy," she gasped. "You are a dear. But don't worry about me. I'll be all right."

"I wanted to take you back with me," he said.

She looked at him earnestly, her face close to his. "I promise, Beefy, as soon as Mother's better, I'll write to you and see whether that job's still open. And if it is I'll come." She stood up. "That all right?"

So Beefy told her to write to him care of Lizzie Tubb, and cam back to Danby, alone, disappointed, lonely.

It was eleven o'clock at night when he returned to the church hall. The front door was open. He went in, and climbed the ladder to the loft. The boys were just getting ready for bed.

They were pleased to see him. "If it isn't old Beefy," they cried. "Back from Ascot."

"Meet any duchesses?" asked Willie One Eye.

"Been hobnobbing with the House of Lords, Beefy?" asked Peg Leg.

"Bloddy capitalist," beamed Joe Vodka. Beefy grinned. He liked being teased.

Heck, combing his hair, brought them back to earth. "How's the undertaking racket?" he asked.

Beefy stopped grinning. "I got the sack," he said glumly.

The boys looked concerned. "Got the sack?" Peg Leg cried. "Already? Why, Beefy, whatever for?"

Beefy looked unhappy. He didn't want to say it was on account of Ida and the boys talking to him. They might feel hurt and remorseful. "I – " he stammered.

"Fancy only keeping a job for a day," said Heck. "You'll have to do better than that if you're going straight."

Lofty had an awful thought. "It – it wasn't anything to do with us coming and talking to you, was it?"

"Well, no," Beefy said, standing first on one foot and then on the other. "No. Leastways – "

Lofty sighed with relief. "I'm glad about that," he said. "We should of felt awful, shouldn't we, boys, if we'd of thought it was anything to do with us."

"Awful," they agreed.

"Well, as a matter of fact," Beefy began.

Peg Leg cut him short. "Ida was a bit worried about it. I think," he said. "She told me she thought that chap didn't quite like us being there. So we're all very relieved to know it wasn't on account of us. Very relieved indeed."

Beefy swallowed. "As a matter of fact," he tried again.

"Now you just stay here as long as you like, Beefy," Peg Leg cut in kindly. "There'll always be a bed for you here, won't there, boys."

"Course there will," they all agreed warmly.

Beefy's eyes filled with tears. He didn't deserve such kindness.

"Thanks, Peg," he gulped. But he couldn't accept their friendship and give nothing in return. "If there's anything I can do any time, don't be afraid to ask me on account of I'm going straight," he said, his breast full to overflowing with love for his comrades.

But Peg Leg was firm. "No, Beefy. We're not going to come between a man and his conscience. If you want to go straight we're the last people to stop you," he said. "Ida wouldn't want us to, anyway."

Beefy slid into his linoleum. "Thanks, Peg," he said from the bottom of his heart. His sorrow at leaving Sally behind, and losing his job, was a little assuaged by the simple warmth of his friends' welcome. He lay, thinking; of Sally, and of how she'd looked in the candlelight with her hair loose about her shoulders; of Heck and the boys, and their kindness, and of how glad he was, after all, that he hadn't hurt them by saying that it was on account of them talking to him that he'd been sacked.

But a problem, that had been worrying him subconsciously for some time, suddenly crystallized. He struggled to put it into words. As always, when he wanted help or advice, he turned to his closest friend, recumbent now on his mossy bank. "Heck," he whispered.

"What?" said Heck.

"Well!" Beefy tried hard to get the words into some sort of order. "When I didn't go straight that judge was cross with me."

"So what?"

"But when I *did* go straight Mr Smith got even crosser than what that judge did."

"So what?" Heck repeated.

"Well, I thought if you went straight, everyone was nice and kind and friendly," Beefy complained.

Heck turned his back on him. "You'll learn," he said unfeelingly.

The next day Beefy went to see Lizzie. He gave her two pound notes. "I thumbed lifts," he explained.

Lizzie drooped the corners of her mouth in disappointment. "I wanted you to have it," she said. "I'd have liked you to use it." For a few moments she held the money in her fingers, looking rather helpless. Then she put it back in the vase. "I wanted you to have it," she repeated. She came and sat down at the table, fingering the edge of the cloth. "What happened about your cousin?" she asked.

"She couldn't come on account of her mother got took bad on purpose."

"Just as well," Lizzie said. "He's got one."

Beefy flushed angrily. "But Sally's coming as soon as she can. She's going to write."

Lizzie plucked at the cloth. "He's got one," she repeated. "Not half! And I wish he hadn't."

"Does she get cross?" asked Beefy unhappily. Everyone seemed to get cross nowadays.

"Get cross? You'd think she owned the place. Natter, natter, natter. I know I'm getting old," she went on. "And perhaps I can't see the dust and dirt as well as I used to. But there's no need to be nasty, is there?" she asked plaintively.

"Course not," said Beefy.

"I can't see me staying long in the vicarage job, not if she stays."

"She won't stay," Beefy said firmly.

But Lizzie's fears were justified.

At the vicarage, the Rev. John Adams looked up from the remains of a well-cooked, beautifully served lunch to the thin, pale lips of his new housekeeper, and wondered, not for the first time, how so cold a person had managed to write such a friendly letter.

"That Lizzie Tubb," said Mrs Phillips. "Is she part of the fittings?"

"Yes," the Vicar said, a little coldly.

"You realize, sir, that she's getting past it?"

"Maybe. But she's a good old soul."

"I have never believed in employing incompetents simply because they are good old souls."

"You are not employing her," the Vicar reminded his housekeeper. "I am."

Mrs Phillips did not say, "More fool you." But her expression implied it.

The Vicar glared. "What is more, I shall continue to employ her," he announced.

Mrs Phillips pursed her lips. She left the room, and the clatter of her footsteps down the stone passage sounded to the Vicar like the crackle of approaching thunder. He sat on, elbows on table, chin in hands. Mrs Phillips certainly didn't let the grass grow under her feet. Only been here a day, and already getting her teeth into staff changes. Well, he'd see about that. Old Lizzie Tubb wasn't going to be sacrificed on anyone's altar of efficiency. Then, regretfully, he thought of the dismal months without a housekeeper. He thought of the excellent lunch he had just eaten. No. He wasn't going to throw his charwoman to the lions. But, equally, he wasn't gong to lose his excellent housekeeper. He decided that he would have to play his cards very, very carefully.

"Board meeting tomorrow morning, boys," Heck said that night, taking off his jacket. Beefy, wrapped in his linoleum, looked up anxiously. "Can I come, Heck?" he asked.

"Course you can't. You're going straight," Heck said.

"Oh," said Beefy unhappily. He didn't like this. All the boys going to a meeting, and him not there! He'd feel lonely, like. Left out of things.

"I thought maybe I could come and listen," he muttered.

"Not ruddy likely," snapped Heck. "These things are in committee. We don't want no outsiders," he added cruelly.

Peg Leg said, "Perhaps he could come *ex officio*."

Beefy brightened. "What's Exo Fishy-O?" he inquired.

"Well," Peg Leg explained vaguely. "You sort of come although you don't come official, see."

"Don't see why he should," grumbled Heck.

"Oh, let him come," said Lofty. "There might be something he could do that didn't involve an infringement of the law."

Heck appeared to consider. "OK," he said at last, with a show of reluctance. "You can come if you like, Beefy."

"Thanks, Heck," Beefy said gratefully. He snuggled happily into his linoleum. He was going to the meeting after all and he was going exo fishy-o. It sounded important. He wasn't sure that going exo fishy-o wasn't even nicer than going just ordinary.

The next morning Lizzie came into the church hall just as the boys were finishing breakfast. She did not seem to see the rest of the gang. She shuffled up to Beefy. "This came," she said pushing a letter into his hand. "I think it must be for you. Nobody never writes me no letters."

Beefy took the envelope and looked at it this way and that. He held it up to the light. No. There was no way out of it. He had got to ask for help.

"I got a letter, Heck," he appealed. "Would you read it to me?"

"You ask me that, just before a board meeting! I've got enough to do without acting nurse to you."

"Sorry, Heck," Beefy said. "I was forgetting you was busy." He wandered off. "I got a letter, Peg," he said. "Would you read it for me?"

Peg took the envelope, tore it open, extracted the letter.

"Dear Beefy," he read. "Mother is much better, and if all goes well I hope to be able to come and see your Vicar in about three weeks' time. If I don't hear from you I shall assume that he is still in need of a housekeeper. Love, Sally."

"Thanks, Peg," said Beefy. He took back the letter, put it in his pocket. "Sally's my cousin," he explained. "But Lizzie says the Vicar's got one."

"What? A Cousin?"

"No. A housekeeper. And Sally wants to be his housekeeper, only she won't be able to on account of he's got one."

"You mean you got to get rid of this dame?"

Beef nodded. "She gets cross with Lizzie, too," he said.

"Soon fix her," Peg said airily. "Leave it to me and the boys."

"Thanks, Peg," Beefy said. It was nice to have friends, always eager to do little services for one! "How do you think you'll get rid of her?"

"We'll think of something," Peg said. "Come on. The meeting's beginning."

They went into the big room. Ida was already seated at the table. She grinned up at Beefy. "Why, Beefy," she said. "I hadn't expected to see you. I'd heard a rumour you was going straight."

"I am," Beefy said. "But Heck said I could come exo-fishy-o."

"Ex what officio?" asked Ida, who had spent an unlikely year at a convent school at the age of twelve, and understood the rudiments of the Latin tongue.

Beefy looked baffled, and began to go red. "We thought he might be useful," Heck said to Ida, quickly and quietly.

"Oh, yes," said Ida, shuffling her papers. "Of course. May we have the minutes, please."

Heck began to read. Beefy, thinking about Sally's letter, was suddenly aware that Heck was reading about him. "The board stood in silent memory of Beefy, who was unavoidably absent. Several members paid warm tributes to his loyalty and selfless devotion to duty."

Beefy's mouth fell open. He beamed, and blushed, and hung his head. He would dearly have liked to ask Heck to read that bit again, but he didn't like. He only hoped the rest of the boys had been listening.

The minutes ended. Ida signed the book. She pushed it away, plumped her elbows on the table, and surveyed her fellow directors. Her moment had come.

"Boys," she said, and her voice was husky with excitement. "Boys, I'm on to something big."

She paused. Expectant silence.

"You couldn't of paid warm tributes when you was standing in silent memory," Beefy, who had been revolving things in his mind, pointed out.

Ida had built up a satisfying dramatic situation. She had taken a preparatory deep breath. She deflated, like a punctured tyre, with a hissing of air. Now she'd got to build up again. "Perhaps the biggest thing we have yet tackled," she said impressively.

"Or maybe what happened was you stood in silent memory, and *then* you sat down, and *then* someone said, 'I wish to pay – ' "

Ida snatched up her cosh gavel and gave the table a blow that would have felled an ox, or even Beefy. "The biggest thing we have yet tackled," she bellowed.

With horror Beefy suddenly realized that Ida was cross. And he was rather afraid she was cross with him. "I – I'm sorry, Ida," he stammered. "I hadn't noticed you was saying something."

Ida fingered her cosh. Then she looked at Beefy's horror-stricken face. "It's all right," she sighed.

"I was trying to get things straight in my mind, see," Beefy explained.

Ida put her chin in her hands. "Can I go on, Beefy?" she asked patiently.

"Yes, Ida, of course. I was only clearing up a few points. Just making – " He caught the chairman's baleful eye, and relapsed into silence, thoroughly ashamed of himself. It must be being exo fishy-o that had done it. Usually he hardly dared to open his mouth at a board meeting. Yet here he was being publicly rebuked for talking too much. He hung his head.

Any dramatic force that Ida's announcement might have had was now irretrievably ruined. And well she knew it. She said in a flat voice, "The Northern Counties Bank are receiving a consignment of £100,000 in one-pound notes on Wednesday."

She had shaken them, after all. Five and a half pairs of eyes regarded her with considerable interest. She saw the word "Pliz" forming on Joe Vodka's lips and hurried on. "Between eleven o'clock and twelve on Wednesday morning a van will drive up to the back door of the bank and deliver one hundred thousand one-pound notes." She was after dramatic effect again now. "There is a tide in the affairs of men, which, taken at the flood, leads on to fortune." She dropped her voice an octave. She slapped the table with her cosh. "Gentlemen, this is *our* tide. This could be *our* fortune."

Beefy was quite carried away. He'd always known Ida was clever, but he'd never known before that she was in the class that could make up bits of poetry. And though he couldn't quite see the connection between tides and floods and a hundred thousand ponds, he had nevertheless grasped one salient fact; Ida was going to make them all that rich they wouldn't know what to do with the stuff.

But Peg Leg Evans was less impressed. "May I ask the chairman the source of her information?" he inquired.

"No," snapped Ida. "You may not. But it's good. That money's going to be at the bank between eleven and twelve on Wednesday. And we're going to get it." She rose to her feet. "I will now call upon the secretary to set the scene." She announced solemnly.

Heck the Sec. rose, and dragged the church hall black-board to the right of the table. Casually he pulled a piece of chalk out of his pocket. He drew parallel lines on the board, and then he turned and looked at the boys importantly, just like Beefy had once seen a schoolmaster do in a film.

"This here's the High Street," he said, just like the schoolmaster. He drew two more lines. "And this here's Market Street, running into High Street." He drew a square where the two streets joined. "And that's the Northern Counties Bank, with the front door in Market Street." He tossed the chalk up and down in his cupped hands, and surveyed the class. "Now, are there any questions, so far?"

"Yes," said Peg Leg jocularly. "Why don't you stop your bit of chalk squeaking?" and was promptly scowled into gravity by Ida and Heck.

Heck coughed delicately, and turned back to the board. "Here," he went on, "in Market Street, is a large gateway. This leads into a big yard at the back of the bank. Delivery vans drive into there, leave their goods at the back door, and have room to turn round and drive out again. But the particular van we are discussing will not drive out again, not for some time, anyway."

He bowed to the chairman. She rose, briskly. "The plan is this, gentlemen," she began. "One, Peg Leg, in his postman's uniform, will lurk in the yard from eleven o'clock onwards. As soon as he sees the van entering the yard, he will knock at the back door of the bank and present their registered letters on all of which the seals will have been broken or tampered with. This will create a diversion. Two. As soon as the van has entered the yard, Heck, Lofty Longbottom, Willie One Eye and Joe Vodka will drive up in a borrowed car, park it in the gateway, take out the ignition key, put on the handbrake, lock all the doors, and, if time permits, let down one or more tyres, thus sealing the gateway. This party will then hold up the men unloading the money, and relieve them of it.

"Three. In the meantime, Beefy's replacement will have driven up in the van, and will be parked just outside the gates, in Market Street, with his engine running. Heck, Lofty, Willie and Joe will by this time have grabbed the money. They will run out of the yard, climb into the van, bringing the cash with them, of course, and Beefy's replacement will drive like the devil to a secret rendezvous where I shall be waiting." She took a sip of water. "Any questions?"

"What about me?" Peg Leg asked promptly.

"You'll be all right. You're in uniform. No one's going to suspect you. By the time they've found that their registered letters contain what they're supposed to, and not Bible leaves, they'll be so thankful they'll be ready to kiss you."

Beefy had listened to all this with growing amazement. That there were people who could understand all this sort of thing! And not only understand it, but work it out in the first place. But amazement gave way to misgiving, misgiving to a lonely foreboding.

"What does 'replacement' mean, Ida?" he asked, very humbly.

"Well," said Ida. "In this case it means the bloke what's going to take your place."

There was a silence. "Wisht I could come after all," Beefy said at last.

"Oh, no, Beefy," Ida said firmly. "We ain't going to tempt anyone who wants to go straight. We respect your decision too much for that Beefy." She turned to the meeting. "We shall be all right, shan't we, boys."

"Course we shall," they said. "Don't you worry about us, Beefy, old boy."

"But I *want* to come," pleaded Beefy.

"No. We'd be glad to have you, of course. But we're not coming between a man and his conscience," Ida said.

Peg Leg shook his head. "Course not," he agreed. "Never get another van driver like old Beefy, though," he added thoughtfully.

Ida appeared to consider. "There's no doubt it would set the seal of success on the venture if Beefy came," she admitted. She considered. She shook her head. "No. I won't come between a man and his conscience," she repeated.

"But I *want* to help," pleaded Beefy. "I don't want to feel left out."

Lofty Longbottom did not often say much at meetings, but now he looked very thoughtful and said, "What we got to consider is this. Should we really be asking Beefy to do anything dishonest? After all, he's only driving the van, mind. He ain't doing any pinching and stealing."

Ida looked at him thoughtfully. "If it comes to a discussion of ethics, there ain't nobody I'd rather listen to than you, Lofty," she said. Earnestly she leaned across the table. "You really feel Beefy wouldn't be doing nothing wrong?"

They regarded each other solemnly. "I really feel that, Ida," said Lofty.

Ida set her plump hands on the table and pushed herself back in her chair.

"Beefy, " she said, her mind made up. "You can drive the van."

"Oo, thanks, Ida," Beefy said. He beamed round at his fellow directors. "You ain't ever seen a van drove like I'm going to drive that van," he told them happily.

CHAPTER 8

Wednesday began ordinarily enough. First, the great and terrible stars were extinguished. Then Earth, revolving in nothing, on nothing, spun England towards the sunlight, and the eastern sky was filled with all the glory of God and His Archangels. In the valleys, treetops floated in white mist that was like pools of milk, and the sun drank up the mist; and farms, and fields and hedgerows appeared new-made. Larks took off urgently, like fighter aircraft, and climbed up, up, up, into the hazy blue. In Danby a thousand alarm clocks burst into frenzied, bouncing life, driving sound waves, like arrows, into a thousand ears. The ears told the brains, and the brains sent out messages here, there, everywhere, so that eyes opened, hands rubbed eyes, hands pushed aside the bedclothes. Feet found the floor, groped for carpet slippers, and carried the body downstairs. Hands turned taps, and filled kettles with water from a lake fifty miles away. They put kettles on gas stoves, and lighted little blue flames. And the blue flames were the burning of a forest whose shade had ceased a million years ago.

Now the brains commanded the hands to put into a teapot dried leaves from the other ends of the earth; and, into cups, milk, that was the grass, and the sunlight, and the soft rain of English meadows. A thousand brains commanded, drink. And a thousand bodies, drugged and heavy with sleep, drank, and were refreshed, and shouldered another day.

Yes, Wednesday began ordinarily enough. The Reverend John Adams went off to early Communion, where he consumed bread and wine that was, in some way that the wise can accept though none can understand, the Body and Blood of the Creator of that bread and wine.

When he returned home, and pushed open the front door of the vicarage, he was greeted by such a smell of frying bacon and eggs, by such an aroma of coffee, that he could have fallen on his knees and given thanks there and then for the loving kindness of a God Who, in His gentle understanding, gives us not only the Blessed Sacrament, but eggs and bacon as well.

His thankfulness was increased by a letter from the architect. Things were moving fast, now. Very soon tenders would be going out to the builders. Very soon the bricks and mortar of the new church hall would cease to be drawings on paper and become reality.

Over breakfast he wondered vaguely who would submit the lowest tender. Somehow he had a feeling it would be Amos Coldbarrow. And he hoped it wouldn't. Not a nice man, Amos. A good builder, undoubtedly, and keen. But a red-faced, hard-drinking, hard-swearing old reprobate who scoffed at the Church and pinned his faith on lucky charms and "What the Stars Foretell". An eighteenth-century character, the Vicar decided, who feared the devil, but did not fear God.

With a sigh of satisfaction he popped the last piece of crisp, marmaladed toast into his mouth, emptied his coffee cup, and dropped his napkin onto the table. Mary Phillips came in. "Everything satisfactory, sir?" she asked.

"Very nice indeed, thank you, Mrs Phillips. Your cooking is excellent."

She began to clear away. "You soon won't have anything to eat it off, at this rate," she said darkly.

"Why?" he asked, knowing the answer.

"That Lizzie Tubb broke two plates yesterday."

"Indeed?"

Mrs Phillips put her hands on the table and looked him full in the face.

She said: "If I am to stay, I demand the right to choose my own staff."

"And Lizzie Tubb would not be your choice?"

"She most certainly would not."

The Vicar rose, and began to pace the room, filling his pipe. "Now look, Mrs Phillips," he said at last. "You are a most excellent housekeeper. There can be no thought of your leaving. But Lizzie Tubb is an old woman, and poor. She has worked here for years; for me, and for Canon Tumble, and for the incumbent before him. To dismiss her now would be a most unchristian act. And I am not prepared even to discuss it." He put his pipe between his teeth, bit on it, and looked gravely and firmly at his housekeeper.

"Then I give a month's notice," Mrs Phillips said promptly.

"I refuse to accept it."

"You'll have to accept it."

The Vicar lit his pipe, and threw the match into the empty grate.

"What have you got against Lizzie Tubb, Mrs Phillips?" he asked.

"Only her incompetence. I cannot tolerate incompetence."

The Vicar looked at the tall, thin, bitter creature before him. "Shall we discuss this when you are a little less overwrought?" he suggested.

"Vicar," said Mrs Phillips, "I have never been overwrought in my life."

I can believe that, he thought, looking at the thin lips. You're the coldest fish I ever met. Aloud he said, "Leave it now, Mrs Phillips. We'll discuss it later."

She bowed coldly, and went out with the tray. But the Vicar thought he had seen a flicker of regret in her eyes as soon as she had given notice; so he was not surprised when, later in the morning, she came into the study and said, meekly, "I am afraid I behaved very impetuously this morning, sir."

The Vicar looked up, but betrayed no emotion. "You wish to withdraw your notice?"

"If I may, sir."

"Very well, Mrs Phillips." He went back to his work. He let her reach the door. He looked up and put down his pen.

"Mrs Phillips," he said. "At this stage it would be possible for you to decide to make Lizzie Tubb's life such hell that she would be forced to resign. You would then have gained your point, and you would still have a comfortable post."

Silence, while Vicar and housekeeper eyed each other.

"I am not a female Himmler," said Mrs Phillips at last.

"But you are a woman of singular determination," said the Vicar.

Mrs Phillips inclined her head. Very quietly and thoughtfully she left the room. For a long time the Vicar sat looking after her. Then, with a sigh, he went back to the proofs of the parish magazine.

To return to the beginnings of Wednesday.

Lizzie Tubb lay under a grey blanket, whimpering and moaning in her sleep. Above her head was a framed text: Be Strong and of a Good Courage, the letters twined with honeysuckle and clematis. On a packing case beside her bed was a mug containing her teeth. There were no other furnishings.

Fear clutched suddenly at Lizzie's stomach, and she thought, Mrs Phillips. She opened her eyes, and saw a square of sunlight clinging to the drab wallpaper, and knew it was another day. Another day of being made to feel old, clumsy and useless. Another reproachful, reproving day. Mrs Phillips! She wished Mrs Phillips was in – Hanover.

Mr Macmillan awoke and thought about overdrafts, and mortgages, and stocks and shares. What was today? Wednesday. Nothing untoward in his diary, he thought. A lot of cash to get in, he remembered. If he wasn't engaged he'd just keep an eye on that transaction. You never knew, these days. Funny things happened.

Beefy greeted the day cheerfully, humming "Yes, we have no bananas", but under his breath, so as not to make his friend Heck mad. He was going to help the boys. Wasn't going to do anything dishonest, either. Just drive the van to a secret rondivoo.

Beefy had never seen a rondivoo. He imagined it as a sort of windmill without sails. And secret! He would tap on the great, iron-studded door. A little panel in the door would slide open, and he would see two eyes staring at him through the slits of a mast. "Who's there?" a foreign sort of voice would ask. "It's Beefy," he'd say. "Why, come in, Beefy," the foreign voice would say, and there would be much drawing of bolts and the great door would be flung open.

And Beefy would step inside the rondivoo, and drop £100,000 onto the stone-flagged floor. But these were dreams, he realized. First, he had to do the job.

So keen was he on his work that he found himself driving the van, a green one, down Market Street before half past ten in the morning. It was a nice van, easy to handle, and the Company had bought it – well, acquired it – specially for the occasion. He was all keyed up. He had collected the van, and Ida had told him where the secret rondivoo was, and then she had put her hand on his shoulder and said, "Good luck, Beefy", very emotional, just like the CO sending his bomber crews off on a raid at the pictures.

Beefy wished he wasn't so early. He didn't quite know what to do for the next half-hour. Slowly he approached the gateway that led into the yard of the bank, and had to brake because a van was turning into the gateway. Then the road was clear again, and he was just about to touch the accelerator when he froze. A van! Going into the yard! And it was half an hour before the boys would be along.

He thought quickly, or tried to. He parked his van, got out, and hurried over to the gateway, trembling with excitement. Yes. As he thought. The van was drawn up outside the back door of the bank. Two men were lifting out big cases and carrying them inside.

Beefy was frantic. All that money, being carried into safety before his very eyes! He peered anxiously up and down Market Street. There was no sign of the boys. Naturally; it was still only ten-thirty-five.

Then a surprising, a wonderful thing happened. Just as the two men were carrying the sixth case towards the door a bank messenger came out with two mugs of tea. Promptly the men put the case down on the doorstep so that they could take the tea. Beefy watched. The men were talking to the messenger now. One of them pulled a folded newspaper from his pocket, showed the messenger an article on the sporting page. The discussion became animated. Beefy caught the words "Danby Rovers", "Cup Final", "Couldn't play pussy". He watched. His mouth was dry with excitement.

The three men went into the bank.

And they left the case standing on the doorstep.

The watcher in the gateway licked his dry lips. "Beefy showed drive and initiative," he whispered to himself. He advanced crabwise into the yard, peered into the doorway of the bank, could not see anyone. He stooped down, put his arms round the big case, staggered out of the yard with it, pushed past a policeman, loaded the case into his van, and then, to his utter astonishment, found himself driving, without let or hindrance, to the secret rondivoo.

There had been £100,000 in six cases. He'd got one. Six into ten goes one, and that leaves four, and you add a nought. Six into forty goes, say, five and then a baffling number of noughts. Probably got £150,000 here, thought Beefy. Roughly that is. Ida and the boys wouldn't half be pleased.

He peered anxiously into his driving mirror. No, he was sure he wasn't being followed. But the traffic was heavy here. He had to drive slowly. A black saloon car was approaching. And suddenly Beefy saw that Heck was driving it. He sounded his horn frantically, waved, and pulled into the side. The boys had seen him. The black saloon stopped, and the occupants leapt out and came running across. "Where the hell are you going?" Heck asked angrily.

"I got the money," said Beefy. "Leastways, some of it. About £150,000," he added airily. "They was early."

"Got the money?" gasped Lofty.

"Yes. They was early, see, so I nipped in – "

"Then what you sitting here for?" shouted Heck. "Go on. You'll have every cop in Danby looking for you." He turned, and raced back to the black saloon. The others followed him.

Beefy started the van, and drove off. He stuck his lower lip out. He was just a trifle hurt. Heck was his friend. There was no need to shout. After all, if he hadn't turned up early and shown drive and initiative, there wouldn't have been no money.

He drove on. There were still no police cars in his driving mirror, only the black saloon. It was drawing nearer, overtaking him, flashing past. Soon it was out of sight.

He was in open country now. Happily he watched the needle flickering on the fifty-five mark. All clear behind. Before long he would be at the rondivoo at this rate.

Actually he was just a bit disappointed in the rondivoo. It wasn't at all what he had expected. It was simply a rather tumbledown old barn that they had used once before on a job, miles from anywhere and big enough to conceal both the car and the van. But never mind! Ida would be there, and the boys, and they would open the case and stare in wonder at the money. Then they would slap him on the back and say, "Good old Beefy."

He could see the barn now, old mellow brick overhung with trees, half-buried in ivy. This was where he had to be careful. But no, the lane was deserted, in front and behind. He turned in at a broken gate, bumped a few yards over a field, stopped outside the barn. The big doors were open. He drove in.

Before he could switch off his engine Heck and the boys rushed up, opened the back of the van, and seized the case. They set it down before Ida on the earth floor. With a pair of scissors she cut the ropes.

Tense, agonized silence while she pulled off the lid. Beefy lumbered up to see them all gazing spellbound into the big cardboard case.

The silence seemed to last for ever. Then: "Collecting-boxes," groaned Heck. "Flaming, perishing ruddy collecting-boxes."

Ida did not say anything. She picked up the lid, and for the first time read the address label. "Edward Macmillan, Esq., Hon. Branch Secretary, Indigent Bankers' Aid Society, c/o the Northern Counties Bank Ltd, Danby."

No one said anything. There was a consignment note in the case for "6 boxes, containing 150 IBAS Collecting-boxes, 50,000 Emblems, for use on Flag Day, May 5th."

"I'm ever so sorry," said Beefy.

It was strangely quiet in the barn, and there was a rich damp smell of earth, and rotting wood, and potatoes.

"It must have been the wrong van," explained Beefy.

Ida looked at her wristwatch. "Twelve o'clock," she said. "They'll have got the money in the strongroom by now."

Six pairs of shoulders slumped.

"Pliz, what is collecting-box?" asked Joe Vodka.

No one answered. Silence built up in the barn. Heavy, oppressive, it was one with the earthy, warm smell of the place. It weighed down on Beefy like water on a deep-sea swimmer, pressing on his temples and his eyeballs.

"I thought they was early, see," he muttered. He swallowed.

Eyes were watching him. Heck's, cold and meditative as a snake's; Ida's bright, amused yet calculating; Joe Vodka's, like black, bottomless lakes among the northern pines.

The silence grew even heavier, more deeply charged. It was like the moment when the great thunderclouds, opposing armies, roll into position, and the birds quake, silent, on the boughs, awaiting the lightning stroke.

The spell was broken by a policeman's head appearing round the door. For perhaps the first time in his life Beefy was glad to see a Bobby.

"What's going on here?" asked the policeman.

Ida rallied. "Just having a picnic, Officer," she said gaily.

He looked round the barn. "Not much sign of food." He sounded suspicious.

Ida patted the lid of the box. "It's in here," she said.

He came into the barn. "Well, you can't picnic here," he said. "Private property."

Ida put on her best convent school accent. "I say, I'm most terribly sorry, Officer. We'd no idea." She gave him a melting smile. "Come on, boys, we'll have to find another picnic spot."

Watched by the policeman, they put the case into the van. Ida seated herself in the back seat of the saloon. The others climbed into the two vehicles. They drove away. The silence was suddenly broken by a throaty chuckle from Ida. "Boys," she said. "There's only one thing for it. We got to have a Flag Day. All personnel will report to me at 0900 hours on Saturday, May 5th. Collecting-boxes will be worn."

The cars hurried homeward through the April noontide.

Beefy thought he would never recover from the disgrace. But the following day he had other things to occupy his mind. Lizzie brought him a letter from Sally, and Peg Leg Evans read it to him. Sally said she hoped to come to Danby on Saturday, May 12th. Her train was due to arrive at 4.15. Would Beefy meet her? As she had not heard from Beefy she assumed the Vicar still needed a housekeeper.

Beefy was filled with excitement. Sally was coming at last. But the Vicar had still got a housekeeper. The boys hadn't got rid of her yet. He mentioned the matter to Peg Leg. "Don't worry," said Peg Leg. "We'll soon fix her."

For some months now Danby had been moving towards the centre of the world stage. Danby Rovers had won round after round in the matches for the FA Cup. They had reached the semi-final, and won. And now, on Saturday, April 28th, they were to play Bolton Wanderers in the Cup Final at Wembley. The excitement was almost unbearable. Solemn articles in the sporting pages of the national press denounced, deplored, accused. The women's magazines carried chatty little articles about what the wives of the opposing centre forwards cooked for dinner. Fifteen Danby men were injured in the rush for Cup Final tickets. A protest march, carrying banners "FA Unfair to Rover Fans" was broken up by police with drawn batons. A Danby Rovers director, believed to have refused to spend £50,000 on a new goalkeeper, narrowly escaped being tarred and feathered. On the Saturday morning fifty special trains left Danby station for Wembley, to an accompaniment of whistles, rattles and general hysteria.

John Adams, feeling that such excitement over a game played with a *round* ball was little short of pagan, went to his study immediately after breakfast and began to write a denunciatory sermon. He had hardly filled his pipe, however, when a knock came at the door and Mrs Phillips entered.

The Vicar gave her good morning warily. What had Lizzie Tubb been up to now, he wondered.

But it wasn't about Lizzie Tubb. "I'm sorry to interrupt you, sir," said Mrs Phillips. "But I have just had a letter from my married daughter at Leicester. Her son is running in the school sports this afternoon, and she asks me to visit them. I wonder if I might ask for the day off. I could leave you a cold luncheon, if that would be convenient."

She stood there stiff and, for once, a little awkward. Evidently asking, or granting, favours did not come easily to her. "I suppose," the Vicar could not help saying, "I suppose this is not a variation of the grandmother's funeral joke, Mrs Phillips?"

For a moment the housekeeper looked puzzled. Then she said, "No, Vicar. I have no desire to visit Wembley."

"Quite right, too," said the Vicar warmly. "Twickenham's one thing. Wembley's another." He came back to the matter in hand. "Yes, of course you can go. And I hope you have a very nice day."

"Thank you, sir," said Mrs Phillips with an effort. "I will leave everything prepared." She went.

The Vicar returned to his sermon. After a time the door opened again. Mrs Phillips, looking very smart in her outdoor clothes, came in. "I'm going now, sir," she said.

"Goodbye," he said. "Enjoy yourself." He gave her a quick smile. "I'm sure you will do your grandson great credit," he added.

She did not smile back. "Thank you," she said. A minute later he heard the front door close behind her.

John Adams refilled his pipe, set a match to it, went on writing. But he was soon disturbed by the sound of shuffling footsteps approaching the study door, followed by a nervous tapping. "Come in," he called cheerfully.

The door opened. The round moon-face of Lizzie Tubb appeared, and gazed at him anxiously through thick pebble glasses.

"Hello, Lizzie," he said, trying to sound as friendly as possible.

She shambled into the room, peering with short-sighted intensity from side to side. She stooped, and her arms hung forward slightly as though she carried an imaginary bucket. John Adams watched her. Why bone meal? he wondered irrelevantly. Rather to his surprise he rose, and pulled a chair up for her. "Sit down, Lizzie," he said kindly.

She flopped into the chair. The Vicar went and sat down at his desk. Lizzie sat and stared at him.

"Well, Lizzie, what is it?" he asked.

She swallowed. She seemed to have difficulty in getting her cracked voice working.

The Vicar said, "What can I do for you, Lizzie?"

Her throat was full of gravel. "I've come to give my notice," she said.

He made his voice very kind. "I'm sorry to hear that. Aren't you happy here?"

Her words came slowly. "It ain't that. You've been nice to me, you have."

"What is it, then?"

There were tears, now, behind the pebble glasses. "I'm getting on, I want a bit o' rest. I got a bit of money. I want a rest," she muttered.

"Mrs Phillips hasn't been – nasty to you?" he asked suddenly.

She gave him a startled look. "I just want a bit o' rest," she repeated stubbornly.

He was suddenly angry, furiously angry with the little Hitlers who rob the lives of subordinates of all their peace and sweetness. Just wait till he saw Mrs Phillips again. He'd have quite a lot to say to her.

"I don't want you to decide anything now, Lizzie," he said. "Wait a few days and think it over. By the way, if it has any bearing, Mrs Phillips may not be staying with me much longer."

He saw a flicker of hope in her eyes. But she said again, "I just want a bit o' rest, see."

Why are decent people so consistently decent? he wondered. Always willing to put themselves in the wrong, rather than give away their persecutors. He rose, and held the door open. "You think it over, Lizzie," he said. "And don't worry."

She did not seem to see the open door. She sat there, ungainly as a hippopotamus, her face blotched and blurred with tears. "I just wanted a bit o' rest," she said.

For all his bluff appearance, John Adams was a man of deep sensitivity. He knew well the cunning self-tortures of the human mind. He knew what Lizzie must have suffered before she came to him today. "Wait there, Lizzie," he said, and hurried to the kitchen and prepared two cups of tea, strong and sweet. For the Lizzies of this world, tea was, he knew, comfort, refreshment, and solace. He came back and put a cup into her hand. She took it silently and gulped it noisily. It pulled her together. She put the cup down on his desk and peered up at him. "I'll be going now," she said. She groped for words. "You been nice to me."

He touched her shoulder. "Why shouldn't I be nice to you? You looked after me, didn't you, when I hadn't a housekeeper."

She put a hand on her knees and pushed herself up out of her chair. "I'll wash them cups up," she said.

"And you won't leave me without thinking it over very carefully?"

"I don't know," she said groping her way to the door. "I'm tired, see, I want a bit o' rest."

He heard her slip-slopping down the stone passage, the cups rattling in her hands. He went back to his sermon. The day wore on.

In the afternoon what remained of Danby sat biting its fingernails, its eyes glued to television sets. Empty buses cruised unhappily through the deserted streets. Traffic lights flickered from red to green, controlling traffic that was not there. And one minute before the end of the game a great, muffled cry went up from the silent town. Danby Rovers had scored. Danby had won the Cup.

The town went mad that night. People danced in the streets. Unmentionable objects were hung on the Town Hall weathervane. The police force finished up twelve helmets short. The special trains from Wembley disgorged their delirious passengers, who rushed off to increase the pandemonium. The Cup was borne in victory through the streets. In the market place the statue of Julius Caesar, who had always thought his own triumphs pretty well staged, turned green with envy.

And in the middle of the excitement there came a peremptory knocking at the vicarage door. John Adams, thirsting to get to grips with Mrs Phillips, hurried to open it. To his surprise a policeman was standing in the porch.

"Good evening, sir," he said. "Do you know this lady?"

The Vicar peered out into the darkness. "I most certainly do," he gasped. "It's my housekeeper."

Between them they helped her in, and let her down onto a settee in the drawing-room. "Found her in the market place, sir" the policeman said. "Suppose we ought to make a charge, really. But – well, it's a special occasion, like, isn't it."

"I hope you won't think of doing any such thing," the Vicar said earnestly. "Er – did she attract any attention, may I ask?"

"Attention! I'll say she did. There was about a hundred of them, dancing the hokey-cokey round her."

John Adams led the way to the front door. "Oh, Lord," he said. He opened the door. "I can be sure that nothing more will be heard of this matter?"

"Quite sure, sir, Goodnight."

"Goodnight, constable. And thank you very much for your help and discretion."

He closed the door. He passed a hand over his eyes. Then he went back and looked at his housekeeper.

She was slumped on the settee, her legs stretched out wide before her. Set recklessly on her head was a paper hat in the Danby Rovers colours. In one hand was a rattle. In the other an empty gin bottle.

And Mrs Phillips was in a drunken stupor.

"God bless my soul," the Vicar said. He felt quite unusually helpless. But there was only one thing to do. He went out into the saturnalian night, and fetched Lizzie Tubb.

The following morning, when the Vicar returned from early Communion, he found a neat breakfast tray awaiting him. A boiled, brown egg under an egg cosy; a well-filled teapot under a tea cosy; thin, well-buttered slices of white and brown bread. Marmalade, strawberry jam, honey.

And a note. "Dear Mr Adams, I wish to tender my immediate resignation. In the circumstances I feel sure you will agree with me that the one month's notice originally agreed between us should be waived. Yours very truly, Mary Phillips."

The Vicar read the note. Then he struck his egg over the head with unnecessary force. He was suddenly tired of Mrs Phillips; didn't mind if he never saw her again. But she came in as he was finishing breakfast. She looked neat and fresh. Her face had its normal smooth pallor. No bleary-eyed dishevelment about Mrs Phillips. She hadn't even the grace to look sheepish.

"Good morning, sir," she said. "Can I get you some more tea?"

"No, thank you, Mrs Phillips." Her composure irritated him. "I have read your note," he said. "I accept your resignation. And I agree that in the circumstances a month's notice would be an embarrassment for all parties."

She inclined her head. "I am sorry about last night's incident," she said coolly.

"I'm quite sure you regret your behaviour bitterly," he said. "Please don't distress yourself by talking about it."

"On the contrary," she said. "I don't regret my behaviour at all."

He looked up at her in astonishment. She was the coolest customer he'd ever met.

She went on: "Would you believe me if I told you that, as I was coming home from my married daughter's, I was set upon by a gang of thugs? One of them – one of them held

118

my nose while another poured half a bottle of what I think was whisky down my throat. Then they seem to have dressed me up like a football supporter and left me in the market place. I have a vague recollection of people dancing some kind of pagan dance round me."

"Did you recognize any of these men?" he inquired.

"No. One was tall and dark, with long side-whiskers. And I imagine one of them had a wooden leg. But I doubt whether I could identify any of them. It was dark, of course, and they were very – efficient."

"And you know of no one who might bear you any ill will?"

"No one."

She was silent. So was the Vicar.

"There is no reason why you should believe me," she said at last.

The Vicar walked over and leaned on the mantelpiece. He took a pipe from the rack and tapped the back of the bowl thoughtfully against his palm.

"I believe you, Mrs Phillips," he said quietly. "But many people in the parish wouldn't. I am afraid that last night's incident has made your position as my housekeeper untenable."

"I realize that perfectly," she said. "That's why I resigned first and told you my story afterwards."

"I appreciate your attitude." He was silent for a moment. "Mrs Phillips," he went on, "I think it only fair to tell you that, even before this incident happened, I was prepared to ask you to leave. I felt that I had to lose either you or Lizzie Tubb. And, excellent housekeeper though you are, I was not willing to lose Lizzie."

For the first time Mrs Phillips showed some emotion. She sneered. "Has she complained about me?" she asked.

"No!" snapped the Vicar with sudden heat. "She hasn't complained. But she said she was tired, and wanted to give the job up. And I thought I knew why."

There was silence between them. Then, on an impulse, John Adams went up to her and held out his hand. "Goodbye, and thank you for looking after me. I shall miss you. I'm sorry things have turned out as they have."

She did not take his hand. She looked into his eyes, and said, "May I ask you one question, sir?" She took a deep breath. "Who – who put me to bed, last night?"

"Lizzie Tubb," said the Vicar evenly.

There was emotion now. There was hatred in her eyes, and in the twist of her lips. She reached for the door handle. "I think you could have spared me *that*," she said, and wrenched open the door, and was gone, slowly, deliberately, and half an hour later she left the house, just as the bells began to peal for Mattins.

In the parish of St Jude the Obscure the affair of the Vicar's housekeeper almost supplanted the Cup Final as a subject for conversation. It had all the elements of a perfect piece of gossip. An aloof, superior stranger came into the parish and took up an important position, looked down on everybody, and talked lah-di-dah. And then, before you knew where you were –

Broke a bottle of whisky over a policeman's head. They put in six stitches.

Climbing on the statue, holding a bottle to J Caesar's lips, swearing at him like a fishwife because he wouldn't drink.

Took six cops to get her down.

Thrown out of the Jolly Sailor.

Made a scene in the Poet and Peasant.

But Lizzie Tubb said to Beefy, "Mrs Phillips was took bad on Saturday. Ever so bad. I felt quite sorry for her."

"P'raps she'd ate something," suggested Beefy.

But on the Monday, when the Vicar came across Lizzie scrubbing his hall, he said, "Lizzie, you've got to look after me until I can get a new housekeeper."

A pair of grateful eyes looked up at him. "You mean – you mean she's went?"

"Yes." He sighed. It was all very well for Lizzie; but it was a bit hard on him. The comfort of well-cooked meals, of an ordered life, was not easily forgotten. "You will stay on, won't you?" he asked.

"If you want me," she said. "I know a Vicar's housekeeper what wants a job," she went on, sitting back on her haunches.

"You do?" he asked eagerly. "Who is she? Where is she?"

"She's the cousin, or aunt, or something of a friend of mine. Comes from away. She's coming Saturday week."

"Bless you, Lizzie," he said fervently. "Can I see this friend of yours? Where does she live?"

"It ain't a she. It's a him. He lives – I don't rightly know where he lives," she added hastily. "But he can come and see you."

Two house later, Beefy, well-scrubbed, in a clean singlet, stood before the Vicar, who looked at him in some surprise.

"Lizzie Tubb tells me a relation of yours is looking for a post as housekeeper," he said.

"That's right," said Beefy.

"Lizzie said she was coming to Danby next week."

"That's right," said Beefy.

"Do you think she'd keep house for me?"

"That's what she's coming for," said Beefy.

"Oh," said the Vicar, even more surprised. "But I had a housekeeper until very recently. Your relation couldn't have known she was going to leave."

"That was before," explained Beefy.

"What was before what?"

ERIC MALPASS

"Before she came."

The Vicar's head was beginning to spin. "I think I'd better see your relation," he said. "Will you bring her to see me when she arrives?" But he didn't want to risk missing this opportunity. "I ought to be able to get in touch with you," he said. "Where do you live?"

Beefy blushed. "Well," he said. "Leastways… You can tell Lizzie if you want me," he finished hastily.

The Vicar watched him go. Extraordinary fellow! Make a good rugger forward if he was in better trim. Buy why all the mystery? Why did he and Lizzie both close up like clams when he asked where Beefy lived? He only hoped that this woman would turn out to be a suitable housekeeper. But he didn't feel terribly hopeful. She'd need to be a great deal brighter than her nephew.

122

CHAPTER 9

Saturday, May 5th, and a bright, breezy day. The flag-sellers were out in force. When Edward Macmillan did a job he did it properly. You couldn't move for flag-sellers. They guarded all strategic points. There was no escape.

But it was a flag day with a difference. Mr Macmillan had more collectors than he realized. Amos Coldbarrow, builder and contractor, saw a plump, smartly-dressed woman smiling at him. He tried to take evasive action. But he was too late.

"Buy a flag?" said the plump lady.

Amos grunted. He produced a threepenny piece.

The plump lady's smile was as bright as Blackpool illuminations while she pinned his flag on. But then a very surprising thing happened. Amos felt something hard pressed against his ribs. The lady's smile had been switched off. "Come on," she hissed. "All you've got, or I'll pump you full of lead. And if you tell the police, I'll get you if it's the last thing I do."

The lady's hand was in the pocket of her loose coat. But he could just see the glint of a black revolver in her hand.

"Is this a joke?" he asked hopefully.

"Brother," she said earnestly. "It's no joke. And I haven't got all day. Come on. Get your wallet out."

Amos looked round for a policeman. *He* wasn't frightened. He didn't know whether this woman was stark, staring mad or just trying it on. But one thing he did know.

She obviously wasn't going to risk shooting him in broad daylight. And he was just going to call her bluff and run for it, when he remembered something he had read in the paper that morning. "May 5th. A difficult day for those born under Taurus. Don't take any risks today. Don't assume that the improbable is the impossible."

Mr Coldbarrow was born under Taurus. Well, it was highly improbable that this lady would pump him full of lead. But, dammit, it wasn't impossible. Life was sweet for a builder and contractor with plenty of money. He pulled out his wallet.

"You don't really expect to get away with this, do you?" he asked, stuffing twenty pounds in five-pound notes into the collecting-box.

"You're going to be sorry if I don't," said Ida grimly.

Trembling with rage, Amos Coldbarrow hurried away. Ten minutes later he approached the same spot with a policeman. Somehow the plump lady had changed into little Miss Titterton, secretary to St Jude's parochial church council.

"Why, Mr Coldbarrow," she cried reproachfully. "You've bought a flag from someone else. I shall never forgive you. Never!" She turned to the policeman. "What about you, Officer? Are you going to help the Society?"

They ignored her. "Is this the woman?" the policeman asked.

"Good Lord, no. She was fat, I tell you."

The policeman turned to Miss Titterton.

"How long have you been here?" he asked.

"About ten minutes. Is there anything wrong, Officer? I can assure you I am an accredited collector."

"Was there anyone collecting here when you arrived?"

"Yes, a lady." Miss Titterton's fingers tied nervous knots in the tapes of her collecting-box. "If you are at all doubtful about me, Officer, Mr Macmillan will vouch for me immediately."

"What happened to this lady?"

"A motor car came and picked her up and drove away. Mr Macmillan knows me very well. If you ring up the bank – "

"What sort of car?"

Really, Miss Titterton didn't know. She used to know all the makes before the war, but nowadays, with all this streamlining, they all looked exactly alike to her. Sometimes, indeed, she wasn't even sure which was the back and which the front. She giggled nervously.

Had she, by some miracle, noticed the registration number?

Yes. Now *there* she could help. It had spelt a word, and she always noticed when car registrations spelt words. Often they were quite amusing. Now they might not believe this, but her friend Carrie had a car DOT something or other. Dot and Carry, you see. She laughed shrilly.

No, the silly thing was that she couldn't remember the word. But it did spell a word. Surely that helped. Now, was the Officer *quite* sure he didn't want to ring up Mr Macmillan. She'd really feel happier if he did. She would hate to have the police on her track.

Mr Coldbarrow and the policeman came away, suffering from a deep sense of frustration. The flag day proceeded. By lunchtime the Indigent Bankers' Aid Society had gained £210 3s. 4d. Ida and her fellow directors had clocked up £75, a gold watch, and a pair of platinum cuff links.

For if Mr Macmillan had organized well, Ida had organized better. A collection of clothing for a forthcoming jumble sale, delivered by the Scouts to St Jude's church hall, had proved invaluable. Heck drove a borrowed car round the town to a fixed and precise timetable, passing the Town Hall on the hour, Market Street at five minutes past,

Woolworths at the quarter, and so on. This meant that Ida's collectors were able to time their demands for money a minute or so before the car was due to arrive, safe in the knowledge that the car would come at a fixed time to whisk them away to St Jude's church hall. Then, a quick change into some of the jumble sale clothing, and off again to a new collecting post in another part of the town. As Mr Macmillan had a hundred collectors, and Ida but six, the police became more and more baffled, and by the time they had arrested three of the more highly respectable citizens of Danby they were in such a state of confusion that, as Constable Moggs put it, they'd have run in Julius Caesar himself if he'd had one of them collecting-boxes.

Beefy was having a lovely time. "Help the Society!" he called gaily. "Help the Society!" Over his striped singlet he wore an enormous black overcoat with an astrakhan collar. His sandy hair was covered by a smart corduroy cap. He wore dark glasses.

He was collecting at the corner of Market Street. So far he hadn't held anyone up with his sweet persuader, on account of Ida begging him not to on account of he was going straight, her not wanting anything on her conscience. But he was itching to do so. Lovingly he fingered the gun in his pocket. He'd just have one go. Just as soon as some prosperous geezer came along.

The Town Hall clock had struck three. Heck was due in less than five minutes. Beefy looked anxiously about him for prosperous geezers. And, to his delight, there was a tall, pale, well-to-do-looking man approaching him now.

Beefy's fingers tightened on the gun. He stepped forward. "Help the Society," he called.

The man pulled aside the lapel of his overcoat to show that he was wearing an emblem on his jacket. He didn't say anything. He didn't feel like unnecessary conversation this afternoon. Mr Macmillan was in a black mood.

To begin with he was twenty-five collecting-boxes short. He'd taken up the matter with headquarters, and they said quite definitely that they had sent him what he asked for. He didn't like that sort of thing. Made him look a fool. And then, this morning! As if he hadn't got enough to do, running a bank *and* a flag day, he had spent the whole morning answering telephone calls. Little Miss Titterton, who seemed to think that the police net was closing about her. Police constables, inspectors, superintendents, all of whom appeared bitterly reproachful that he had organized a flag day at all. So he had come out to see for himself what was happening.

He was about to walk on when he suddenly noticed that the man in the astrakhan coat was gazing at him with horror. He couldn't see the eyes, because of the dark glasses, but the mouth had sagged open, and the man looked frozen to the spot.

Mr Macmillan remembered all the frantic telephone calls of that morning. He turned to look at the man more closely, but at that moment a black saloon car drew up at the kerb, the man ran across the pavement and jumped in, the car drove away.

Mr Macmillan took careful note of the number. Then he looked for a policeman. There wasn't one. He hurried back to the bank and rang up the police station.

Ida and Peg Leg were in the back seat of the car, both clutching valuable collecting-boxes. Beefy climbed in beside the driver. "Go quick," he panted. "That was old Mac."

Ida sat forward. "Did he recognize you?" she asked urgently.

"I don't know," said Beefy. "He didn't say."

"Listen," Ida said. "He'll take the number of the car. He's that sort. Then he'll ring up the police. Even if he's only a bit suspicious. Before we know where we are the town's going to be full of police cars looking for us."

They drove on in worried silence. The Town Hall clock struck the quarter. They stopped outside Woolworths. Lofty Longbottom climbed aboard. "The police are after us," said Ida. "We think they've got the car number."

Lofty reached for the door handle. "I'm getting out," he said.

"We're all getting out," said Heck.

"No, we ain't," Ida said firmly. "We should attract too much attention. And if they find the car abandoned they'll be round it like flies round a honey pot. No," she explained, "Heck's got to drive us to a nice, quiet side street where we can all get out unobserved. All, that is, except the driver. He's got to drive on and warn the others, and then abandon the car as far from where we got out as possible. It's going to be dangerous for the driver," she added thoughtfully.

They were cruising up the Derby Road now. Suddenly they all saw it; a police car approaching from the opposite direction. Heck swung into a side street. Through the back window they watched the police car flash past the end of the street. Sighs of relief went up from five anxious company directors. But suddenly Heck jammed on the brakes and brought the car up on its haunches. "It's no good," he gasped. "I can't go on. It's one of my turns."

"Didn't know you had turns," said Peg Leg with interest.

Ida kicked him sharply on the ankle. "Course he has turns," she said. "It's his heart. Can't drive when he's got a turn coming on. Next thing you know he's unconscious and the car's climbing up a lamp-post."

"This'd be a good place to get out," said Lofty. "Nice and quiet."

"But somebody's got to take the car on," Ida said firmly. "Someone cool and resourceful."

"Wish I could drive," said Peg Leg.

"I'd do it myself," said Ida, "if I hadn't let my licence lapse."

They waited. They knew they would not wait in vain. They could hear a whirring noise emanating from Beefy's head as he marshalled facts, got them into some sort of order, prepared for speech. At last: "I'll take the car on if you like," he volunteered.

"But you was going straight, Beefy," said Ida.

Beefy swallowed. "It don't matter," he said. Actually, he'd just been considering that point. He didn't want no more judges getting cross with him. On the other hand, he kept thinking about that board meeting where they'd all stood in silence and said, "Good old Beefy." Leastways, they'd stood in silence, and *then* they'd sat down, and *then* they'd said, "Good old Beefy." That had been nice. He'd been proud. And perhaps if he took the car on now they'd do it all over again. Only he hoped that this time he would be there to see for himself.

Another point weighed with him. It was his fault that they had had to organize a flag day at all. If he hadn't taken the wrong box that day they'd all be riding round in Daimlers now, telling their chauffeurs to get out and give the poor flag-sellers half a crown. His disgrace weighed heavy upon him. Here was a chance to wipe out the memory for that terrible mistake.

"Sure you don't mind, Beefy?" Ida asked anxiously.

Heck clutched his heart and gave an awful groan.

"That's all right," Beefy said. "You lot get out. I'll take the car on."

Three doors were flung open. Beefy found himself alone in the car. "Good old Beefy," called Ida from halfway up an entry. Beefy watched Heck legging it up the road and felt vaguely surprised. He hoped Heck would be all right. He'd always imagined that people with bad hearts had to go slow and careful.

In a matter of seconds Beefy's fellow directors had disappeared. He let in the clutch and set off. First he'd got to find Joe Vodka and Willie One Eye. Then, abandon the car and scatter.

But he hadn't gone half a mile before he saw a police car in his driving mirror. To his horror it was gaining on him rapidly. He pressed his foot down hard. The speedometer needle crept up. Forty, forty-five, fifty. But the police car was still gaining on him. And, ahead of him, he could see traffic lights. Remorselessly they changed to red. He was caught. Unless he could ignore the lights. Drive straight through. But now a stream of traffic was beginning to move across the road, blocking his way. He'd just pile up if he didn't stop.

Then he saw a possible chance of escape. There was a side street off to the right, just before the main crossroads where the traffic lights were. With a screaming of tyres he swung across the road, missing a lorry by inches, and into the side street. In his driving mirror he saw the lorry halt, either through alarm or anger, and neatly block the entrance to the street he was in. He swept on, and round into another street, a quiet, tree-lined avenue. Halfway up this road were some wrought-iron gates, open. Beefy turned in, and found a number of cars parked outside a high, red-brick building. He parked his car with the others, ran through another gate, and found himself in a large field where a number of schoolboys and their parents were watching a cricket match. They looked at his astrakhan collar, his dark glasses, with some surprise. But at that moment, the batsman, with a vicious drive, knocked one of the umpires, an unpopular physics master, unconscious, and Beefy was forgotten in the gleeful concern of the onlookers.

He pressed on, out through another gate, and into a private road that ran beside the school grounds. This brought him to a piece of waste land. More people here, and a big tent with banners with words on. Beefy wished he could read them. Perhaps it was a circus. If he went in there he'd be safe for a bit. They'd never think of looking for him in there.

And then he realized he couldn't go in. He hadn't any money. He'd just got to go on, hunted like an animal, with the net closing about him all the time.

But a surprising thing happened. There was a man standing in the doorway to the tent. He beckoned to Beefy. He smiled. Beefy sidled nervously up to him.

"Coming in?" the man asked.

"I can't," said Beefy sadly. "On account of I ain't got the money, see."

The man's voice was kind. "You don't need money to come here," he said. "Just step inside, brother."

Beefy stepped inside.

When Ida left the car she returned, by devious and quiet ways, to her hotel room.

She was anxious, and disappointed. She was afraid. The day hadn't been a success. For one thing, they had had to leave the collecting-boxes in the car. It would have been too dangerous to carry those through the streets. Thus, not only were profits lost, but valuable clues were left for the police to find.

She wondered how the boys had fared. Poor Beefy was almost certain to be caught, but the others might be all right. Poor Beefy! Still, you couldn't make an omelette without breaking eggs, she told herself, and, after all, he had volunteered to take the car on. No one had forced him.

While she thus meditated, she was busy packing. In the car that afternoon she had had a sudden vision of a quiet little pub, not far from the Tottenham Court Road, where she could lie up for a couple of weeks, and no questions asked. She was tired of the provinces, of the parochialism of a Midland town, where everyone knew your business, or, anyway, wanted to. She longed for the impersonal bustle of London. It drew her as the sea drew Masefield, as the lake isle of Innisfree drew Yeats.

But she did not write a poem. She packed her bags. As soon as it was dark she would go out, catch the bus to Leicester, and board a London train. For she was in a quiet reflective mood. She did not want to face the tumult of Danby Station, where she might meet people. She just wanted to slip away quietly. No questions, no farewells.

She was fastening her suitcase when a timid knock came at her door. She froze. It wasn't a copper's knock, but nevertheless she was scared. She crouched over the suitcase, holding her breath. The knocking came again. She took her gun in her hand, stole over to the door, opened it a crack, and peered out.

Beefy stood there, a very worried-looking Beefy.

She gave a great gasp of relief, and flung the door open. He edged inside. "Ida," he asked. "What's saved?"

She locked the door behind him. "What on earth do you mean?" she asked.

His worried eyes gazed into hers. "I mean, what's saved? What does it mean?"

She sighed. She knew her directors hadn't had Oxford and Cambridge educations, but she did expect them to understand words of one syllable. "Well," she explained. "It's like when the police are after you and you give them the slip, and then you're saved, see."

"No. I know *that* sort of saved," Beefy said with a touch of hauteur. "I mean churchy sort of saved."

Ida looked at him with sudden foreboding. "Beefy, you ain't been and got yourself saved?"

"Sort of," he admitted miserably.

Ida groaned. "What happened?" she asked, sitting down on the bed.

"Well, I hid in a tent. On account of the cops was after me. And there was a lot of people, and a bloke at the front, and the bloke says, 'Stand up all them as wants to be saved,' and some people stood up." He paused, and moistened his lips with his tongue.

"Go on," Ida said grimly.

"Well, the bloke turns to us lot who hadn't stood up, and he says, 'You miserable bunch of Good Time Charlies, one day you ain't half going to regret not being saved,' he says. 'Especially when you're dead,' he says. And he goes on at us like that for ever so long. It was like that judge." Beefy shuddered at the memory. "And then he looks at me ever so nasty, and he says, '*Now* will you stand up?' "

He paused. Ida looked at him anxiously. "Beefy," she asked, "You didn't – ?"

Beefy blushed furiously. He looked at the toes of his boots. He balanced on one leg. "Yes, Ida," he confessed. "I – I stood up."

There was silence in the drab little room. At last: "You didn't ought to have done that," Ida said reproachfully.

"But what's it mean?" implored Beefy. "What's it mean I got to do?"

"Nothing," Ida said promptly. "It don't mean anything It's just a way of saying."

But Beefy had got his teeth into something. "I got to go through with it," he muttered.

Ida groaned. Once let one of her lieutenants get religious and you never knew what might happen. You couldn't run a criminal organization on those lines. "Look, Beefy," she said irritably. "There ain't anything to go through with. You're saved, ain't you? Well then, what you beefing about?"

"Got to follow it up," Beefy said firmly. "Bloke says, 'Follow it up,' he says, 'or you won't half regret it when you're dead.' What's following it up, Ida?"

This could clearly go on all night. And it was almost time for the Leicester bus. Ida had had a difficult day. She felt tired, and very, very irritable. She tried a new approach. "I'll tell you what following it up means," she snapped. "It means behaving holy. It means no more crime." She paused to see what effect her words were having.

"I was going straight, anyway," Beefy said apologetically.

"Oh no you wasn't," Ida said, throwing off the mask. "Not if I could help it. Going straight isn't your line, Beefy." She tried flattery. "It's all right for some people. But you've got too much about you."

Beefy gulped. "I got to go straight now," he said miserably.

Ida shrugged helplessly. But she had one trump card left. "I'll tell you what else it means," she said savagely. "It means going to church every Sunday."

Beefy paled. "Every Sunday, Ida?"

"Every Sunday," she said firmly.

Beefy spoke with quiet dignity. "If I got to, I got to," he said. "I don't want to regret nothing when I'm dead."

"Tcha!" Ida was furious. She looked at her watch. Only five minutes before that bus went. She grabbed her suitcase. "I'm going," she said. "Tell the boys I'm having a few days' change. It's either that or a complete breakdown, and I prefer a holiday."

She flounced out. Beefy followed unhappily. Ida was cross with him, and he couldn't help the boys any more, and his friend Heck was poorly with a heart attack, and he'd got to go to church every Sunday. The future was indeed black.

Then he remembered one cheerful fact, and he brightened up. Sally was coming next Saturday, and he was going to introduce her to Lizzie and the boys, and perhaps take her to a Western at the pictures sometime. Very softly he began to whistle, "Yes, we have no bananas." Perhaps life wasn't so bad after all.

CHAPTER 10

May 4th is the Feast Day of St Jude the Obscure, as any reputable hagiologist will confirm.

It follows that, on the Sunday following the flag day, St Jude's celebrated its patronal festival. There were great preparations. On the previous Sunday evening the choirboys had gleefully presented their Mums with surplices to be washed and ironed. Banners were taken out of their plastic covers. Cubs and Brownies were scrubbed and inspected. Extra chairs were set in the aisles. The choir practised an anthem until they were in a state of near mutiny. At evensong a vast congregation poured into the church.

And one of the congregation was a shy and bewildered Beefy.

Now Beefy had always regarded himself as a Methodist, on account of, when he was a boy, a friend had once taken him to the Shepherd's Warning Methodist Sunday School Anniversary. But he was no rigid sectarian, and when he found himself suddenly face to face with the prospect of regular church attendance, he decided to try St Jude's.

When the sidesmen saw his blue and white striped singlet, his bristly cranium, his bent nose, it gave them rather a turn. But they soon rallied. You got all sorts at a festival, they reminded themselves. They gave him a friendly smile, and two books, and told him he could sit where he liked.

Beefy was pleased. He hadn't expected them to be friendly. He went and perched at the back, and gazed round the church. It was nice, big and cool, and there was a huge gold cross at the far end that kept drawing his eyes. Then a boy in a long black frock came out and lit two candles, one on each side of the cross, and the flames stood up straight and still, like soldiers. And there was a man playing an organ, like at the pictures except that there wasn't any tune particularly. Then the organ was silent, and the bell stopped ringing. The Vicar, all in black and white, came out of a door and announced the hymn, and everyone stood up and began to sing.

It was nice. Beefy, his prayer book clutched upside down in his great fist, la-la-la'd with the best of them. He was enjoying himself. It made a nice change from "Yes, we have no bananas."

The choir processed round the church, singing sweetly. Before them went the crucifer. Behind, the slow pomp of flags and banners. Beefy was entranced. He wondered why he hadn't come to church before.

The service moved on. At last the Vicar entered the pulpit. This was the Feast Day of St Jude the Obscure, he said. Now St Jude was a humble man. So humble, indeed, that nothing whatever was known about him. So what could we learn from St Jude the Obscure, on this his day? Why, surely, that we too must be humble.

Beefy gazed, mouth open, up to the pulpit. Wisht I was humble, he thought. Must be nice to be like this Jude. And then, suddenly, he remembered something. That's what Sally had said *he* was. What was it? The gentlest and humblest man she'd ever met. Humble. That's what he was. Like this Jude.

He wished he knew what it meant.

The sermon ended. The closing hymn began. Beefy sang happily, filled with a warm glow by the singing, and the stately ceremonial, and the knowledge that he shared some unknown quality with this Jude.

But then a terrible thing happened. There was a sort of rustle among the singing congregation. The men were groping in their pockets, the women searching in handbags. And men with plates were moving inexorably up the church, collecting money from everybody.

You had to pay!

And the only thing in Beefy's pocket was a huge hole.

The men were nearer now, only two rows away. Beefy's instinctive reaction to this crisis was to run for it. But he knew he couldn't. Not in church.

The plate was in his row now. It was coming nearer. It was being handed to him. He shied away from it like a frightened horse. This was one of the most awful moments of his life. "I – I ain't got no money," he stammered to his neighbour. "On account of I didn't know you had to pay."

"Pass it on," hissed the man.

But Beefy was far too flustered to do anything sensible. The man kept shoving the plate at him. Beefy refused to touch it. "If I'd knowed I'd of brought some," he explained.

Then the sidesman leaned over and said firmly, "Pass the plate on, please."

And Beefy looked at the sidesman.

It was fortunate that he was not holding the plate, or he would most assuredly have dropped it.

For the sidesman was Mr Macmillan, old Mac, whom Beefy had kidnapped, and half-starved, and threatened with his sweet persuader; and who, only yesterday, had seen Beefy acting suspiciously at the flag day.

Somehow they managed in the end to get the plate past Beefy, and at last, to his intense relief, the service ended. His one idea now was to get out of the church as soon as possible, and never enter it again. But it was a slow business, and before he could reach the door he saw, to his horror, Mr Macmillan bearing down on him.

There was no escape. Beefy looked up at the tall man, his eyes frightened. "Could you spare me a moment?" said Mr Macmillan.

Beefy's mouth was too dry for him to speak. He nodded. "Come this way," Mr Macmillan said, and led him into a little dark room at the back of the church. Beefy looked round immediately for ways to escape, but the room had only one door, and no windows. If they were going to lock him in here while they fetched the police, here he would have to stay.

He found Mr Macmillan's eyes on him, and squirmed under their gaze. It was a long time before Mr Macmillan spoke. At last he said, stiffly, "I wanted to say how pleased I am to see you in church. Does this mean that you intend to go straight in future?"

This speech was so unexpected that Beefy could only stare. At last he managed to say, "That's right. On account of I been saved, see."

"Oh." Mr Macmillan decided to leave that. "I wanted to make quite sure that seeing me here wouldn't stop you coming again. What passed between us before," he added awkwardly, "is over and done with. You have nothing to fear from me on that score."

Beefy went on staring.

"Will you promise to come again next Sunday?" Mr Macmillan gave a wintry smile.

Beefy nodded.

"And you really intend to go straight?"

Beefy nodded.

"Good." He looked intently at Beefy. "By the way, you weren't selling flags yesterday, were you?"

Beefy gulped, and shook his head.

"Must have been someone else, then," said Mr Macmillan. He held out a hand. "Goodbye, Beefy," he said. "See you next week."

Beefy stuck a limp fist feebly into Mr. Macmillan's. "I'll bring some money, next week," he said. "Two lots." He walked out, dazed and bewildered, into the clear evening.

Vicar and People's Warden strolled home together. "Quite a few strangers in church tonight," the Vicar said.

"Yes," agreed Mr Macmillan. He paused. "You remember that extraordinary fellow who tried to – er – abduct me? He was there."

The Vicar looked at the warden in surprise. "What on earth was he doing?"

"I think he's come to join us."

"Good Lord. Did he see you?"

"Yes."

"Then I shouldn't imagine we shall have him again."

"I thought of that," Mr Macmillan said. "So I approached him and told him that I regarded the former incident as closed."

The Vicar looked at Mr Macmillan admiringly. "That was very decent of you," he said.

Macmillan laughed shortly. "It wasn't easy," he admitted. He coloured slightly. "I just felt it was my duty as a warden of this church – and as a Christian."

"Good for you, my dear fellow," John Adams said warmly. "Good for you." The warden was a better man than he had imagined. A sudden warmth sprang up between the two men. When they reached the Vicarage door John Adams said, "I suppose you wouldn't care to drop in for a sherry?"

"Love to," said Macmillan. They went inside. The Vicar produced a bottle and two glasses. They sipped. " 'I often wonder what the vintners buy, one-half so precious as the goods they sell'," the Vicar said appreciatively.

Macmillan looked blank. "Sorry," the Vicar said. "Bad habit of mine. Just quoting." He changed the subject. "What's he look like, this bloke?"

"A beefy-looking individual. You couldn't miss him. He turned up in a blue and white striped singlet."

"Oh, no," gasped the Vicar, and Macmillan was surprised at the astonishment in his face. "Not him?"

"Why? Do you know him?"

"I was hoping a relation of his – aunt, cousin or something – was going to be my housekeeper."

Macmillan paused with his glass halfway to his lips. "Good Lord," he said. "You'll have to be careful, won't you?"

The Vicar peered into his sherry. "Honestly!" he said. "I spend a whole winter without a housekeeper. I get one and she stays about a week. I have the chance to get another, and she turns out to be a crook's aunt. Dash it, it's a bit hard."

"A reformed crook, of course," Macmillan pointed out, not very hopefully. "And, anyway, *she* may be a perfectly respectable old lady."

"Maybe," agreed the Vicar. "But it's not an awfully good recommendation, I must say."

The two men sat silent, then, enjoying the sudden feeling of friendship they had for each other.

"Who's going to get this contract?" the Vicar asked eventually.

"For the church hall? I don't know. But I've a feeling it may be Coldbarrow."

"I'm afraid you may be right."

Macmillan raised his eyebrows. "He's a good builder. Good businessman, too."

"He's an old reprobate."

"That won't make the church hall tumble down any sooner."

The Vicar sighed. "I suppose you're right. I just don't like it, that's all." They relapsed into silence again, while the shadows gathered about the big room, and another Sunday slipped quietly away into the past.

Beefy, meanwhile, was meditating on life, and his own life in particular. It was a still, peaceful evening, and he thought how nice it would be at Shepherd's Delight, leaning over the pigsty door and scratching the back of Emily the pig. The shadows would be long, and there would be the laughter of children in the distance, sounding sort of sad, somehow. Then he'd go inside, light the lamp, draw the red curtains and settle down with his Western.

Beefy sighed, and the sigh drifted, like a puff of smoke, into the rain-washed blue of the evening sky, up into the cold wastes of infinity. It had been all very well dreaming about Shepherd's Delight when he was in crime, when he was dealing in thousands and tens of thousands. He could have pulled off a big job almost any time he liked, then, and gone and bought a cottage and a pig just like that. But now he was going straight. He wanted to, of course, but he'd got to, anyway, on account of being saved. And where you got the money to retire on when you was going straight, Beefy didn't know. There just didn't seem any money at all in going straight, he decided. No money at all.

He began to grow melancholy, began to wonder whether he'd ever get that cottage at Shepherd's Delight. A life of respectability stretched before him, weary, stale, flat and, worst of all, unprofitable. Didn't seem much to look forward to, somehow. Toiling all week, church on Sundays.

He brightened a little. Church hadn't been so bad, after all. In fact, he'd really enjoyed it. The singing had been a proper treat. And old Mac, nice as pie! Or, anyway, as nice as you could expect an educated geezer like him to be to someone what wasn't educated.

Suddenly his mind, that could never cope with more than one fact at a time, if that, admitted another thought. Sally was coming! Only five, or was it six, more days, and she'd be here, installed at the Vicarage, shining like a second sun, a second moon, through the smoke and grime of Danby.

CHAPTER 11

On Saturday, May 12th, thousands of people, packed in little padded boxes, were trundled this way and that, North, South, East and West, across the kingdom. Great, panting engines drew them, hundreds at a time, into the lofty, blackened cathedrals of the London termini. Little engines, with tall chimneys like old-fashioned top hats, chugged and chuffed them into the mountains, through cuttings deep and tangled with weeds, over banks whereon the wild thyme grew, along tracks that seemed as ancient and as timeless as the Roman roads. They were whisked from the grim cities of the Midland plain to the edge of the crawling sea, from lovely hamlets to hideous towns, from ringing pavements to springing turf, from hell-on-earth to heaven, from heaven-on-earth to hell. Most of them had luggage; and most of them clutched tightly a little invisible luggage, too; gay little packages, drab, bursting-at-the-seams cases, black, heavy trunks that seemed too big to handle on one's own. There was job; a whole forty-eight! First thing I'll do, I'll go up to my room, all on my own, and change into civvies. Then I suppose we'll have supper. But Ma's made a steak and kidney pie. Tells everyone, "If there's one thing our Dave likes it's steak and kidney." Never had the heart to tell her I ain't gone on it. See the boys, perhaps, after. And a good lay-in tomorrow morning…

There was sorrow; turned me right over when I got the telegram. Yes, Tom said he'd be at the station. Yes, he's all right, Tom is. Bit wild, perhaps, but he's all right at a time like this. Kind, and quiet like. Understanding. Yes, I'm glad Tom said he'd be at the station. He'll tell us about it, before we meet the others...

There was despair, in a big, black trunk; yes, I think the change has done me good. It was a nice rest, anyway. No, I still seem to get tired. No, I haven't put on any weight. I weighed myself on the pier before I came away. Actually, I'd lost five pounds. But those machines aren't always correct, are they? Or perhaps I'd got some lighter clothes on. Yes, that'd be it. I'd got some lighter clothes on, I bet. The rest was nice, anyway. I couldn't really have lost another five pounds, could I – ?

But Sally, rattling down through the proud hills, into the smoky plains, Sally clutched a little parcel of hope. Mother was better, and had given her her blessing. And now she was coming, away from the restricted world of Shepherd's Delight, into the busy, bright world of the towns. She was going to be happy in Danby. She knew it. She'd been happy at home, of course. But this was something new, exciting. She'd got a smart little navy-blue costume, and a new hat, and white gloves and handbag, and she really felt that she looked rather nice.

And Beefy would be at the station to meet her. She liked Beefy. He was funny, of course, and amused her quietly, but he was kind, and gentle, and treated her like a queen. She hoped the old clergyman would like her, and make her his housekeeper. It would be an interesting job, in a big industrial parish. She'd meet all sorts of people, perhaps be able to go to dances occasionally. Life was unfolding for her. Life was going to be something very wonderful.

The train began to slow down. She looked at her wristwatch. They were nearly due. Her fellow passengers began to lift cases down from the rack, to put on coats, to powder noses. She felt a sudden tremor of excitement, a sudden nervousness. She stood up, and collected her luggage. The train rattled into the station. She saw the exciting name DANBY. "Danby," shouted the porters. A loud, synthetic voice cried, "The train new entering platform four is the 4.20 train for Euston." The train stopped. There was a furious hissing of steam. Tremendous excitement. Doors were opened. Sally stepped down onto the soil of Danby.

And there was Beefy, shining and beaming like the morning sun, hurrying to meet her. She had never seen anyone look as pleased to see her as Beefy did at that moment. Smiling, she held out her hand, and then, suddenly he was shy, and looked down, and wiped his palm on his blue serge trousers. Then he grabbed her hand and stood grinning at her, wiping his boots on an invisible doormat.

"Hello, Beefy," she said happily. "It is nice to see you. Thank you for meeting me."

"I've made all arrangements," he said proudly. "I'm going to take you to see Lizzie Tubb, and then you can go and see the Vicar and get taken on."

Sally laughed. "He won't want to bother with me tonight. He'll be writing his sermon. I'll go on Monday."

Beefy looked crestfallen. "Where can you stay till Monday?"

"I've written to a hostel. It's in Market Street. Do you know where that is?"

"Yes," said Beefy. He picked up her luggage, and they set off. They soon found the hostel. At the entrance Beefy hung back. "I'll wait for you," he said.

So while Sally went inside he waited outside the door, thinking how nice it was going to be when he took her to see his friend Lizzie. He hadn't told Lizzie. He meant it to be a surprise.

At last Sally reappeared. Proudly he let her through the streets. She gazed round her, her lips slightly parted. She was interested in everything. Beefy fidgeted while she inspected the Julius Caesar statue.

"Why Julius Caesar?" she asked. "What did he do for Danby?"

"I don't know," said Beefy, who had never given it a thought. He considered. "I think he's dead," he said helpfully. That reminded him of something. "How's Auntie Nellie?" he inquired.

"Oh, she's quite better, thank you, Beefy."

He grinned mischievously. "You'll have to tell her when you write that I ain't dead of face-ache yet," he said. He chortled happily.

They were in Rockefeller Avenue now. Beefy led his cousin up an entry, through a rotting wooden gate into a grimy back-yard. He knocked on a door from which the paint was flaking. There came a barking from inside the house. "That's Whitey," Beefy said proudly.

Shuffling footsteps approached the door, which opened to show Lizzie's startled moon-face.

"Hello, Lizzie," said Beefy. "This is my cousin." He stood there, proud and happy. But thanks to the uproar from Whitey, Lizzie didn't hear a word. She slapped ineffectually at the dog. "Be quiet," she said. "Never heard such a row."

The dog went on barking. Speech was impossible. Lizzie looked bewildered. "Are you coming in?" she shouted.

They entered the dark little kitchen. Whitey, having made his protest, curled up in his basket. Lizzie studied Sally from under her brows. Suddenly realization dawned. "You ain't Beefy's cousin?" she asked.

"I am," the girl said.

147

"Not the one who's going to the Vicarage?"

"I hope I am."

Lizzie looked at her curiously. She seemed at a loss for words. At last: "I'll make you a cup of tea," she said. Her voice was disapproving.

This was not at all the friendly sort of tea party that Beefy had expected. Embarrassed, he pulled Whitey's ears, while Lizzie put the kettle on and got out three plain white cups and saucers.

Lizzie said, "Wisht you'd told me you was bringing your cousin, Beefy. I could of smartened up." She looked down at herself. "Me in all me old working clothes." She sounded ashamed.

"I thought you always wore them things," Beefy said. "I ain't never seen you in nothing else."

"Well, I don't," Lizzie snapped. She turned to Sally. "I got ever such a pretty frock," she said. "Blue, with little spriggy flowers."

Sally said, "I'm awfully sorry we've broken in on you like this. I'd no idea Beefy hadn't told you we were coming. These men!" she said severely.

Lizzie's face softened immediately. "It don't matter a bit. Beefy knows he's welcome any time. *And* his friends."

The atmosphere had cleared suddenly. Lizzie poured tea. Beefy took a noisy gulp. Then he said to his cousin, "Lizzie and me's got something to ask you."

"Yes?" Sally smiled brightly, and wondered what on earth was coming.

"What's that what's wrote on her stummick?" Beefy asked. He waited hopefully. At last he was going to find the answer to something that had worried him for months.

Sally looked in bewilderment from one to the other, "What?" she gasped.

Beefy stood up and jabbed a thick finger at Lizzie's apron. "What's it say?" he asked.

"Oh, Beefy, don't be so silly," said Lizzie. "I'm sure I don't know where to put myself."

Sally's smile was becoming a little strained. "I think you're teasing me," she laughed. "It only says '1 cwt Finest Bone Meal'." She looked from one to the other, to see whether she'd said the right thing.

There was stunned silence. Lizzie sat, her fingers plucking at the tablecloth, and gazed in wonder at the inscription. But Beefy was sticking his lower lip out. "What's it say that for?" he asked.

Sally, out of her depth, said nothing. Lizzie said in a small voice, "I suppose it just happens to be there, like."

"I think it's a silly thing to have wrote on your stummick," Beefy went on sternly. "I don't see no point in it."

"Look, Beefy," Sally explained soothingly. "Lizzie wanted something for an apron, so she used this. And it just happened to be something that had once been used for bone meal. What are you getting into such a state about?"

Beefy glared at her. He was very put out. Ever since he'd seen the old charwoman, pottering in and out of the church hall, he'd been intrigued by that printing. His imagination had toyed with the subject for hours. And then, when at last the moment of revelation came, it was nothing but bone meal. He was disappointed in Lizzie, having that wrote on her stummick. It didn't make sense. He'd thought better of her.

"We better be going," he said miserably. He'd looked forward so much to introducing Lizzie to his pretty cousin. But everything had gone wrong. Strange undercurrents, that he could not understand, had swept them far off their expected course.

Sally stood up, and held out her hand. "Goodbye, Lizzie," she said. "And thank you very much for the tea."

Lizzie heaved herself to her feet, and took Sally's hand. "I'm sorry I wasn't smartened up," she said. "I ain't used to visitors. I should of put my blue dress on."

Sally smiled. "It was lovely," she said. "I'm so glad to meet a friend of Beefy's."

"So long, Lizzie," called Beefy, trying vainly to shake off the cloud that hung over him. His eyes strayed uneasily to the "1 cwt Finest Bone Meal", and looked away. He couldn't see any point in it. He sighed, and followed Sally out into Rockefeller Avenue.

They strolled back to the hostel. "She's a nice old thing," Sally said.

Beefy agreed, a little doubtfully. "Silly, having that about bone meal wrote on her," he muttered. "I can't read, see, and I always thought it was something nice."

Sally took his arm. "For goodness' sake stop grumbling," she laughed. Then she said, suddenly, "You haven't shown me where you live, yet."

Beefy went red. "It's not far away," he muttered. "Leastways, it is really. I'll show you one day, when we got more time."

To his relief she said, "Yes, I must go in and unpack. And I ought to write and let Mother know I've got here safely."

Beefy, with his cousin's soft hand touching his arm, was beginning to cheer up. "You won't forget to tell her, will you," he said.

"Tell her?"

"About me not dying of face-ache."

"Oh, no, I'll tell her." They had reached the hostel now. Beefy stood on one leg. He swallowed. He had prepared a speech. He said, "I don't suppose you'll want to see much of me, Sally. On account of you're so pretty, and you talk nice, and you're smart and you dress nice, and I ain't educated, see. I'm just – nobody, like. But – well, I got to go to church tomorrow night. I been saved, see, so I got to go, and it's nice. They sing things, and they march round the church with big sheets with things wrote on them, and there's candles and things. I don't suppose you'd want to go with me," he finished anxiously, "but, well if you wouldn't mind it would be nice, see."

She put her hand on his. "Oh, Beefy, I'd love to," she said.

His face lit up. "It don't matter," he said. "You don't have to say yes if you'd rather not."

"But I *want* to come with you," she said.

He still couldn't quite believe it. "It'll be all right if you change your mind," he said.

"I shan't change my mind," she laughed. "You call for me. What time? Six? Quarter past?"

"Quarter past," breathed Beefy. He walked home, whistling happily.

The Reverend John Adams climbed into his pulpit during the last verse of the hymn.

Entering his pulpit was still an exciting and rather frightening thing. It was surprising how those few feet of height lifted him, mentally and spiritually, as well as physically, above his congregation. In these egalitarian days, when Jack was as good as, if not a great deal better than, his master, the Vicar was just one more paid servant of the people, a sort of archaic welfare officer. But, once in his pulpit, he put on some of his former authority. He was there to instruct; and though people nowadays understood almost everything, from "How to Fiddle your Income Tax" to "How to Make a Small Hydrogen Bomb", there were, perhaps, one or two basic truths they did not understand. So, by Jove, he would instruct them. They might wriggle, look at their watches, fidget, pretend to sleep, but he'd got them. They couldn't escape. They were going to be instructed.

He looked round, a faint smile on his squarish, youthful face, and his heart warmed to them. They were a good crowd, even though they did all protest that they hated sermons. Little Miss Titterton, singing away in a thin, reedy soprano. George Bloodshot and Bert Briggs, deep and heavy as euphoniums in the choir. Willie Ironmonger, his humbug bulging like a gumboil in his left cheek. Old Lord Wapentake, in the front pew, reading the Commination Service, digging Lady Wapentake in her high-born ribs to point out interesting bits. Edward Macmillan, whose cold paleness hid, the Vicar now knew, if not a heart of gold, at least a Christian conscience. That odd fellow Beefy; the Vicar could hear him singing above all the rest. Yet surely that was a prayer book open in his hand! Must know the hymn by heart, John Adams decided. Church upbringing, apparently. Or perhaps he learned it in prison, he thought less happily.

And then, just as the congregation were singing the Amen, he saw Sally.

The music faded into silence. Hymn books were closed. The congregation stood with bowed heads, waiting. They went on standing. Suddenly John Adams was aware that one or two heads were being raised to look inquiringly in his direction. He pulled himself together. "In the name of the Father – " he said, and crossed himself, to the satisfaction of fifty per cent of his congregation and the intense chagrin of the other half.

The people sat down, safe in the knowledge that, for the next twenty minutes, they would not be required to stand up, kneel down, sing, or even, unless they wanted to, think. John Adams went on to preach a sound and sincere sermon. But his emotions were turbulent. He had seen beautiful women before, and remained unmoved. He had never before seen such beauty, calm, repose in one face as he now saw in Sally's. She was like a bowl of daffodils in a drab room, a breeze of morning after a dark and shuttered night, spring of clear water on a thirsty hillside.

The service ended. As was his custom, John Adams stood at the south door to say goodnight to his people. A little wind came in at the door and played around his surplice, and ruffled his hair. Despite himself, he could not help waiting anxiously for the lovely stranger to come out. The congregation filed slowly past him, smiling, nodding, bowing. Who was she? She'd been sitting next to that chap Beefy. Surely they couldn't be together? Anyway, where were they both? The church was almost empty now. The sidesmen had finished putting the books away, were collecting their hats and saying goodnight.

Then, at last, he saw her. She and Beefy were half-hidden by a pillar. They seemed to be arguing. Then, slowly, they turned and walked towards the south door.

When the service ended, Sally whispered to her cousin, "What a nice young clergyman. Where does he come from?"

Beefy looked at her in surprise. "He don't come from nowhere. He's the Vicar."

"But," said Sally. She drew him into a quiet corner. "You don't mean he's the one I've come all this way to be housekeeper for?"

"Yes." Beefy was puzzled. "He's nice. Lizzie says he's ever so nice."

To his horror Sally stamped her foot. "Oh, Beefy," she said. "You know I couldn't keep house for him. I thought you meant an old man."

"It's nicer him being young," Beefy said. "More company, like."

"But think what people would say."

Beefy couldn't make head or tail of all this. It seemed to him an ideal arrangement. But he knew that women were strange creatures, and that once they dug their toes in you just couldn't shift them. He had an unhappy feeling that his plans were going to be ruined by a woman's whim.

They were nearly at the south door now. The Vicar stood there, looking very boyish and eager, a prayer book under his left arm, his robes billowing in the wind.

"Hello, Beefy," he said. He smiled at Sally, and gave her a friendly good evening.

But, under that beautifully laundered surplice, a heart beat with most unclerical thumps. She was even lovelier than he had imagined. Her complexion was peach-perfect, her manner demure but possessed. Yet it was her expression that captivated him; serene as the moon, reposeful as a summer sea, it nevertheless gave an impression of strength. She's a very fine person, he thought. She must be, with a face such as hers. Then he remembered that she was one of his flock, and, being a Vicar, he was able to say the one thing that really mattered.

"I hope we shall be seeing you again," he said.

She did not speak. She shook her head, and smiled, and passed on. He was puzzled. He watched her go, escorted by a most miserable-looking Beefy, and suddenly he had an idea that almost made his hair stand on end. He put his head out of the church door. "Beefy," he shouted, in the sort of voice he had once used to rally the forwards.

Beefy leaped as convulsively as if he had felt a policeman's hand on his shoulder, or a gun in his back. Apprehensively he turned. The Vicar beckoned. " 'Scuse me," Beefy said to his cousin with old world courtesy. He sidled back warily to the Vicar.

"Come in here," said John Adams. He led him into the dark little room that Mr Macmillan had used.

"Who is that young lady?" the Vicar asked.

"That's my cousin," said Beefy.

"Not – not the person you were proposing as my housekeeper?"

"That's right."

"But I couldn't have her. Don't you see? She's far too young."

"She's had a lot of experience," Beefy said.

"I don't mean that. Can't you imagine what my parish would say if I took a girl of her age as my housekeeper?"

Beefy scratched his head. Then he shook it. "No," he said.

The Vicar looked at him keenly. "I'm afraid everyone isn't as pure-minded as you, Beefy," he said quietly. "They'd probably report me to my Bishop."

Slowly the meaning of the words sank in, and a crimson flush spread slowly over Beefy's face. He was speechless. At last he said, slowly, "But Sally's a nice girl. It'd be all right. She's not that sort of girl. It'd be all right. Besides, you're a Vicar." Beefy was shocked to the very core of his being.

"Things must not only be all right. They must be seen to be all right," the Vicar said. "Did – did your cousin say anything when she saw how old I was?"

Beefy stuck his lower lip out. "She said you was too young," he admitted.

The Vicar, who had been sitting on a table, stood up and put a hand on Beefy's shoulder. "I'm sorry," he said. "I'd had great hopes of getting a housekeeper. But you see how impossible it is."

"I think it's daft," Beefy muttered. He was bitterly disappointed. To have his plans brought to nothing just because of what people might say! People ought to mind their own business.

Together they walked across to the door, and out into the church garden. Sally was still there. She smiled at them as they approached. John Adams said to her, "There seems to have been some confusion about our ages."

"I thought you were seventy," she said.

"And I expected you to be at least sixty-five." They laughed, looking for a long moment hard into each other's eyes; and suddenly, Beefy was lonely, forgotten, hating the laughter and the quick silence that followed.

"You do agree that it's impossible, of course?" the Vicar said.

"Good heavens, yes."

"And you've come all this way. What are you going to do now? I don't like to think of you just going back again. I feel responsible."

"I'm not going back for a few days," she said, and her words were like the song of nightingales in the Vicar's ears. "I'll just see whether I can find a post in Danby."

"Perhaps I can help," he said quickly.

"Thank you very much. If you should hear of anyone old and respectable who wants a housekeeper, or anything in that line – "

"I'll let you know."

She held out her hand. "Goodbye," she said. "And thank you."

For a moment he held her fingers, and they were strong and friendly. "Goodbye," he replied. "I'm sorry the conventions – " They laughed. She withdrew her hand. Beefy fell into step beside his cousin, and walked moodily beside her to her lodgings.

When they reached the door she gave him a smile that turned his heart clean over, and said, "I haven't thanked you yet for trying to find me a job."

"That's all right," he said.

"It *was* sweet of you. But it wouldn't do, you know. I should be thrown out of the parish."

"Wisht people would mind their own business," he said gloomily. Then he brightened. "Are you really going to try and get a job in Danby?"

Yes, she'd just stay a few days. She would like to get something. It would be rather disappointing now if she had to go home again. Yes, she'd be seeing Beefy. She'd let him know if she changed her address. Oh, but of course, she didn't know where he lived. Very well, she'd tell Lizzie. But she looked at him curiously. "I'm beginning to think you live in a monastery," she said.

"Sort of," said Beefy. He came away.

He was strangely depressed. Sally and the Vicar had seemed to like each other. Bet she likes him more than me, he thought sadly. And, of course, it was only natural that she should, on account of the Vicar dressed nice, and could read and write. But it didn't make it any easier.

In his unhappiness he knocked on Lizzie Tubb's door. "Come in," she said in a flat voice.

Beefy went in. "Oh, it's you," Lizzie said without enthusiasm.

"You've got your spriggy frock on," said Beefy.

"I should have had it on yesterday if you'd of let me known you was coming."

There was a heavy silence. "You didn't ought to of asked her what was wrote on my apron," grumbled Lizzie. "I didn't know where to put meself."

"I thought it would be something nice. Not just bone meal," he said with a touch of asperity.

"I didn't know where to put meself. I didn't really."

There was an irritated silence. Beefy broke it by saying, "She ain't going to the Vicarage."

Lizzie exploded. "I should think not neither. Not at her age." Then, having got it all off her chest, she softened. "I got some bad news for you, Beefy," she said gently.

He looked at her in alarm. "They got the tenders out for the new church hall," she said. "Mrs Fosdyke told me."

Beefy's heart sank. "What's tenders?" he inquired.

"Reckon they're those holes what they put the foundations in," said Lizzie.

So it was coming at last. Despite Heck's delaying tic-tacs, work on the new hall was begun. Before winter came the old hall would be sold to a factory. Beefy's cosy roll of linoleum would be cast onto the rubbish heap, Beefy and the boys would be homeless. He felt too sick at heart for further social intercourse. "Think I'll be going," he muttered. "Goodnight, Lizzie." He went across the road, climbed the ladder into the loft, and slid, supperless, into bed. But he did not sleep. The friendly laughter of Sally and John Adams was in his ears, and the sound of pick and shovel as the men dug out the tenders; but the grunting of his pig Emily, and the song of the lark ascending over Shepherd's Delight, these seemed to him tonight to be very, very far away.

CHAPTER 12

Up at the towers, Lord Wapentake was drenching his wife's tulips in weedkiller. Not deliberately, of course, for he was a kindly man. He'd just got the packets mixed.

To him entered Lady Wapentake, wringing her hands. But when she saw what he was doing she stopped wringing. "What are you putting on my tulips, Mortimer?" she asked suspiciously.

"Fertilizer, my dear. Do them a power of good."

She looked dubious. "I really wish you'd leave them to Walters. After all, he's paid to look after them." She remembered what she'd come for. She went on wringing. "I didn't come to talk about tulips," she said. "Mortimer, something dreadful's happened. Carson's given notice."

"Who's Carson? asked Lord Wapentake, trying to see a rainbow in his spray.

Lady Wapentake sighed. "Do try to concentrate, Mortimer. Carson is our housekeeper, our treasure."

Slowly, the tall old man straightened up. He glared at his wife.

"I am not exactly an imbecile," he said with quiet dignity. "I am quite well aware of the name of my own housekeeper. Bless my soul, she's been with us years. And her mother before her."

"She's given *notice*, Mortimer," Lady Wapentake almost shouted.

"So did her mother. Went and married some feller. Can't remember his name. Whatever was it? He used to carve chessmen out of bits of wood. Damned awful things they were, too."

"Mortimer! Carson, our housekeeper, has given notice."

"What's she want to go and do a thing like that for? Not been beating her, have you, Alice?" he asked suspiciously.

"She wants to get married."

Mortimer stirred his hell brew. "Tell her she can't," he said, dismissing the matter.

"Listen," hissed Lady Wapentake, gritting her aristocratic teeth. "We've got to get another housekeeper. And you know how difficult it is these days. I shall approach the agency, but I want you to keep your ears open when you're in town. For instance, the Vicar might know of someone."

"Very well, my dear." He went on with his work of destruction. Lady Wapentake hovered anxiously for a few moments. Then she went indoors. She did hope Mortimer knew what he was doing with those tulips. More important still, she hoped that she had got her message through about the housekeeper. Goodness, they were going to miss Carson. And it was so difficult nowadays to get anyone satisfactory. Thoughtfully she picked up the telephone. She spoke to the agency. No, they were so sorry. Just at the moment they had no one they would care to recommend. Yes, they would most certainly bear it in mind. They would make every possible effort.

Lady Wapentake replaced the receiver. She sighed.

A head came round the door. "Just remembered that feller's name," said Lord Wapertake. "It was Carson."

A few days after this the Vicar of St Jude's was working in his study when the front door bell rang. He was about to jump to his feet when he heard shuffling footsteps in the hall and realized that Lizzie was in attendance.

Now the front door was being opened. Then the shuffling footsteps approached his study door. Lizzie came in.

"It's that cousin of Beefy's," she said.

"Oh, ask her to come in," cried John Adams, leaping to his feet, wondering whether Lizzie could hear the sudden pounding of his heart.

Lizzie showed the visitor in. John Adams put out his hand. "This is a great pleasure," he said warmly.

"I know I shouldn't trouble you," Sally said. "But I wondered whether you happened to have heard of any jobs yet."

He set a chair for her. Then he sat down at his desk, crossed one leg over the other, and pulled his pipe out of his pocket.

"I'm awfully sorry," he said. "I've tried. But I've not had any luck."

"Thank you for your help," she said quietly. "The fact is, I saw a post advertised in *The Times* and it's quite near my home. I travelled up to see the people last Monday, and they would like me to go."

"You didn't promise anything?" the Vicar asked quickly.

"I said I would think it over and write to them in a few days. They were nice people but, well, I rather like Danby. If there were a job here I think I'd prefer to stay."

"I'd like you to stay," John Adams heard himself saying.

She raised her eyebrows. He saw her colour slightly. There was a silence in the sunlit study. "I must go where my bread and butter is," she said in a small voice.

"How long before you need to decide about this other post?" he asked.

"I don't know. I can't keep them waiting very long."

"Give me a couple of days," he said.

The front door bell rang, to the Vicar's annoyance. He would have liked this interview to go on and on. But he heard Lizzie Tubb letting the new visitor in, he heard the shuffle of Lizzie's feet approaching the study door. A nervous tapping. "Come in," he called.

Lizzie put her head round the door. "It's the Lord," she said in an awestruck voice.

Sally stood up. "No, no," said John Adams, motioning her back into her chair. "I'm engaged at the moment, Lizzie. Ask – "

But he was too late. Lord Wapentake was already in the room. "Morning, Vicar," he cried. "Thought I'd just drop in for a moment." He saw Sally. "Sorry," he said. "Didn't know you'd got a visitor."

"This is Miss – er?" began the Vicar.

"Bryan," said Sally. "Sally Bryan."

"Thank you, Miss Bryan. Miss Bryan, may I introduce you to Lord Wapentake."

"How do you do," said Lord Wapentake.

The Vicar had an idea. "Miss Bryan is looking for a post as housekeeper," he said. "I suppose, Lord Wapentake, that none of your friends happens to be in need of one."

Lord Wapentake considered carefully. "Can't think of anyone," he said at last. He went on thinking. "Now if you'd said a gardener, I'd have said we wanted one ourselves. Guess what that feller Walters has done now. Killed my old China's tulips stone-dead."

"How on earth did he manage that?"

"Lord knows. But they're all as dead as doornails this morning."

"I must be going," said Sally.

"Come and see me in a couple of days," John Adams said, opening the door for her. "Thank you," she said. For a moment they smiled into each others' eyes. Then she was gone, taking some of the sunlight with her.

For the next two days the Vicar's mind was in a turmoil. It was in his power to keep Sally in the parish; but only if he could find her a post. The thought of losing her was becoming unbearable. They had met only twice, but already he was beginning to wonder whether he were not in love with her. He spent long hours remembering the way she moved, the loveliness of her eyes, the serenity of her face, the softness of her voice. And yet, what did he know of her? Nothing, except that her cousin went about kidnapping bank managers. She had appeared out of the blue. And, if he didn't do something about it, she would return whence she came. And that must be prevented at all costs, even if her whole family made a living by kidnapping bank managers.

He grew frantic. He rang up his dentist. Did he need a receptionist? No. He called to see Edward Macmillan. No, they had all the girls they needed in the bank. He spoke to the Postmaster. But no one wanted Sally.

When, after two days, she called to see him, she had a letter in her hand.

"I don't suppose you've had any luck?" she asked.

"I'm terribly sorry. I've tried everywhere," he said.

"Thank you," she said. "Then I'm going to post this. It's accepting that other job." She held out her hand. "Goodbye," she said. "You've been awfully kind."

"No," he said. "Wait. There must be something in Danby." He stroked his chin. "I've got an idea," he said slowly. "I'll ring up Lady Wapentake. She might be able to help. His Lordship's a dear old boy, but – well, his wife might be more useful."

"Are you sure it's not too much trouble?"

"Trouble?" He looked at her gravely. "I'd do a lot more than that for you," he said, and reached for the receiver.

He dialled the number of the Towers. He heard a click at the other end. "Who the devil's that?" inquired Lord Wapentake's voice.

"The Vicar here. Could I speak to Lady Wapentake, please?"

"You want my old China? Certainly, I'll fetch her. Hold on."

The Vicar held on. Now we may be getting somewhere, he thought, with sudden hope. He ought to have done this before, instead of asking the old boy. He put his hand over the mouthpiece, and smiled at Sally. "He's gone to fetch her," he said. "I've got a feeling she may be able to do something for us."

Five minutes later Sally said, "I'm afraid he must be going to an awful lot of trouble to find her."

Ten minutes later she said, "Is it a very big estate?"

The Vicar sighed, and replaced the receiver. "He must have gone to look for her and then forgotten all about it," he said. Idly, he dialled the number again. He got the engaged signal. "I'll cycle over and see her," he said.

"Indeed you won't," Sally said. "You've gone to quite enough trouble over me as it is." She picked up her handbag. "It's no good," she said. "I'm going to take this other job. It really did look rather attractive."

"Can't I persuade you to give me another day?" he pleaded.

She gave him a smile that tore at his heartstrings, "Listen," she said. "You've got a whole parish to look after. I can't have you spending all your time over my affairs. I'm not even one of your flock."

Don't go. I want you to stay. I love you, his heart pleaded. But he did not say the words. He said, "May I walk as far as the postbox with you?"

She looked pleased and surprised. "I'd love you to," she said.

They stepped out into the morning air. John Adams wished the postbox were five miles away, instead of just at the end of the road.

They were nearly at the postbox now. And this, thought the Vicar, is the end of things. In a few seconds the letter will be on its way, and then, tomorrow perhaps, she will follow it. I shall remember her, and the memory of her will grow fainter, and I shall always wonder what might have happened had she stayed. But I shall never know. And the future is grey, and forlorn, and I do not care for anything any more, for my parish will be empty without her, and my people will be short of the one person who matters, and even my calling will be dust and ashes until I have overcome this sickness in my soul.

"Will you write and give me your address?" he asked.

"Yes, of course, if you'd like me to," she said eagerly.

They were at the letterbox now. Sally checked the address on her letter. She made sure the envelope was sealed. And the big red pillarbox stood there with its mouth open, waiting to be fed.

Meanwhile Beefy had been doing his little best. "Has that cousin of yours got the job at the Vicarage?" Peg Leg had asked, one evening before lights out.

"No," Beefy said miserably.

He felt the boys looking at him. He wriggled farther into his linoleum.

"On account of why not?" Heck inquired nastily.

"On account of she ain't old enough," said Beefy.

"Why? How old is she?" Peg Leg asked.

"Twenty-five."

"I should of thought that was an ideal age for a housekeeper," said Peg Leg.

"The Vicar ain't old enough, either," explained Beefy.

The boys looked hurt. Peg Leg said slowly, "Do you mean to say, Beefy, that we subjected that poor old lady to shame and ignominy to no avail?"

"*And* wasted a good half-bottle of whisky on an uneducated palate," added Lofty.

"It ain't my fault," Beefy complained.

"Well, it certainly ain't ours," said Lofty.

There was a strained silence in the loft that night. But the next day Beefy had an idea that cheered him up tremendously. It was a wonderful, idea, involving the killing of two birds with one stone.

Mr Macmillan was having a busy and difficult morning. As if he hadn't got enough to do, one of his cashiers entered his room and said, "Excuse me, sir. There's a Mr Jones to see you."

"Jones? Jones? Do I know him?"

"I don't think so, sir. He's a stranger to me. He certainly hasn't an account."

"Oh, very well," sighed Mr Mcmillan. "Show him in."

The cashier showed Mr Jones in, and to his delighted astonishment he heard his manager cry, "Beefy! What the hell are you doing here?"

Beefy edged in, looking flustered. On the way to the bank he had prepared a neat little speech. But now it was all gone with the wind. "I got a cousin what can read and write," he stammered.

"I congratulate you," said Mr Macmillan.

There was silence, while Beefy quarried a few more words.

"She's looking for a job," he said at last.

"I have no vacancies," Mr Macmillan said firmly. He touched a bell. "Run along now, there's a good chap."

Beefy reached the door. "I'm looking for a job, too," he said.

Mr Macmillan looked at him. "I'm afraid you wouldn't do for a bank, Beefy," he said, not unkindly.

"I didn't mean figuring. I meant wearing one of them silk titfers."

Mr Macmillan shuddered. He stood up. "No, Beefy. Thank you all the same." He opened the door. "Goodbye," he said.

Dejectedly, Beefy left the bank. It would have been nice, him and Sally working in the same bank, him making tea and going for walks in a silk hat, and Sally doing figures and writing things. It would have been nice. But it was not to be. He only hoped Sally had had more luck. He didn't want her going back to Shepherd's Delight and leaving him here alone.

But the days passed, and there was no sign of Sally. He daren't go to her lodgings. He began to wonder, desolately, whether she had gone home without saying goodbye to him. He was very unhappy.

Sally and the Vicar had to wait at the pillarbox. Someone else was posting a letter.

The Vicar was in no mood for polite conversation. He wanted these last few minutes with Sally alone. But he could not ignore one of his flock. He raised his hat. "Good morning, Miss Carson," he said. He remembered something. "Miss Bryan," he said. "You'd be interested to meet Miss Carson. She is housekeeper at the Towers, Lord Wapentake's home."

"How do you do," said Miss Carson. "As a matter of fact, Vicar," she added rather coyly. "I shan't be housekeeper there much longer."

She was surprised to see the Vicar gaping at her. "Hadn't you heard?" she laughed. "I'm getting married."

For a fraction of time all movement was suspended. The clouds stood still in the sky, the distant roar of traffic ceased, birdsong was silent. Sally, with the letter halfway through the mouth of the box, failed to give it the final push that would have deflected the course of several lives.

All movement was suspended. Then, like a halted cinematograph film, it began again. Sally withdrew the letter, the Vicar murmured congratulations, grabbed Sally's arm, and before she knew what was happening they were both hurrying back to the Vicarage as fast as they could go.

The Vicar dashed in, seized the telephone and dialled the number of the Towers.

He got the engaged signal.

He slammed down the receiver. "Come on," he said. "We'll catch a bus."

"But I don't know whether I want a post at a big place like that," said Sally. "With butlers and maids and so on. I should be scared."

"They haven't got a butler. Only a housekeeper and a maid and a gardener. They're terribly poor. In fact, his Lordship's always threatening to give up the Towers and retire to a smaller place of his in the north of England."

By this time he was again in the street, dragging Sally after him. He pushed her on to a bus. Ten minutes later they were walking smartly up the weed-infested drive of the Towers.

Lord Wapentake, who was laying about him with a hoe, paused in his labours and said, "Morning, Vicar." He looked at Sally with interest. "I've met you before, young lady," he said.

"That's right. In the – " began Sally.

"I know. Don't tell me." He regarded her keenly. "You're Birchington-Smythe's eldest."

"No. I'm Sally Bryan."

The old man shook his head. "Think you're mistaken, my dear," he said kindly.

"Miss Bryan is seeking a post as housekeeper," the Vicar said patiently. "I wondered – "

"Wish you'd said gardener. Have you heard about that fellow Walter's latest? Killed my old China's tulips stone-dead. I've sacked the feller."

"Would it be possible to see Lady Wapentake?"

"You come and see her tulips first. Dead as doornails."

He led them round the hideous red-brick Gothic monstrosity that was his home, and into a large and somewhat tangled garden. Suddenly he turned to Sally. "How's your father?" he asked.

Sally looked puzzled. "I – I'm afraid he's dead," she said gently.

Lord Wapentake stared at her with bulging eyes. "Good Lord," he said. "Good Lord." He looked lost. He sliced at a peony with his hoe. "Better go and find my old China," he said in a subdued voice.

But at that moment Lady Wapentake, looking like a rather bedraggled sparrow, came in the garden, and greeting the Vicar warmly.

The Vicar said, "Lady Wapentake, may I present Miss Bryan. She is seeking a post as housekeeper. I wondered whether– "

"May heaven bless and reward you as you so richly deserve," Lady Wapentake said devoutly.

"Poor old Birchington-Smythe's been called home," said Lord Wapentake.

His wife brushed aside this irrelevancy. She turned to Sally. "Come into the house, my dear. Let us see whether we cannot come to some mutually satisfactory arrangement. Mortimer, ask the Vicar to help you mend the lawnmower."

The ladies went towards the house. The Vicar stood watching them, admiring the grace of Sally as she walked, and the straightness of her carriage, listening to the fading sweetness of her voice. She couldn't be away long, he told himself. Ten minutes, half an hour at the most, and he would once again be able to look into the deeps of her eyes, to smell the delicate fragrance of her, to hear her laughter and her speech.

Lord Wapentake brought him back to earth. He said, confidentially, "You know, I always used to tell Birchington-Smythe that he didn't eat enough fruit. Always." He paused. He shrugged. "Wouldn't listen, of course. And now look what's happened."

This, thought the Vicar, is not going to be easy. He took a deep breath. "You are mistaken, Lord Wapentake," he said, clearly and distinctly. "Colonel Birchington-Smythe is not dead."

There was a stunned silence. An irritable pair of grey eyes looked searchingly at the Vicar. "Which of you am I to believe?" Lord Wapentake asked coldly. "You, or that chit of a girl?"

"Miss Bryan didn't tell you that the Colonel was dead. She said her own father was dead."

"Who the devil's Miss Bryan?"

"That young lady who has just gone into the house with her Ladyship."

"Ah. So she's Miss Bryan, is she?" Lord Wapentake looked cunning. "Then why," he asked, with the air of one making a mating move at chess, "why did she come here masquerading as the Birchington-Smythe girl?"

Outwardly the Vicar was cool. But inwardly he was raging. That anyone could so speak of Sally! Chit of a girl, indeed! Masquerading, indeed! He would have liked to grab the hoe and strike his exalted parishioner smartly on both ankles with it.

But at that moment Lady Wapentake and Sally came out of the house. They were both smiling happily. Sally appeared to be walking on air. "Vicar," cried Lady Wapentake, "subject to the formality of references, Miss Bryan will be starting work here almost immediately. Carson is not leaving for a few weeks, but she will be able to show Miss Bryan what is required of her." She lowered her voice to a stage whisper. "I think she's charming, Vicar. I'm deeply grateful to you."

Sally gave him a wonderful smile. "So am I," she said.

Only Lord Wapentake was out of tune with the general rejoicing. "Tcha!" he said, driving his hoe into the ground with considerable force, "Tcha!" He turned to his wife. He pointed dramatically at Sally. "This young person comes here," he said, "pretending to be someone she isn't. She tells me some trumped-up story about an old comrade-in-arms. And then, the moment my back is turned, you engage her as a housekeeper." He gave the hoe a savage twist. "I won't have it," he said. "I don't intend to be murdered in my bed, even if you do."

"But – but I don't understand," Sally said piteously. "I don't know what I've done."

Lady Wapentake looked worried. "What is all this, Mortimer?" she asked.

"I am not having this young person at the Towers," Lord Wapentake said firmly.

The Vicar had had enough. His fingers groped for the hoe. He ordered them back.

He said, "Lord Wapentake is entirely mistaken. Miss Bryan did not claim to be anyone but herself. And I myself can vouch for her absolute integrity."

As he said these words, her cousin Beefy the Crook stepped into his mind. "Go away, you," snapped the Vicar. "Oh, sorry," said Beefy. He went away.

"Her absolute integrity," John Adams repeated, reassuring not only his hearers but himself.

"Then that's quite good enough for me," Lady Wapentake said. She turned to her husband. "Mortimer, you'd better ask Miss Bryan's pardon."

Mortimer sulked. But he was looking keenly at Sally. Suddenly he smiled. "Dammit," he said. "It wasn't the Birchington-Smythes who had those girls. It was the Fordingham-Joneses." He put out his hand and shook Sally's warmly. "I remember now. Birchington-Smythe went in for spaniels," he said.

"So you are quite satisfied about Miss Bryan's bona fides?" the Vicar asked, a little coldly.

"Perfectly, my dear feller, perfectly." He turned to Sally. "Be delighted to have you with us, my dear," he said warmly. He thought of something. "You'll be able to tell me about old Fordingham-Jones. Not seen him for years."

Later, walking back down the drive, Sally said, "I really don't know why you have gone to all this trouble for me."

"I regard it as my best morning's work for a long time," John Adams smiled. "I've increased my congregation by one."

And what a one, he thought, Beautiful, intelligent, sweet and gentle. He couldn't just regard her as one of his flock. Already he was wondering when she would have a day off, whether she would let him take her out, what the parish was going to say if he did.

Oh, blow the parish, he thought. Aloud he said, "What's the next move?"

"Give up my rooms tomorrow. Take my luggage to the Towers. Settle in. Learn the job."

They were at the bus stop now. "I *am* grateful to you," she said.

"So is Lady Wapentake."

"Thank you. She's rather sweet, isn't she?"

"Very charming woman. He's all right, too. Don't let him scare you. He – er – gets a bit muddled, sometimes, and it makes him cross, but it doesn't last."

The bus came in. Let it be full, thought John Adams, happy to have her on his own. But there was plenty of room. The short journey was over all too quickly. He walked with her to her lodgings. "You're just in time for lunch," he said. "When shall I see you again?"

She looked at him long and thoughtfully. "I hope to attend evensong on Sunday," she said demurely.

"I didn't mean that." His strong, weather-brown face was flushing slightly. "I – I wondered whether you would let me take you to the theatre one evening."

Don't let her refuse, he thought. And don't let her be coquettish. It would spoil her.

She looked at him gravely. "I should enjoy that very much," she said. "But – can you do that sort of thing? Without gossip, I mean?"

"We can try," he laughed. "When's your evening off?"

"Really!" she said. "Time enough to begin thinking of days off when I've started work."

"Then may I telephone you? At the Towers?"

"Please do." She held out her hand. "And thank you so much." She lowered her eyes. "I'm glad I'm not leaving Danby," she said.

"So am I," agreed John Adams fervently. He coughed, tried to add something, found his mind was ecstatic but blank, and turned and hurried away, watched by a dozen fascinated eyes.

CHAPTER 13

"Your cousin's been," said Lizzie.

"Sally? Here?" Beefy beamed all over his face. "I thought she must of went home," he said.

"She's working up at the Towers. She says go and see her some time. Thursday's her day off."

"What's the Towers?"

"It's Lord Wapentake's house. Lovely. It's as big as a railway station."

Beefy's face fell. "But I couldn't go there," he said. "They'd throw me out."

"Course they wouldn't. Don't go marching up to the front door. Go round to the backyard."

"I don't think I dare," said Beefy.

But he wanted to see Sally so badly that the following Thursday afternoon he put on a clean singlet and set off for the Towers. He wasn't going in, of course. He was just going to hang about at the gates in the hope that she would come out.

Lizzie had said that the Towers was on the Leicester Road.

It was a long road. When he had walked a couple of miles he came to some big gates, with a house at the end of a long drive. This would be it. He waited.

He waited a long time. But there was no Sally. Then, at last, a bell rang in the house, and children began to appear in the drive.

Lord Wapentake must have a big family, Beefy thought at first. But when about a hundred children had appeared he began to wonder whether he had not, perhaps, made a mistake. Diffidently he approached an objectionable-looking child and inquired whether this was the Towers.

The child scowled at him, shook his head, and passed on.

Beefy hurried off along the Leicester Road. The houses began to give way to fields and spinneys. And then, at last, he came to a high wall, and in the wall two wrought-iron gates, set between pillars on each of what perched a pig. A stone one.

This must be it. But Beefy had wasted so much time at the school that he was afraid he might have missed Sally. Terrified though he was, he decided to go in.

There was a lodge beside the gates, and he was sure a man with a shotgun would step out and bar his path. But the door of the lodge looked as though it had not been opened for many years, and the windows were blind eyes, curtainless and dark. Boldly he set off up the drive. It curved, between high, untrimmed bushes of rhododendrons, and at last brought him in sight of the house.

Beefy gasped. He had never seen such splendour. A doorway through which you could have driven a single-decker bus. Red-brick towers, picked out tastefully in geometrical patterns of blue brick. A hundred windows, a hundred chimneys. And somewhere, behind one of those lofty windows, was Sally. If she hadn't gone out. He could hardly believe it. It was like having a relation in Buckingham Palace.

A little path, even higher in weeds than the drive, wandered off to the left. Perhaps that led to the backyard.

With his heart in his mouth he followed it. He came to a coachhouse with a stopped clock, stables, a big paved yard. And the back door of the house.

Astonished at his own temerity, he knocked. Oh, let it be opened by Sally, by kind, gentle Sally.

The door was flung open by a tall old gentleman who sagged slightly at the knees.

"Who the devil are you?" asked the old gentleman. "Laundry?"

Beefy swallowed. "I'm Sally's cousin," he said.

"Never heard of you. Know anything about gardening?"

"No."

"Come with me," said the old geezer. He led Beefy out of the yard, along another little path, and into a flower garden. He pointed to a dreary patch of withered leaves. "Look," he said. "Tulips. My old China's tulips. Now, what would you say was wrong with those?"

Beefy was too scared to be able to think clearly. He stammered, "I reckon they're dead."

"Dead? Of course they're dead. Anyone can see that. Question is, what killed them?"

Beefy remembered how, in a youthful prank, the lads of Shepherd's Warning had poured weedkiller all over the Rectory garden; he remembered the result. "They've been poisoned," he said promptly.

Lord Wapentake's slightly protuberant eyes gazed at him with immense respect. He smacked one hand into the palm of the other. "Just what I said myself. Just what I told my old China." He looked shrewdly at Beefy from under bushy brows. "Where did you learn your gardening?" he inquired.

Beefy wasn't used to being regarded with immense respect. He liked it. He liked this old geezer, too. He said, proudly: "My Grandma learnt me."

Lord Wapentake led Beefy to a rusty, rustic seat. The two men sat down side by side, hands on knees, and gazed at the encroaching wilderness.

"What's your name?" asked Lord Wapentake.

"Beefy. Beefy Jones."

"Where are you from?"

"Shepherd's Warning."

Lord Wapentake swivelled round and gazed at Beefy in astonishment. "Well, damn my eyes," he said. "I've got a little place up there myself. Warning Hall." He edged up closer. "Between ourselves I'm going to sell this great barracks one of these days and take my old China to live up there."

"That'll be nice," Beefy said enviously.

The two men sat there in the afternoon sunlight, but the sunlight was no warmer than the friendship that had suddenly glowed into life at the mention of Shepherd's Warning.

Lord Wapentake put a hand on Beefy's shoulder. "Do you wear sock suspenders?" he asked.

"No," said Beefy. He hitched up a trouser leg. "On account of I don't wear socks, see."

"Got a drawer-full upstairs," said Lord Wapentake, a little sadly. "My old China buys me a pair every Christmas. Never wear them. Thought you might like some."

Beefy couldn't remember anyone offering him a present before. Not even his dear friend Heck. He was deeply touched.

"Let's go and spray something," said his Lordship, rising. They went to one of the outhouses, and found a bright and shining spray, and filled a bucket with water. They came back into the garden. "Now, what shall we spray?" Lord Wapentake asked eagerly. "I know, roses."

He sent a fine jet into the air. "You got a rainbow," said Beefy.

"Got one the other day," Lord Wapentake said proudly. "How many colours can you see?"

They watched, fascinated. "Knew a feller in Simla who was colour-blind," went on his Lordship. "Couldn't tell crimson from flaming yellow." He gave Beefy a mischievous glance. "And the joke was, the joke was, the feller was a colour sergeant." His Lordship doubled up with a great bellow of laughter. He slapped his thigh. "Colour sergeant," he repeated, "and he couldn't tell crimson from flaming yellow." He continued to chortle.

Terrified by the uproar, rabbits bolted for their holes. Rooks, dozing in the immemorial elms, rose and circled with annoyed clatter. Spiders legged it for safety across their corpse-strewn webs.

"What's a colour sergeant?" asked Beefy.

His Lordship mopped his streaming eyes. "Thought you'd appreciate that," he guffawed.

They were sitting down again now. His Lordship edged a little closer. He swept a hand towards his rolling acres.

"How'd you like to look after this lot?" he asked. "Three pounds a week and midday dinner?"

Beefy goggled. Was this nice old geezer offering him three pounds a week? No. He just couldn't believe it. "How – how much?" he gasped.

"Three pound ten," said Lord Wapentake hurriedly.

"But – but I ain't no gardener," stammered Beefy.

"Bet you know more than that feller Walters," said his Lordship. "Come on, my dear chap. Let me show you round."

Dazed and bewildered, Beefy followed his new friend round the estate. Overgrown lawns, parkland disfigured by crashed elms, an ornamental garden, a lily pond in which Beefy was fascinated to find frogs in all stages of development. At last they came back to the flower garden. "What my old China wants here is a blaze of colour," said

Lord Wapentake. "Now, what would you suggest?" He waited hopefully.

Beefy thought of a joke. He wondered whether he dare. But his new friend was so nice that he decided to risk it. "Reckon we ought to ask that colour sergeant," he said.

He looked anxiously at Lord Wapentake. Two grey eyes regarded him in slight bewilderment. Then his Lordship saw it. He shouted with laughter. The rooks, who had only just settled down after the last outburst, rose up again, complaining bitterly. The rabbits decided they might as well give up trying to feed in these circumstances, and went home. Several spiders' webs were damaged in the stampede for safety. "Oh, damn good," cried his Lordship. "Damn good. Ask the colour sergeant! I must tell that one to my old China." He came back to earth. "When can you start?" he inquired.

"You – you really mean I can work here?" Beefy asked rapturously.

"Be damned hurt if you don't, my dear feller."

"I could start tomorrow," Beefy said.

"That's the idea. I like keenness. Eight o'clock tomorrow morning, then?" He rose, and shook Beefy's hand.

But for some time Beefy had been growing more and more intrigued as to the identity of his new friend. At first he'd thought he was a gardener; but from the way he talked he seemed to be someone more important than that. There was only one way to find out. "Are you the foreman?" he asked.

The rooks, who had just been coming in to land, took off for the third time. Lord Wapentake's laughter shook a decayed branch from a neighbouring elm. "Me?" he roared. "A foreman? Dammit, man, I'm the blasted Earl." He wiped his streaming eyes. "Never laughed so much since old Tumble dropped the baby in the font," he sobbed.

But Beefy's knees had turned to water. "You – you mean you're a Lord?" he gasped. He felt he'd been tricked. Lords didn't ought to go about dressed like tramps. You didn't know where you were.

But the Earl put a friendly hand on his arm. "Don't you worry, my dear feller," he said. "You come along at eight o'clock tomorrow morning and we'll set you on. Goodbye."

"Goodbye," said Beefy weakly. He came away, along the tousled path, down the long drive, past the stone pigs. But as he walked the Leicester Road, with its streams of home-going traffic, he began to recover from his shock. He'd been talking to a Lord, as friendly as you like; a Lord who had offered to give him a present of sock suspenders, a Lord who had given him a job. More! He would be working at the same place as Sally. He might see her often. He gave a little skip and then, deeply ashamed, tried to pretend he hadn't.

He could hardly wait to tell the boys. They wouldn't half tease him. "I been talking to a Earl," he'd say, and they'd say, "Good old Beefy. You'll be dining at the House of Lords next," and he'd pretend to be cross, but really he'd be ever so pleased.

The church hall was empty. He let himself in with a new key they'd had made for him. In the kitchen he prepared himself a nice supper of cocoa and baked beans, and took it up to bed with him.

It was still early. He watched the yellow sunlight of evening creep sadly up the dingy walls. He watched the swallows, in their faultless evening dress, dart and curve against the sky. He heard the cries of children at play. He shovelled the hot, aromatic beans into his mouth, and supped his cocoa, and was content. Sally, and that nice old geezer of an Earl, and a steady job. The future was unclouded. True, he didn't know much about gardening; but neither did Adam and Eve at first. And they must of learnt.

And they hadn't got a Earl to show them how. He'd be all right.

A door opened downstairs. He heard the clattering of the boys' footsteps on the ladder. They crowded in. "Why, hello, Beefy," they said. "You're early. What you been doing?"

"I been talking to a Earl," said Beefy.

They were immediately interested. "Nice work, Beefy," said Peg Leg, impressed. "It ain't everybody talks to Earls. Any chance of using him?"

"He wanted to give me a present," Beefy said.

"One of his cast-off yachts?"

"Sock suspenders," said Beefy.

There was a horrified silence. "Sock suspenders!" Heck said scornfully. "He goes hobnobbing with Earls, and all he gets is sock suspenders."

"Only I didn't get them, on account of I don't wear socks."

They looked at him pityingly. "But I got a job," he added proudly.

"What sort of job?" Heck asked quickly.

"Gardening." He said importantly, "I got to be up early tomorrow, on account of I start work at the Towers at eight o'clock."

There was an interested murmur. "We must see he don't oversleep, boys," said Heck. He combed his lank hair.

"If Beefy wants to get a job and go straight it's up to us to help him," said Lofty.

"Reckon we all ought to be very proud of Beefy," Peg Leg said. "Going out and earning a honest living by the sweat of his brow."

"Beefy the Breadwinner!" cried Willie One Eye. The boys laughed. Beefy's face, protruding from its roll of linoleum, beamed like the rising sun. "You don't half tease," he said happily.

But Heck, to everyone's surprise, had gone to the loft door and was descending the ladder. This was unusual. If Heck wanted something he didn't go himself. He sent Beefy. That was understood.

They went on preparing for their rest. But they wondered.

It was nearly ten minutes before Heck returned, carefully carrying one of the Mother's Union cups. "Here you are, Beefy," he said. "I've brought you a nice cup of cocoa. As a small token of our respect for someone who is not afraid of honest work."

He had said it same as like he was making a speech, loud and important. All the boys clapped.

Beefy blinked away his tears. "You shouldn't of went and done that, Heck," he said.

"You drink it down," Heck told him. "You got to keep your strength up nowadays."

Beefy drank, watched by all. He'd never been waited on like this before. And it was a lovely cup of cocoa. Just a slightly unusual taste about it somewhere, but that didn't mater. Heck had made it with his own hands, hadn't he.

He drained the cup. He wiped his mouth on the back of his hand. "That was nice, Heck," he said, deeply grateful. "But you shouldn't of."

"Nothing like a good, nourishing cup of cocoa," said Peg Leg. He began to descend the ladder. "I'll put the lights out tonight, Beefy. You better get some sleep."

Beefy yawned. "I mustn't oversleep in the morning," he said. "Got to be there by eight o'clock." He yawned again. His roll of linoleum had never felt so comfy. And his old hassock was like swansdown. He just couldn't keep his eyes open. "Goodnight, boys," he murmured.

"Goodnight, Beef," they said kindly.

Others in the parish of St Jude were not sleeping so peacefully. That evening the Vicar and wardens had opened the returned tenders, and, as John Adams had foreseen, that of Amos Coldbarrow was the lowest. And now the Vicar lay awake, wondering. Was it right to give the contract to a notorious evil liver? On the other hand, even if the church council would agree, was it right to add to the church's commitments by accepting a more costly tender? It was a difficult problem. Still, he consoled himself, things were moving. Whatever was decided, the building would be started soon. The Lord Bishop of the Diocese had already consented to lay the foundation stone. The new hall would be roofed before winter set in. Yes, things were going well.

Sally, never very far from his thoughts, came into his mind. How did she like the Towers, he wondered. Would she really let him take her to the theatre? He tried to imagine her face, her voice, her laughter. But he could form no clear picture. He murmured her name softly as he drifted into sleep.

Not far away, in Rockefeller Avenue, Lizzie Tubb lay with a bedfellow – pain. Nasty. In her inside. Like needles. She'd had it, on and off, for some time, now. Suppose I ought to go and see a doctor, she thought. But they'd only one idea, nowadays. Hospital. Lizzie shuddered. She wasn't going to no hospital.

The light from the street lamp outside fell on the text: Be Strong and of a Good Courage. Nice, she thought. Nice how that honeysuckle climbs round the words. She'd always wanted a honeysuckle She'd brought some back once, when she went on a church outing into the country. Smelt lovely. She'd stuck some bits in the black dirt of her yard, and watered it when she remembered. But it hadn't growed. Not that you could expect it to, really. That had been a nice outing. Before the war. Things had been nicer, somehow, before the war. They'd got a sort of glow about them, when you looked back. There didn't seem to be that glow any more.

Nice, that outing had been. There'd been a chap with a mouth organ. Regular scream. Lovely weather, too. Didn't seem to get weather like that, nowadays. The sun was less bright, the sky less blue, the earth less green. S'pose I'm getting old, she thought.

That pain was nasty. She wished it was morning. You could get up and do some work, then. Nothing like work, when you was worried.

Cup of tea might be nice, she thought. Sort of comforting. She went down to the kitchen. Whitey would be a bit of company. But he only cocked an eye at her and went to sleep again. She made the tea, and sat in her nightie sipping the hot, strong brew.

And, outside, the setting moon was a washed pebble in the misty sky.

Beefy's eyeballs, pressed against translucent lids, were suddenly aware of great brightness.

They went into immediate action. They drew up the quivering, fleshy blinds. They woke Beefy. Look, they said. Look at the sun, high in the sky, shining down on your hassock. Look at the empty loft. The boys always wait for you to fetch them a cup of tea. Where are they? You must have overslept, they said accusingly.

Beefy shot out of his roll of linoleum like a ball from a cannon. He was trembling violently. I must of overslept, he muttered. I'd got to be there by eight. His trembling fingers fumbled with buttons, with bootlaces. He clattered down the ladder, into the deserted kitchen. He rinsed his face, and dashed out of the building, and set off for the Leicester Road. He wished he knew what time it was. But when he came within sight of the Town Hall clock, he hardly dared to raise his eyes. When he did so, his stomach gave an awful lurch. Nine fifteen. He was going to be two hours late. He was going to lose his job. The old geezer was going to be cross with him.

Perhaps he wouldn't go. There didn't seem much point, just going there to be told off. But all the time his short legs were hurrying him along the Leicester Road. Yes, he'd just go, and say he was sorry, and then come quietly away and try to get another job. Not such a nice one, of course. And it wouldn't be with Sally. But perhaps he'd get one.

The big, green buses swept past him. But he hadn't any money. He trudged on, every now and then breaking into an anxious trot. But he was at last beginning to realize that he had a very nasty pain behind his forehead. He couldn't understand it. He never had headaches. Heck had once said that there wasn't anything inside there that *could* ache, and Beefy had accepted this fact.

And his limbs felt weary and drugged. He must have slept too heavy; so heavy that he didn't even hear the boys go out in the morning. It was all very funny.

He came to the gates of the Towers. He turned in, taking his courage in both hands. There was no sign of life. He went up the little path to the outhouses. His heart was pounding uncomfortably. Any moment now he was going to meet the Earl, and the storm was going to break about his aching head.

He came into the coach yard. Lord Wapentake was there, his head inside the bonnet of a veteran Rolls.

Beefy coughed. His Lordship looked up testily. Then he saw who it was. His face wreathed in smiles. He glanced at the coach-house clock, which hadn't gone since one night in 1910 when his Lordship, kept awake by its striking, had risen, put on his dressing gown, seized his shotgun, and given it both barrels.

"Quarter to eight," he said appreciatively. "You're early. Know anything about motor cars? She won't go."

Beefy felt he ought to explain that he wasn't really early; he was late. But it looked like being very difficult. So he investigated the car instead. Two minutes later he said, "The petrol tank's empty."

Lord Wapentake regarded him with awe. "You can look after the car as well," he said decisively. "Give you another pound a week."

Beefy felt quite faint. "Another pound?" he gasped.

"That's right. You clean the car today. Never mind the garden."

Beefy had a lovely day. He polished the Rolls until he could see his face in every inch of it. He'd always liked messing about with the Company's van. But a Rolls Royce! He was in the seventh heaven. When, tired and happy, he returned to his bed, the boys looked at his beaming, oil-smudged face with surprise.

Peg Leg was the first to pull himself together. "Here comes the breadwinner," he cried.

"The ploughman homeward plods his weary way," said Heck.

"I ain't been ploughing," Beefy explained. "I been cleaning a car; a Rolls Royce."

"Whose?" demanded Heck.

"That Earl's."

Peg Leg heaved a sigh of relief. "Oh, that's good," he said. "You know, Beefy, we was awfully afraid you might get into trouble for being late this morning. Willie thought you'd said something about having to be there by eight o'clock. But we weren't sure, and we just hadn't the heart to wake you. You was sleeping so peaceful."

"Sleeping like a baby," said Lofty Longbottom gently.

"Heck quoted some poitry at you," said Peg Leg. "What was that poitry you quoted at him, Heck?"

Heck cleared his throat. "I said, 'What? Art thou poor, and hast thou golden slumbers?' " he told his delighted friend.

"And then we all crept out as quiet as mice, and left you to your slumbers," said Peg Leg, tears in his eyes.

Beefy was deeply touched. He could see the picture quite clearly. There he was, like a sleeping cherub in a roll of linoleum, eyes gently closed, his cheek resting upon his folded hands; while his dear friends tiptoed quietly down the ladder, each sparing a wishful smile for their sleeping comrade.

But Heck changed his bliss to anxiety by saying, "I've heard some news today. They're going to start building that new church hall. Given the job to a bloke called Coldbarrow."

There was an anxious silence. "We got to stop them," Peg Leg said at last. "We shall never get another place like this." He meditated. "But what can we do?"

"Delaying tic-tacs?" Beefy suggested helpfully.

Joe Vodka broke into a spate of violent Russian, during which he flung imaginary bombs, fired imaginary tommy-guns, and drew his finger several times across his throat.

"Joe ain't what you'd call subtle, is he?" said Peg Leg, a note of reproof in his voice.

"What say we burn the new hall down?" suggested Willie One Eye.

"You'd have a job. It ain't built yet," pointed out Lofty.

"Well, when it is built," said Willie with some irritation.

"Too risky," said Heck. There was a meditative silence. Oh, let them think of something, thought Beefy. The world was hard; and the thought of losing his nightly refuge terrified him. What its hole is to a rabbit, so was the linoleum to

Beefy. He didn't like this silence. They weren't getting anywhere. He cleared his throat. "Reckon you can't beat delaying tic-tacs," he muttered.

He was ignored. Several further suggestions were dropped into the prevailing silence, like pebbles into a well, and the resultant ripples died, and the silence prevailed once more.

Then Peg Leg spoke the words that have brought comfort and peace of mind to ten thousand baffled meetings. "I move," he said, "that a small committee be appointed to go fully into the matter, and report back."

There was a gratified murmur. But Heck, peering into the mirror at his gold teeth, shook his head. "Can't do it," he said firmly. "This ain't a properly constituted meeting. It ain't got power to appoint committees."

Silence fell, disappointed and helpless. And as it went on the boys began, shamefacedly, to realize something. They couldn't manage without Ida. They needed their Brain. Even Heck was no good without Ida.

Peg Leg was the first to grasp this fact. He stopped carving his initials on his wooden leg and looked up. "We got to ask Ida," he admitted mournfully.

"She wouldn't help last time we raised the matter," pointed out Lofty.

"Perhaps she'll be feeling more co-operative after her holiday," Heck said, not very hopefully. "I'll have a word with her when she comes back."

Beefy waved his head about anxiously, like an upside-down tortoise. "We *got* to do something," he said. "Delaying tic-tacs or something."

"Oh, put the light out and stop beefing," said Heck.

CHAPTER 14

Under the loving care of Lord Wapentake and Beefy the grounds of the Towers became rapidly more desolate.

The pair were inseparable. And at last the happy day came when his Lordship led Beefy to the rustic seat and said, "Isn't it about time I gave you some wages, my dear feller?"

"Well," said Beefy. "If you're sure? I mean – "

But Lord Wapentake had already pulled out an ancient wallet, and was counting ten-shilling notes. "There you are. Four pound ten," he said. "Suppose you don't believe in this damned National Insurance nonsense, do you?" He did not wait for a reply. "Knew you wouldn't. Neither do I." He put a hand on Beefy's knee. "But do you know," he went on slowly. "That feller Walters used to make me pay contributions. Spite, Sheer spite, if you ask me. Meant he had to pay himself, too, of course. But that didn't worry him, so long as he injured me. Cutting off his nose to spite his face, that's what I called it. Told him so, too."

"It don't worry me," said Beefy, wondering what it was all about. Ida had never suggested that the board of directors should pay contributions.

"Of course it doesn't. You're a sensible feller." His Lordship shook his head. "That Welsh Wizard has a lot to answer for."

Beefy wondered vaguely how wizards had crept into the conversation. "Saw a wizard once, he mused. "At the theatre. Sawed a lady clean in half." He shuddered. "Surprised me they allowed it."

"Allow anything, nowadays," agreed his Lordship sleepily. "No moral standards." His head fell forward. He slept in the hot sunlight.

But Beefy sat on in a happy daze, nine ten-shilling notes clutched in his great fist. He had never had such wealth. He didn't quite know what to do with it. He'd really got everything he wanted.

Then he had a lovely idea. He would buy something for Whitey. A collar, perhaps. And some cigarettes for his friend Heck. How pleased they would be. He could hardly wait until evening to rush off to the shops.

Then he had an even more wonderful idea. He would take Sally to the pictures. If she'd go with him. Anyway, he was going to ask her. Sally was nice. Even if she didn't want to go, she wouldn't laugh at him. What day was it? Thursday. Perhaps she'd let him take her tonight.

But he didn't quite know how to get in touch with her. All his work was out of doors, and to his disappointment he had not met her once since he had come to work at the Towers. Still, perhaps the Earl would be able to do something about it. Impatiently he waited for the old geezer to wake up.

And, while he waited, John Adams sat in the Vicarage study and nervously dialled the number of the Towers.

The clear, unmistakable voice of Sally answered. Yes, this was Miss Bryan speaking. Yes, she was very happy indeed at the Towers. And very grateful to the Vicar. The theatre? Yes, she would love to go. Tonight? It should be possible. How very kind. Yes, she would meet him by the Julius Caesar statue at 7 p.m. Till this evening, then. Goodbye.

The Vicar replaced the receiver. He mopped his brow. Then he rose, grabbed a cushion, and drop-kicked it over the desk. He pounced on it and passed it, swift and low, to the bust of Milton, who ignored it.

Probably a soccer man, thought the Vicar, without rancour.

Then, very deeply ashamed of this lonely, joyous outburst, he sat down to write his bit for the parish magazine.

Beefy fidgeted. But the old Earl slept on.

And Sally came into the garden to gather flowers.

Beefy leapt to his feet. He ran across to her. She looked up. "Why, Beefy," she cried, smiling and laughing. "Whatever are you doing here?"

He was one huge beam. "I work here," he said. "In the gardens. I came to see you, and the old gee – his Lordship took me on."

"How awfully nice," said Sally. It was a great relief to find that her cousin was gainfully, and honestly, employed. She had always wondered just how he did make a living.

"I got some wages," Beefy rattled on. "And I wondered – I did wonder if you'd like to come to the pictures tonight on account of it's your day off only it don't matter if you say no."

Her face fell. "Oh, Beefy, I'd love to," she said. "But I'm afraid I can't. I'm going out."

There was a moment's silence. "It don't matter," said Beefy brightly. "It don't matter a bit, Sally. I only wondered. But I don't mind, really I don't."

"Oh, I am sorry. I'd have loved to come," she smiled at him and touched his sleeve. "Ask me again, won't you?"

"If you really want me to. Course I will."

"Of course I want you to. Now, what about helping me to pick some flowers? Or are you busy?"

Beefy had a gloriously happy time helping his cousin gather flowers. The sun shone, and the birds sang, and the bees were a loud murmur of content. It was not until she had left him, and had gone into the house, that he felt disappointment gnawing at him like a pain. As the long day wore on he became more and more lonely and depressed. Even the presence of his new friend failed to cheer him. When knocking-off time came he trudged aimlessly back to Danby, a lonely, miserable evening before him. Nothing to do. He could go to the pictures, he supposed. But, having hoped to take Sally, he found the idea of going alone quite unbearable. No, he'd just have a cup of tea and a sandwich at a milk bar, and then look round the town, and get off early to bed. After all, he thought, the way things are going I ain't even going to have a bed much longer. I'd better make the most of it.

In his loneliness he had quite forgotten that he was going to buy presents. Now he remembered. It cheered him up a bit. He got twenty cigarettes for Heck, and had them wrapped up nice. He bought a massive, brass-studded collar for Whitey.

"Do you want the name engraved?" asked the assistant.

Beefy shook his head. He couldn't wait for things like that. He was suddenly eager to see Lizzie's face when he arrived with this present. She'd be pleased. She'd say, "That's nice of you, Beefy," in a sad, pleased sort of voice.

He hurried round to Rockefeller Avenue. He went up the entry, and into Lizzie's backyard. He knocked on her door.

There was a perfunctory barking from Whitey; then the sound of Lizzie's plimsolls shuffling across the kitchen. She opened the door, and gave him a mock-reproving smile. "Come on in," she said. "I thought you was lost."

"I been working," he said proudly. "Got my wages today, too." He began to drag something out of his pocket. "I bought Whitey a present," he said, handing a little brown paper parcel to Lizzie.

She opened it, her fingers trembling slightly. She peered inside. She looked up at Beefy's beaming face. "He don't smoke cigarettes," she said in a puzzled, disappointed voice.

Beefy, still beaming, began dragging at his pocket again. "That was a joke," he explained kindly. "I knowed all the time, really. Thought it'd make you laugh." He gave her another screwed-up parcel. "Here, give him this."

Lizzie, rather dubiously this time, undid the parcel. She looked at the enormous collar. She looked up at Beefy. "It's nice. He'll like that," she said. She sat down suddenly, and began plucking at the tablecloth.

"You didn't ought to of," she said. "Spending your wages on me."

"Ain't you going to try it on?" asked Beefy.

They hung it round the unfortunate animal's neck. He put up his front paws and struggled to get it off. Unsuccessfully. He wandered dejectedly round the kitchen.

"It's nice," said Lizzie. "You like that, don't you, Whitey?"

"Do you think he's a bit weighed down, like?" Beefy asked anxiously.

"No. He likes it." She rose, and lifted the kettle onto the fire. "I got a bit of brawn to my tea. Are you stopping?"

They had a cosy, friendly meal in the dark kitchen. Lizzie kept looking fondly, first at her dog, and then at Beefy.

"You didn't ought to of," she said. "Spending your wages."

It was a nice bit of brawn. And there were good thick slabs of bread and marge and a couple of mugs of strong tea. Beefy enjoyed it hugely. This was nicer than being alone in a milk bar. But at last the meal came to an end, and a lonely evening began to loom ahead once more.

And then Beefy had a beautiful idea. "I suppose you wouldn't like to come to the pictures, Lizzie?" he inquired.

She peered up at him eagerly. "Tonight? You and me?"

"I asked Sally, only she couldn't come," explained Beefy. "And it's lonely going by yourself. You could put your spriggy frock on," he added.

"Ar," said Lizzie. She thought. "I ain't been well, lately. Had a pain. Here. Like needles. Do me good to see a bit of life." Her thick lenses flashed with gratitude. Beefy glowed.

"You go and put your spriggy frock on," he said kindly. "I'll wash up."

"Shan't be long," said Lizzie. She almost ran upstairs. When she reappeared she was wearing a shapeless frock, a hat like a coalscuttle, and pointed, jumble-sale shoes. There were streaks of powder on her blob of a nose.

Beefy said: "There's a Western at the Majestic. Seen a picture advert. Red Indians war-dancing horrible."

"I been thinking," Lizzie said. "Pictures make my eyes ache something awful. I – I suppose you wouldn't like to go to the theatre instead?"

Beefy hid his disappointment. He'd been looking forward to them Indians. "Course we'll go to the theatre," he said. "Be nice."

"You sure you don't mind?"

"Course not. I like the theatre. I seen a wizard saw a lady clean in half once."

"I'll just get Whitey's supper." Lizzie said. "He likes that collar, don't you, Whitey?"

Nobly the dog wagged his tail. "I got my spriggy frock on," Lizzie pointed out.

"Looks nice," Beefy said. He looked at her thoughtfully. "My Grandma had a hat just like that. Got it at a jumble sale. Ninepence."

"Goodnight, Whitey," Lizzie said. "Be a good dog."

Together they went out, the Well of Life to taste.

The Theatre Royal, Danby, has come down in the world. The stage that Irving trod has since been subjected to every possible indignity; circuses, ice shows, crooners, panel games. Now, however, it has settled down to a fairly steady routine. It presents variety in the winter, and in the summer it is handed over to a young and adventurous repertory company.

This company pleases itself, as well as its patrons. Its productions range from *Ghosts* to *The Ghost Train*, from *The Seagull* to *Seagulls over Sorrento*. If some of the plays are way above the heads of most of the audience, well, the audience don't usually find that out until after they've paid their entrance money. And as Ethel, who swept up, pointed out to Mabel, who sold the programmes, a bit of culture never hurt nobody.

Beefy and Lizzie stood among the throng before the imposing frontage of the theatre.

"Wonder what's on," said Beefy.

"Ask him." Lizzie jerked a thumb at the commissionaire, in his plum and gold.

Beefy didn't quite like troubling so ornate a personage. But he edged up, coughed nervously to attract attention, and asked, "What's on?"

The man looked at him in surprise. Then he looked at the huge advertisement that was just in front of Beefy's nose. He read out, "*The Cherry Orchard*, by Anton Chekhov."

"Is it funny?" asked Beefy.

"You'll laugh your flipping heads off," the man said with a pitying look.

They went into the foyer. Proudly Beefy bought two tickets for the pit stalls. Then they passed, trembling slightly with excitement, into the auditorium. Beefy bought a programme.

"What you bought that for?" asked Lizzie.

"Fan myself with," said Beefy.

Idly they watched the rich taking their seats in the orchestra stalls. And suddenly Beefy said. "There's Sally." And Lizzie said, "There's the Vicar." Beefy stuck his lower lip out. "They're together. She said she was going out. She didn't say she was going with *him*," he grumbled.

Sally was in a white frock, cool and radiant. It would have been nice, bringing her to the theatre. He'd have felt proud. It was nice with Lizzie, of course. But he wished he was with Sally. And he didn't like her being with the Vicar, somehow. After all, there'd been all that fuss about she couldn't be his housekeeper. And now here they were at the theatre together, where everybody could see them. He couldn't understand it. It didn't make sense.

But now there was a ripple of excitement in the theatre. The footlights were glowing on the red curtains. The gramophone, that had been playing gloomy music, broke into a roll of drums. Everybody stood up, uncomfortably clutching programmes, handbags, boxes of chocolates and coats.

The National Anthem ended. With a sigh of expectation the audience relaxed into its seats. The curtain rose.

It was a queer sort of play. Beefy couldn't quite understand all of it, on account of you couldn't see it through twice like you can a cowboy film. But he enjoyed it. There was one bit where a lady put a top hat on and did some conjuring tricks, but she wasn't as good as the wizard who sawed a lady in half. In fact, Beefy found himself hoping that she *would* saw a lady in half, but she didn't. Perhaps she wasn't clever enough.

Or perhaps they was short of ladies.

And at the end there was a sad bit about an old geezer who should of went to hospital only they forgot to order an ambulance. Beefy was very annoyed. "They didn't ought to

196

of forgot about that ambulance," he complained as they pushed their way out of the theatre. "The poor old geezer looked to me as though he wouldn't last long."

But he was also thinking about Sally. He kept his head down. He didn't want to see her tonight. She looked far too grand. He wouldn't know what to say. Besides, he still felt disapproving. He couldn't laugh and joke with people when he felt disapproving.

But at last they were safe, out in the bustle of the darkening streets. And Beefy had another idea. There was still plenty of money burning a hole in his pocket. "How'd you like a fish supper?" he asked.

Lizzie slowed down. "You don't want to spend all your wages on me," she said. "Let's go home and I'll make us some cocoa."

But Beefy was firm. They entered the Elite Fish Saloon.

Later, Beefy looked at Lizzie over two plates of fish and chips, a vinegar bottle and a salt pot, and asked. "Did you like that play?"

"Yes, said Lizzie, "It was nice." She ate a succulent piece of fish. "It was funny," she qualified. "Not funny so it made you laugh, but – well, funny."

"Liked that bit where something went ping," said Beefy.

"Reckon somebody dropped summat behind the stage," Lizzie said.

Beefy considered. "No. It was supposed to be. 'Cos that old geezer said he reckoned it was something at the colliery."

"Just covering up. They do that," said Lizzie knowledgeably.

But Beefy was not convinced. "Could have been a angel's harp string," he said with rare imagination. "Busting," he explained.

Lizzie sniffed scornfully, and sprinkled some more vinegar on her chips.

Sally and the Vicar had also enjoyed the play.

When he rang up to book the seats, he had been rather disappointed to find what the play was. He preferred something a bit more English and robust. But when he met Sally, so lovely in her white dress, with her brown arms, her sunburnt, smiling face, he forgot his disappointment. In her company he would have enjoyed the play in the original Russian.

When they took their seats she said, "I love the theatre, don't you?"

"Rather!" He was terribly happy. She was very close, and there was a fresh, open-air fragrance about her. "I always like the moment just before the curtain rises," he said.

"So do I. It's like being a child, and coming into a room with a sparkling Christmas tree, and wondering what's in all the parcels."

"I hope you'll like the play," he said. He didn't want to give the impression that he thought it might be over her head. "It's not everybody's cup of tea, you know."

She looked at him, and her face was eager. "Oh, but I've always wanted to see a Chekhov play. I've heard them on the wireless, but this is the first I've seen."

He began to reorientate his ideas about Sally. That she was a beautiful and intelligent woman he had known. But from the fact that she was Beefy's cousin he had assumed that her outlook and tastes would be fairly limited.

"He fascinates me," she went on eagerly. "With other playwrights, even Shakespeare, you can see how they get their effects. But Chekhov – no. His characters sit around, talking commonplaces, and suddenly there is a sound in the distance; peasants singing, a screech owl; or even just a silence on the stage. And he's made magic."

"You're very perceptive," he laughed. A good deal more perceptive than I am myself, he thought ruefully.

When the play began he watched her. She sat back in her seat, relaxed, absorbed. Her eyes were shining, her lips slightly parted. Her hands, strong and generous, lay in her lap.

Seeing her sitting thus, he knew that he loved her; and, loving her, he put out a hand and placed it on one of hers.

She started, turned quickly with a warm smile, and gave him her hand, firm and friendly. She did not withdraw it until the first act came to an end.

"Are you really enjoying it?" he asked anxiously.

"Immensely. And you?"

"Immensely. Though I must say I'm glad I haven't got this lot in my parish. Irritating crowd, aren't they?"

"I think they're delightful."

He said: "One of the troubles with Imperial Russia was that they never introduced Rugby football. If that chap Leonid had gone to a rugger school as a boy he might have had a bit more about him. Given them something to think about, too. Stopped them getting so infernally bored."

Her laughter was like a running brook. "I'm sorry," she said, seeing his look of surprise. She touched his hand. "I was just imaging Piotr Trofimov going in for a low tackle."

He took her hand in wonder. "Do you like rugger?'

"Rather! I saw the All Blacks once."

You wonderful girl, he thought. "We'll go and see a game next winter," he said.

The happy evening came at last to an end. Arm in arm they walked briskly through the fresh night air. When they reached the gates of the Towers they stopped. She put out a hand. "Goodbye," she said. "And thank you for a wonderful evening."

The moon was wearing a cheerful expression tonight. The wind tormented the trees and ran away, like a schoolboy tugging the girls' pigtails. Little clouds swam across the sky, like white ducks on a pond.

It was a night to dance barefoot in the dew.

It was a night to climb a mountain, and pluck down a burning star to light your pipe.

It was a night to kiss the pretty girl standing close to you under the sighing boughs.

John Adams put out his arms. His hands were about her shoulders. He looked down at her laughing mouth, and then, suddenly, she was away from him, away from his arms. "We've been quite foolish enough for one evening," she laughed, and was gone, faded like a ghost into the darkness of the drive.

He stood there for a long time, angry with himself for not having managed things better. Still, he'd made a start. She seemed to like him; and, as for himself, he was in love with a beautiful and charming woman, and the moon was full. He ran lightly home, along the moonlit road, until, coming to the houses and the lamps, he slowed to a walk more befitting his cloth.

CHAPTER 15

"And what," asked Ida, "do we know of this Coldbarrow?"

The deputation shuffled their feet in silence. Even Heck looked sheepish.

Ida waited. At last she said, "As I thought, nothing." She went and sat on her bed. She glared. "How many times do I have to tell you boys that you got to study your opponents? Cast your minds back to the war."

She was interrupted by a sigh from Heck. He's remembering the dear old black market, she told herself. "Montgomery used to have a picture of Rommel over his bed," she went on.

"Lofty's got one of Diana – " began Beefy, but was cut short by a painful kick on the ankle.

"Used to study his features," Ida said, with a scowl for Beefy. "Tried to discover his weaknesses, see. That's what we've got to do, if we're going to stop him building this hall."

There was a helpless silence. "Very well," Ida said wearily. "I'll see what I can do. Though I don't know why I should. Comes of being good-natured, I suppose. Now you'd better get along. I've got to unpack."

The deputation of directors sighed with relief. "Thanks, Ida," they said. They filed out of the presence.

The chairman of the board sighed too. Just back from a well-earned holiday, and she finds Heck, Lofty and Beefy in her hotel bedroom, waiting for her with a problem like this.

Her first reaction had been to tell them to go jump in the cut. But she couldn't really do that. The church hall was very useful. It kept them together. Once get them scattered, and you never knew what might happen. She'd seen too many promising lads drift into respectability, just through lack of control and direction.

This reminded her of Beefy. There was a typical case of drifting for you. Unstable, that was the word. No matter how much care you bestowed on him, you could never be sure that he wouldn't go off and do something straight.

She picked up the telephone and asked for Reception.

"I've just had visitors," she said. "Three men. Have they left?"

No. They were just passing the desk now.

"The tall, dark one. Heck. Send him back," she ordered.

"Heck," she said when he came in. "I'm worried about Beefy. Has he got over this nonsense about going straight?"

"Got over it? He hasn't. He's working."

Ida looked incredulous. "You mean he's actually holding down a job?"

"Been there since soon after you went on holiday. Gardening at the Towers."

Ida's jowl quivered with annoyance. "And you did nothing to stop him?"

"I drugged his cocoa," said Heck sulkily. "Made him a good two hours late on his first morning. But it didn't seem to make no difference."

They shook their heads. "After all I've done for him," Ida said bitterly.

"Blow, blow, thou winter wind," Heck said.

"Pardon?"

"Shakespeare. Man's ingratitude," he reminded her.

"Oh, yes,"

They thought for a few moments. "He's a straying lamb," Ida said. "A poor, straying lamb."

"What wants bringing back to the fold," added Heck.

"He wants prodding back with a blasted pitchfork if you ask me," Ida said grimly. "Mr Secretary, I leave it to you."

"Very well, Mr Chairman." Heck bowed himself out.

A few mornings later Beefy and Lord Wapentake sat on their favourite seat, resting from their labours. But although the sun shone, and the flowers, such as were left, were as gay as ever, there was a dark mist of constraint between the two men this morning. Lord Wapentake seemed to have something on his mind. Several times he turned to Beefy as though to speak, but the words did not come. Instead, he would put his hands on his knees, and look about him, and whistle something that might have been the National Anthem. But at last he made a supreme effort. He swallowed. He put a hand on his friend's knee and said, "Beefy, my dear feller, have you ever been in prison?"

Something came between the earth and the happy sunlight. The birds stopped singing, and waited anxiously. It was Beefy's turn to swallow.

"Once," he said in a small voice.

The old man's hand was still upon his knee. "What was it for?" asked the Earl gently.

"Kidnapping bank managers," said Beefy.

Lord Wapentake sat back on the seat. "Oh, is *that* all," he said with relief. "You – you've never stolen jewels, or anything?"

"Me?" said Beefy indignantly. "Of course not."

His Lordship nodded his head. "Good," he said. "Good. Hope you didn't mind my asking, but – well, I had a couple of plain-clothes men to see me this morning."

Beefy looked startled. "What did they want?" he inquired.

Lord Wapentake said slowly: "They came to warn me about a character called Beefy Jones. Apparently his line is to take a menial post at one of the stately homes, spy out the land, and then make off with the family jewels."

Beefy blushed furiously. "It ain't true," he shouted excitedly. "I never pinched no jewels. I ain't never pinched no jewels." He sat staring angrily into space, his breathing loud and quick.

"Course you didn't," his Lordship said soothingly.

"Did they go away?" asked Beefy in a worried voice.

"They did. I told them I'd only one male servant, a gardener; and that he'd been with me for fifty years and came of a long line of bishops."

There was silence, while Beefy slowly calmed down, like a boiling kettle taken off the fire. At last Lord Wapentake said thoughtfully: "Beefy, you ever seen a plain-clothes man with a wooden leg?"

"No," said Beefy.

"You ever seen a plain-clothes man with black side-whiskers and gold teeth?"

"No," said Beefy, wondering where this was leading. "Have you?"

"Not until this morning," Lord Wapentake said, gazing meditatively at an immemorial elm. He changed the subject. "My old China's on the warpath," he said. "Wants a good supply of produce for the church garden party. She looks after the vegetable stall, you know."

"We better plant something," said Beefy, still smarting.

"Bit late for that. It's in a fortnight or so."

They thought. "I know," Beefy said. "Radishes. Let's plant lots and lots of radishes."

"Come on, my dear feller. We'll go and investigate." They pottered off to the kitchen garden.

But Beefy simmered and worried all day. He wanted to see what Heck thought about all this. He didn't like having his name bandied about by the police. He didn't trust them.

He went to bed early, and waited for the boys. But when at last they came in, Heck wasn't there.

"He's gone to see his poor ole Mother," Peg Leg explained. "On account of she's sick."

Beefy looked forlorn. "I wanted to see him," he said. "What time's he coming?"

"He ain't. He's staying the night."

Beefy groaned. "I wanted to ask him something," he said. "Two cops have been up at the Towers telling Lord Wappitake I go pinching jewels."

Peg Leg looked horrified. "Well, that ain't a very nice thing to say. You ain't ever pinched jewels, have you?"

"Course I ain't."

Peg Leg turned to the others. "Here's poor old Beefy, trying to go straight, and they say things like that about him. It fair makes your blood boil."

"What you think I ought to do?" Beefy asked miserably.

Peg Leg considered. "You might try suing them for slander," he suggested. He considered. "No. Wouldn't do you no good. The scales would be weighted against you."

"I'd like to," Beefy said sulkily.

"Wouldn't do you no good," Peg Leg said judicially. "Just you carry on, Beefy, going straight and holding your head high. That way you'll make them ashamed of their base insinuations."

"Thanks, Peg," said Beefy. He sighed. It made you feel better, having friends who believed in you, friends who helped you to go straight in spite of everything. "Don't you worry," Peg Leg went on. "Just you go back to work tomorrow as though nothing had happened." He composed himself for sleep. "Goodnight, Beefy."

"Goodnight, Peg," Beefy said gratefully.

But when he reached the Towers the following morning he found things in a state of uproar. Police were all over the place. Lady Wapentake was wringing her hands in the kitchen. Sally, pale and anxious-looking, was in the flower garden. His Lordship was marching up and down with a double-barrelled shotgun over his shoulder, bravely fighting against a temptation to shoot every policeman in sight.

"Ah, my dear feller," he cried when he saw Beefy. "Come here."

Warily, Beefy edged up to him. Lord Wapentake put a friendly hand about his shoulder. "Look at 'em," he said scornfully. "Searching for clues! Why, they couldn't track an elephant through a foot of snow."

Beefy asked apprehensively: "What's happened?"

"Happened? Why, we've got the whole blasted force camping out here. Never been asked so many tomfool questions in my life."

Beefy persevered. "What are they looking for?" he asked.

Lord Wapentake stared at him as though he were half-witted. "Why, this feller who tried to pinch my old China's jewels, of course." He spoke petulantly. "What the devil do you think they're looking for? Mushrooms?"

Beefy felt himself trembling. "You mean – you mean someone tried to pinch jewels? Here?"

"That's what I keep telling you." His Lordship was beginning to sound exasperated.

"It wasn't me," said Beefy.

"You? Course it wasn't you. Tall, dark feller. Caught him in the act." He patted his gun. "Got away, but I winged him. Both barrels. Bet he won't sit down comfortably for a few days." He chortled.

But now Beefy saw, to his horror, a large detective approaching. Lord Wapentake saw him, too. "I'm off," he said. "If anyone asks me any more questions I shan't be able to keep my fingers off this trigger."

"But what shall I say?" Beefy asked miserably.

"Baffle him," said his Lordship firmly. "Just baffle him. It won't be difficult," he called over his shoulder.

The detective's eyes bored into Beefy. "Can I have a word with you?" he asked.

Beefy looked like a caught rabbit. "I got to plant some radishes," he said.

"They can wait. What's your name?"

"Beefy."

"Beefy what?"

"Er – Jones. Leastways – "

"How long have you been working here?"

Beefy was trapped. Lord Wapentake had told those policemen yesterday that his gardener had been working at the Towers for fifty years, and if he said anything different now they'd check up and be suspicious. Yet he knew it would be difficult to make it sound convincing.

He compromised. "Nearly fifty years," he said.

"It will pay you not to be facetious with me," said the detective.

"I wasn't," pleaded the terrified Beefy.

"Then how long have you been working here?"

"About a fortnight," Beefy said in a small voice.

"In the gardens? Do you ever go into the house?"

"Only for dinner."

"Have you ever been upstairs?"

"Once," Beefy admitted grudgingly.

"What for?"

"Lord Wappitake asked me to fetch the weedkiller. On account of he wanted to put it on some weeds."

"And where was the weedkiller?"

"In the bathroom cupboard."

The detective sighed. He shut his notebook. "Thank you," he said wearily. He sought out Lord Wapentake. "Where do you keep your weedkiller?"

His Lordship glared. "In the larder," he hissed through clenched teeth. "In a bottle labelled 'Health Salts'."

"You are making things very difficult for us, my Lord," sighed the detective. "We are only trying to do our duty, and incidentally, help you."

Lord Wapentake relented immediately. "Sorry, old feller," he said contritely. "Bit on edge this morning, I'm afraid."

"That's all right, my Lord. Er – where *do* you keep the weedkiller."

"Damned if I know." He considered. "Yes, now you mention it, I believe it's in the bathroom cupboard. Yes, it is, because I sent that feller Beefy for it one day, and then later on I found he'd been spraying the weeds with solution of my old China's bath salts."

Better than finding your old China bathing in weedkiller, thought the detective grimly. He wandered off. Lord Wapentake called him back. "Look, old feller," he said kindly. "I keep telling you. All you've got to do is go out and find a tall dark feller who lets out a yell every time he tries to sit down."

The detective did not answer. He'd had enough of the aristocracy for one day. He was beginning to realize what the French Revolution had been about.

Beefy, to his surprise, was not arrested. All day he toiled, with his head well down, and when evening came he made for home as fast as his short, thick legs would carry him. The church hall was empty. He dived in, climbed up the ladder, and burrowed into his linoleum like a homing rabbit. What a day it had been! Beefy, surrounded by policemen, was as ill at ease as a mouse in a cats' home. He was suffering from a sense of strain.

But when the boys came in he had another shock. His friend Heck was limping. Beefy was worried. "You had an accident, Heck?" he asked solicitously.

Heck, who was peeling off his jacket, paused. "No," he said quickly. "Why?"

"Thought you was limping," said Beefy.

Heck said nastily: "I suppose I can have a blister on my heel without everyone making a song and dance about it, can't I?"

"Sorry, Heck," Beefy said humbly. "I just thought you might have had an accident, see."

"It's on account of he had to go and see his poor old Mother," Peg Leg explained. "It was a long way, wasn't it, Heck?"

But Heck seemed to be in a bad mood tonight. He did not reply. He lay down on his mossy bank. "Are we going to have that light on all night?" he asked querulously.

Beefy climbed out of his linoleum. "I'll go," he said. He looked down at his friend. "Why you lying on your stummick, Heck?"

But the only reply was an exasperated snort. Beefy hovered. Then he went down the ladder and put the light out. He was worried about Heck. Perhaps going to have another of his nasty turns, and lying on his stummick so that his friends would not see the suffering in his face. Beefy lay awake a long time, in case his friend should need anything. But Heck was silent through the long night hours.

Silent, but not asleep. His thoughts were too bitter for this. It had been such a clever plan. It would bring an erring fellow director back to the path of duty, and at the same time augment the Company's profits by a nice collection of jewellery. And, if it hadn't been for that homicidal old maniac with the gun, he'd have done it. It wasn't the first time he'd helped himself to jewels. He had a nose for that sort of thing. But never again, he wouldn't lift a finger now if the whole board of directors joined the Salvation Army. He was through.

CHAPTER 16

The church garden party, held in Mr Macmillan's garden, was a great success.

Star-scattered on the grass, pretty girls in pretty frocks drank lemonade through straws. Young men and maidens tired the sun with dancing, and sent him down the sky. There was laughter, and the sweet music of the dances, the contented click of woods from the bowling green. The bees, ignoring the whole affair, created a drowsy hum as they clocked up untold bee-hours in their food-production drive. Wolf Cubs ran round with cakes, inviting the parish to guess the weight, laboriously writing down the calculated, facetious, or half-baked answers. Trestle tables were loaded with the kindly fruits of the earth.

Lizzie Tubb, in her spriggy frock, helped with the sandwiches, and forgot, for a few sweet hours, the pain that gnawed at her body and her mind.

Beefy, wearing a top hat and a fatuous grin, stood in an enclosure of wire netting, looking not unlike an amiable gorilla in a zoo, while people tried to knock his top hat off with tennis balls. He was deliriously happy. His friend Mr Macmillan had asked him to do the job. Beefy had accepted with delight. And people in the parish were getting to know him now. "Good old Beefy," they cried, as they knocked his hat flying. They fed him monkey nuts through the wire. He was on top of the world.

So was the Reverend John Adams; for Sally, helping Lady Wapentake on the vegetable stall, had smiled at him.

So was Sally; for John Adams had bought a pound of peas and had stayed chatting for twenty minutes.

So was the whole parish; for their nice young Vicar, who had worked so hard to give them a new church hall, was now turning his thoughts to gentler matters, apparently; to that nice-looking girl from the Towers, in fact. Romance, it seemed, was in the air; and they were glad of it.

But Amos Coldbarrow did not share in the general well-being. He didn't like this sort of goings-on. You'd got your hand in your pocket the whole time, if you weren't careful.

He was aware of a timid hand tugging at his coat. "Would you like to guess the number of sweets in this jar?" piped a little Brownie. "It's only threepence a go."

"No," said Amos. He wandered on. They'd only asked him, and he'd only come, because he'd started building the church hall. But he'd get away soon, now, before they had the coat off his back.

He heard his name being called. He looked round. The Vicar, in a cream linen jacket, was approaching. "Hello, Amos," he greeted him. "How's the building?"

"The usual snags," said Amos. "But nothing serious."

"We shall be on time for the stone-laying ceremony?" the Vicar asked a little anxiously. He'd got the Bishop all lined up for the job. He remembered the Archdeacon's acid amusement over the lost sketch plans. He didn't want the Bishop to be kept waiting.

Amos said: "Don't worry. I've never let anyone down yet."

"I'm sure you haven't." The Vicar felt reassured. Not a bad chap, Amos, when you got to know him. He was glad now that the church council had insisted on giving Amos the job. It did mean that a start was being made. This time next year, he thought eagerly, we should be well settled in. No more worry about cramped conditions, and lack of room; on more depression of spirit caused by that monstrosity in Rockefeller Avenue. This time next year it would be a factory. It should never have been anything else.

By a strange coincidence he was quite close to the vegetable stall again. "Hello, Sally. How's it going?" he asked.

"Very well, thank you, Vicar," she said.

"They're playing a waltz. I suppose you couldn't leave your post for ten minutes, and come and dance?"

"I don't see why not," said Sally. She spoke to Lady Wapentake, who smiled and nodded. Then, together, a young and graceful couple, they walked through the crowds and on to the lawn.

She slipped into his arms, and they were away, under the long shadows of the poplars.

"You dance well," he said.

"Thank you," she said, smiling up into his face.

"Your cousin's enjoying himself, isn't he."

"Beefy? He's having a lovely time. I'm so glad. He's such a simple soul."

"Yes," agreed the Vicar absently. But his mind wasn't really on Beefy. He was too happy. Her hand was warm in his, and his arm, strong and protecting, was about her waist. I could dance like this, he thought, until the sun goes down, and the moon climbs up behind the poplars, and the stars are hung, like fairy lights, among the trees; until the bat and the moth take over from the swallow and the butterfly, and the dew lies heavy on the daisied lawn.

But the music came to an end. "I must go now," said Sally.

"One more dance," he pleaded. But at that moment Amos Coldbarrow came up and said, "I want a word with you, Mr Adams." And Amos Coldbarrow's face was pale and set, and his hand trembled.

Amos, having escaped from the importunate Brownie with the sweets, and having set the Vicar's mind at rest, had just decided to go home, when he saw something that drew him as surely as the candle draws the moth. It was a gaily striped booth, on which hung a card, "Madame Ida, Fortunes Told".

Amos Coldbarrow pulled aside the flap of the tent, and went in.

It was dark inside. Madame Ida sat at a card table, on which stood a crystal. Her head, and most of her face, was covered with a brightly coloured cloth. She held out a plump, and businesslike, hand. "Cross the gypsy's palm with silver," she said.

Amos sighed, and produced half a crown. Madame Ida dropped it into her voluminous wrappings. "Sit you down," she said.

Amos sat down, facing her across the card table.

"You wish to tear aside the veil and peer for a few moments into the future?" she inquired.

"I want to see you do your stuff, if that's what you mean," said Amos.

Madame Ida pushed back her chair. Elbows out, she leaned forward and grasped the crystal. She gazed.

"You are seventy years of age. You are a builder of some sort," she declared.

"Anyone in Danby could have told me that," he said. "I want more than this for my half-crown."

And by Jove, you're going to get it, Madame Ida said to herself. She went on gazing. "I see building in progress," she said. "Foundations being laid. A large building; a factory, or a school. No. I see a bishop now, laying a foundation stone. It must be a church."

"Or a church hall," suggested Amos drily.

"Or a church hall. Now the walls are going up. Now the girders are going up to support the roof. Heavy, iron girders."

"You've seen the specifications," said Amos.

"They're having a bit of trouble, getting one of the girders into position. Now someone in authority has come to advise." She peered through the gloom of the tent at Amos, and then back to the crystal. "Yes, it's you," she said. "You're underneath the girder now. You're pointing upward with your stick. You're, Oh!" She screamed, and flung a cloth over the crystal.

"What?" demanded Amos. "What happened?"

She sat back, breathing heavily.

"Nothing," she said quickly. "Nothing. The crystal went dark. I couldn't see."

He rose, and seized her shoulders. "What did you see?"

"Nothing, I tell you. Let me be. Go."

"What did you see?" he repeated, shaking her.

She stood up, clutching the table. "Please go away," she cried. "I am not well. Please go." She flung an arm across her eyes. "Oh, it was horrible, horrible."

"*What* was horrible?" asked Amos, beginning to feel ill himself.

"The girder. It fell. It came tearing down from the roof." She looked at him, wide-eyed. "It crashed into the floor, crushing all in its path."

Amos was clutching the table by this time. "Was – was anyone hurt?" he asked.

"You were squashed like a beetle." She sobbed.

Amos shuddered. He heard his own voice, harsh and beseeching. "Are you sure of all this?"

She nodded, a handkerchief to her eyes. "Your head was all stove in," she informed him.

Amos groped his way out of the tent. "Would you like to buy a raffle ticket?" asked a Brownie. But Amos went on his way, unseeing. He leaned heavily on his stick. He put a hand up to the back of his head. "All stove in," he muttered. There was only one thing to do. He sought out the Vicar. There he was, dancing on the lawn, just as though nothing had happened. Fortunately, at this moment, the music stopped. Amos staggered up to the Vicar and said, "I want a word with you, Mr Adams."

"I want a word with you, Mr Macmillan," the Vicar said, ten minutes later.

"What is it?" asked Macmillan, sensing a crisis. "Run out of ice cream?"

"Coldbarrow's given up the contract."

"What?" The blood drained slowly from the churchwarden's face. "But why? He must be mad."

"He refused to give any reason. Less than half an hour ago he was assuring me that everything would be ready for the bishop. And now he's just come up and washed his hands of the whole affair."

Macmillan rubbed his chin. Then he said more hopefully, "I should think someone's put his back up. He'll get over it."

"I hope you're right. But I don't think so. He was trembling all over. He looked really ill. Simply refused to give any reason whatever."

The two men looked at each other. "What do we do now?" asked Macmillan.

"Go back to the beginning, I suppose," sighed the Vicar. "Get someone else on the job. Put the Bishop off." He lifted a hand to his eyes. "Dammit, Macmillan, I knew these building projects were difficult, but I didn't expect all this trouble. Are we ever going to get this hall built?"

Mr Macmillan put a hand on his arm. "Don't worry," he said kindly. "We're not going to be beaten."

There was a silence. Then the Vicar looked up. "That's the spirit," he said with a sudden grin. "We'll get this hall built come hell or high water." He glanced towards the platform. "They're getting ready for the prizegiving. I'd better go."

People were beginning to group themselves round the platform, on which stood Lord Wapentake behind a table of prizes, a list of winners in his hand. The Vicar jumped up beside his Lordship, and announced into the microphone that the prizegiving was about to begin.

There was desultory applause. His Lordship looked at the list of prizewinners and found he couldn't read a damn word. Left his glasses at home, of course. He was just about to ask the Vicar to call out the names when he saw a top hat among the crowd. "Hey, Beefy," he bellowed. "Come up here."

Beefy was horrified. Him, on that platform, with all those people looking at him. Even his silk titfer didn't give him confidence. But he couldn't ignore the old geezer. With trembling knees he ascended the scaffold, and stood awkwardly, blinking nervously at the crowd.

To his delight there was a burst of good-natured clapping. There were even cries of "Good old Beefy". He grinned down at them, and saw Sally on the front row put up her hand and wave. He waved back. And then, to his horror, Lord Wapentake pushed a paper into his hand and said, "Here you are, my dear feller. Call these names out."

Beefy took the paper. He looked at it. He turned it over. Then he said in a hoarse whisper, "I can't. I can't read, see."

But there was no point in whispering, for the microphone took his voice and handed it to the loudspeakers; and the loudspeakers opened their metal mouths and shouted to the people, "I can't read. I can't read, see. I can't read."

"Shouldn't need glasses at your age," Lord Wapentake said severely.

"It ain't glasses. It's on account of I ain't educated. I ain't never been learnt, see."

The loudspeakers shouted to the people, "I ain't never been learnt, see."

There was an embarrassed silence. Beefy, covered with confusion, saw Sally smiling bravely up at him. Then the Vicar came to the rescue. He took the paper, and said, kindly, "Let me do it, shall I, Beefy?"

He began to call the names, while Beefy clattered blindly down the steps, and hurried round behind the platform, and through the gardens, meeting no one, and out into the quiet streets. His face was crimson. He wouldn't of minded so much if Sally hadn't been there. But she had been in the front row to witness his shame. Worse, everybody knew she was his cousin. They'd say, "You know that nice girl, Sally? Well, she's got a cousin what ain't educated. She's got a cousin what can't read." Yes, he'd let Sally down all right. She'd never speak to him again, he was quite sure. He hurried home, into the deserted church hall, and climbed the ladder to the cool, friendly gloom of the loft, and sat, with burning cheeks, brooding upon his shame.

As soon as the prizegiving was over, the Vicar jumped from the platform and hurried over to Sally. "I'm an awful clot," he said. "I should have realized sooner what the trouble was."

Her smile was a little too bright and fixed. "Don't be silly," she said. "You did your best." She turned away. "I must go and clear up," she said.

"No. Just a moment. I wanted – "

Her head was down. "I don't think we ought to be seen together," she said quietly. "People so soon jump to conclusions."

"What do you mean?" He couldn't understand why she had changed towards him so suddenly. "You – you're not ashamed of your cousin, are you?"

She looked at him then, her eyes flashing. "Me? Ashamed of Beefy? Of course I'm not. Beefy's a gentleman."

"Then what's all this about not being seen together?"

"You're the Vicar of this parish. You have a position of authority. People aren't going to respect you if they think you're running round with one of the servant class."

"Bosh and fiddlesticks," cried John Adams. "You're talking like a Victorian novelette."

"No, I'm not," she said patiently. "In your position you can't afford to be too friendly with the cousin of an illiterate."

The garden party was breaking up now. People were drifting away. Others were busy taking down trestle tables, collecting unsold goods. From the lawn still came the sad, drowsy notes of a waltz.

"Look," pleaded John Adams. "I was going to ask you to let me take you out to dinner next Thursday. Will you come?"

"No, thank you," she said. She moved away. "I really must give a hand with this packing up."

"But Sally – " he pleaded, hurrying after her. He was too late. "Ah, there you are," cried Lady Wapentake to Sally. "Just help me with these radishes, will you. I'm sending them to the hospital."

"What about these tables, Vicar?" asked George Bloodshot. He was caught up. A few minutes later he saw Sally being whisked away in the Wapentake Rolls.

CHAPTER 17

The crew of a Martian reconnaissance saucer, hovering twenty miles above England, gazed through their powerful binoculars with astonishment.

"Something seems to have disturbed the Earthmen properly this morning," said the pilot. "Just look at them."

Out from the great cities poured the Earthmen, on foot, on bicycles, in cars and trains. Some fled into the country. Others made a beeline for the coast, not pausing until they reached the water's edge, some even plunging into the sea.

"Better radio a report," said the pilot. As a result the Martians read in their evening newspapers, "Disaster Strikes England. Earthmen Flee Cities."

But the Martians were wrong. It was not disaster that had struck England. It was August Bank Holiday.

By eight o'clock in the morning the sun was already hot, for an anticyclone had drifted lazily up from the Azores and perched on our doorstep. Already the streets were arid, sun-scorched canyons. Houses were airless boxes. Townsfolk heard the call of running water, the fairy tinkle of harebells on empty moors, the insistent crying of the sea; and by noon the Dales of Derbyshire were as crowded as Danby High Street on a Saturday afternoon, and on the beaches the people were thicker than the pebbles.

Lizzie Tubb looked at the clock. Half past eight. She was probably the happiest person in Danby that morning, for Beefy was coming at nine to take her to the seaside.

Lizzie had never been to the sea. She'd seen it at the pictures, of course, and thought it looked nice. But she'd never been. So when Beefy had said he would take her in the Company's van she'd been ever so pleased. She had thought of little else. They were going to take Whitey. "Be nice," Beefy had said. "We'll throw sticks in the sea for him to fetch."

"He'll like that," said Lizzie. "And we might go on the pier, perhaps." She looked anxiously at Beefy. She'd always wanted to go on a pier.

"Course we will," agreed Beefy, beaming all over his face. "We'll go anywhere you like."

Twenty-five to nine. Lizzie hummed a little tuneless tune to herself. She'd got her spriggy frock on, and the hat that was like Beefy's Grandma's jumble-sale hat, and a pair of smart, pointed, patent leather shoes. The ride would be nice, too. She'd only been in a motor car once, at her sister's funeral, and she'd enjoyed it, then, though she'd felt she didn't ought to of, on account of it was a funeral.

Quarter to nine. "We're going to the seaside, Whitey," she said. "You'll like that, won't you," and Whitey wagged his tail with a pleased expression, though quite frankly he hadn't the faintest idea what she was talking about.

He might be early, thought Lizzie, and went into the fusty-smelling front room and peered out through the aspidistra leaves. The street was empty. Still, it wasn't time yet. She waited patiently.

Her heart beat more quickly. She had heard the sound of a motor car. At last it came into sight. No, it wasn't Beefy's. It went on and stopped farther up the street.

Her clock gave nine angry little pings. He'd be here soon now.

She waited, gazing out in the hot, dusty street. Ten past nine. Perhaps he'd had a bit of a puncture, or something. She began to grow anxious. It was such a nice, hot day. It would be nice at the seaside. Not to go, after all, would be unbearable now.

At nine-thirty she went to the front door, and listened. She heard a stream of traffic passing the end of the road, but none of it turned into Rockefeller Avenue.

At ten o'clock she thought, perhaps he'll say it's not worth going now. She did hope not. It would be nice to be able to say she'd seen the sea, and you never knew, it might be her last chance. That brought her back to her pain. She ought to see a doctor. She knew that, but they'd only got one idea nowadays. They weren't getting her into hospital.

She wandered back into the kitchen. Whitey stood up and wagged his tail. "He's late, isn't he, Whitey?" she said. "Won't be worth going if he doesn't come soon." Back she went into the front room, and stood, her fingers tugging at the aspidistra leaves.

At eleven o'clock she returned to the kitchen and took her shoes and hat off. "He won't be coming now, Whitey," she said. Well, perhaps it was nice, not having to turn out after all. It would have been very hot, travelling; and all them people! She didn't know that she liked crowds. It was nice and peaceful in the house. Never had she known it so quiet, for all Rockefeller Avenue must have gone into the country or the seaside. They'd be there, now, sitting on the sands, with the sea sparkling and dancing like she'd seen it on the pictures.

She went upstairs and took her spriggy frock off, and put her old clothes on. She got herself a bit of dinner. It was nice and restful. She didn't have to talk to nobody, and after dinner she'd have a bit of a lay down.

Beefy arrived, hot and dishevelled, just as she was washing up.

"I'm sorry," he said. "I'm ever so sorry."

"That's all right, Beefy. It don't matter a bit."

He sighed with relief. "Thought you might be cross," he said. "But I'm ever so sorry."

"We've had a nice rest," she said. "Haven't we, Whitey?"

He came in. "It seems a bit flat when you was going to do something and then you don't," he said. "The gardens at the Towers is open to the public. I wondered if you'd like to have a look round."

"I suppose – I suppose it's too late to go to the seaside?" Lizzie said.

Beefy looked embarrassed. "It's on account of I ain't got a van, see."

"You didn't have an accident?" she asked anxiously.

"Not what you'd call an accident." He swallowed. "It ain't our van, really. We sort of – borrow it, see. The geezer who owns it keeps it in a lock-up garage, and when he ain't using it, we borrow it, see."

"A sort of understanding," suggested Lizzie.

"Sort of," said Beefy. "Leastways, it's an understanding on our side, only he don't seem to understand the understanding, 'cos when I was letting myself into the garage this morning he come along and shouted."

"Fancy him wanting his old van on a bank holiday," said Lizzie. "What did you do?"

"I runned away. And he hollered for a policeman and they chased me. I been hiding down by the canal."

"Poor old Beefy," said Lizzie, her eyes bright with gratitude. "Doing all that so you could take me to the seaside."

Beefy said, "It'll be nice at the Towers. I'll show you the radishes what I planted."

Yes, it was nice at the Towers. A thousand children milled about the lawns, under the shocked glances of the rooks. They reduced the frogs in the fountain to a state of nervous prostration, while Lord Wapentake lurked in the baronial doorway with a loaded shotgun, prepared to repel boarders.

But it wasn't quite like the seaside. Lizzie said gratefully, "It's nice, Beefy. Them's lovely radishes," and she thought of the shimmering sea, and of Whitey, scampering out with a stick in his mouth, shaking himself, while the sands turned golden in the setting sun.

"You know," said John Adams, "this is the one bank holiday of the year that the Church has had nothing to do with. I disclaim all responsibility." He settled himself more comfortably in the driving seat of his new sports car, put a little more pressure on the accelerator, and began to whistle rather cheerlessly.

Sally, her dark hair ruffled by the wind, smiled wanly but said nothing. He glanced at her out of the corner of his eye. She wasn't being terribly friendly, he thought, and his heart sank. Persuading her to come at all had been difficult. Ever since that ridiculous business of the prizegiving she'd avoided him like the plague, and only by means of insistent telephoning had he been able to talk her into coming. As if it mattered whether her cousin could read and write! He wasn't in love with her cousin. He was in love with her.

They drove on in silence, swept over an ancient, lovely bridge, and swung right into a lane that followed the swirling river. Then, at a point where the lane left the river to wander up a hill, he stopped the car. "This is where we walk," he said, grasping the picnic basket.

He helped her over a stile, and they set off along a path that dived into the depths of a wood. Fresh and cool in a white dress, she strode along beside him, her brown arms swinging. Once he tried to take her hand, but she smiled gently and pushed him away. "You're very aloof, today," he complained.

She gave him a friendly smile, then. "Not really," she said. She changed the subject. "Where are we going?"

"You'll see," he said. "I think you'll like it." They came out of the woods, and climbed a little hill, the sun hot on their cheeks, and from the top they looked down on the meanders of the river, and the wide, sun-sleepy valley, and the hills beyond. Then they dropped quickly down to the river, and to a clump of ancient willows. The water chuckled and gurgled, and the gnats danced in little clouds, and the coloured cattle stamped and wallowed in the silver stream, and swished their lazy tails. The noontide lay hot and heavy on the land. There was the smell of hot grass, and the strong dank smell of the river.

"Will this do?" he asked.

"I think it's lovely," she said. They sat down, on the very edge of the stream. They unpacked the picnic things, and he lit the primus stove, and put the kettle on, and then lay back, his hands folded behind his head, and watched the smoke from his pipe curling upward into the sky.

How quiet it was! Wherever the bank holiday crowds had gone, they had not come here. Far up in the blue, infinitely remote, a shining aircraft crawled across the emptiness, and drew a white vapour trail, like a chalk line, across the canvas of the sky. The distant aeroplane made the silence and loneliness even more intense.

He turned and looked at Sally. She was gazing sadly across the water-meadows. One hand trailed in the running water. She caught his eye, and the sadness left her face, and she smiled at him. He sat up, and took his pipe from his mouth. He put out a hand. "Sally," he said, moved by her loveliness, his voice unsteady with emotion. Suddenly there were tears in her eyes. "Oh, my dear," he said. He scrambled to his feet and knelt before her, taking her in his arms, and holding her close. "What is it?" he asked, kissing her brow, burying his face in her sweet-smelling hair.

For a moment she clung to him. Then she lifted her face, and dabbed away her tears. "I'm sorry," she said. "You must think me an awful fool."

"Of course I don't," he said. "I think you're the most wonderful person I've ever met." He held her limp hand tight in both of his. "What's the matter, Sally dear?" he asked gently.

"Nothing. The – the kettle's boiling."

"Oh, blow the kettle." He lifted it down from the stove. He sat down beside Sally and concentrated on pulling up a blade of grass. "Sally," he said slowly. "I'm only a very ordinary sort of bloke. I'm not very clever. I often don't know what to do next, and I get cross and irritable. But – will you marry me?"

It was her turn to concentrate gravely on pulling up a blade of grass. Her lips parted, but she did not speak. She simply shook her head, gently and sadly.

"I love you," he pleaded.

She did not look at him, but went on shaking her head. The cattle splashed in the river. A little cloud crept up and touched the sun, and shrivelled away.

"Do you love me?" he asked.

Still she did not reply.

"Why won't you marry me, Sally?"

She opened her lips, and swallowed. "It wouldn't work," she said, speaking with difficulty. "Our worlds are poles apart. When I was a little girl I – I suppose I was fairly clever.

I won a scholarship to a grammar school. So I suppose I acquired a certain manner. I received a vague sort of education. But – " her voice broke. "I'm the type to be a Vicar's housekeeper, not a Vicar's wife."

"Why? Because you happen to have a cousin who can't read, do you mean?" This was ridiculous. He'd soon settle this nonsense.

To his surprise she said heatedly, "Because none of my family can do much more than write their own names. Because my mother lives in a little country cottage and does the Vicarage washing; because I should let you down at every turn."

He'd never heard such nonsense; but he was beginning to realize that he'd have to take it seriously. "Listen," he said earnestly. "You're behind the times. People don't think like that any more. No one cares tuppence what anybody's father was. And as for letting me down – " He laughed. "It's more likely to be the other way round."

"I'm getting hungry," she said. "I thought we'd come for a picnic."

"Not till we've settled this," he replied firmly. "Do you love me, Sally? That's all that matters."

She looked down. "No," she said quietly. "I don't love you, John."

He picked up the kettle, and put it back on the primus. "I'm sorry," he said. "Then there's nothing more to say, is there."

She said: "No. There's nothing more to say."

They ate their lunch, slowly, as though the sandwiches would choke them. They said little. As soon as they had finished, they stood up and began to clear away the remains of the meal. A swan, white and wonderful, sailed up to investigate, and they threw bread on the water for him. He ran his painted beak over the surface like a vacuum cleaner, and sucked in the bread, and drifted away, a white-sailed galleon. They watched him go. "Lovely, isn't he," said John making strained conversation. "They say they're monogamous."

"Yes," she said. "They keep to the same mate all through their lives."

They watched the bird until it disappeared round the bend of the river. Then, neither knowing how it happened, they were in each other's arms, and he was kissing her lips and murmuring her name. "So you do love me, after all," he said.

"Yes. Oh, yes. Of course I do. I've loved you from the first day I saw you." She sighed. "But I won't marry you. It wouldn't be fair to either of us."

He laughed now. "Oh, yes, you will. I'm going to wear you down. I shall ring you up every day until you say yes."

"I shan't, John," she said seriously.

"Rubbish! Come on, let's leave the things here and go for a walk." He was like a schoolboy in his happiness. They set off, in the quiet afternoon sunshine, his arm about her waist, her head on his shoulder. At last they returned, and he picked up the basket and they went back to the car. He drove gaily to the main road, and they joined the tired, irritable stream of returning traffic. Into the setting sun they crawled, and when eventually they turned in at the gates of the Towers there was a sudden peace. He stopped the car in the drive, beside a little arbour, and switched off the engine. Neither of them spoke. At last: "Thank you for a lovely day," she said, "I shall always remember it."

He laughed. "You sound as though it were our last."

"It is," she said. "We mustn't meet again, John."

"You forget that I've asked you to marry me, and that you've said you love me."

"But I'm not going to marry you."

"Oh don't be so exasperating," he cried. "You weren't like this before that ridiculous business at the garden party. Do you really want to spoil both our lives, just because your cousin broadcast the fact that he couldn't read?"

She opened the car door and got out. She held out her hand. "Don't be cross, John," she pleaded. "Goodbye."

He left the car and took her arm, and walked with her towards the house. Inside the arbour, where Beefy had taken Lizzie so that she could rest her hot feet, inside the arbour they had heard every word. Beefy's face was burning painfully. He looked down at his boots. So he'd made Sally ashamed of him. He'd let her down. On account of him she couldn't marry the Vicar. He didn't want her to marry the Vicar, but he didn't want her not to if she wanted to. And now she couldn't, anyway, on account of he'd let her down. He'd got to do something about this. He'd got to think.

Lizzie broke the heavy, troubled silence. "We better be going," she said gently.

"Yes," agreed Beefy sadly. "We better be going." Together they trudged back along the Leicester Road.

Beefy did not sleep that night. He lay awake with his shame, and by the time the dawn showed grey through the fanlight he had realized that there was only one thing for him to do. He must leave Danby. With him out of the way people would soon forget that she had a cousin what couldn't read. Then she could marry the Vicar and live happy ever after.

But it was a hard decision. It meant leaving so much. He wouldn't see Sally again, or the boys, or Lord Wapentake. He would lose the first real job he had ever had. Even his roll of linoleum and his hassock would have to be left behind. Or would they? In the cold, discouraging light of dawn he decided on action. He could do no other. He owed it to Sally.

Quietly he slipped out of bed. He picked up his precious roll of linoleum and his hassock. He tiptoed to the door, and took one last, long look at the familiar room. The boys were snoring as one man. Heck lay on his stomach, a lock of black hair across his forehead. Beefy swallowed. Then, the linoleum over his shoulder, the hassock in his hand, he descended the ladder, went out into the quiet greyness of Rockefeller Avenue, and made his way towards the Leicester Road and to a future unfriendly and unknown.

About the same time the Vicar awoke, and thought immediately of Sally; of her loveliness, and of how he had kissed her, and of the quiet, troubled day they had spent beside the river. Surely she couldn't mean this nonsense about refusing to marry him! He fought an impulse to ring her up and ask her. He must wait for a more civilized hour. Nine-thirty, he decided, was the first possible moment that he could telephone.

The minutes dragged slowly by, while Danby came to life and greeted another blue day with its usual loathing. Bank holiday was over; the hills, the river and the sea were put away until Easter. Ahead lay work, and winter, with only Christmas, like a lighted tree, shining through the gloom.

Nine-thirty. John Adams, having prepared and eaten a lonely breakfast, sat in his study and reached nervously for the telephone. He dialled the number of the Towers.

Sally's voice answered. "John here," he said. "Will you marry me?"

He heard a sigh at the other end. Then she said, "John, you mustn't ring me up again, please."

"I'm going to ring you twice a day until you promise to marry me."

"Then I shall give my notice to Lady Wapentake and go home."

"I shall follow you."

She sighed again. "It wouldn't be any use. My mind's quite made up, John. Goodbye."

"Wait," he cried, "wait," and heard the telephone go dead at the other end. Frantically he dialled the number again. There was no reply.

What now, he thought. There must be an answer. But, short of dragging her to the altar by the hair, he couldn't think of one. Wearily he came back to earth, and with part of his mind still on Sally began to work on the question of the new church hall.

Another builder had taken over from Mr Coldbarrow. The work was going ahead, and in a month's time the Bishop was coming to lay the foundation stone. This time there must be no mistake. John Adams had put his Lordship off once, and his Lordship was not a man to be treated lightly. Brisk and efficient himself, he expected his parish priests to be the same. Imagination boggled at what he would say to a second postponement.

But there wasn't going to be a second postponement. This new chap was getting on with the job. After all, other people had built church halls, though sometimes during the past few months he had wondered how. And if other people could, so could St Jude's. John Adams stuck out his jaw, and settled down to his correspondence.

By this time Beefy, well on his way, was beginning to wonder whether he had not acted precipitately. His feet hurt, the linoleum was unwieldy, and swayed in the breeze, and the hassock was a most awkward burden. Policemen in the villages through which he passed looked at him with considerable interest.

He was overcome by a great sadness, being haunted by the memory of the church hall loft, seeing, in his imagination, the boys leaving it in the morning sunlight, and returning to its quietness in the evening. He thought of his cottage at Shepherd's Delight, and of how, if he kept on giving up jobs like this, he'd never be able to save enough money for it. Sally came into his mind. She would marry that Vicar, and live happy ever after, and they would both forget Beefy, and never know the sacrifice he had made for them. He was nearly in tears.

His mind went through the processes that, for him, passed for thought. Had he done any good by coming away like this? Suppose Sally still refused to marry the Vicar? Perhaps he should have told her he was leaving Danby for ever. Then she would have known that he would soon be forgotten. But now, for all she knew, he might turn up again any day, and spoil everything. Another dreadful thought struck him. Perhaps Lord Wapentake and the police would think he really had tried to pinch them jewels, and was running away. In that case they'd be after him.

To his horror he heard a fast car approaching. Cops! He panicked, and would have dived into safety. But the road was bounded by wire fences, which afforded no cover. He began to run, aimlessly, like a rabbit caught in headlights. The car was slowing down. They *were* after him, and there was no escape. He turned an anguished face to the car. Already, in his mind's eye, he saw that judge being cross again.

"Why, if it isn't old Beefy," cried a pleased voice. "We was looking for you, Beefy."

He stood, blinking, and clutched the swaying linoleum. It took him some moments to grasp the situation. Then his face lit up. He cried, "Why, Heck! Peg Leg! Lofty! What you doing here?"

"Get in," said Peg Leg. They helped him into the back seat. The linoleum was a problem. At last they opened the sunshine roof and stuck it through. "Lucky we borrowed a car with a sunshine roof," said Lofty.

"We been all the way to Nottingham looking for you," said Peg Leg.

"*And* all the way to Birmingham," Lofty added.

"Ida's just the tiniest bit hurt, you walking out like that," Peg Leg warned. Beefy felt his stomach give a lurch. He didn't like people being hurt on account of him. It made them cross.

Heck came down to business. "What the hell you playing at, going off like that?" he inquired.

This, Beefy realized, was not a question to which there was any clear-cut answer. And the fact that Heck sounded cross sent his thoughts whirring away like startled birds.

"I was going away," he began.

"Why?" asked Heck, turning the car round in the road.

"I got to go away," said Beefy. "I – I don't want to come back."

Heck snorted, and put his foot down on the accelerator. They leapt for Danby. Peg Leg said consolingly, "You come and have a nice quiet talk with Ida, Beefy. She'll soon straighten out any trouble."

It was nice to think of going back where he belonged. There he'd been thinking till it hurt of the boys in the loft, all together, and him not there. And now he was going to be there, after all. Just couldn't help himself, it seemed. Then he remembered Sally, and how she wanted to marry the Vicar, and couldn't on account of Beefy was her shame. He sighed. "I got to go away," he repeated. "It's on account of my cousin, see."

"What about your cousin?" asked Heck, unwrapping a piece of gum.

233

"She wants to marry the Vicar, but she can't on account of I'm her cousin and Vicars can't marry people what's got cousins like me," Beefy explained with astonishing lucidity.

There were tears in Peg Leg's eyes. "So you were going away, Beefy," he said quietly. "You was going away rather than be an embarrassment to your cousin."

Heck said, "A director of a company can't just walk out for reasons of sentiment. He's got responsibilities."

"I ain't got no responsibilities," Beefy said unhappily.

"But you have, Beefy." Peg Leg took up the argument. "We all have. Maybe you ain't the brains of the Company," he conceded. "But you got your part to play, a very important part. And if you ain't there to play it, well, the Company just ceases to function."

"You mean – you mean if I wasn't there it wouldn't work no more?"

"Course it wouldn't. The Company would go into – what would the company go into if Beefy wasn't there, Heck?"

"Perishing liquidation," said Heck, spitting neatly out of the window.

Beefy gazed at his boots with a pleased expression. "Huh! You're kidding," he said, hoping they would say that they weren't.

They did. "Course we ain't kidding," Lofty said reassuringly.

Beefy beamed. Then he remembered Sally. "But what about my cousin?" he asked.

"Don't you worry about her," Peg Leg said. "Ida'll fix that. Ida would get her married to the Archbishop of Canterbury if she wanted to."

By this time they were in the outskirts of Danby. Heck drove them straight to Ida's hotel. "I'll take the car away, and lose it," he said. "You boys go on up with Beefy."

234

They unshipped the linoleum and the hassock, and went up to Ida's room. Beefy was suddenly nervous. Ida was hurt. She'd be cross with him. But there was no escape now. They knocked, and went in.

Ida, in a brilliant green and red kimono, went on polishing her nails. At last, after an awful silence, she looked up and scowled.

"So you found him, did you," she said. "Beefy," she snapped. "I'm just about tired of all this. I pick you up from the gutter, I try to make an honest criminal of you, I appoint you a director of this Company, and what happens?"

"I – I don't know," stammered the wretched Beefy.

"No?" Ida's face was furious. "Then I'll tell you. As soon as my back's turned you start trying to go straight. You get yourself saved. You meet an Earl, and instead of using him you let him exploit you by giving you an honest job. And then, to crown everything, you simply walk out on your friends and fellow directors." She quivered with rage. "Have you no moral sense at all?"

She glared at the crimson Beefy. She was deeply hurt. If it were not for the principle of the thing she would have let him go hang. But she couldn't stand on one side and see a good man seduced by respectability. Besides, there was the Company. It was her life's work to hold that together. Great things remained to be done. True, they hadn't been terribly successful so far. Teething troubles, she told herself. All companies had them. But with her brains, and the loyal co-operation of her lieutenants, they would yet conquer. If, that is, her directors didn't go wandering off down the primrose path of respectability.

This outburst reduced Beefy to an incoherent jelly. There was so much he wanted to say. Everything could be explained, if only he could find the words. He opened his dry mouth. "I – I wasn't going straight," he stammered.

"Leastways I was, only I wasn't when I went away. Leastways, I didn't went on account of I was going straight."

He was sweating profusely. He wished Ida would stop glaring at him. But those cold, angry eyes continued to bore into him. "Why," demanded Ida, "did you clear off in the middle of the night?"

But Beefy's mind was trailing after another line of thought. "You said once it was all right if I did go straight," he remembered.

"Don't prevaricate," snapped Ida, banging her dressing table with a hairbrush.

Beefy, feeling more and more hopeless, swallowed. He didn't think he was explaining things very well. "I didn't went on account of I was going straight," he said. "I went on account of my cousin, see."

"What abut your cousin?"

"She wants to marry the Vicar."

Ida's patience was becoming exhausted. "I see. Your cousin wants to marry the Vicar. So you get up in the middle of the night and take your bed and go off without a word to anyone." She turned to Peg Leg and Lofty. "Does that make sense to you boys? Am I getting dim in my old age?"

To Beefy's immense relief Peg Leg said, "Beefy was being noble and self-sacrificing, Ida. He thought the Vicar couldn't marry his cousin if he was around, him being low in the social scale, see. So – he went."

Ida was unmoved. "Just the tomfool sort of thing he would do, too," she said. "I suppose loyalty to the Company can go hang so long as Beefy's friends and relations are all right."

"I didn't think anybody would miss me," said Beefy.

"As a matter of fact, I told him that if he came back you'd fix it so that his cousin could marry the Vicar," Peg Leg said.

It was his turn to receive Ida's withering glance. She jabbed the dressing table savagely with a nail file. "How many times do I have to remind you boys that I'm your chairman, not your grandmother?" she demanded. "I'm your Brain. Not a matrimonial agency."

"Beefy might settle down more comfortable, like, if his cousin was happily married," Peg Leg said.

Despite her irritation, Ida saw his point. A good general knew that the morale of his men was of the utmost importance. Yes, she decided reluctantly, it was her job to try to help in this matter. "Tell me about your cousin, Beefy," she said in a more kindly tone.

"She wants to marry the Vicar," said Beefy.

Ida gazed at him with mingled astonishment and fury. "I know that, you great oaf," she roared. "Tell me what I can do about it."

Beefy was disappointed. It was no good asking him things like that. He wasn't a Brain. "I thought you'd of knowed," he said miserably. "Peg Leg said you could marry her to the – the Archbishop of Canterbury if she wanted, only she don't want that. She wants to marry the Vicar."

The chairman's eyes narrowed. She ran her fingers along the edge of her nail file as though it were a dagger. "Beefy," she said quietly, "if you tell me once more that she wants to marry the Vicar I will not be responsible for my actions." She appealed to Peg Leg Evans. "Peg, what can we do?"

"Knock-out Drops," Peg Leg said promptly. "Reckon you can't beat Knock-out Drops."

"Taken in water?" asked Ida.

"Taken in water," said Peg Leg. They looked at each other knowingly. They nodded. "Draw up a detailed scheme and submit it to me before Sunday," Ida commanded. "And march this defaulter back to barracks. And if he tries to escape again, shoot." She had second thoughts. "No, dammit, give him his train fare to Land's End. I've had enough."

"Thanks, Ida," Beefy said humbly. Fancy, the chairman of the Company, going to all this trouble just to help him. He was very, very grateful. And that evening, as he carried his linoleum and his hassock up the ladder, and saw the dear old loft, filled with his dear old friends, his eyes were wet with tears.

Chapter 18

The Reverend John Adams was not sleeping well. He was worried, and frustrated. He was in love, and never saw the beloved, except in church on Sundays. He daren't ring her up, in case she went away as he had threatened. There must be some way, he kept telling himself, some way to make her forget this nonsense and marry him. It would be so wonderful to be married to Sally; he'd do everything to make her happy. He imagined her, filling the great, gaunt Vicarage with her freshness, smiling at him across the dinner table, cooking for him in the big kitchen. There must be some way, he repeated sadly.

He was also worried and nervous about the building scheme, for the laying of the foundation stone was fixed for September.

And September came, golden and mellow, with a flutter of falling leaves. The swallows began to spend long hours sitting on the telephone wires outside the Vicarage, studying imaginary maps, listening to imaginary weather forecasts, arguing about routes, and navigation, and wind speeds. The sun crept southwards, and the chrysanthemums were a ragged glory, and everyone said it was nice to see a bit of fire these evenings.

It was a perfect day for the stone-laying ceremony. The sky was a powdery blue. The mean streets of Danby were touched with gold. One of those still, dreaming days, when all sound seems softened by distance. John Adams, robing in the vestry, the Bishop of the diocese, tall and impressive, by his side, John Adams began to feel that everything was going to be all right. From outside came the murmur of an eager, but reverent crowd. And when Mr Macmillan came in and said, "Excuse me, Vicar, but could I have a word with you?" he had no sense of disaster. "Certainly," he said. "What is it, Mr Macmillan?"

His churchwarden gestured to him to go outside. Even then, he did not suspect anything. He walked out of the vestry. "Yes?" he said, and then he saw Macmillan's face.

"Good heavens," he asked, "what's wrong?"

Mr Macmillan opened his mouth to speak, but the words did not come. First he looked as though he were going to laugh; then as though he were going to cry. Then he flapped his hands helplessly. "Oh, it's too preposterous," he said.

The Vicar felt his stomach muscles bracing themselves as for a physical blow. "What is it?" he asked. "What's preposterous?"

Macmillan took a deep breath. He said, "Look. We didn't tell you before. It seemed so ridiculous. But – well, the fact is, we've lost the foundation stone."

For a few moments the Vicar gazed at him in stupefaction. Then: "Don't be so ridiculous," he snapped. "You can't lose foundation stones." He strode out of the church, and on to the building site.

There was no foundation stone. Only a few members of the church council gazing in a lost sort of way at the place where it should have been.

John Adams felt quite ill. But he made an effort. "A foundation stone can't just disappear," he said. "Where have you looked?"

Everywhere, they told him sadly.

A foundation stone can't just disappear, John Adams assured himself again. Neither could sketch plans, he reminded himself; yet his sketch plans had never been found. Dazedly he began to walk back to the vestry. Macmillan went with him, as silent as the friends of Job.

"Mac," the Vicar asked thoughtfully. "Do you believe in the Devil?"

"No."

"Well, you should. I do. I believe in the Powers of Evil. And I'm beginning to think they're taking a special interest in our church hall."

The churchwarden put a hand on his shoulder. "It isn't the Devil, Vicar," he said kindly.

"Then who is it? Look, Mac. Every single move we've made to build this hall has been countered. It's been like playing chess against a master." He remembered something else. "And what in Heaven's name am I going to say to the Bishop?"

Macmillan considered. "You'll have to tell him the truth," he said. "I'll come with you."

The two men entered the vestry. The Bishop was looking slightly annoyed at having been left alone. "I'm quite ready, Adams," he said with a touch of impatience.

"And I'm afraid we're not, My Lord. Something very disturbing has happened. The – the foundation stone has been removed."

There was an astonished silence. The Bishop was looking far from pleased. "What on earth do you mean? You mean it isn't there?"

"It's simply disappeared. They've looked everywhere." The Vicar suddenly groaned, as though he could stand no more. "I think it's the Devil," he said wearily.

The Bishop exploded. "Don't talk such nonsense, Adams. I could think of a lot of things it might be, including downright incompetence, but it certainly isn't the Devil." He began to disrobe. John Adams looked at him in consternation. "You're disrobing, my Lord?"

He received a nasty look from his Lordship. "I'm a busy man, Adams. It takes me all my time to lay foundation stones that are there. I certainly don't propose to waste my time on those that are not."

John Adams said, "I'm most terribly sorry about this, my Lord. The whole thing is quite beyond me."

The Bishop looked at his suffering face. He softened. "Worse things have happened," he said, putting a hand on the Vicar's arm. "I've no doubt we shall get over it."

"Thank you, my Lord." They went with him to his car, and watched him drive away. Macmillan touched the Vicar's shoulder. He said, "Don't worry. He won't unfrock you."

"I don't suppose he will. But oh, Mac, I do feel a fool," John Adams said.

September wore on. Some years grow bitter and shabby before August is out. Others live out a majestic old age, building up a sweet store of golden days. So it was this year. The swallows lingered on the telephone wires, as sleek as the members of an orchestra. The sun was a golden apple in the sky, and, clustered on the trees, the apples were little golden suns. Pears, and plums, fat and luscious, vegetable marrows, cucumbers and tomatoes, all approached a climax of maturity, and the wasps, pulsating, dug into the pears, and the white butterflies fluttered lazily about the cabbages.

In the hedgerows, blackberries, shining and clean, caught the sunlight, and the bitter elders hung in gleaming clusters from their shoddy branches, and the hazelnuts were there for the gathering. All was ripeness, and ripeness was all.

The sun, drifting ever southward down the sky, like a burning boat on a summer sea, peered through the Vicarage windows where the Vicar sat, pining for Sally. It even managed to send a tiny shaft into Lizzie Tubb's dark little kitchen, where Lizzie was telling herself that the pain wasn't really any worse than it had been in July. It was just that she noticed it more. The sunlight lay on the floor of the church hall loft, and threw into sharp relief the wording on a stone that lay there: "This stone was laid by the Lord Bishop of the Diocese, September – " It was spread like butter over the rolling, devastated acres of the Towers, where Lord Wapentake and Beefy had discovered a new delight: bonfires.

They were burning everything in sight. The blue smoke climbed up briskly to the blue heavens, and the flames leapt, and crackled, and died, and the smell of the smoke was the smell of all the autumns that have ever been. Sometimes Beefy saw Sally, pale and sad-looking, and he knew why she was pale and sad-looking. It was on account of she wanted to marry the Vicar. But he didn't like to say anything about it, so he would just say, "Hello, Sally", in a kindly voice, and she'd look pleased and say, "Hello, Beefy, how's the gardening?" and she would go on her way. Wisht Ida and the boys would do something, Beefy thought. Ida had promised to get Sally married to the Vicar, so he knew it would be all right eventually. And they were working on it, because they'd asked him some funny questions, such as whether Sally always went to church on Sunday evening, and whether the Vicar ever had a drink to help him on with his sermons.

It was taking a long time, however, and Beefy began to grow despondent. He didn't like to see Sally pale and sad-looking, and yet the only cure was for her to marry the Vicar and Beefy didn't want her to marry the Vicar, not really, on account of – well, on account of he didn't quite know what, but he just didn't. Winter, too, was coming, and the long darkness of winter, and so was the time when they were going to sell the church hall to a factory, and the boys would be scattered, and Beefy would be homeless. And Shepherd's Delight was far away, as far away as ever. Beefy shivered. Despite the lovely autumn days, winter, and the long darkness of winter, lurked in the folds of the valleys, it lurked in the mist of morning and the dusk of evening.

Throughout September the teeming earth had been moving to a climax of maturity. Now the climax was reached, and all over England the kindly fruits of the earth were being borne into churches, into cathedrals and tiny chapels, into great minsters and remote shrines, there to be blessed.

Everyone agreed that the Church of St Jude the Obscure was a picture. Shocks of corn stood about the pulpit; and the lectern eagle, surrounded by flaming beech leaves, was like a phoenix rising from the fire. The rough, robust flowers of autumn were everywhere, chrysanthemums, bronze and white and yellow, Michaelmas daisies, dahlias, many-coloured. The altar steps, as Lord Wapentake unkindly remarked, looked like a high-class fruiterer's, with peaches and pears, and pomegranates, plums and oranges, grapes and grapefruit, and the innocent apple, the fruit of youth, that yet is popularly supposed to have started all the trouble, so long ago in Eden.

The minute bell was ringing now, and people were still pouring in. The organ played, and the sidesmen, in a reverent scurry, brought out extra chairs, while a choirboy, in black cassock, fetched the processional cross, and another hung out the hymn boards. It was the first time this autumn that the lights had been lit for evensong, and everyone felt cosy, happy, and excited. The light gleamed on brass and silver. It fell softly on leaf and fruit and flower, while on the altar, the candle flames stood up straight and still, like the spears that guarded the Cross.

The minute bell was silent. The organ was silent. The people were silent. John Adams came to the vestry door. He announced the hymn, "Come, ye thankful people, come." And the people sang, from a full heart, while the processional cross was borne, glinting and gleaming, round the church, and the sweet singing of the choir moved westward, and southward, and then a long march eastward, until it reached its home in the brightly lighted chancel.

The hymn came to an end. The people stood for the exhortation. Everyone was there. Lord Wapentake, absent-mindedly eating the grapes that festooned his pew; Lady Wapentake, trying to stop him without creating uproar; Mr Macmillan, pale and proud; Lizzie Tubb, with a grey wool cardigan over her spriggy frock; next to her Beefy, gazing wide-eyed at so much beauty, like a child gazing at a Christmas tree; next to him Sally, in her neat, navy blue costume, trying not to look too often at John Adams.

At last the time came for the Vicar to enter the pulpit. He took as his text the words of the first hymn, "Come, ye thankful people, come." He concentrated on the word "thankful". It was a subject dear to his heart. He never failed to be moved by the bringing together of God's gifts at the harvest festival. He himself possessed the thankful heart, the eye of wonder, and if he could help his congregation to share his point of view even once a year, then he would feel that he had not altogether failed.

He warmed to his subject. He had been speaking for twenty minutes now, and his throat was getting dry. He looked enviously at Lord Wapentake, munching grapes. There was a bunch hanging temptingly on the pulpit. He imagined the juicy flesh within the cool green skins. This would never do. He took up the carafe of stale, tepid water that stood at his hand. Still speaking, he poured some into the glass, sipped, sipped again. Suddenly, to his horror, the lighted church went black, began to revolve slowly. He gripped the sides of the pulpit, lost the thread of his words. He saw the congregation watching him with considerable interest. Ah, thank goodness. He could see more clearly now. The church was on an even keel again. He took another sip of water, just to steady himself, and the church spun like a teetotum. The lights whirled about him. He was at a fair, on the roundabout, going faster, faster, so fast that in the end he was flung out and away, out and away through the darkness and the plunging lights and the wheeling stars, out into the waiting silence of the night.

For a dreadful moment no one moved when John Adams fell. Then a dozen men, led by Mr Macmillan and George Bloodshot, hurried to the pulpit. They lifted the unconscious form of the Vicar down the steps, carried him to the priest's vestry, and laid him on the floor. The congregation remained seated, anxious and troubled, not knowing what to do next. Then it was given something else to think about. That nice girl who was housekeeper at the Towers stood up, pale and tense, and hurried into the vestry. Everyone's heart went with her in her grief. The men surrounding the Vicar stood aside, in silent sympathy. She fell on her knees beside him, gazed into his pale face, touched his cold brow.

Mr Macmillan said kindly, "We've tried the usual remedies, and they don't seem to work. But don't worry. We've sent for a doctor. He should be here very soon now."

"But can't you do something?" she pleaded. "Perhaps he's only fainted. It must have been the heat."

"It's something more than a faint if you ask me," said George Bloodshot comfortingly. "Our Fred used to look just like that when he had one of his turns."

Sally looked up at him piteously. "What caused it?" she asked. "In – in the case you're speaking of."

"Can't remember." He shook his head sadly. "Poor old Fred. He didn't last long." He sighed.

"Oh, be quiet, you idiot," Macmillan said angrily. He turned to Sally. "Don't worry, Miss Bryan. I'm certain it's nothing serious. The Vicar's a very healthy young man, I'm quite sure."

Sally took the Vicar's cold hand in both of hers. "I do hope you're right," she said. She looked down at the face of the unconscious man. "Oh, John, John, John," she murmured softly.

At that moment John Adams, who had lain as one dead, groaned. His eyelids fluttered. He opened his eyes, and lay staring at nothing. Sally threw her arms about him. "John, my darling. Look," she cried. "It's me, Sally."

For a long time he lay in her arms, staring at her, unseeing. Then his lips moved. He spoke her name.

She buried her face in his shoulder. "You gave me such a fright," she said. "You will get better, won't you."

"Yes," he said slowly. "Yes." Everything was very difficult to understand. There had been the accident on the roundabout; that was the last thing he could remember. And now here he was, in his own vestry, robed, being embraced by dear, darling Sally under the interested gaze of half the parochial church council. He was obviously dreaming, and, being in a dream, where nothing mattered, he asked, "Will you marry me, Sally?"

Yes, he must be dreaming, for she said, "Marry you? Of course I'll marry you, John darling. I'll do anything if you'll promise to get better and not give us such dreadful shocks." And she flung her arms tightly about him, and burst into tears of pure relief, and buried her lovely face in his white surplice. John Adams held her close, murmuring words of comfort and endearment, and hoped that this dream would go on for a long, long time.

Slowly, very slowly, he began to realize that the dream was, after all, reality. The doctor came, examined him, and assured Sally that her beloved would be as right as ninepence after a Goodnight's sleep. Then, supported by Macmillan and George Bloodshot, he was allowed to stand on the altar steps and let the people go with the blessing. Then Macmillan took him to the Bank House in his car and put him to bed, where he lay in the darkness and tried to absorb the joyful news that Sally had said she would marry him.

Sally walked home, saying to herself, "He loves me, and he's not going to die or even be ill, and I've done it now. I'm going to marry him and I don't care what happens, and I don't care what anyone says."

They extinguished the candles. They put out the lights in the church. The people left, slowly, reluctantly, little groups standing at each street corner, loath to break away, hungrily sucking every drop of emotion and excitement and drama out of the events of the harvest festival. And throughout the evening the news spread like a forest fire through the parish; men, taking their dogs for a walk, met other men, and passed it on; one tongue brought it to the Poet and Peasant, and a hundred tongues bore it away; women slipped out to the dustbin, and whispered to neighbours, emptying the teapot at the drain; the news went running and scuttling down a thousand telephone wires; the news that the Vicar, at death's door, had proposed to Sally in the vestry, and had been joyfully accepted.

The parish was delighted. The Vicar was popular, and they liked Sally. She's all right, they said; you can tell she's educated, they said, but she ain't got an ounce of side. Laughs and talks to you just like one of ourselves. And that funny cousin of hers! It was going to be nice and homely having a Vicar's wife whose cousin was as ignorant as oneself. A nice change from the days of Mrs Tumble, who had a viscount for a cousin, or so she said, and never let you forget it.

The Vicar recovered quickly from his Knock-out Drops, and went about the Vicarage singing cheerful selections from Hymns A. and M. at the top of his voice. At the first opportunity he drove Sally into Birmingham and bought her the most beautiful engagement ring that either of them had ever seen, and took her out to lunch, and allowed himself to be dragged round the shops, and then drove her home through the blue mists of a still September evening.

"When shall we marry? Next week?" he asked.

"Don't be silly," she laughed. "Why, we hardly know each other. Let's get married in the springtime."

"Darling, I want to marry you tomorrow. I'm tired of cooking my own breakfast."

"Silly." She laid her head on his shoulder. "Spring will be soon enough. I've got to consider Lady Wapentake for one thing."

So spring it was to be. Spring, so far away, at the other end of the tunnel of winter; but already the swallows had darted away on their long flight over the sunlit sea, and the children, going to school, scuffled their feet in the brittle leaves, and hunched their shoulders against the morning chill.

Nights grew cold in the church hall loft. Beefy dusted the cobwebs off his ginger-beer bottle, and began to fill it with hot water in the evenings. The warmth was nice, but he needed the comfort, too, for Lizzie Tubb had told him the news about the Vicar and Sally, and the news had made Beefy sad. "What's biting you?" Peg Leg asked one evening, seeing the unhappiness in Beefy's face. "You look about as cheerful as you did when you was undertaking."

"Nothing," Beefy said, stretching his face into a grin. "Nothing, really."

Peg Leg looked at him suspiciously. "You ain't going off again?" he asked.

"No. Course I ain't."

"Then what you looking so perishing miserable about?" Heck put in.

Beefy was being edged into the wrong. He began to get flustered. "It's my cousin," he said. "It's on account of she's going to marry the Vicar."

There was a shocked silence. Then: "Well, I'll be damned," Heck cried. "You hear that, boys. There's the serpent's tooth for you."

Beefy looked worried. He wondered what serpents had got to do with it. But now Peg Leg was taking up the accusations. "First we get rid of that housekeeper at the Vicarage. And are you satisfied? Oh no. Your cousin don't want the job after all. Then we risk hellfire by administering Knock-out Drops to a Vicar. And are you satisfied? No. Now it turns out you don't want your cousin to marry the Vicar."

"I do," said Beefy. "Leastways I don't want her to because I don't want her to, but I want her to on account of she wants to. See?" he added, not feeling quite sure that his audience was with him.

"Oh, shut up and go to sleep," snapped Heck.

"Heck's right," said Peg Leg. "You got that job on tomorrow, Beefy. You want to be fresh."

"Wisht I hadn't got to do it," grumbled Beefy. "Suppose something goes wrong?"

Heck sat up and pounded his mossy bank. "That's right," he said. "You like living here, of course, but when it comes to doing anything about it, then you don't want to do it."

"I don't mind that," Beefy said hastily. "I just thought – well, I ain't very clever, see, and if anything went wrong I shouldn't know what to do."

"When the chairman and me have organized anything," Heck said, "things don't go wrong. Not if the executives do their stuff," he qualified.

"What's them? Executives?"

"You will be one tomorrow."

Beefy half shot out of his linoleum in his amazement. "Me? One of them?" he cried. He felt very proud. It would be nice being whatever it was. "I'll try ever so hard not to let you and Ida down, Heck," he said humbly. "And I'm ever so grateful. About the Knock-out Drops."

"You sound it," Heck said scornfully.

"I am, really. It's just that, well, she's my cousin, see, and, well, I'm sort of losing her, like."

"Go to sleep," shouted Heck.

"Sorry, Heck," Beefy said humbly. "I just wanted to say I was ever so grateful about the Knock-out Drops."

Heck rolled over, humped an aggrieved shoulder at Beefy, and gave a loud snore. Beefy decided it might be better if he tried to explain matters some other time. Soon Heck began snoring in earnest. One by one the other members joined in, until the whole orchestra swept into a crescendo of noise. But Beefy lay awake through the uproar, wondering why he didn't want Sally to marry the Vicar. He was deeply ashamed of himself. He ought to be ever so pleased. And so he was, of course, he assured himself. Very pleased.

He sighed dismally in the lonely, comfortless night.

And the Vicar, who, according to Beefy's reckoning, should have been the happiest man in the world, was also tossing and turning. Tomorrow the bishop was coming to lay that confounded stone again, and the Vicar was nervous. True, he'd got the new stone, and he'd set a strong watch of

Boy Scouts over it; but he still wasn't happy. Too many things had gone wrong with this church hall. He'd be very, very thankful when tomorrow was over and the stone laid.

He had another worry. The Bishop was coming to the Vicarage for lunch; and what on earth, John Adams wondered, did a bachelor incumbent give a bishop to eat. It was a very serious question. And there was but one answer, he decided: ham, tongue and salad.

"I'd better have a good breakfast today," the Bishop said, a few hours later. "I'm lunching with young Adams, and it's certain to be ham, tongue and salad."

His wife said, "Poor boy, I do hope he hasn't mislaid the foundation stone this time."

"I'll drum him out of the diocese if he has," said his Lordship. He helped himself to another fried egg. "How *does* one lose a foundation stone?" Suddenly he laughed. "You know, I wouldn't tell poor Adams, but actually it did make rather a refreshing change."

Bishop and Bishop's wife looked at each other gravely over the breakfast table. They smiled. They chuckled. "Who'd be a parish priest?" said his Lordship. He picked up the *Daily Telegraph*. He remembered something. "I wonder if you'd ask Simpson to bring the car round at twelve-fifteen," he said to his wife.

At twelve-thirty John Adams panicked. No mustard. He had just been congratulating himself on a well-laid luncheon table. Then he noticed that there was no mustard pot. He hurried into the kitchen. The tin was empty.

The Bishop was not due until twelve-forty-five. He dashed down to Mrs Hickman's little shop, past the site of the new hall, where he was relieved to see the Scouts keeping untroubled guard, met someone whose parish magazine had been delivered three days late and who needed placating, waited in Mrs Hickman's shop while four children decided what to buy, sympathized about Mrs Hickman's sciatica, and finally galloped home, clutching a tin of mustard, at twelve-forty-four.

To his immense relief the Bishop's car had not yet arrived. He dashed in, mixed the mustard, and stood by to open the door to his Lordship.

Time passed. No Lordship. One o'clock came, one-thirty, two. The Vicar wasn't terribly concerned that the Bishop hadn't managed lunch; but the stone-laying ceremony was at two-thirty. Surely there were not going to be any more snags! He wondered whether he ought to ring up the Palace.

Ten minutes later he knew he ought to. He dialled the number.

The Bishop's wife answered. Yes, the Bishop had left at twelve-fifteen. She herself had told Simpson, that was the chauffeur, to bring the car round. She certainly hadn't seen the Bishop get into the car, but as a matter of fact she had just caught sight of the Austin turning out of the drive. Yes, he certainly intended to have lunch with Mr Adams. She was really rather worried. If he did arrive would Mr Adams be so good as to give her a ring? Yes, she would make what inquiries she could.

John Adams put the telephone down. Two-fifteen. He daren't go to see whether the bishop was on the site, in case he turned up at the Vicarage. He would have to wait here. Then he had an idea. He telephoned Mr Macmillan.

"Mac," he said. "Will you do something for me? Go down to the site as soon as possible?"

"What's happened?" Macmillan's voice, untroubled and amused, came over the wires. "Don't tell me we've lost another stone."

John Adams said shortly, "No. We've lost the Bishop."

There was a snort of laughter from the other end. "You're getting jumpy, Vicar," said Macmillan. "He'll be at the church, robing. I'll go and have a look for you."

The Vicar put the telephone down. Immediately it rang again. "I thought I'd better let you know," said the Bishop's wife. "Something rather serious has happened."

"Oh, I am sorry. I do hope – not an accident?"

"No. But we've just found Simpson in the garage. All tied up with rope and with a bit of oily rag in his mouth."

The Vicar's heart sank. "Have you told the police?"

"Of course."

"Does your chauffeur know who tied him up?"

"No idea. Apparently it was done very expertly, from behind."

"I'll come straight over," said John Adams. He ran his little car out of the garage, and drove to the Palace, pausing only to call out to the waiting crowds, at the church hall, "The ceremony is postponed. The Bishop has been unavoidably detained." He would have liked to add, "And if anyone still wants the church hall they can jolly well take the job over; because I've had about as much as I can stand."

But he kept his defeatism to himself.

The Bishop was due to leave at twelve-fifteen. At twelve-fourteen he was ready. He glanced out of the window. The car was waiting in the drive, with Simpson, in peaked cap and blue mackintosh, at the wheel. The Bishop walked towards the door. And at that moment the telephone rang.

He hesitated; but his secretary was away for the day. There was nothing for it but to answer it himself.

The call was an important one. By the time he put the receiver down it was nearly half past twelve, and if there was one thing the Bishop hated it was unpunctuality. He almost ran out of the house, and noted with displeasure that

Simpson, instead of holding the car door open for him, was still at the wheel. He'd have something to say about that later, though as a matter of fact it would save a few seconds. He wrenched the car door open and hurried into the back seat. "Don't waste any time, Simpson," he said. "We're late."

Simpson said nothing, but they shot out of the drive at about fifty miles an hour, and took the Danby road at the same speed. His Lordship's mind was busy with the recent telephone call, but he saw with satisfaction that they seemed to be breaking all records for the run to Danby. Only ten miles now, seven, five, three. Soon they would be in the suburbs.

And then, with a squeal of tyres, the car suddenly swung off the Danby road into a lane. "Simpson, where are you going?" his Lordship cried.

Simpson did not reply. The car went faster. The Bishop grasped the front seat and pulled himself forward. For the first time he had looked at Simpson. There was something unfamiliar about those thick shoulders. The Bishop stared. He was not a man to acknowledge fear, but he felt a touch of horror when he realized that he was being driven by a complete stranger. "Stop! At once," he cried, in the voice that he used for quelling archdeacons.

He did not quell Beefy. Beefy kept his foot on the accelerator. "It's all right, Mister," he said soothingly. "There ain't nothing to be frightened about. We're just going to ride round till it's too dark to lay foundation stones."

"You will stop immediately," ordered the Bishop.

Beefy went faster.

His Lordship sat back and considered. The car had come on to a main road now, and was heading north at an alarming speed, away from the towns, out into the open country. Clearly it would be foolhardy to try to overcome the driver while travelling so quickly. The only thing was to wait until they came to some form of traffic control, lights, or policemen, and then act quickly and decisively.

But the driver had obviously thought along the same lines. Whenever they seemed to be approaching a town he would swing off into the lanes; but always the nose of the car would come back to the north, away from Danby, while the Bishop's watch ticked inexorably on.

Then, at last, his Lordship was filled with hope. They were on a long straight road, and half a mile ahead he saw a beautiful sight: a level crossing with closed gates, and a goods train lumbering peacefully across the road.

They drew nearer. The driver began to slow down. The Bishop, peering ahead, felt sure there were no side roads. He grasped the door handle, ready to jump out as soon as the car had slowed down sufficiently. And then, to his horror, he saw the guard's van move across the road. The gates began to open. There was just room for the car to slip through now. Beefy accelerated. They went through, scraping one wing of the episcopal Austin. The Bishop sank back on his seat, exhausted with emotion. The car swept on.

There must be an answer, the Bishop thought. But what? He looked at his watch. Two o'clock, and he must be fifty miles from Danby. He gazed ahead. They were in a pretty lane, but he had no eye for natural beauty at the moment. Some way ahead, a man was opening a gate into a field. Slowly and nonchalantly a cow wandered out into the road. Another, and another. Soon the lane was full of cows. Frantically Beefy sounded his horn. The cows gazed at him with mild surprise. The man leaned on the gate. The car was slowing down now. It had to. Cows were all around it. The Bishop grasped the door handle, and pushed. Nothing happened. There was a cow pressed against the door. He leapt out at the other side. "Stop!" he shouted, but the car nosed through the herd and was away. The Bishop turned to the cowman, who eyed his gaiters with interest. "Quick!" he said. "I must have transport immediately." The man pointed to his ear. "Ain't got me hearing aid," he said helpfully.

It was five o'clock before the Bishop got back to Danby. The stone-laying ceremony had been abandoned. But he had already stirred up the police of three counties so effectively that Beefy was picked up that same evening.

Even so, the police were not satisfied. Beefy, they decided, was the leader of a gang, a gang that was responsible for all the trouble in Danby. They arrested Ida just as she was leaving for another little holiday. They collected Heck and the boys in a milk bar. Ida was furious. Getting pinched just because they'd taken a bishop for a little ride round Derbyshire! If it had been one of the really big jobs she wouldn't have minded so much. It was a risk that any Company had to take. But to slip up over the mere temporary removal of a bishop! She was livid; livid with herself as much as with her directors and the police.

The gang were found to have been responsible for most of the criminal activity in Danby during the last twelve months. When they were at last all safely put away a deep sigh of relief went up from the police; and the walls of the new church hall began to rise by leaps and bounds.

CHAPTER 19

At last the golden autumn days began to falter. Winter, tired of sending out skirmishing parties at dusk and dawn, mounted a frontal attack. It sent great winds to tear the leaves from the trees. It stretched out the black, starless nights, and drove the sun towards the southern horizon. The sodden fields turned flat and grey, and the streets of Danby glinted dully in the rain. Men helped the decay by putting back the clocks, much to the relief of Lord Wapentake, who had omitted to move his forward in the springtime, and had been in a state of bafflement ever since.

The Vicar had to put in some hard work to persuade Sally, deeply distressed by Beefy's downfall, not to break off the engagement; but he won, at last, and they settled down to a pleasant winter of hard work in the parish, and occasional quiet dinners, and dances, and visits to the theatre.

Lizzie Tubb got worse. Her round moon-face fell in, and her eyes behind the pebble glasses grew big and dark, and her hands waxy and transparent. The winter wore on, plunging into a pit of darkness; and then, just when everything seemed lost, the change came, and the colour crept slowly back into earth and sky.

And with the coming of spring Lizzie spent more and more of her time in bed, watching the sunlight and the moonlight creep over the text on the wall, fighting against her sickness and her pain, remembering the little backyard where she had played as a child, where, it seemed now, the sun had shone without pause on the broken asphalt and the peeling paint of the coalhouse door; thinking of Fred Spragget, fat and bald, who yet had once been the loveliest of God's creatures, and had kissed Lizzie under the mistletoe on a white and spangled Christmas long ago.

Lord Wapentake looked at the untilled earth and the springing weeds, and wondered when the devil that gardening feller was coming back. He'd never heard such damned nonsense; putting a really decent feller inside just because he'd taken old Ted a little ride round. As for the little matter of tying up and gagging that feller Simpson; Lord Wapentake would have liked to do more than that. Simpson had worked for him once, till his Lordship sacked him, and binding and gagging was nothing to what the feller really deserved. In fact, the old gentleman had astonished the court, and risked both a charge of perjury *and* the Wrath to Come, by asserting that he himself had instructed his chauffeur to go and give old Ted a bit of a run round, since old Ted, in Lord Wapentake's opinion, was looking a bit peaky and needed some fresh air.

And, when the yellow daffodils bobbed and curtsied in the yellow sunlight, John Adams took his lovely dark-haired bride to the white, soaring cathedral church of the diocese, and there the Bishop married them, before the great high altar of God, and sent them out into the world again with his most willing blessing. John, coming out of the cathedral into the sudden sunlight, his new wife on his arm, murmured to himself, "My cup runneth over." Nothing mattered now. Sally was his wife, unbelievable though it seemed; and together they could face anything that man and the Devil could devise.

It was an April evening, when the rain fell soft and warm on the roofs of Danby, and the trees stood absolutely motionless, only a leaf jerking occasionally at the fall of a raindrop; it was an April evening, quiet, unutterably sad, when Beefy came home.

He was a remorseful and shaken Beefy. His happy, peaceful little world had fallen about his ears. He was alone, and frightened. The judge had been even crosser than the first time. Beefy had felt himself blushing furiously while he was being sentenced, and he didn't like blushing in front of people. It made him feel silly. And he couldn't really see why they'd sent him to prison. After all, Lord Wappitake had told them that he'd asked Beefy to take that Bishop for a nice ride. They ought to have believed Lord Wappitake. If people didn't believe a lord, Beefy felt dimly, the Constitution was threatened and the gates were thrown open to anarchy and chaos.

But sentenced him they had; and here he was, months later, a free man, but not knowing what had happened to his friends, his cousin, his roof, or his bed. Had Ida and the boys also been caught, and locked up? Had Sally cut herself off from him forever by marrying the Vicar? Had the church hall, despite Heck's delaying tic-tacs, at last become a factory? Beefy wondered, and feared, as the grey rain fell upon his head.

His fears were justified. When he came into Rockefeller Avenue, the first thing he saw was a big notice outside the church hall, together with piles of bricks, and sand, and timber, all wet and depressing under the April rain. The door through which he had passed so many times was boarded up. Beefy felt that sickening shock of incredulity when the thing long-dreaded really comes to pass. The nearest approach to a home that he had known for many years was destroyed. He had become, in that moment of looking, a homeless wanderer, cut off from his friends, unable to make contact with those who might help him.

He stood for a long time, his lower lip thrust out, staring at the notice, at the builders' materials, at the ruins of his home. The rain tickled his nose, and ran down his neck, and soaked persistently through his thin clothes. He did not notice. "What they want a factory for?" he muttered sulkily. "What they want to go and turn it into a factory for?" Then a watchman came out, and gave him a suspicious look. Beefy shambled off.

Still, he had one friend left. Lizzie Tubb. She'd give him a cup of tea, perhaps, and let him dry his clothes a bit before he had to face the coming night. He hurried away, frightened lest the watchman follow him and make trouble, and went up the entry and into Lizzie's yard, and knocked on the back door.

He stood there, under the sad sky, and waited. The dog barked, but no one came to the door. His heart sank. Lizzie was out. His one friend was not there to take him in. He daren't go up to the Towers. They wouldn't want him there; and Sally was probably married, anyway. He knocked again, hopelessly. The dog gave another bark, more from a sense of duty than in anger, and was silent. Beefy was just turning away when he thought he heard something, a slow shuffling. Hope sprang up in his heart. He heard the drawing of bolts, the turning of a key. The door opened a crack. Lizzie, an old coat over her nightdress, stood there peering. She looked funny without her pebble glasses. Beefy hardly recognized her. "They've took it for a factory," he said.

"Why, it's Beefy," she said, unsmiling. "Are you coming in?"

He stepped into the remembered kitchen. Whitey sniffed at his legs. "I'm going back to bed," Lizzie said. "I ain't been well. You'll have to come and talk to me up there if you want to. Just give me time to get into bed." She saw Beefy's eyes turning to the teapot. "You can make us a cup of tea if you like. Be nice."

She heaved herself up the creaking stairs. Beefy put the kettle on the flicker of fire. He found two mugs and put them on the table. It was nice in the kitchen, quiet and peaceful like. At last the kettle began to boil. He made the tea. On the table was an opened tin of condensed milk, with a spoon embedded in the milk. He put a spoonful in each mug, filled up with tea, carried the mugs upstairs.

Lizzie was sitting up in bed, slewed round uncomfortably on one elbow. She looked as though she couldn't find an easy position. Without teeth and glasses she seemed naked. Beefy felt embarrassed. "I brought you some tea," he said, to hide his shyness.

"That's nice," she said. "I been wanting a cup of tea." She took the mug in a trembling hand and drank noisily. She gave him the empty mug and lay back on the pillow. "I feel better for that," she said.

There was silence; only the soft fall of the rain in the street, the angry ticking of the alarm clock, Lizzie's painful breathing. Beefy didn't know what to say. He had had very little experience of sick visiting. As last he inquired, "What happened to the boys? You know, Heck and that lot."

Lizzie turned her head slowly and looked at him. Her processes, never quick, were slowing down. She absorbed the question, found an answer with difficulty, and with difficulty enunciated it. "They was copped," she said.

Beefy groaned. Lizzie gathered her strength to pass on further news. "That cousin of yours got married last week," she said. "They was supposed to be coming back from the honeymoon today."

Beefy did not hear these words with surprise, but suddenly he saw his little dream cottage at Shepherd's

Delight, and he was there, and Emily his pig, and the red curtains were drawn against the night, all just as he had hoped for and longed for and imagined; yet the vision was dust and ashes, and that future Beefy, like Beefy present, was lonely and forlorn. Then he saw St Jude's Vicarage, and the Vicar, pen in hand, seated at a desk, while Sally stood behind and ruffled his hair. Imagined laughter filled the dusk-laden bedroom in Rockefeller Avenue, and Beefy knew the pain and the loneliness, but not the anger, of jealousy.

"He's been good to me, the Vicar has," Lizzie mumbled on. "Ever so good. Begged and prayed of me to go into hospital before they went off and got married." She almost managed to laugh. "But they wasn't getting me into no hospital."

"You'd of been comfortable," Beefy said, looking at the tousled bed.

"I'm comfortable here, thank you. Or I should be, if it wasn't for this pain. Sally used to come in every day before they got married. She was good. And she wanted to arrange for someone to come in and tidy up every day while she was away. But I wasn't having anybody in but her. Oo, she has been good."

"She was good to me too," said Beefy. "At the trial. They both were. You wouldn't believe."

Silence fell in the darkening room. Suddenly the street lamps were switched on, and the light shone into the room, onto the drab, ancient wallpaper; on to the flaking ceiling; onto the honeysuckle and clematis that wove about "Be Strong and of a Good Courage".

Beefy looked up at the text. "That's nice," he said. "It's pretty."

Lizzie dragged herself onto one elbow so that she could see it. She gazed at it long and thoughtfully. "Yes," she said. "It's nice. I've always liked that. It's company like."

"Them flowers are nice, crawling about the letters," Beefy said, pleased to have found a subject of conversation.

Lizzie seemed to reach a sudden decision. "I want you to have that, Beefy, if anything happens to me."

Beefy was deeply touched. "Me? Have that?" He remembered something. "I ain't got nowhere to hang it," he said sadly. He was very upset. It would have looked ever so nice over his roll of linoleum, and now it was too late.

But Lizzie said fiercely, "I want you to have it. It's yours, see. If anything happens to me, tell 'em it's yours, see."

"It's nice," Beefy looked at it appreciatively. "What's it say?"

" 'Bless This House'," said Lizzie.

"That's nice. I like that. 'Bless This House'," he muttered. It would be a nice thing to hang in his lonely cottage at Shepherd's Delight when, at last, he came there. Make it sort of peaceful and homely.

He came back to earth. He remembered that his cottage at Shepherd's Delight was miles, and years, away, and that his linoleum in the loft was gone forever. "I ain't got nowhere to sleep," he said. "They've took it for a factory."

"You better sleep in the kitchen. It'll have to be in a chair, or on the floor, but there's been a bit of fire. It'll be warm. And you can bring me a cup of tea in the morning."

"Oo, thanks, Lizzie," Beefy said, delighted by this solution to his difficulties for at least one night. He went downstairs, and slept on the floor with Whitey, and in the morning he lit the fire and made some tea, and took a mug up to Lizzie.

But Lizzie had drunk her last mug of tea this side the grave. She lay bunched up on the bed, stiff, cold, untidy, ugly. All the winters of her working life she had risen early on dark, bitter mornings, so that she could work, so that she could eat; and she ate so that she could live to rise on dark, bitter mornings, and shuffle off to work harder than her body was intended to work. Why she sought to maintain this dreary cycle no one knew, or even wondered; least of all Lizzie Tubb. And now it was over. The weary soul fluttered, like a bewildered moth, back to the comfort of the Presence of God.

Beefy was flustered and frightened. He looked in horror at the still bundle on the bed. He put out a hand and touched the cold, crumpled face. "Lizzie," he whispered. "What's the matter?" But he knew what was the matter. He turned away, and lumbered downstairs. Whitey met him, tail-wagging. Beefy looked at him pityingly. "I think – I think something's happened her," he told the dog. He stood irresolute, but he had to get help from someone. He hurried to the Vicarage.

Sally opened the door. "Why, Beefy," she cried, her face lighting up. "This is a pleasant surprise." She wondered whether he were straight from prison. "Come and have some breakfast," she said.

"It's – it's Lizzie," stammered Beefy. "She's – something's happened to her. I think she's dead."

"Oh. Poor Lizzie, come in Beefy. I'll tell John."

Matters were quickly taken out of Beefy's hands. There was an inquest, for Lizzie had refused to take her illness to a doctor. The bereaved Whitey was adopted by a kindly neighbour. Enough money to bury her was found in the vase on the mantelpiece, and those who serve the dead cared for and dressed her body as none had ever cared for her in life. On a wild and gusty spring day they carried her to St Jude's, where John Adams, youthfully solemn in his wind-tossed robes, met her at the gate, and escorted her slowly into the church.

"I am the resurrection and the life," John Adams began, and Beefy, following the coffin, felt his eyes filling with tears. He had never heard or seen anything so beautiful. He couldn't understand it at all. Poor old Lizzie Tubb, in her cheap coffin; poor old Lizzie Tubb, whom nobody loved, and who went and died. And now they were weaving about her a beauty, a dignity, such as Beefy had never known. Lizzie Tubb, alive, had been no one. Dead, she was being escorted with all honour to the Gates of Heaven, to be received with trumpets.

They took her to the dreary cemetery and lowered her into the wet clay. The one floral tribute, a vast bunch of arum lilies, bought by Beefy with the last of his wages from Lord Wapentake, went with her. The earth clattered and spattered on the coffin. Beefy wept openly. Poor old Lizzie. It wasn't very nice, when you came to think of it, being dropped into a hole.

They wrapped her in clay, and sealed her off from the sunlight and the breeze of morning. Then everyone went home for tea; everyone except Beefy, who had no home, who had said a polite "no thank you" to a most pressing invitation to tea at the Vicarage, and who had heard, for the first time, the beating of the wings of the Angel of Death. With no more reason or direction than a dog wandering on a beach, Beefy set off along the Birmingham Road, slept, supperless, in an old barn, and then shambled on, breakfastless, to Birmingham.

The next months were the most miserable of Beefy's life. He got one job after another; but his employers were all men interested primarily in the making and amassing of money; impatient men, who had no time to seek out and develop Beefy's gifts, if any. They just sacked him instead. What worried Beefy was that they usually got very cross before they sacked him. Job followed job. The stone that was Beefy rolled, like Iser, rapidly, and gathered no moss. So little moss did he gather, in fact, that a September morning found him leaning over a canal bridge, his sole possession, Lizzie's text, under his arm. He was at the end of his tether. He hadn't been able to find a job for a week now; even Birmingham was beginning to know him. Naturally, his money was gone. There were nasty, jumping pains in his stomach on account of he hadn't eaten anything since breakfast yesterday morning. His clothes were damp and chilly through sleeping in a park. His mind was aggrieved. He had at last cut himself off completely from his old life of crime; he'd really gone straight; and what happened? He was painfully hungry, and just didn't know where his next meal was coming from. He was frightened and bewildered. There didn't seem to be a solution. If he didn't work he would starve, and he didn't want to starve. It already began to feel as though it would be very painful. But if no one would give him work, what then? It only left crime. But he couldn't think of a remunerative crime. He just hadn't any ideas. Without Ida and the Company to direct his efforts, he was lost.

He looked down into the black, oily waters of the canal. But that way out never occurred to him. It called for too much imagination. Instead, he ran away from his trouble. He began to think of food until the saliva ran down his stubbly chin; of fish and chips, hot and vinegary, and tasting of the hot newspaper; of sausages, doughnuts, ice creams; strong, scalding cups of tea; of everything that warmed and strengthened and comforted the belly and the soul of man. He thought of Sally, living happy ever after with that Vicar. Tears came into his eyes when he remembered Ida, and the boys, and his roll of linoleum under the sloping roof of the church hall loft. Why couldn't he have been left alone in that idyllic life? He'd been so happy. He hadn't asked for anything more. And he hadn't been doing no harm to nobody. But no. Mysterious forces that he could not understand had driven him out. The toe of Fate had taken a flying kick at his particular anthill. And here he was.

He was as helpless as a stranded whale, an upturned sheep. He did not know how to begin to help himself, and no one else was interested in coming to his rescue.

A motor boat came up the canal, chuff-chuffing smoothly between the stone banks. Beefy liked boats. In happier days he had often leaned over bridges in Danby, hoping to see one pass. This was a nice green one, newly-painted. An auburn-haired woman was at the tiller. A man with black side-whiskers reclined gracefully on a tarpaulin. The boat came nearer.

Beefy peered. He hung dangerously over the parapet the better to see. Then: "Ida!" he yelled. "Heck, it's me, Beefy."

The note of the engine changed. "Well, if it isn't old Beefy," answered Ida from the boat. She hove to. Beefy went scampering down the decaying steps that led to the canal bank. They pulled him on board.

They were all there, in the little cabin; Joe Vodka, grinning so much that you felt the top of his head might become completely detached; Peg Leg, Lofty, Willie One Eye, all beaming and saying, "If it isn't old Beefy! Fancy seeing old Beefy." Even Heck came inside off his tarpaulin, and Beefy laughed and smiled and cried all at the same time, and decided this was the happiest moment of his life.

"Bet you'd like a cup of tea, wouldn't you, Beefy," Ida said.

"Well, if it ain't any trouble," Beefy said politely.

"Course it ain't any trouble. Lofty, make us all a cup of tea. We got to celebrate." So Lofty made them a cup of tea on the stove, and they all sat around in the cosy gloom of the little cabin and lifted their cups to Beefy and said, "Cheerio, Beefy," and Beefy held up his cup to them and said, "Cheerio, boys," and was as happy as a king.

When they had drunk their tea Ida said, "You know, Beefy, we can't tell you how glad we are to meet you like this. Aren't we, boys."

"That's right," they said.

"The fact is," Ida went on, "we got a job to do, and just before we met you we was saying, 'Beefy's the man for that job.' Weren't we, boys?"

"That's right," they agreed.

"I said: 'The whole success of the enterprise will be in jeopardy without Beefy.' Didn't I, boys?"

"That's right."

Beefy glowed with pride. "What you want me to do?" he asked importantly.

Ida remembered Beefy's predilection for going straight. She decided to feel her way carefully. "Well," she said. "It's like this, Beefy. We've been to a port and we've picked up a little packet of stuff that someone in Danby happens to want very much. So we're going to Danby in this boat, and then we want you to go and deliver the stuff. One of us would go," she hurried on to say, "But – well, the police might be looking out for us. But it's different with you."

Beefy couldn't quite follow this argument; but that, after all, was nothing new, and what Ida said must be right. "I'll go, Ida," he said earnestly. "Just you leave it to me."

Ida looked at him doubtfully. "You sure you don't mind, Beefy? Of course I'm not asking you to do anything dishonest. It's only a case of delivering ever such a little parcel, and getting the money for it."

"That's all right." Beefy was only too delighted to help. But it was funny, all the gang and a boat being required to bring a little parcel all the way from a port. "What's in the parcel?" he asked.

"Oh, only some white powder. It's – it's a sort of medicine, and this geezer and his friends have to take it, see. If you deliver it and don't make any mistakes we shall probably get this job for the rest of our lives. Easy money," she added appreciatively.

"Couldn't they get it from a chemist's?"

Ida began to feel the irritation that Beefy always seemed to inspire in her nowadays. "It's cheaper this way," she said shortly.

"But – " began Beefy. He saw the gleam in the chairman's eye. He changed the subject. "Fancy you having a boat," he said.

"It's ours," Ida said proudly. "We ain't borrowed it. It was just being left to rot, so we baled it out, and Peg Leg painted it up, and Heck and Lofty borrowed the engine out of a motorbike in a car park, and fitted it up beautiful. He's clever with anything mechanical, Heck is."

Beefy could hardly believe the change in his fortunes. Half an hour ago he hadn't known where to turn, and now here he was, back among friends, with a job for life; the delightful job of drifting along the canals and rivers of England, taking medicine to poor sick geezers.

They chugged happily on through summer fields, through a quiet evening and a silver morning. They came into the squalor of Danby, and tied up. They gave the proud and excited Beefy a little parcel, and made him memorize an address, and sent him off. He walked through the familiar streets. The address he had been given was in a decaying street at the far end of the town. He had to go through the market place, and as he was passing the statue of Julius Caesar a terrible thing happened. He met a man, and the man looked at him very long and hard. Beefy turned his face away and hurried on. To his horror he heard a cry of "Hey". He pressed on. But the man came running after him and barred his path.

Beefy would have run for it but there was a policeman standing two yards away.

Now Ida had said that there was nothing dishonest in what Beefy was doing. Nevertheless, when people started shouting "Hey", and barring his path, he felt that neither honesty nor dishonesty entered into it. It was just trouble. With unusual presence of mind he shot his little parcel into the mouth of an adjacent pillarbox.

The man was still standing in his way. "Are you Beefy Jones?" he asked.

"No," said Beefy firmly. The man looked at him closely. "I think you are," he said. "I want you to come with me. There's nothing to be afraid of."

Unwillingly, watched by the policeman, Beefy went. The man took him into a nearby office where another man was sitting at a desk with a lot of books and papers.

"This is Mr Beefy Jones," the first man said. "I've found him at last."

"We've been looking for you for months," said the second man. "Have you any means of identification?"

"What say?" asked Beefy.

"Can we prove that you are Beefy Jones?"

"No," Beefy said. He wasn't anybody's fool.

The man sighed. He looked at the apprehensive Beefy. I shall have to use words of two syllables here, he thought. He looked again. Monosyllables, he corrected himself.

He cleared his throat. "Mr Jones," he began. Beefy brightened immediately. "Mr Jones, we believe you were acquainted with the late Elizabeth Lavinia Tubb."

"No," said Beefy, determined to deny everything, whether he understood it or not.

The man looked up irritably. "Come, come," he snapped. "You knew Lizzie Tubb?"

"Oh, yes." He wasn't going to deny Lizzie, even to save his own skin.

"Miss Lizzie Tubb, you may be surprised to hear," the man went on, tapping his desk with a paperknife, "was not in the impoverished circumstances that most people imagined."

Beefy thrust out his lower lip. No one was going to say anything against Lizzie in his presence. "Lizzie was nice," he said.

"I mean she wasn't poor," the man almost shouted. "I am a solicitor. I am also Miss Tubb's executor. In your absence I sold her house, and the value of the estate is now £500 2s. 11d."

"You – you mean Lizzie had all that money?" gasped Beefy. He couldn't have been more surprised if they'd told him that Joe Vodka was Czar of all the Russias.

"Moreover," went on the man. He paused for effect. "She made you her sole beneficiary."

He was disappointed by the reception of this news. "Is that good or bad?" Beefy asked politely.

The man sighed. "It means that Miss Tubb has left you £500," he said succinctly.

"And two and elevenpence?" asked Beefy, trying to have everything straight.

"And two and elevenpence."

There was a long silence. Beefy's face crumpled slowly. "I never wanted nothing," he managed to say. "I never wanted nothing."

"Well, you've got something," said the solicitor. "You've got £500."

Beefy stood there, awkwardly, his face working. "I never wanted nothing," he repeated. "I never wanted Lizzie to leave me nothing."

The solicitor had had quite enough of this client. He was a busy man. "If you will wait a few minutes I will make out a cheque for the amount, and get you to sign an official receipt. Just sit down, will you?"

Beefy perched on the edge of a chair. The man went into an outer office, and soon came back with a cheque and a typewritten sheet of paper.

"Just sign this receipt, will you," he said.

Beefy hung his head. "I can't write," he admitted.

"Oh, Lor'." The solicitor put his head round the door of the outer office. "Jenkins, just come and witness Mr Jones' mark, will you."

So Beefy made his mark, and the solicitor handed him a cheque. "Don't spend it all at once," he said.

Beefy gazed at the little piece of paper. "What do I do with this?" he asked.

The solicitor remained outwardly calm. But he had been told in the outer office that a very important client was waiting to see him. He didn't like to keep important clients waiting. "Jenkins, take Mr Jones along to the bank and open an account for him," he ordered. "Goodbye, Mr Jones." He put out a perfunctory hand, and with the other pressed a bell.

"I never wanted nothing," said Beefy.

They worked him towards the door. And at that moment a knock came, and a girl entered and announced, "Lord Wapentake, sir."

"Well, damn my eyes," cried Lord Wapentake. "What the devil are you doing here, Beefy?" To the solicitor's astonishment he half-embraced Mr Jones. "When did they let you out? Bad business, that. Very bad business. Gross miscarriage of justice, eh, Fortescue?"

"I – I really couldn't say, my Lord," said solicitor Fortescue uncomfortably.

"I bet you couldn't. Never commit yourselves, you lawyer fellers." He turned to Beefy. "When are you coming back to be my gardener?"

But Beefy's mind had grasped the fact that his heart's desire was in his grasp. "I – I dunno, I got some money now. Reckon I might go back to Shepherd's Delight. Buy a

273

cottage. And a pig. Thought I might call the pig Emily." He trailed off.

Lord Wapentake became excited. "Shepherd's Delight? Dammit, my old China and I are going to live at my place at Warning. We're selling the Towers to the Coal Board. Too damned expensive to live there any longer. That's what I've come to see this lawyer feller about."

Beefy goggled. "You mean – you mean you're going to live at Shepherd's Warning?"

"That's what I'm telling you. You'll be able to live at Delight and work for me. Admirable arrangement. Now that's settled. Don't you go taking a job with anyone else."

Beefy's eyes were shining. "Course I won't," he said fervently.

Mr Fortescue coughed. "Perhaps Mr Jones would like to go to the bank now," he suggested hopefully.

"That's right, my dear feller." Lord Wapentake put a hand on Beefy's shoulder. "You pop along to the bank. I'll expect to see you at Sheherd's Warning."

They hustled Beefy out. Mr Jenkins took him to the bank, told the cashier that the gentleman wanted to open an account, and went back to the office.

The cashier, little knowing what was in store, took out a signature card. "What is your name?" he asked.

"Beefy Jones."

"And your address?"

"What say?"

"Where do you live?"

"On a boat."

"I'm afraid we shall want some address."

Beefy tried to be helpful. "It's green," he said.

"What is?"

"The boat."

The cashier sighed. "We'd better leave that and come back to it later. What's your occupation?"

"Say?"

"What do you do for a living?"

Beefy said very proudly, "I'm a company director."

The cashier looked at him with a mixture of respect and astonishment. "May I ask which company?"

"Well, it ain't really got a name. Leastways – " He petered out. The cashier waited. "Matter of fact," Beefy said at last, "What I'm doing now is taking medicine to poor sick geezers."

"Ah." The cashier seized on this in desperation. "Shall we say medical orderly?"

"Sort of," agreed Beefy.

The cashier wrote it down. "Now just sign your name here," he said more hopefully, feeling that his fearful task was done.

"I can't write," said Beefy.

There was a numbed silence. "Then will you make a cross there," the cashier said through his teeth. "And I'll put your address as 'Poste Restante, Danby'. Call in and tell us as soon as you get a permanent address."

Beefy shambled out. He'd got five hundred pounds, two shillings and elevenpence. He was going to buy a cottage at Shepherd's Delight, and a pig, and Lord Wapentake was going to give him a job. His future was at last settled. Everything was coming his way, and wouldn't the boys be pleased to hear his news. "Good old Beefy," they would say. "Going to live like a gent. We'll all come and spend our summer holidays with you, Beefy."

Then a horrible thought struck him. The little parcel! He'd quite forgotten about posting it in the letterbox. He hoped the poor sick geezers wouldn't die if they didn't get their medicine. And Ida was going to be cross. And the boys. They were going to shout at him.

Need he go back? Yes. He'd left Lizzie's text on the boat. He'd got to fetch that. Ida and the boys wouldn't want it on account of it said "Bless This House" and they lived on a boat. Besides, he wanted it. Lizzie had give it him. Reluctantly he returned to the boat, and went aboard.

Ida and the boys were waiting in the little cabin. "Well, got the money?" Ida greeted him sharply.

Beefy shuffled his feet. "No," he said. "Leastways – "

"No? Why not?" she cut in furiously.

"I put the medicine in a pillarbox. On account of I met a geezer and – "

"You – what?" There was a cold, menacing silence in the tiny cabin. "You put that parcel in a pillar box?"

Beefy swallowed. "Maybe if you asked the post office they'd give it you back," he suggested.

Silence. Cold, dreadful silence.

It was broken by Ida. "This ain't the first time you've tried something like this on. But by Jiminy it's going to be the last."

"Who was this geezer?" Heck asked.

"He took me to see a chap who gave me five hundred pounds two shillings and elevenpence."

The menacing silence changed to a fascinated silence. At last: "Five hundred pounds!" sneered Heck. "What ever would anyone give *you* five hundred pounds for?"

"And two and elevenpence," corrected Beefy.

"What was it for?"

"Lizzie Tubb left it me. I never wanted nothing, but she left it me."

This was too much for Beefy's fellow directors to absorb. "You – you mean you've really got five hundred pounds?" said Ida, recapping.

Beefy nodded.

"You mean you've got it on you?"

"Well, not really. I put it in the bank."

Heck gave a horrified groan. "You *never* did?" he cried.

Beefy began to look anxious. Peg Leg said, "You didn't *really* trust a bank with all that money, Beefy? You're pulling our legs, aren't you? Trying to frighten us?"

"Did they give you any receipt?" asked Ida.

"They gave me this," said Beefy. With trembling fingers he produced a passbook.

Heck looked at it contemptuously. "Not worth the paper it's written on." He dismissed it. "Best thing you can do is go straight to the bank and get it back again. If it's not too late," he added darkly.

Beefy by now was sick with anxiety. "I thought banks was honest," he stammered.

"Honest!" Heck would have spat if he hadn't been cultured. "They did my poor old Mother out of fifty thousand pounds. That's how honest they are. She paid it in. And what happened when she went to draw it out again? They laughed at her. Just laughed at her."

"I thought it was all right," said the wretched Beefy.

"You get it out if you can," counselled Ida.

"I'll come with you," said Heck. "See there's no funny business."

"No you won't. I'm going," Ida contradicted him with authority.

Peg Leg said, "Perhaps Beefy would prefer me to go. We've always been good friends, ain't we, Beefy."

Chairman and secretary scowled at Peg Leg. Peg Leg glared at them both. "We'll all go when we've had dinner," Ida said firmly.

But Beefy was in a panic. "Reckon we ought to go straight away," he said. He was horrified. That money represented life happy ever after at Shepherd's Delight. It represented a cottage, and a pig, and security; and the bank wasn't going to give it him back. He couldn't argue with a bank. Ruin stared him in the face.

"We'll go after dinner," Ida repeated.

Beefy said "But – " Ida gave him a look. They had dinner.

After dinner, Ida said, "Gentlemen, I wish, as chairman of the Company, to interview Beefy. Will you please leave us alone?"

The directors muttered. They scowled. They went.

Beefy and Ida looked at each other across the dark little cabin. Beefy swallowed. Ida was going to be cross. She was going to bring up the question of him putting the poor sick geezers' medicine in the pillarbox. She was going to shout; and, to add to his troubles, instead of sitting here they ought to be going to the bank to make a desperate bid to get his money back.

His relief when Ida smiled was tremendous. She even put a hand on the sleeve of his striped singlet. "Beefy," she began. "This Company wants a blood transfusion."

He sat gazing at her, his hands on his thighs, his mouth slightly open. He wasn't quite with her.

"You'd be surprised if I told you how many companies fail every year through lack of capital," she continued. "You get a company with expert direction, with ideas, with able and willing executives. And what happens? It fails because it lacks the capital to carry out its plans."

Beefy breathed heavily. He still wasn't quite with her.

Ida put her hand back on his sleeve. "That is the position in which our Company finds itself. We need additional capital, Beefy."

"I see," said Beefy, who didn't.

She leaned forward and put her face close to his. "Beefy, I am prepared to issue to you five hundred fully paid ordinary shares of one pound each at par."

She had made her momentous offer. She sat back, and waited for the reaction.

Beefy felt very uncomfortable. It was nice of Ida, and he very much appreciated her offer even though he couldn't understand it, but he didn't want no shares. He wanted a cottage and a pig.

He shuffled his feet. "You mean I should have to pay for them with my five hundred pounds?"

Ida shrugged. "Well, nominally, I suppose. But they'd appreciate. They'll be worth a thousand at least this time next year."

Beefy hung his head. He felt terribly ungrateful. "I – I thought I might buy a cottage and a pig," he muttered. "I didn't want no shares."

"You'd be chief shareholder," she pointed out, and added, confidentially. "You'd have the Company in your pocket."

"I was going to buy a cottage and a pig," Beefy muttered.

Ida had sown her seed. She rose, and put a friendly hand on Beefy's shoulder. "You think it over," she said kindly, "and come and see me. With the money. You wouldn't like to see the Company go through and know that you could have saved it, would you? Why, you'd never forgive yourself."

"No," said Beefy. "Leastways – " He groped for the door handle, and escaped into the sunshine. He was sad. He supposed he'd have to buy them shares. And he didn't want no shares. He wanted a cottage and a pig.

A deep sigh brought him back to earth. He turned, and found Heck leaning over the side of the boat, gazing disconsolately into the green waters of the canal. He didn't like to see his dear friend so obviously distressed. "What's the matter, Heck?" he asked.

Two mournful eyes turned and gazed at him. "It's my poor old mother," said Heck, with a helpless shrug.

"Is she poorly again?"

Heck sighed even more deeply. "Worse than that. She's in trouble. She needs money. Needs it bad."

Beefy's heart sank. "Does – does she need a lot of money?" he asked.

Heck turned and leaned over the side once more. "Oh, it's impossible. She needs at least five hundred pounds to save her from the shame of the prison house. Yet where can I get five hundred pounds?"

"Well," began Beefy. "Leastways – "

But at that moment Peg Leg came up and said, "Could I have a word with you, Beefy? In private?" he added, with a baleful glance at Heck.

The baleful glance was returned. Peg Leg took Beefy firmly by the elbow and led him to the stern. "Beefy," he began. "You never knew I was married, did you?" He sighed. "Sweetest little woman you could wish to meet, my wife. And the kids! Little angels come to earth, all seven of them." He wiped his eyes. For a moment he was too moved to carry on. Beefy nearly cried, too, in sheer sympathy.

Joe Vodka, watching them from his resting place on a tarpaulin, groaned with frustration. He'd thought up a most convincing story about needing five hundred pounds' worth of roubles to help his aged grandparents to escape from the salt mines; but he lacked the English to make anyone understand it, least of all Beefy.

The Reverend John Adams was so happy that he was almost afraid. Surely such happiness in this vale of tears was more than a miserable sinner ought to expect.

The frustrations and difficulties that had attended the early stages of the building of the church hall had suddenly fallen away; the work was finished, most of the money was to hand, and tomorrow the Lord Bishop would give the hall his blessing and declare it open. His vision of the new church hall, with its bright, clean rooms, its big windows, its laughing children, had come true. He had achieved an ambition that would benefit generations still unborn.

But he had another, greater source of happiness. Sally. His lovely bride had turned the grim old Vicarage into a place of gaiety and sunshine. She sang as she worked in the kitchen. She smiled at him as she dusted his study. She laughed as she faced him over the dinner table, or across the fireplace in the autumn evenings. She was, he thought, even more beautiful than when he had first met her. No one, he was quite sure, had ever had a wife so lovely, so kind, so cheerful, so utterly and absolutely delightful.

Now as they swung, arm in arm, through the streets of Danby, he glanced down at her eager face, the eyes bright, the lips slightly parted. He felt proud when he saw other men staring at her in admiration, when he saw women glance enviously at her beauty. Soon, he thought, she will look even more beautiful, for he was taking her to buy a hat for tomorrow's ceremony, and he was jolly well going to see that she bought a nice one.

Even as he watched her the expression of her face changed. He felt her fingers tighten upon his. "Look, John, it's Beefy," she said.

An extremely worried and dejected-looking Beefy was approaching. Walking with him, almost like an armed escort, were an auburn-haired woman, a man with black side-whiskers, and a man with a wooden leg. At that moment Beefy saw them. His face lit up. He grinned from ear to ear. "Sally," he cried.

"Beefy," cried Sally. She ran up impulsively and kissed him. "Wherever have you been? We've done everything to try and find you." Then there was an awkward pause; but Beefy made no attempt to introduce his cousin to his friends, so with an apologetic smile in their direction Sally dragged him away. "Come and see John," she said.

"But – we was going to the bank, on account of I gave them some money and I didn't ought to of."

"Oh, that can wait," she said cheerfully. "You're coming to the Vicarage. I've just got to buy a hat, first."

"Hello, Beefy," said John. "Come and have some tea at the Vicarage."

"I got to go to the bank," said Beefy. "I gave them the five hundred pounds Lizzie Tubb left me and Heck says I didn't ought to of, on account of they ain't honest, and Heck and Peg Leg want to borrow some and I'm going to buy some shares in the Company."

John Adams looked at him keenly. "Who's Heck?" he asked.

Beefy jerked a thumb at his friends, who had wandered across the road and now stood irresolute, waiting for him. "That nice-looking one with the side-whiskers," he said.

John Adams strode across. "Beefy is coming with me," he said coldly. "There's no need for you to wait."

Ida drew herself up to her full height. "Our friend has a most urgent business engagement," she said. She raised her voice. "Hey, Beefy," she yelled. "The banks close at three."

Beefy, sick with anxiety, began to cross the road. Sally pulled him back. "Beefy," roared Peg Leg. Ida glared at John Adams. "If you don't stop interfering I shall call the police," she said, game to the last.

"Splendid," said the Vicar. "And I shall tell them that you have all been trying to obtain five hundred pounds by false pretences." He looked Ida straight in the eye. "Whose word do you think would carry more weight, yours or mine?"

Ida saw his point. She lowered her eyes. Call this a democracy, she thought bitterly. One law for the rich and another for the poor. It was as true today as ever it was. "Come on, boys," she said at last. The boys shrugged. They thrust out their lower lips. They did not move. "Come on, boys," Ida repeated. "We've got to think. We ain't going to let him get away with this." Sulkily they turned and wandered off down a side road, muttering.

John Adams smiled. He came back to Sally and the anxious Beefy. "That's that," he said. "Now we'll buy this ridiculous hat."

Later, in his study at the Vicarage, John Adams said, "So Lizzie Tubb left you five hundred pounds?"

Beefy nodded.

"What did you think of doing with it?"

"Well, I thought I might buy a cottage and a pig at Shepherd's Delight, but they want to borrow it on account of they've got wives and children and mothers. But I reckon it's no good talking. The bank's got the money now. Heck says I didn't ought to of let them have it."

"Now listen. That's absolute nonsense. You can withdraw that money any time you like. But you keep it there for the time being."

A great load fell from Beefy's mind.

"What would you do for a living at Shepherd's Delight?" went on the Vicar.

"Lord Wappitake said I could be his gardener. He's going to live up there."

John Adams drummed on his desk. He wanted to help Beefy to settle down comfortably at Shepherd's Delight, for he liked him, and he hated to see anyone being fleeced.

He had other reasons, understandable though less altruistic. An illiterate cousin-in-law who kidnapped bank managers was an embarrassment for any Vicar; a cousin-in-law who kidnapped bishops was a downright menace. Any incumbent would have jumped at the opportunity of transporting such a relative to the other end of the country.

He made up his mind. He said: "Beefy, I want you to stay with us until Monday. Then my wife and I will take you to Shepherd's Delight in my car, and we will stay up there for a few days and try to help you to find a house and get settled down. But in the meantime I want you to stay in the Vicarage and avoid your friends, in your own interests."

Beefy assimilated this. Then he said: "I got to see my friends. They got my tex'."

"Which text?"

"The tex' Lizzie give me."

"Now, look, old man." John Adams crossed his legs. "You just forget about that text and stay here. It'll be much better for you."

At that moment Sally came in and heard her husband's plans with delight. "You may be able to get poor old Mordecai Wainwright's cottage," she said. "Mother happened to mention in her last letter that it was still for sale."

So Beefy stayed with them, and the next day the Vicar and Sally went off to the new church hall and saw the results of John Adams' efforts officially blessed, amid general rejoicing and the final discomfiture of all who had forecast ruin and disaster as the result of the scheme.

Beefy, however, left in the great, empty Vicarage, thought of his tex', and of his dear friends, who were all so sad and sorrowful, and whom he might never see again. At last he could bear it no longer; he opened the back door and crept out, and found his way round to the street. He set off. He wanted to see his friends again. He wanted his tex'. But he wasn't looking forward to the interview. They all needed his money far more than he did, but he daren't let them have it, or that Vicar would be cross. So he'd got to tell the boys and Ida that he couldn't help them.

He avoided the market place and the main streets. He crept along quiet back streets, which became more and more mean and dreary, and at last he reached some steps that led down to the canal. He went down, down the slippery stone steps, and when he reached the bottom he looked with a sinking heart at the place where the little green boat had been moored. The mooring was empty, and the place where the little green boat had been knew it no more. For a long time he stood there, gazing up and down the squalid reaches of the canal. Then he turned, and walked sadly back to St Jude's Vicarage.

When the Vicar snatched Beefy from his friends, like a brand from the burning, Ida, Heck and Peg Leg felt frustrated. They didn't like giving best to a mere parson; on the other hand, short of making a scene in public they couldn't very well have kept Beefy. And they were in no position to make scenes in public. So they wandered back to the boat, and ten minutes after they went aboard Ida called an extraordinary meeting in the cabin.

She came straight to the point. She said: "Gentlemen, one of our directors is in possession of the sum of five hundred pounds. He has not, perhaps, the *savoir faire* one would expect of a company director, and I am afraid that he may very soon fall a prey to unscrupulous characters." She coughed, and took a sip of water. "Now you will agree that, in normal circumstances, it would be our duty to stay and succour our friend and colleague. Our duty and our desire.

"But, gentlemen, circumstances are not normal. There is a sizeable packet of cocaine lying in a pillarbox in this town. Eventually the post office, or the police, are going to find out what it is. Then they will start asking questions. Awkward

285

questions. Gentlemen, will someone propose that, despite Beefy and his five hundred pounds, we up anchor and away?"

She sat down and looked round the table.

"I propose that," Heck said promptly. "If we stay here, we shall all be in prison again before the end of the week. But if we go, we go as free men; and with our brains and abilities there ain't nothing can't stop us. We shall soon find other ways of making a fortune; they're all around us, like" – he almost blushed – "like daisies in a meadow. All we got to do is stoop down and pick the one we like." He sat down.

Peg Leg rose immediately. "Five hundred pounds is five hundred pounds," he said. "I move that we stay here till we've got hold of Beefy."

The rest of the meeting began to look undecided; but Heck, hearing the canal water slapping and lapping against the side of the boat, remembered his half-hours with the perishing poets when he was prison librarian. He put up a warning finger. "Listen!" he cried sepulchrally. " 'The Deep moans round with many voices'." He leapt to his feet, and flung out a dramatic arm. " 'Come, my friends, 'tis not too late to seek a newer world'."

Heck's eloquence won the day. They cast off, just when the workers of Danby were walking and cycling home to tea through the autumn sunset. The engine began to chug. The bows of the little boat nosed out into midstream. Slowly they began to move forward, and slowly the stone banks gave way to reeds, and the factories gave way to trees and fields, and the people gave way to quiet cattle, knee-deep in white mists. And the little craft crept away, carrying Ida, of the flame-coloured hair, and her board of directors, carrying them down the molten gold of the canal into the cauldron of the sunset, bearing them on to strive, to seek, to find, and not to yield.

" 'Come, my friends, 'tis not too late to seek a newer world'," quoted the Vicar, on the morning of the following Monday.

"What did you say, darling?" asked Sally, just getting into the car.

"Only quoting," he called, as he poured water into the radiator. He replaced the radiator cap, took the watering can back into the garage, locked up, came and leapt into the driving seat. "All right, Sally?" he asked, putting a friendly hand on her knee.

"Yes, thank you, John."

"All right in the back there, Beefy?"

But Beefy was too happy to answer. The car leapt forward, to seek a newer world. Slowly the parish of St Jude's fell away; St Jude's was left behind, the living and the dead; Mr Macmillan, and the church council; poor old Lizzie, facing the winter in her overcoat of clay; the ugly church and the fine, cheerful new hall; the chip shops and the pubs and the garish cinemas; the stupidity and silliness and quiet decency and patient courage; the squalid ugliness and the blue, soaring, English heaven. Danby fell away; and Beefy's eyes turned forward, to Shepherd's Delight, with its blue mountain, and its blue smoke standing up from the chimneys; and he knew that soon, very soon, he would be in his own little garden. He saw the scene so clearly, as he leaned over the pigsty door and scratched Emily's back until, with a smile of ineffable delight, she fell down and lay, entranced, in the mud. It was Sunday evening, and from the nearby church came the sound of his favourite hymn, "Erbye Dwid Mee". And, as he listened, the sun sank behind the blue mountain, and Beefy went inside, into his little cottage, and drew the red curtain, and settled down with the Western that, somehow, he did not quite know how, he would by now have learnt to read.

And John Adams was happy because he was sitting next to Sally, his wife. Sally was happy because she was going to Shepherd's Delight to see her Mother. And Beefy was happy, unutterably happy because at last, at long last, he was going to buy a cottage and a pig. His lips moved.

"Reckon I'm going to call my pig Emily," he muttered, and his eyes filled with tears of pure joy.

Eric Malpass

The Lamplight and the Stars

Nathan Cranswick's third child comes into the world on the day of Queen Victoria's Diamond Jubilee. Whilst the Empire celebrates, Nathan's concerns are about his family's future. A gentle and wise preacher, he gratefully accepts the chance to move from the dingy, cramped house in Ingerby to the village of Moreland when he is offered a job on the splendid Heron estate. Anticipating peace and tranquillity for his wife and young family, his hopes are cruelly dashed when their new life is beset by problems from the beginning. A family scandal and the Boer War menace their whole future, but finally it is the agonising choice facing his gentle daughter which threatens to tear the family apart…

Morning's at Seven

Three generations of the Pentecost family live in a state of permanent disarray in a huge, sprawling farmhouse. Seven-year-old Gaylord Pentecost is the innocent hero who observes the lives of the adults – Grandpa, Momma and Poppa and two aunties – with amusement and incredulity.

Through Gaylord's eyes, we witness the heartache suffered by Auntie Rose as the exquisite Auntie Becky makes a play for her gentleman friend, while Gaylord unwittingly makes the situation far worse.

Mayhem and madness reign in this zestful account of the lives and loves of the outrageous Pentecosts.

ERIC MALPASS

OF HUMAN FRAILTY
A BIOGRAPHICAL NOVEL OF THOMAS CRANMER

Thomas Cranmer is a gentle, unassuming scholar when a chance meeting sweeps him away from the security and tranquillity of Cambridge to the harsh magnificence of Henry VIII's court. As a supporter of Henry he soon rises to prominence as Archbishop of Canterbury.

Eric Malpass paints a fascinating picture of Reformation England and its prominent figures: the brilliant, charismatic but utterly ruthless Henry VIII, the exquisite but scheming Anne Boleyn and the fanatical Mary Tudor.

But it is the paradoxical Thomas Cranmer who dominates the story. A tormented man, he is torn between valour and cowardice; a man with a loving heart who finds himself hated by many; and a man of God who makes the terrifying discovery that he must suffer and die for his beliefs. Thomas Cranmer is a man of simple virtue, whose only fault is his all too human frailty.

ERIC MALPASS

THE RAISING OF LAZARUS PIKE

Lazarus Pike (1820–1899), author of *Lady Emily's Decision*, lies buried in the churchyard of Ill Boding. And there he would have remained, in obscurity and undisturbed, had it not been for a series of remarkable coincidences. A discovery sets in motion a campaign to republish his works and to reinstate Lazarus Pike as a giant of Victorian literature. This is a cause of bitter wrangling between the two factions that emerge. For some, Lazarus is a simple schoolmaster, devoted to his beautiful wife, Corinda. For others, who think his reputation needs a sexy, contemporary twist, he is a wife murderer with a deeply flawed character. What follows is a knowing and wry look at the world of literary make-overs and the heritage industry in a hilarious story that brings fame and tragedy to an unsuspecting moorland village.

SWEET WILL

William Shakespeare is just eighteen when he marries Anne Hathaway, eight years his senior. Anne, who bears a son soon after the marriage, is plain and not particularly bright – but her love for Will is undeniable. Talented and fiercely ambitious, Will's scintillating genius soon makes him the toast of Elizabethan London. While he basks in the flattery his great reputation affords him, Anne lives a lonely life in Stratford, far away from the glittering world of her husband.

This highly evocative account of the life of the young William Shakespeare begins the trilogy which continues with *The Cleopatra Boy* and concludes with *A House of Women*.

Eric Malpass

The Wind Brings Up the Rain

It is a perfect summer's day in August 1914. Yet even as Nell and her friends enjoy a blissful picnic by the river, the storm clouds of war are gathering over Europe. Very soon this idyll is to be swept away by the conflict that will take millions of men to their deaths.

After the war, the widowed Nell leads a wretched existence, caring for her husband's elderly, ungrateful parents, with only her son, Benbow, for companionship and support. But Nell is a passionate woman and wants to share her life with a man who will return her love. Meanwhile, Benbow falls in love with a German girl, Ulrike – until she is enticed home by the resurgent Germany.

This moving story of a Midlands family in the inter-war years is a compelling tale of personal triumph and disappointment, set against the background of the hideous destruction of war.

TITLES BY ERIC MALPASS AVAILABLE DIRECT
FROM HOUSE OF STRATUS

Quantity		£	$(US)	$(CAN)	€
	AT THE HEIGHT OF THE MOON	6.99	11.50	15.99	11.50
	THE CLEOPATRA BOY	6.99	11.50	15.99	11.50
	FORTINBRAS HAS ESCAPED	6.99	11.50	15.99	11.50
	A HOUSE OF WOMEN	6.99	11.50	15.99	11.50
	THE LAMPLIGHT AND THE STARS	6.99	11.50	15.99	11.50
	THE LONG LONG DANCES	6.99	11.50	15.99	11.50
	MORNING'S AT SEVEN	6.99	11.50	15.99	11.50
	OF HUMAN FRAILTY	6.99	11.50	15.99	11.50
	OH, MY DARLING DAUGHTER	6.99	11.50	15.99	11.50
	PIG-IN-THE-MIDDLE	6.99	11.50	15.99	11.50
	THE RAISING OF LAZARUS PIKE	6.99	11.50	15.99	11.50
	SUMMER AWAKENING	6.99	11.50	15.99	11.50
	SWEET WILL	6.99	11.50	15.99	11.50
	THE WIND BRINGS UP THE RAIN	6.99	11.50	15.99	11.50

ALL HOUSE OF STRATUS BOOKS ARE AVAILABLE FROM GOOD BOOKSHOPS
OR DIRECT FROM THE PUBLISHER:

Internet: www.houseofstratus.com including author interviews, reviews, features.

Email: sales@houseofstratus.com please quote author, title and credit card details.

Hotline: UK ONLY: 0800 169 1780, please quote author, title and credit card details.
INTERNATIONAL: +44 (0) 20 7494 6400, please quote author, title, and credit card details.

Send to: **House of Stratus Sales Department**
24c Old Burlington Street
London
W1X 1RL
UK

Please allow for postage costs charged per order plus an amount per book as set out in the tables below:

	£(Sterling)	$(US)	$(CAN)	€(Euros)
Cost per order				
UK	1.50	2.25	3.50	2.50
Europe	3.00	4.50	6.75	5.00
North America	3.00	4.50	6.75	5.00
Rest of World	3.00	4.50	6.75	5.00
Additional cost per book				
UK	0.50	0.75	1.15	0.85
Europe	1.00	1.50	2.30	1.70
North America	2.00	3.00	4.60	3.40
Rest of World	2.50	3.75	5.75	4.25

PLEASE SEND CHEQUE, POSTAL ORDER (STERLING ONLY), EUROCHEQUE, OR INTERNATIONAL MONEY ORDER (PLEASE CIRCLE METHOD OF PAYMENT YOU WISH TO USE)
MAKE PAYABLE TO: STRATUS HOLDINGS plc

Cost of book(s): _____ Example: 3 x books at £6.99 each: £20.97

Cost of order: _____ Example: £2.00 (Delivery to UK address)

Additional cost per book: _____ Example: 3 x £0.50: £1.50

Order total including postage: _____ Example: £24.47

Please tick currency you wish to use and add total amount of order:

☐ £ (Sterling)　　☐ $ (US)　　☐ $ (CAN)　　☐ € (EUROS)

VISA, MASTERCARD, SWITCH, AMEX, SOLO, JCB:

☐☐☐☐☐☐☐☐☐☐☐☐☐☐☐☐☐☐☐

Issue number (Switch only):

☐☐☐

Start Date:　　　　　　Expiry Date:

☐☐/☐☐　　　　☐☐/☐☐

Signature: _____

NAME: _____

ADDRESS: _____

_____

POSTCODE: _____

Please allow 28 days for delivery.

Prices subject to change without notice.
Please tick box if you do not wish to receive any additional information. ☐

House of Stratus publishes many other titles in this genre; please check our website (**www.houseofstratus.com**) for more details.